TRUE COLOURS

STEPHEN LEATHER

ISIS

LARGE PRINT

Oxford

First published in Great Britain 2013
by
Hodder & Stoughton
an Hachette UK Company

Published in Large Print 2014 by ISIS Publishing Ltd.,
7 Centremead, Osney Mead, Oxford OX2 0ES
by arrangement with
Hodder & Stoughton
and Hachette UK Company

CIP data is available for this title from the British Library

ISBN 978–0–7531–9256–6 (hb)
ISBN 978–0–7531–9257–3 (pb)

Printed and bound in Great Britain by
T. J. International Ltd., Padstow, Cornwall

For Edith

AFGHANISTAN/PAKISTAN BORDER, 2002

The Chinook cleared a low ridge, dropped to the floor of a plateau and then rose again, following the steep slopes of a round-topped hill. The helicopter came to a hover and landed as the groundwash of the twin rotors stirred up a storm of dust and debris.

Jock McIntyre, Geordie Mitchell, Jimbo Shortt and Lex Harper jumped down and went into positions of all-round defence while Dan "Spider" Shepherd and Captain Harry Todd unloaded six mopeds that had been lashed to the tailgate of the Chinook. They remained crouched and watchful as the Chinook took off, then took a few more minutes to watch and listen, allowing their hearing to become attuned to the quietness of the night after the din of the helicopter. They scanned the surrounding countryside for any movement or sign that might suggest they had been spotted. All was dark and quiet, and eventually McIntyre signalled to them to move out. He led the column of mopeds down the hill before looping around to make their way to the target.

McIntyre and Shepherd rode at the head of the column, with Harper, Todd and Shortt behind them and Mitchell as "Tail-end Charlie" at the rear of the line. They rode without lights, their Passive Night

1

Goggles allowing them enough vision to avoid potholes and obstacles in the path.

The night was icy, the wind stinging their faces as they cleared the top of a ridge. McIntyre checked his GPS, signalled to the rest of the team, silenced his engine and freewheeled down the slope, towards the dark, indistinct shape of a tall building set into a fold of the hills.

They hid the mopeds in a clump of trees a hundred yards from the target and moved forward on foot, carrying the sections of ladder and the prepared charges, and leaving a faint trail of their boot-prints on the frost-covered ground. Shepherd caught a whiff of woodsmoke on the breeze as they approached from downwind, and a moment later, the tall shape of the target building loomed out of the surrounding darkness, the wall facing them glowing an eerie yellow through the goggles as it caught and reflected the moonlight filtering through the clouds.

There was a straggle of huts and outbuildings surrounding it and a pile of rubble that might once have been another house. While the others kept watch on the main building, Shortt and Mitchell made sure that all the outbuildings were deserted.

They dug in and watched the main building. In the early hours of the night, two small groups of men arrived and left again. Another hour passed and then a solitary figure, shrouded by a black cloak, emerged from the door and disappeared into the darkness. After that, there was no more traffic, and the faint glow of a lantern inside the building was extinguished well before midnight.

Eventually the area was in darkness, the cloud cover masked the starlight. They waited another full hour before assembling the ladder. Shepherd and Todd crept silently towards the building while the others set up a cordon and covered them. Even if any of the Taliban managed to escape before the charges were detonated, they would not avoid the deadly crossfire from the waiting soldiers.

Shepherd and the captain placed the ladder against the wall and, after listening for any sound from within the building, Shepherd climbed up and began to place shaped charges against the wall on each floor. He allowed the cables of the initiators to trail over his shoulder as he moved up. When he'd finished, he slid back down the ladder without using the rungs, slowing his descent by using his hands and feet on the outside of the uprights as brakes. He glanced at Todd and mimed protecting his ears.

Todd slipped round the corner and Shepherd followed him, pressing his fingers into his ears to protect them from the shock wave as he triggered the charges. The blasts of the three shaped charges came so close together that they could have been a single explosion.

Within seconds of the detonation, Shepherd was on the move, rushing up the ladder with Todd hard on his heels. The two men stormed through the gaping hole that had been blown in the top-floor wall. A thick fog of dust and debris still hung in the air as they swung their

Kalashnikovs around. Four Taliban lay on the floor, killed as they lay sleeping, their internal organs pulverised by the devastating concussive force of the blast wave. They moved slowly through the building, clearing the rooms one at a time.

The top two floors were sleeping areas, littered with Taliban dead, but the ground floor was where the cash was stored and disbursed. As they blew in the walls, the shaped charges had created a blizzard of hundred-dollar bills. The cash was all in US dollars, traded for drugs in Pakistan, extorted from businesses in the areas they controlled, or plundered from the avalanches of cash that the Americans had been pouring into the country in their attempts to buy the loyalty of warlords and tribal elders. Stacked on the floor were crates of ammunition, a few rocket-propelled grenades and a rack of AK-47s.

Shepherd looked over at the captain. "No point in leaving what's left of the cash and weapons and ammo for any Taliban who turn up later," he said. "Flip your goggles up or turn your back while I get a nice fire going for them. The flare in your goggles will blind you for ten minutes if you don't."

He dragged a few bits of bedding, rags and broken chairs and tables together into the centre of the room, kicked the embers of the fire across the floor and then stacked boxes of the Taliban's ammunition next to the pile. He surveyed his handiwork for a moment, then scooped up a stray $100 bill and set fire to it. He dropped it on to the pile of debris and waited until it was well alight before murmuring into his throat mic, "Coming out."

Todd climbed out through the hole in the wall first. As Shepherd moved to follow him, he heard the whiplash crack of an assault rifle and saw Todd fall backwards. There was a second crack as the captain dropped to the ground, gouts of blood pumping from his throat. Shepherd had seen no muzzle flash but heard answering fire from the SAS cordon and swung up his own weapon, loosing off a burst, firing blind just to keep the muj heads down before he slid down the ladder and ran over to Todd and crouched next to him.

Todd lay sprawled in the dirt, blood still spouting from his throat. The first round had struck his head, close to the left ear, gouging out a chunk of skull. The second had torn out Todd's larynx. Either wound might have been fatal, the two together guaranteed it. Shepherd cursed under his breath, took a syrette of morphine and injected him, squeezing the body of the syrette to push out the drug like toothpaste from a tube. He began fixing a trauma dressing over the wounds, even though he knew he was merely going through the motions, because nothing could save the captain now. Death was seconds away, a minute or so at the most.

Once the dressings were in place he cradled Todd's head against his chest, listening to the wet, sucking sound of the air bubbling through his shattered larynx as blood soaked his shirt.

The captain grabbed at his arm as his body began to shudder. There were more bursts of fire off to

5

Shepherd's left. Todd was staring at Shepherd, his eyes fearful. "You did good, Captain," Shepherd said. "You did good."

A fresh spasm shook Todd, his eyes rolled up into his head and he slumped sideways to the ground.

As Shepherd looked up, he saw a movement in the shadows by a pile of rubble at the edge of the compound. A dark shape resolved itself into a crouching figure and Shepherd saw a milky-white eye staring at him, though, seen through his goggles, it glowed an eerie yellow. Shepherd grabbed his weapon and swung it up, but in the same instant he saw a double muzzle flash. The first round tugged at his sleeve, but the next smashed into his shoulder, a sledge-hammer blow knocking him flat on his back, leaving the burst of fire from his own weapon arcing harmlessly into the sky.

A further burst of fire chewed the ground around him, and his face was needled by cuts from rock splinters, though they were no more than gnat bites compared with the searing pain in his shoulder. Out of the corner of his eye, Shepherd saw McIntyre swivelling to face the danger and loosing off a controlled burst of double taps, but Ahmad Khan had already ducked into cover behind the rubble.

Shepherd looked down at his shoulder. There was a spreading pool of blood on his jacket, glistening like wet tar in the flickering light of the muzzle flashes as his team kept up a barrage of suppressing fire.

Shortt ran over, pulling a field dressing from his jacket. "Stay down," he shouted, and slapped the dressing over the bullet wound. Shepherd took slow, deep breaths and fought to stay calm. "Geordie, get over here!" shouted Shortt. "Spider's hit!"

Geordie sprinted over, bent double. He looked at Todd but could see without checking that the captain was already dead. He hurried over to Shepherd. "You OK?" he asked.

Shepherd shook his head. He was far from OK. He opened his mouth to speak but the words were lost as he coughed. Helpless, he saw the dark shape of the Taliban killer move away, inching around the rubble heap and then disappearing into the darkness beyond. He tried to point but all the strength had drained from his arms.

"I'm on it," said Shortt, standing up and firing a burst in the direction of the escaping gunman.

Spider tried to sit up but Mitchell's big, powerful hand pressed him flat again. "Keep still and let me work on you," he growled. Mitchell clamped the trauma pad over the wound, compressed it and bound it as tight as he could. "Oboe! Oboe! All stations minimise," said Mitchell into his mic, SAS-speak ordering all unnecessary traffic off the radios. Mitchell looked down at Shepherd and slapped him gently across the face. "Stay with me, Spider. Just stay with me."

LONDON, PRESENT DAY

There were four of them sitting around the table in the corner of the pub, half-full pints of lager in front of them. A football match was playing on a television mounted above the door but they paid it no attention. Dennis Weaver was holding court. He was a big man gone to fat, with a gut as large as a full-term pregnancy that bumped the table each time he moved. He was wearing an England football shirt and gleaming white Nike trainers but it had been years since he had taken part in any exercise that hadn't involved lager or cigarettes. Weaver was in full flow, jabbing a nicotine-stained finger in the air to punctuate his angry words. "Yasir Chaudhry. The guy's taking the piss. Did you see him on TV last week? The council knocked two houses together so that he had a place big enough for him and his wife and eight kids."

"Bastard," muttered Stuart Harris, a heavy-set man with a shaved head and a tattoo of a cobweb across the left-hand side of his neck. He had the words LOVE and HATE tattooed across his knuckles. Like Weaver, he was wearing a football shirt, but his was the claret and blue of West Ham.

"Then one of the papers finds out that he's got another wife living nearby in another council house and she's got four kids. And who's paying for all his little bastards?" Weaver jabbed a finger at his own chest. "We are," he said. "Do you think he pays tax? Does he hell. Benefits, that's what he gets. Benefits and free houses and free health and free schools for his bastard kids."

Flecks of spittle erupted from between his lips and he wiped his mouth with the back of his hand before draining his pint. "Then do you know what the raghead goes and does? Stands in front of his house and tells a group of his raghead mates that they should all go on benefits. Jihad Seekers Allowance, that's what he called it. And you know what he called us? Us Brits? Kuffars, that's what. He hates us, but he's happy enough to take our money." He banged his hand down on the table. Several heads turned to look at him, but just as quickly turned away. Weaver had a reputation as being a man who didn't like being looked at, in pubs or out of them.

The men at his table all nodded in agreement. "Bastards," muttered Harris again. "Fucking bastards," he said, louder this time, as if gaining confidence.

"Whose round is it?" said Weaver, pointing at his empty glass.

"Barry's up," said Harris, gesturing at Barry Connolly, a diminutive Irishman with a straggly moustache and a greying ponytail. He was wearing a battered black leather vest over an Irish rugby shirt and had a pack of cigarette papers and pouch of tobacco on the table in front of him.

"I got the first round," whined Connolly.

"Bollocks, I got the first one," said Harris. "You went straight to the shithouse and I got them in. And you were in the shithouse again when Stuart got the second round."

Connolly rubbed his stomach. "I had a bad curry last night, I've had the runs all day."

"More information than we need," said the fourth man at the table. His name was Andy Taylor. Like Harris he had the words LOVE and HATE on his knuckles. The ink had faded over the years and both Es had all but gone. "I'll get them." He headed over to the bar, pulling a nylon wallet from the back pocket of his baggy jeans, which were hanging so low his underwear was visible.

"What's your problem, Barry?" Weaver asked Connolly. "You're always ducking your round."

"Dennis, mate, I'll get the next one," whined Connolly. "Cross my heart." He made the sign of the cross on his chest.

"Make sure you do," said Weaver. "It's bad enough with these ragheads sponging off us without you not paying your way."

"Short arms and long pockets," said Harris. "I thought it was the Scots that were tight fisted, not the Paddies."

"I'll get the next one, swear to God," said Connolly. He stared sullenly at the floor. A cheer went up from a group of football supporters standing at the bar and they began jumping up and down and punching the air. The men at the table looked up at the television in time to see the goal-keeper retrieving the ball from the back of the net.

"Who scored?" asked Harris.

"Who cares?" said Weaver. "It's only the bloody Eyeties. Who gives a toss about the Eyeties?"

Taylor returned with four pints of lager and placed them carefully on the table before sitting down.

"Anyway, tonight's the night," said Weaver. "We're going to burn the bastard out."

"Are you serious?" asked Harris, his hand suspended in the air as he reached for his pint.

"Do I look like I'm joking?" said Weaver.

Taylor leaned forward, his eyes burning with a fierce intensity. "Tonight?"

"Tonight," repeated Weaver. "I've got the address and I've got the petrol. We're going to burn the bastard's house down with him and his bastard family in it."

Taylor formed his right hand into a fist and punched the air. "Yes," he hissed.

Connolly grinned. "Woof!" he said. "Woof, woof, woof!"

Taylor frowned. "Woof? What do you mean?"

"Woof!" repeated Connolly. "It's the sound that petrol makes when you set fire to it." He held up his hands and splayed his fingers as he said "woof!" again. "Get it?"

Taylor sneered in contempt. "Yeah, I get it." He looked at Weaver. "What's the plan?"

"First, I need you all to hand over your phones," said Weaver.

"Why?" said Connolly.

"Because they track phones these days," said Weaver. "If we go there with our phones the cops will know." He grinned. "But if we leave them here, it'll look like we never left the pub."

"What, we're just going to leave them on the table?" asked Harris. "They'll be gone in a minute."

"Give me some credit, mate," said Weaver. He reached under the table and pulled out a black Adidas kitbag. "We'll put them in here. The landlord's a pal, he'll keep them behind the bar. And there's half a dozen guys here who'll swear we never left the place." He unzipped the bag and held it open. One by one the men put their mobiles inside. Connolly switched his off and Weaver glared at him in disgust. "Didn't you get what I just said? What's the point of switching it off? It has to be on so that it shows up."

Connolly grimaced, switched the phone back on and dropped it into the bag. Taylor tossed in an iPhone and reached for his pint. "Don't forget the other one, Andy," said Weaver.

Taylor frowned as if he didn't understand.

"You've got a Nokia as well."

"That's a throwaway," said Taylor. "I use it for stuff I don't want traced. It's not in my name and I change the SIM card every couple of weeks."

"Didn't realise that selling used cars meant you had to behave like James bloody Bond," said Harris. His eyes narrowed. "What do you need a throwaway phone for?"

Taylor took out a battered Nokia and dropped it into Weaver's bag. "Let's just say that sometimes I might sell a motor that's less than kosher and I wouldn't want an angry buyer turning up on my doorstep," he said.

Weaver zipped up the bag and looked at his watch. It was just after eleven. "Right, the pub's closing at one this morning and it'll take half an hour to get to the raghead's house. Let's move." Weaver drained his glass

12

and the rest of his men did the same. He stood up and took the kitbag over to the bar.

The landlord, a balding man in his fifties, nodded and took it from him without a word and put it down behind the bar. He winked at Weaver. "Be lucky," he said.

Weaver caught up with the men at the door, buttoning their coats and pulling on leather gloves. "We need to pick up Colin," he said.

"Colin's got the flu," said Connolly.

"Man flu," said Weaver. "I spoke to him on the phone this afternoon, he's sniffing a bit but nothing major. We're the five musketeers, all for one and one for all and he's coming along."

They walked out of the pub and over to Weaver's car, a ten-year-old Jaguar. They climbed in, Taylor sitting in the front passenger seat next to Weaver, with Connolly and Harris in the back.

Weaver drove the short distance to where Colin McDermid lived in a small flat in a terraced street. Both sides of the road were lined with cars so Weaver had to double park while Taylor ran over to the house. He rang the middle of three bells and shortly afterwards disappeared inside. Weaver drummed his gloved hands on the steering wheel as the seconds ticked by. He looked at his watch and then at the clock set into the dashboard and swore under his breath.

"Do you want me to go and get them?" asked Harris.

"Give them a minute," said Weaver. "McDermid's probably getting his trousers on."

"You sure you want him along?" said Harris. "We hardly know the guy."

"Colin's sound," said Weaver. "And he needs to get bloodied." He looked at his watch again. He was about to open his mouth to speak when the door opened and Taylor emerged, followed by a gangly man with a greasy comb-over wearing a blue anorak and black tracksuit bottoms. McDermid pulled the door closed and he and Taylor jogged over to the car.

McDermid climbed into the back, forcing Connolly to move closer to Harris. "What's going on?" asked McDermid, wiping his nose with the back of his hand. Taylor got into the front seat and Weaver drove off.

"Yasir Chaudhry, that raghead who keeps giving speeches about our dead soldiers burning in hell, we're going to give him a taste of his own medicine," said Weaver.

McDermid sniffed noisily. "Are you serious?"

"Serious as a can of petrol and a lighter," said Weaver. "We're going to burn the bastard's house down."

"About bloody time," said McDermid. He banged the roof of the Jag with the flat of his hand. "He's been due for a while, that one."

"That's the truth," agreed Harris.

"Why do I always have to sit in the bitch seat?" whined Connolly.

"Because you've got the smallest arse," said Weaver. "And because you're so short I can still see out of the mirror with you sat there."

Connolly folded his arms and scowled. "It's not fair."

"Life's not fair," said Harris. "Get over it. And if you don't stop bitching we'll send you back to live with Snow White."

Taylor laughed out loud and Connolly folded his arms and cursed under his breath.

Weaver twisted around in his seat and looked at McDermid. "You left your phone in your flat, yeah?" he asked.

McDermid jerked a thumb at Taylor. "Andy took it off me," he said. "Said I had to leave it in the flat and switched on."

"He's right," said Weaver. "If the cops check on you they'll find your phone was in your flat and you can say you were in all night watching TV or internet porn or whatever you do when you're in there on your own."

"We're sitting in the Bleeding Heart right now," laughed Harris.

Weaver drove at just below the speed limit and all the men in the car kept a look out for police vehicles. They all tensed when they saw a car with fluorescent stripes turn into the road ahead of them but they quickly realised it was a paramedic and relaxed.

"So what's the plan?" asked McDermid. He pulled out a pack of cigarettes and slipped one between his lips.

"You'll find out soon enough," said Weaver. "And don't even think of lighting that, not with the amount of petrol I've got in the boot."

McDermid put the cigarette back in the packet and the packet back in his jacket pocket and stared sullenly out of the window.

Taylor looked at his watch, a cheap Casio. "You sure he's home?" he asked.

"Sure I'm sure," said Weaver. "Had a guy around there this evening. He sent me a text while I was in the pub."

"Texts can be traced," said Taylor.

"I'm not stupid," said Weaver. "It's the same as your Nokia, a pay-as-you-go, untraceable." He reached into his pocket and held it up. "It's switched off now and I'll dump it later tonight."

"Looks like you've thought of everything," said Taylor.

"Andy, when you've known me a bit longer you'll know that planning is what I do best. Planning and burning out ragheads and Pakis."

"You've done this before?"

Connolly laughed and jiggled up and down. "This is my third," he said.

"Sit the fuck down, Barry," said Weaver, glancing in the rear-view mirror.

"Seriously? This is your third?" Taylor asked Weaver.

Weaver grinned. "Barry's third. I've done half a dozen."

"Good for you, mate," said Taylor. He beat a quick tattoo on the dashboard with his gloved hands. "They need showing who's boss."

"Damn right," said Weaver.

Taylor sat back, nodding. "That Paki family in Southall, was that you?"

"Bloody right it was," said Harris, punching the back of Taylor's seat. We showed them what for, didn't we, Dennis?"

"That we did," said Weaver. "The trick is waiting until they're asleep and then doing the front and back door. That way there's no way out."

"Brilliant," said Taylor, looking at his watch again.

"Don't worry, mate," said Weaver. "We've plenty of time, and Chaudhry and his bastard brood are already tucked up in bed."

Fifteen minutes later, Weaver pulled up in front of a patch of waste ground. Half the street lamps were off but there was enough light to illuminate a burnt-out car and an old boiler and what looked like the insides of a washing machine next to it. The ground was littered with beer cans, discarded needles and fast food wrappers.

Weaver switched off the engine. "Right, lads, let's get this done," he said. He popped the boot, climbed out and walked around to the back of the car. The four men joined him. Connolly was bobbing from side to side as if bursting to go to the toilet. There were four red plastic fuel cans with black spouts lined up in the boot. "Take one each," said Weaver, standing aside so that the men could get to them.

"Where did you get the petrol from?" asked Taylor.

"Why?" said Weaver.

"CCTV," said Taylor. "The cops will ask around to see if anyone bought petrol local. They always do."

"They can ask all they want," said Weaver. "I got this a month ago, took a drive up the M1 and bought it at a couple of service stations. The CCTV will be long gone."

"Smart," said Taylor.

Weaver grinned. "Like I said, this isn't my first time." He slammed the boot shut. "Right, here's the SP. It used to be that they were two semi-detached houses but the council has made it into one house. They knocked down a few walls inside but they left in the front and back doors. Get that? The house has two front doors and two back doors. So to make sure, we need to do all four doors. Right, Colin, you and Barry head around the back of the house. Pour it all around the doors and get as much inside as you can. Do the windows as well. If there's an open window, use that."

Connolly nodded eagerly. He was still switching his weight from leg to leg like an overexcited toddler. "Can I light it?"

Weaver ignored the Irishman. "Once you're set, listen for me," he said to McDermid. "As soon as you hear mine go up, drop a couple of matches and leg it back to the car." He patted McDermid on the shoulder and he and Connolly hurried towards the house. It was in the middle of a row of semi-detached houses that had been built of brick but over the years all had been either painted or clad in stone. A few of the houses had been well maintained and had new roofs and wood and glass porches built around the front doors, but most had fallen into disrepair and had gardens full of children's toys and household rubbish.

"Right, lads," said Weaver. "Let's get this done and then we can get back to the pub." He headed down the street with Taylor and Harris close behind him. Connolly and McDermid had already opened the wrought-iron gate that led to the garden and were walking around the side of the house. A dog barked down the road but then went quiet.

Weaver held the gate open and Taylor and Harris walked by him, the only sound the sloshing of the petrol in the cans. A siren burst into life somewhere in the distance and the men tensed, but within seconds it was clear that whatever it was it was moving away from them.

The two gardens had been merged into one and then paved over. There were spindly conifers in earthenware tubs either side of the front doors. Weaver gestured at the letterbox. "You can be mother," he said to Harris. "I'll get the other one."

All the lights were off in the house and the downstairs curtains were open. As Weaver tiptoed across to the second front door, Taylor looked through the window. There was a large dining table with eight chairs around it and the remains of a meal. There was another table piled high with schoolbooks next to half a dozen backpacks.

Harris grinned and crouched down. He put the can on the ground and unscrewed the cap. The smell of petrol immediately assailed their nostrils.

"Smells like victory," said Taylor.

Harris frowned and looked up. "What?"

"That movie. *Apocalypse Now*. But he was talking about napalm."

"What is napalm exactly?" asked Harris, screwing the black spout into place. "I've never understood that."

"It's petrol mixed with a gel," said Taylor. "It makes it sticky so that it burns longer."

"We should try that one time," said Harris.

"Nah, it's a bugger to pour and there's less vapour so you don't get that 'whoof' that gets Connolly so excited," said Taylor.

Harris straightened up. "You know a lot about it," he said.

"I had an interesting childhood," said Taylor. "Had a mate who got a kick out of blowing things up." He gestured at the house. "For something like this, petrol is best."

"Get yours ready, Andy," said Harris, looking around. "We need to get it poured quickly, we don't want anyone waking up and smelling the fumes."

Weaver was already at the second front door, unscrewing the cap of his petrol can. He looked over at Harris and gave him a thumbs-up.

"Right," said Harris. "Here we go. Open yours and pour it over the window."

Taylor nodded, bent down and began unscrewing the cap.

Harris shivered in the cold night air and then froze as he saw Connolly appear at the side of the house. "What the hell are you doing?" Harris hissed.

Connolly said nothing. He wasn't carrying his petrol can and his hands trembled at his sides.

"What's the problem?" hissed Harris.

McDermid appeared behind Connolly, his face as pale as the moon overhead. Something prodded Weaver in the back and he lurched forward and stumbled into Connolly and then Harris saw the armed cop, dressed in black with a carbine up against his shoulder. "Cops!" he shouted, and turned towards the gate.

Weaver had already begun pouring petrol through the letterbox but he stopped when he heard Harris shout. He pulled the can away from the door. "What's happening?"

"Cops!" shouted Harris, sprinting for the garden gate, the petrol can in his hands.

Weaver swore, dropped his can and started running towards the wall. He stopped short when he saw the armed cop standing in the road. The cop was aiming his gun at Weaver's chest, over the waist-high brick wall. Weaver slowly raised his hands.

Harris reached the gate but as he pulled it open he saw a third armed cop, with silver sergeant's stripes on the shoulders of his black overalls. Taylor came up behind Harris. "Cops?" he said. "Where the hell did the cops come from?"

"Put down the can!" shouted the sergeant.

Harris threw petrol at him and it splattered across the pavement and on to the policeman's boots.

"Put down the can!" shouted the sergeant again. He was aiming his gun at Harris but he could see that he was unarmed.

Harris grinned and threw more petrol at the policeman. The sergeant took a step back. "This is your last warning, put down the can!"

"You can't shoot me, I'm not armed!" shouted Harris.

"Stuart, mate, he will shoot you," said Taylor, raising his hands.

Harris took a cigarette lighter from his pocket and held it up. "Come near me and this place goes up!" he shouted. It was a stainless-steel Zippo and he flicked up the cap.

"The house is empty," said the sergeant. "We got the family out before you got here."

"It'll still burn!" said Harris. "And you'll go up with it."

"Don't be a twat, Stuart," said Taylor. "Burning to death isn't a pleasant way to go."

Harris ignored him and brandished the lighter in the air. "I'm serious," he said. "Get away from me or we'll both go up in flames, the house too." He splashed more petrol across the pavement and it splattered over the sergeant's boots again.

The sergeant looked over at his colleague. "Arm your taser, Den!" he shouted.

The cop let his carbine hang on its sling as he pulled his yellow taser from its holster on his belt.

Taylor looked over his shoulder. The third cop had pushed Connolly and McDermid forward and they were now standing close to the front door. Connolly darted to the side and grabbed the can that Taylor had been carrying and with a loud whoop threw petrol over the cop next to McDermid. Petrol splashed over his bulletproof vest and overalls and the man staggered back, cursing.

"Go on, Stuart, do it!" shouted Connolly. "Woof, woof!"

"Put the lighter down, Stuart," said Taylor. He still had his arms in the air.

The cop with the taser was moving closer to the sergeant.

"I'm warning you. We'll all go up together if you don't put the guns down!" shouted Harris.

Connolly turned around and threw petrol towards the two officers, but most of it splashed over Taylor, who jumped to the side, swearing. "Bloody hell, Barry, watch what you're doing."

There was a crazed look in Connolly's eyes and he threw more petrol at the sergeant.

"Put down the cans!" shouted the cop with the taser, his finger tightening on the trigger.

"What do you want me to do, Sarge?" asked the cop closest to McDermid.

"We want you to fuck off, that's what we want!" shouted Connolly, whirling around and throwing petrol at him.

"This is your last warning!" shouted the cop with the taser. "Put down the can and the lighter."

"I'd be very wary of firing a taser at a man soaked in petrol," said Taylor quietly. He lowered his hands.

"Put down the cigarette lighter," said the sergeant, but his voice was shaking and lacked conviction. "No one needs to get hurt."

"You put the guns down," said Harris. "Put the guns down, and move back."

"That's not going to happen," said the sergeant.

"Then we'll all burn together," said Harris. He flicked the lighter once and it sparked but not enough to set it aflame. "I'm serious, get the hell away."

"Shall I put him down, Sarge?" asked the officer with the taser.

"You really don't want to be pulling that trigger," said Taylor.

The officer scowled and aimed the taser at Taylor's chest. "You keep quiet," he shouted.

"I'm covered in petrol, too," said Taylor quietly. He slowly raised his hands again. "I'm just saying, there's no need for anyone to get hurt here. Least of all, me."

"Get the hell away from us now or we're all going up in flames!" shouted Harris.

"Put down the lighter," said the sergeant.

"You put down the gun!" shouted Harris. He flicked the lighter again and it sparked.

"Stuart, mate, this isn't helping anyone," said Taylor.

"I'm not going back to prison!" shouted Harris.

"They're not going to let you walk away," said Taylor. "They've got guns. You've got a lighter."

"I've got fire, that's what I've got," said Harris. He waved the lighter around. "I'm serious, you move back now or we're all going up in flames."

Weaver made a dash for the gate, reached the pavement and began running full pelt away from the house. The cops turned their heads to watch him go but quickly turned their attention back to Harris.

Connolly swung the can and a plume of petrol splattered over the pavement near the sergeant. "Come on, then, take a shot and we'll all burn!" he said. Weaver's rapid footfalls faded into the distance.

"Drop the can!" shouted the sergeant.

Connolly laughed and tossed the can in the air. Petrol sprayed out of the spout as the can spun towards the policemen. The officers scattered.

"Let them have it, Stuart!" shouted Connolly.

Harris roared and flicked the Zippo. A flame flickered and Harris tossed the lighter at the can, which had landed at the sergeant's feet. The petrol vapour ignited in a loud whoosh and the policeman disappeared in a fiery orange ball.

The sergeant dropped to the ground, screaming, and began rolling over to extinguish the flames.

McDermid started to run but the cop behind him was too quick and he kicked McDermid's feet out from underneath him, then planted his foot in the middle of McDermid's back.

Connolly looked around, his mouth open in shock. The cop with his foot on McDermid's back pointed his gun at Connolly. "I will fucking shoot you!" he screamed, and Connolly raised his arms.

A sheet of flame rippled back from the pavement towards Harris and then his trousers caught fire. He flailed around, screaming as the flames spread up to his coat.

"Get down on the ground!" shouted Taylor, but Harris either couldn't hear him or was too panicked to react. Taylor cursed and dashed through the flames, barrelling into the burning man and pushing him away from the flaming petrol. Harris was screaming and flapping his arms around, which only made his clothes burn more fiercely. Taylor kicked the man's legs from underneath him and Harris hit the ground hard. Taylor immediately rolled him over, beating the flaming jeans with his bare hands.

Harris carried on rolling until he hit the wall and lay still. Most of the flames had gone out but the coat was still smouldering.

Taylor stood up, his chest heaving from the exertion. As he turned to face the road, a small red dot danced on his chest. He opened his mouth to shout but before he had even drawn air into his lungs the barbs of a taser impaled themselves in his shirt. He just had time to see the two wires trailing through the air to the yellow taser in the hands of the armed policeman, but then he was hit by fifty thousand volts and his whole body went into spasm.

"Spider? Spider, can you hear me?" Dan "Spider" Shepherd groaned. He wanted to open his eyes but somehow his brain had forgotten how to do pretty much anything. He couldn't feel his arms or his legs; in fact the only sensation he had was a burning pain in his chest. "Spider, come on, take deep breaths, you'll be just fine."

Shepherd took a deep breath but there was a stabbing pain in his chest and he went back to tidal breathing. He tried wriggling his toes but there was no feeling at all below his waist.

Something soft patted him on the cheek and he caught a half-remembered fragrance. "Charlie?"

He heard a laugh, and then felt a pat on his shoulder. "Thank God for that," said Charlotte Button. "I thought they'd killed you."

Shepherd's eyelids flickered open. "I can't believe they shot me," he said, his voice a strained croak. He was lying on a stretcher in an ambulance. The doors were shut. The engine was running, he could feel the vibration through his shoulders.

"You were tasered," said Button. "That's not quite the same as being shot."

Shepherd forced a smile. "Suddenly you're an expert on being shot?" he said. "Trust me, I've been shot and I've been tasered and they both hurt like hell." He took a deep breath. "The house is OK, right? It didn't go up?"

"We had the fire brigade on stand-by and they were in with extinguishers as soon as the police had finished. But the family were never in any danger. As soon as I got your text I phoned Mr Chaudhry and got him to get his family out."

"And the cop who caught fire, he's OK?"

"Their overalls are fire retardant," said Button. "He's fine. Just a bit shaken."

"Would have been nice if there had been enough cops to have put the lid on the situation right away," said Shepherd. "It got completely out of control because there weren't enough of them to maintain control, even with guns."

"I got straight on to the Met as soon as I got your text but there have been gang shootings in Brixton and Harlesden tonight so armed response vehicles are in short supply."

"I saw one," said Shepherd. "Three guys. Who the hell thought three guys would be enough? There were five of us."

"That was all we could get," said Button. She looked at her watch. "You sent the text less than half an hour ago," she said.

"Best I could do," said Shepherd. "Weaver took our phones. When I went around to pick up McDermid I managed to use his mobile. I had just enough time to send you a text."

"I'm glad you did," said Button. "Without your warning, Mr Chaudhry and his family would probably have died."

Shepherd groaned. He could feel his feet again and he wriggled his toes inside his boots.

"Are you OK?"

"I've just been hit with fifty thousand volts after putting out a fire with my bare hands, so no, I'm not OK."

"Your hands are fine," she said. "A bit singed, but no major burning. Which is more than can be said for Harris. He's going to be hurting for a few weeks and he's got months of skin grafts ahead of him. But you saved his life."

"Yeah, well, I'm sure he'll be grateful. What about Weaver?"

"An ARV ran into him at the end of the road," said Button. "Literally. He ended up on the bonnet."

"Better late than never," said Shepherd. He tried to sit up and Button helped him. "He bought the petrol a week ago, some service station on the M1. They should have CCTV footage." He touched his chest and winced. "That bloody hurts."

"Well, don't touch it," admonished Button. "And they say it won't hurt for long and there'll be no lasting effects."

"I presume by 'they' you mean the bastards who shot me," said Shepherd. He winced again. "Oh, and Weaver and Harris were behind that arson attack on the Pakistani family in Southall. Connolly knows what's going on and he'll roll over, guaranteed. He's as weak as dishwater."

"That's something," said Button. "Though frankly this is all a bit of a disappointment. The whole point of penetrating Weaver's nasty little gang was to get close to his fascist German contacts in Frankfurt. They're the ones planning the real atrocities. Weaver is just small time."

"He was planning on killing a whole family tonight," said Shepherd.

"I'm not saying we didn't do the right thing in stopping him," said Button. "But there were bigger fish to fry and now we're going to have to find another way of catching them." She looked at her watch, a sleek Cartier on a blue leather strap. "We'll stay in here until the cops have finished," she said. "Might as well maintain your cover. The fact you were tasered means

Weaver and his pals won't ever think that you were an inside man. You might even be able to use the Andy Taylor legend again down the line." She nodded thoughtfully. "If we play it right, we might be able to use it to our advantage. Use it as a badge of honour with the Germans."

Shepherd took a slow, deep breath. His chest wasn't burning as much and the feeling had almost returned to his fingers and toes. "I still can't believe they tasered me with all that petrol around," he said.

"It was either that or a bullet," said Button. "Be grateful for small mercies. They saw you helping Harris and then you moved towards them."

"I was unarmed, Charlie. And I was just about to put my hands up." He ran his hands through his hair. "Still, you're right. It could have been worse." He winced as a sudden pain lanced through his chest, just below his heart. He took slow shallow breaths, panting like a dog.

"Are you OK, Spider?" asked Button, putting a hand on his shoulder.

"I just need a shower," he said. "I feel dirty."

"Yeah, they were a nasty bunch," said Button. "But they're off the streets now and they'll be going away for a long, long time. Job well done, seriously. Bit scrappy at the end, I can't argue with that, but you saved lives and put the bad guys away. There aren't many men who could have done what you did tonight."

Shepherd forced a smile, acknowledging the compliment. "I don't understand how they can set fire to a house with kids and babies inside," said Shepherd.

"Men hating men, OK, I get that, but how can you hate a baby?"

"There's no logic to what they do," said Button. "All we can do is try to stop it from happening."

"Yeah, well, we stopped it tonight but they've burnt other families in the past," said Shepherd. "And what's crazy is that most of them are fathers themselves. Weaver's got three kids, McDermid's wife gave birth a month ago and Connolly's got two daughters with one on the way." He shook his head. "I just don't get it."

"There's no point in looking for an explanation," said Button. "They're just racist haters, with no rhyme or reason."

"People aren't born hating," said Shepherd. "Kids of all races and colours play happily together when they're toddlers. They have to be taught how to hate." He looked at his tattooed knuckles and grimaced. "I can't wait to get these off," he said.

"One laser treatment will do it," said Button. "Two at the most."

"I've never liked tattoos," said Shepherd. He turned his hands over and examined the reddened palms. They were greasy and he realised that the paramedics must have rubbed some ointment over the burns. Button was right, the damage was only superficial.

"They were camouflage, and they worked," said Button.

"I want them off tomorrow, first thing," said Shepherd.

"No problem. Go home. Have that shower. I'll call you first thing and I'll have a laser clinic fixed up. And take a few days off, you've earned it."

Yuri Buryakov stifled a cavernous yawn and glanced down at his watch, a Patek Philippe Tourbillon that had cost him over a million dollars. The conference had been going on for over eight hours now, with only a one-hour recess for lunch providing any relief. He had sat through a succession of speakers, listening to the simultaneous translation in his earpiece, but all he had heard was one piece of bluster or special pleading after another, one more reason why Russia should let the West have its gas, coal and oil for nothing.

He allowed his gaze to wander for what seemed like the thousandth time that day. He knew, because his German hosts had told him so over and over again until he could almost have recited it in his sleep, that the Sanssouci Palace in Potsdam was a rococo masterpiece built by Frederick the Great and rivalling Versailles for its opulence and extravagance, if not its size, but all that ornate plasterwork, marble, silver and gold was like too much rich food to him and left him feeling just as queasy. There was a certain irony that this pleasure palace, created by Frederick as a place to escape the burdens of state — its very name, Sanssouci, meant "without care" — should now be playing host to a collection of politicians, officials, functionaries and flunkies, who could not have been less carefree, nor more dull and dour, if they'd tried.

The German Chancellor was the host of this international conference, called to discuss the future security of power supplies for the West. The US Secretary of State, the female head of the CIA, the British Foreign Secretary and the head of MI6, and the leaders or foreign secretaries and spy chiefs of all the EC and NATO countries, had been wrangling all day with the delegation from the major oil, gas, coal and electricity producers of Russia and half a dozen other states of the old Soviet bloc. Buryakov had no interest in spending any more time listening to the turgid speeches and debates, nor in gazing at the lavishly gilded interiors and the immaculate terraced gardens, ornamental fountains and sweeping vistas outside. Culture of all kinds — even the Bolshoi — left him cold. It had been a long day and he just wanted to get back to his hotel on Kurfurstendamm — the Knightsbridge of Berlin — and find some more congenial company than politicians, diplomats and bureaucrats. He would eat some oysters and caviar, drink some ice-cold schnapps or vodka, and then, if the mood was on him, have his bodyguards bring a whore to his suite.

He left the selection to his bodyguards; they knew his taste in women — stick thin, very young and almost androgynous blondes — and he took his pleasures with them the way he took his business opportunities, with a single-minded, ruthless self-interest, indifferent to who he might hurt in the process. If the whores were sometimes a little bruised or bloody after their encounters with him, then a tip of a couple of hundred dollars more would usually stifle their complaints, and if not, well, they were only whores after all, and he was a billionaire, an oligarch, one of the richest men on the planet. His money, his influence and, if necessary, his lawyers could make almost any problem go away.

The sound of a fresh voice, as irritating to him as the whine of a mosquito, intruded on his thoughts. The "Hausfrau", as he called her — the German Chancellor — had risen to her feet and was now bringing the proceedings to a close for the day but, to her visible frustration, the meeting was breaking up without having reached any significant agreement on a way forward.

Buryakov listened with mounting irritation as the Hausfrau repeated her earlier demands for guaranteed power supplies to the West. Buryakov knew that by the West she mean Germany, as Germany had just pulled the plug on their nuclear power programme and needed to replace that power from somewhere. She ended her address with a call for further talks between the officials — "This evening, and all night if necessary," she said, rapping the edge of the podium with her knuckles for added emphasis — in order to conclude some form of compromise agreement that could then be announced to the waiting media before the conference broke up at noon the following day.

Despite his irritation with her, Buryakov smiled to himself. The Hausfrau was desperate for something she could sell to her electorate as a success, but making the German voters happy with their Chancellor was neither in his own commercial interest, nor that of the Russian government. If she wanted an agreement, there would be a heavy price to pay for it.

All through the Cold War, the West had lectured the Soviet Union on the merits of the capitalist system and they had treated the fall of the Berlin Wall as its ultimate triumph. They could hardly complain now, he thought, if their former adversary had learned the lesson so well that it was now using the capitalist system to its own considerable advantage. His smile broadened. He would let the Hausfrau and her allies fret and sweat into the small hours as they tried to find some common ground, while he enjoyed an untroubled night, and in the morning he would see what price he could make her pay for the piece of paper she would wave before the television cameras at the end of the conference.

As the meeting broke up, he pushed back his chair and began making his slow way out of the conference room. As he emerged, his bodyguard team leader, who had been waiting outside the room with the other heads of security while their principals argued inside, took his place alongside him. They made their way through the crowds filling the cavernous foyer of the palace. The rest of his security team had been required to wait outside the building, stamping their feet in the cold for hours.

There was semi-organised chaos inside and outside the palace, with everyone milling about in the foyer, waiting for word that their own limousines had reached the entrance before venturing outside, while the security personnel outside tried to bring some order to the logjam of vehicles. Inevitably the politicians whose vehicles were first in the queue would have paused on their way out for a final discussion with an ally or foe, and the other cars would be blocked, unable to move.

The Cold War was long over, but the tensions between East and West were still there, and Buryakov's lip curled as he stared out of the great windows at the queue of luxury cars and limousines. All of them — Mercedes, BMWs and even the Rolls-Royces — made by German companies. The thought of that flagship British brand being bought from under their arrogant noses only briefly lightened Buryakov's mood and his frown deepened as he saw the Hausfrau standing in the doorway of the conference room, still arguing her case with another Russian oligarch. He was a close friend and ally of Buryakov's and he knew that he shared Buryakov's contempt for the German politician.

The Germans were not to be trusted, Buryakov knew. Not after two world wars. His own father had taught him that. He could remember many years ago sitting on a threadbare sofa with father in front of a black and white television set watching what passed for the news in Soviet Russia. "When a Russian stranglehold is on their throat, the Germans will roll over and beg, but they will never stop looking for a chance to put their own foot on the throat of the Russian bear instead," his father had growled, grabbing young Yuri by the scruff of the neck and shaking him to make his point. "If we allow them to, they will make use of our natural resources to make their own economy even more powerful, and then one day, when they are ready, the German armies will once more roll eastwards to attack Mother Russia yet again."

"I don't like this, we should be allowed our men inside," muttered Buryakov's head of security, a burly Latvian. Andris Gordin had served Buryakov for more than ten years, first as a driver then as a bodyguard and for the past three years as his head of security, and at times seemed to regard Buryakov less as a boss and more as a younger brother to be taken care of. Buryakov was sure that given the chance, the Latvian would happily have wiped Buryakov's arse and flushed the toilet for him.

"You worry too much, Andris," admonished Buryakov. "It's protocol."

"Fuck protocol," said Gordin. "They shouldn't keep us standing around like this."

Buryakov chuckled quietly. "My friend, if they were going to kill anyone here it would be the politicians," he said. "Not the businessmen."

Gordin stared stone-faced at the queue of cars outside. One of the bodyguard teams waved and Gordin waved back. He hadn't been allowed to bring his transceiver into the building so hand signals were the only way of communicating with his team. The bodyguard outside shrugged and Gordin raised his hands in an exaggerated show of frustration.

They moved slowly towards the exit, Gordin clearly uncomfortable at being surrounded by so many people. "This is madness," he muttered.

Buryakov nodded but said nothing. He looked to his left. Standing close by was a powerfully built man in an immaculate pinstriped suit. He had the ice-cold eyes of an international banker and he looked right through Buryakov. He was carrying a furled umbrella, a good call as the sky was threatening rain. Buryakov smiled and nodded, acknowledging their mutual frustration, but the man ignored him and looked away. Typical banker, thought Buryakov. Thought he was better than everyone else.

They were making slow progress towards the exit when everybody stopped dead as the American Secretary of State emerged from an anteroom. As usual she was surrounded by her phalanx of crew-cut, huge and hostile bodyguards. Only the Americans were allowed to bring in their own people, a ruling that Gordin had taken as a personal insult. "Fucking Americans," Gordin muttered. "They act like they own the world." And to add to the insult, the American bodyguards were allowed to carry weapons.

As usual the American contingent made straight for the doors at high speed, barging straight past those in front of them and knocking them out of the way. As they passed through the metal detectors, all hell broke loose. The entrance to the building had been set up with security screens, scanners and metal, gas and explosive detectors, but they were designed to stop people getting in, not getting out. As the heavily armed American bodyguards barged their way through, the alarm on every metal detector in the place began shrieking. Within seconds the entrance hall had dissolved into complete chaos, with people trying to shout above the noise of the detector alarms, and bodyguard team leaders and delegates jostling and shoving, trying to regroup after being elbowed aside by the Americans.

Gordin bellowed in frustration and Buryakov was just about to tell him to calm down when he felt a sharp pain in his right calf. Buryakov yelped and Gordin immediately looked around. "What's wrong?" he asked.

The pain had gone and Buryakov wondered whether it had just been a cramp. The big man with the umbrella was moving away, his face impassive.

"I don't know. Nothing. I'm not sure." Buryakov was finding it hard to breathe. The alarms all went off together. The American contingent ducked into a fleet of black limousines and sped off flanked by German motorcycle outriders with sirens blaring.

"Thank you so much for fucking off," Gordin muttered at the departing vehicles.

Buryakov's chest felt suddenly tight, as if something was pressing on him. He tried to take a deep breath but stopped when a searing pain shot down his left arm. "Andris," he said, his voice a hoarse whisper.

Gordin turned towards him. "Boss, are you OK?"

Buryakov opened his mouth to say that no, he wasn't OK, when his legs buckled beneath him and he hit the marble floor with a dull thud.

Gordin knelt down next to him and began screaming for a medic, first in Russian and then in English. The designated doctor on duty rushed over with her medical bag. She was a middle-aged German woman

39

with badly dyed hair that had probably been advertised as red but had turned out purple. She carried out an immediate visual and touch check, running her hands down Buryakov's front, sides and back, searching for major injuries, but found no blood and no sign of trauma. She cleared Buryakov's airways, but noted his shallow, irregular breathing, and at once inserted a cannula and set up a saline drip. Buryakov's pulse continued to be very rapid and increasingly erratic, and when the doctor checked him again a minute later, she noted that it had now become even more feeble and irregular.

"What is it, what's wrong?" asked Gordin in English.

"Heart attack," said the doctor brusquely. "Please keep back, give him air." She pulled a transceiver from her pocket and began to talk into it in rapid German. *Ambulanz* was one of the few words that Gordin recognised.

Two hours later, Yuri Buryakov was lying in a hospital bed, connected to a drip and several monitoring machines. He was in a private room and Gordin was sitting outside, glaring at anyone who came near the door.

A doctor in a white coat with a stethoscope around his neck and holding a clipboard walked up. He looked over the top of his horn-rimmed spectacles and said something to Gordin in German. The German shook his head. "*Russkij*," he growled. "Russian."

"I don't speak Russian," said the doctor in accented English. "You can speak English?"

"Some," said Gordin. He stared at the ID badge clipped to the pocket of the white coat. *Dr Bernd Jaeger. Kardiologe.*

"How long will you be sitting here?" asked the doctor.

"So long as Mr Buryakov is here, I will be here," said Gordin. "I am in charge of his security."

"Mr Buryakov is a very sick man," said the doctor. "He may be here for several days."

Gordin shrugged. "Then I will be here for several days."

The doctor nodded. "If it would help, I could ask for a small bed to be put in the room so that you can spend the night. Would that be agreeable?"

"You can do that?"

The doctor nodded and wrote something on his clipboard. "Of course. Mr Buryakov has had problems with his heart before?"

"No. Never. He had a medical last month and his heart was fine. A heart like a lion, the doctor said."

"A very sick lion, perhaps," said the doctor, putting his pen in his pocket. "I shall be with him for a few minutes, if you need to go to the bathroom or get a coffee."

"I'm OK," said Gordin, folding his arms.

"Mr Buryakov is lucky to have a man as loyal as you," said the doctor, and he smiled as he opened the door and went inside.

The doctor took off his spectacles and put his clipboard at the bottom of the bed. Buryakov was lying on his back, his eyes closed, his chest rising and falling with each breath. The doctor took a syringe from his pocket, pulled off the cap, and looked for a vein in the patient's right arm. Buryakov grunted as the doctor injected the contents of the syringe, then put the cap back on and pocketed it.

He walked around the bed and switched off the machines. The drug he had injected into Buryakov was a powerful tranquilliser that would render him immobile without inducing unconsciousness. The doctor slapped Buryakov, left and right, and Buryakov groaned. "Wake up, Yuri," said the man in Russian. "You're not dead yet."

Buryakov opened his eyes and blinked.

"That's good," said the man. "Now look at me closely."

Buryakov tried to focus on the man's face. "Do you remember me?" The man asked.

Buryakov shook his head. He tried to speak but his mouth was too dry. His arms lay like dead weights at his side.

"I don't have many friends, but the friends that I do have call me Monotok. The Hammer." He held up one of his massive hands. "My party trick is to hammer six-inch nails into planks of wood with my bare hands." He grinned, showing white slab-like teeth. "To be honest, it's more about technique than it is about strength." He cocked his head on one side. "What about my name? Does my name mean anything to you? Kirill Luchenko?" He looked for any sign of recognition but there was nothing in Buryakov's eyes. Monotok shook his head sadly. "That's a pity. You fucked up my life, I mean totally fucked it up, and you have no idea who I am." He smiled and patted him roughly on the cheek. "But that's why I'm here, Yuri. That's why I put you in hospital and didn't kill you in the street. I could have done. So easily. I know of a dozen poisons that could have killed you within five minutes, but only one that would put you in hospital with the symptoms of a heart attack." He patted him on the cheek, harder this time. "Your security is good, though. The best. Your head of security is to be commended. The street was the only place I could get near you. And I've been trying for a long, long time." He smiled again. "Still, you're here now." He reached into the pocket of his white coat and pulled out another syringe.

"First we're going to talk. Well, actually I'm going to talk and you're going to listen. I'm going to explain to you what you did to me and how what you did made me the man I am." He held up the syringe and waved it back and forth in front of Buryakov's eyes. "Then I'm going to inject this and you're going to have a fatal heart attack." He grinned, the smile of a shark about to bite. "So if you're lying comfortably, let's get started, shall we? Once upon a time . . ."

Button had been right about the tattoos — after just fifteen minutes in a Harley Street clinic a young Asian doctor with a German-made laser made short work of LOVE and HATE. The skin was red and sore around the knuckles but Shepherd could see that the ink had all gone. The doctor's pretty blond assistant gave him a tube of ointment to rub into the skin and a business card with a phone number to call in the unlikely event of him developing a reaction to the laser.

It was just after two o'clock in the afternoon when he walked out of the surgery, so he decided to pop into a pub for lunch before catching the train back to Hereford. He was just tucking into steak and kidney pie and chips when his phone rang. The caller was withholding his number so Shepherd just said "hello".

"Spider?"

Shepherd frowned. He didn't recognise the voice. "Who is this?" he asked.

"Is that Spider Shepherd?"

"Who's calling?"

"I'm calling. Look, don't fuck around, either that's Spider or it's not and if it's not tell me so I don't waste any more of my time."

Shepherd smiled. "OK, yes, that's me, but if you try and sell me a Sky subscription I'll track you down and shove this phone up your arse." He popped a chip into his mouth.

The man laughed. "Well, I can tell civilian life hasn't sweetened your personality," he said. "But then as the last time I saw you there was a bullet in your shoulder, I suppose that's to be expected."

Shepherd's jaw dropped. There were only four men who had been in the belly of the Chinook the day that he'd taken a bullet and one of them had died in Iraq. "Lex?" said Shepherd. "Lex Harper?"

"Cheers, mate," said Harper. "I just hope your phone isn't bugged."

"It's not," said Shepherd.

"Yeah, well, as a spook you should know," said Harper.

"Where the hell are you?"

"Not far away," said Harper. "I need to see you."

"I'm in London," said Shepherd.

"Yeah, I know," said Harper. "Can you get to Hyde Park?"

"Bloody hell, Lex, let's just meet in a pub. In fact I'm in a pub near Harley Street right now. You're in London, right? Come by now, I'll buy you a pint."

"I'll explain when I see you, but I'd prefer it to be out in the open. Sorry to make it all cloak and dagger, but that's the way it has to be. Make sure you're not being followed, then enter the park at the north side and head for the Serpentine."

"Where will you be?" asked Shepherd.

"I'll be watching you to make sure you don't have a tail."

"Why would I have a tail? I'm not a bloody golden retriever."

"I know what you are, mate. Just better safe than sorry. It's half past two now, can you make it by five?"

"Sure."

"See you then," said Harper. The line went dead and Shepherd stared at his phone, wondering how the hell Harper had managed to get his unlisted number. And how a man he hadn't seen for more than ten years knew that Shepherd was working for MI5.

Shepherd took a black cab to the north end of Hyde Park. He paid the driver and as the cab went on its way he turned up the collar of his coat. It was a cold day and the grey sky overhead threatened rain. He headed for the Serpentine, the forty-acre recreational lake that curved its way through the middle of the park. Despite the chill in the air there were plenty of joggers and rollerbladers on the path, along with dog-walkers and pram-pushing mothers.

Shepherd walked slowly. He couldn't see Harper but the hairs on the back of his neck were standing up and he was sure that he was being watched. He was wearing a heavy overcoat but he kept his hands at his sides. Harper had sounded anxious on the phone and Shepherd didn't want him worrying about what was in his hands.

There was a rapid footfall behind him and Shepherd half turned, his hands instinctively coming up to protect his face, but it was only a jogger, a tall blond man in his twenties wearing oversized Sony headphones. He missed Shepherd by inches and it took all Shepherd's self-control not to kick the man's legs from underneath him as he went by. Joggers could be as aggressive as cyclists, and the man passed so close to a woman pushing a stroller that he brushed her coat and she shouted after him to mind where he was going.

A figure ambled across the grass from the direction of a clump of trees, and even though the man's face was obscured by the fur-lined hood of a green parka, Shepherd instinctively knew that it was Lex Harper. He had put on a few pounds since they had served together in Afghanistan, but he had the same lanky stride and the way of bending slightly at the knees with each step so that his head was constantly bopping up and down as he walked.

Shepherd stopped and waited. Harper was wearing brown cargo pants and Timberland boots and had his hands thrust deep in his pockets. He didn't look up until he reached Shepherd. "Long time no see, mate," he said, in a voice that sounded less Scottish than Shepherd remembered. He tilted his chin up and looked at Shepherd with an amused smile on his face.

"You've put on weight," said Shepherd.

"You haven't," said Harper. "Are you still running with that rucksack of bricks?"

"Not as much as I used to."

Harper laughed and stepped forward to hug Shepherd. There was something awkward about the way that Harper moved and for a brief moment Shepherd tensed, but then realised that Harper wasn't a threat, he was just nervous. He patted him on the back and then stepped away. "What's going on, Lex?" he said.

Harper nodded at a bench at the edge of the path that cut through the park towards the lake. "Let's have a sitdown," he said. They walked together to the bench. As they sat, Harper looked at Shepherd's reddened knuckles and frowned. "You been fighting, Spider?"

"Had some tattoos lasered off."

"Bollocks," said Harper. "You were never one for tattoos."

"Yeah? Well, I was never one for fist fighting, either."

"Aye, that's the truth," said Harper. "A sniping rifle was always your weapon of choice." He chuckled.

"Those were the days, huh? You the sniper and me the spotter, watching your back."

Shepherd nodded. "You were good, Lex. Bloody good. Remember how dubious I was when we first met?"

Harper shrugged. "You didn't know me from Adam. I was just a wet-behind-the-ears Para and you were an SAS superhero."

"Yeah, but I needn't have worried. You did good." He sighed. "So you never went for Selection?"

Harper chuckled. "Come on, mate. Are you telling me you didn't ask around about me after I called?"

"Why would I?"

"You're a spook, right? That's what spooks do."

Shepherd shook his head. "Lex, you're a mate. I'm sorry that we lost touch and that, but when a mate calls me out of the blue I don't run a PNC check on them."

"Are you serious? It's the first thing I would have done."

"Lex, what the hell is going on? What would I have found if I had checked up on you?"

Harper laughed softly. "Hopefully not much, as it happens. But there was a small matter of an armed robbery or two a few years back that is still on record."

"Armed robbery?"

"Allegedly," said Harper. He put up his hands in mock surrender. "All right, Officer, I'll come quietly. I've been a bad, bad boy."

"What the hell happened, Lex? You were one of the best lads out there in Afghanistan."

48

Harper shrugged. "Didn't seem like a long-term career, the way they were cutting back."

"And what, armed robbery offers better career prospects?"

"Don't start getting all judgemental on me, Spider. And I've given up blagging. I'm more into import-export these days."

"Drugs?"

Harper grinned. "Allegedly."

"What the hell happened, Lex? Soldiering pays OK and there's plenty of opportunity to go private."

"Why did I choose the dark side, is that what you're asking?"

"You were a bloody good soldier. You were the best of the Paras out there."

Harper flashed him a mock salute. "Thank you, kind sir."

"You know what I mean. You were a natural. You'd have made it through Selection, no bother. I'd have put a good word in for you. The major, too."

Lex shook his head. "I wasn't even given the chance," he said. "I was part of the cutbacks."

"What?"

"Cost savings, they're cutting the army to the bone. That's what the colonel said to me. There was nothing wrong with me, I could walk out with my head held high, a question of numbers, and all that crap."

"They sacked you?"

"They sacked thousands of us, mate. Haven't you heard? The economy's fucked. Those bastard bankers screwed the economy and I was given my marching orders. I told the colonel that I wanted to try for the SAS and he said I should give the TA a go." Lex smiled. "I told him to go fuck himself and that was pretty much the end of my military career."

"I'm sorry, Lex. Seriously."

"Not your problem, mate."

"You could have spoken to Major Gannon. He might have been able to pull some strings."

"That boat's sailed," said Harper. He shrugged. "Anyway, a group of us figured that if it was the banks that had fucked us over, we should give them a taste of their own medicine. Make a few unauthorised withdrawals, if you like."

"With shotguns?"

"With AK-47s, as it happens," said Harper. "Some of the guys had brought guns back over as souvenirs. We had all the guns we needed. The ammo we had to get here, but ammo's easy enough to get. Though to be honest we never had to fire a gun in anger. Point and shout and they hand over the cash without a fight. That's what they're trained to do."

"Health and safety," said Shepherd. "They're not allowed to put up a fight."

"Yeah, well, we did a dozen or so banks, up and down the country. Then we used that money to get into the drugs game and that's what we've been doing ever since. We keep a low profile these days, but we're making money hand over fist. Millions, Spider. We're making millions."

"Yeah, well, that's good to hear," said Shepherd, his voice loaded with sarcasm. "Drugs, Lex? Bloody drugs?"

"You're looking at it from the point of view of a cop, or a former cop," said Harper. "Drugs is the modern prohibition. If this was in the States back in the 1920s we'd be heroes."

"What, like Al Capone? You're breaking the law. Don't expect me to approve of what you're doing."

"I'm not asking for your approval, Spider. I'm just explaining the way things are. And that's why I've got to keep my head down. I'm still wanted in the UK."

"So where are you based now?"

"Thailand, most of the time."

Shepherd turned to look at him. "Are you serious? I was over in Thailand a few years back. Bangkok and Pattaya."

"I know, mate. I saw you."

"No bloody way," said Shepherd.

"Saw you and kept well away," said Harper. "You were hanging around Mickey and Mark Moore and I figured you were up to something. I asked around and you were using some fake name or other so I figured you wouldn't want to have to explain how come you know a former Para."

Shepherd sat back and ran his hands through his hair. "I don't believe this," he said.

"Believe it," said Harper. "You were with a guy who was a few years older than you. You kept meeting up with him."

"Razor," said Shepherd. "He was my wingman."

Harper chuckled. "He spent most of his time in massage places when you weren't around."

"You know the Moore brothers?"

"Sure. Been to some great parties at their place."

"How are they?"

"Same old," said Harper. "They've given up blagging. Like me, they finance the odd import-export thing now and then. Enough to make a good living but not enough to attract attention. You were a cop then, right?"

"SOCA," said Shepherd. "Serious Organised Crime Agency. Supposed to be the British FBI but it turned out to be the Keystone Kops."

"Is that why Mickey and Mark are still living the life in Pattaya?"

"It's complicated," said Shepherd. "But I owe you one for not blowing my cover." He looked around the park. A woman in a Chanel suit walked by with two chihuahuas in matching pink jackets. "Can't we go to a pub? Or a coffee shop." He jerked a thumb to the north side of the park. "Bayswater's over there."

"I'd rather not, mate," said Harper. "There's CCTV everywhere these days. That and face recognition could have me behind bars faster than you could say . . ." He laughed. "Dunno how to end that sentence."

Shepherd laughed. "Yeah, you were never a great talker. But you were one hell of a soldier." He stood up and stretched. "Seriously, mate, two grown men sitting on a bench talking looks a bit weird, don't you think." He nodded at the Serpentine in the distance, the water as steely grey as the overcast sky. "We can sit outside at the Lido Bar. There's no CCTV, you can smoke and at least we can have a drink. Keep the hood of your parka up if it makes you feel better."

"OK, OK." Harper sighed. He pushed himself up off the bench and the two men headed over the grass towards the bar. He took a pack of cigarettes from his pocket, tapped one out and offered it to Shepherd. Shepherd shook his head so Harper slipped it between his lips and lit it with a yellow disposable lighter. "How did you know I was a smoker?"

"I can smell it on you, and you've got nicotine stains on your fingers," said Shepherd. "Elementary, dear Watson. What's the story? You never smoked in Afghanistan."

"Never wanted to," said Harper. "But most of the guys I hang out with now are smokers and I sort of got pulled into it." He held up the burning cigarette. "It feels good. If it didn't, people wouldn't smoke, would they?"

"There's no accounting for folk," said Shepherd. "I hear a lot of people like Marmite, but I've never seen the point of that."

"Now Marmite, there I agree with you. Never seen the point of it either."

They found a quiet table in the outside area of the bar and ordered coffees. "I'll have a brandy as well," said Harper. "Take the chill off it." He pushed his hood down and shook his head. His hair was starting to grey at the temples but he looked pretty much the same as he had when they had served together in Afghanistan. He had the same lean, wiry frame and his habit of jutting up his chin as if expecting an argument at any moment.

"I'll have a Jamesons," said Shepherd.

As the waitress walked away, Shepherd stretched out his legs and folded his arms. "Why are you here, Lex? If being seen in the UK is such a big thing, why are you putting yourself in the firing line?"

"Because of this," said Harper. He reached into his parka and pulled out an envelope. He gave it to Shepherd. Inside was a newspaper cutting with a photograph of a man in a grey shell suit trying to hide his face with an umbrella.

Shepherd read the story. There were just a few paragraphs. The newspaper said the man's name was Wayne McKillop and that he was accused of ripping the head-scarves off two Muslim women in the Westfield shopping centre. According to the article, McKillop had pleaded not guilty and had told police that it had only been a joke and not a racial attack. "So?" said Shepherd.

"You're not looking carefully enough," said Harper.

Shepherd stared at the cutting, rereading it slowly. Then he moved his face closer to the photograph. There wasn't much to see of the man's face. There were two women in the background, and a man. Shepherd's breath caught in his throat as he stared at the man. He was Arabic looking with a straggly beard and a woollen Muslim cap. The man didn't seem to be aware of the photographer; he was striding along the pavement, staring straight ahead. In his right hand was a bulging white plastic carrier bag. In profile his hooked nose

54

gave him the look of a bird of prey, but the most distinctive feature was his milky eye. "No bloody way," whispered Shepherd.

Harper took a long pull on his cigarette and blew smoke before speaking slowly. "Ahmad Khan," he said. "The bastard who killed Todd and put a bullet in your shoulder. And shot three of my mates in the back."

The breath caught in Shepherd's throat. "Bloody hell."

"He's alive and well and living in London. Or at least he was when that photograph was taken. That's him walking by West London County Court. And the paper's dated exactly one week ago."

Time seemed to stop for Shepherd as the words sank in. There hadn't been a day when he hadn't thought of Ahmad Khan. The wound in his shoulder had long healed, but the scar was still there, an ever-present reminder of the night in October 2002 when the bullet from Khan's AK-74 had come within inches of ending his life. As he sat on the bench, his left hand absent-mindedly rubbed his shoulder. There were some mornings when he'd stand in front of the bathroom mirror, staring at his reflection and wondering whether there had been anything he could have done differently that day, anything that would have stopped Khan from killing Captain Harry Todd and almost ending his own life. He looked at the top of the cutting. The name of the paper was there. The *Fulham and Hammersmith Chronicle*. And Harper was right about the date. So within the last couple of weeks, Ahmad Khan had been walking the streets of West London.

"You OK, mate?" asked Harper.

Shepherd stopped rubbing his shoulder. "You definitely think it's him?"

"I wouldn't have come all the way from Thailand if I didn't," said Harper.

"How the hell does a muj fighter end up in the UK?" asked Shepherd.

"I figured you'd be the one to answer that," said Harper. "You've got access that I haven't."

"How did you get this?" asked Shepherd, holding up the cutting.

"Just one of those things," said Harper. "I was in an English bar for my morning fry-up and the guy next to me is reading the paper. Turns out he's lived in Pattaya for fifteen years but every week he has the local paper flown out to him. When he'd finished he left the paper and I grabbed it for a read. That piece was on page seven or so. Recognised him straight away. That milky eye."

Shepherd stared at the picture. His memory was close to photographic but ten years was a long time and people changed.

"It's him, Spider. I'd stake my life on it."

Shepherd nodded. It definitely looked like Ahmad Khan. "What do you want to do, Lex?"

"At the moment, just check that it's true, that he's in the UK. Maybe it is just someone who looks the spitting image of him. They say everyone's got a double, right? A doppel-gänger." He gestured at the newspaper. "Maybe there's another guy with a milky eye and a straggly beard."

56

"Fair enough, I can do that," said Shepherd.

"To be honest, mate, I hope it's not him," said Harper. "I hope he died back in Afghanistan. I'd hate to think of him living the life of Riley all these years in the UK. There'd be something very wrong with that."

"That's for sure," said Shepherd, scanning the article again, even though his photographic memory had kicked in the first moment he'd set eyes on it. "And what if it is him, Lex? What then?"

"Let's cross that bridge when we come to it." Harper took a small Samsung phone from his pocket and gave it to Shepherd. "Soon as you know one way or another, send me a text on that. I've put the number in. I'll call you back."

Shepherd weighed the phone in the palm of his hand. "You really are into this cloak and dagger stuff, aren't you?"

"I know that phone's clean and it's a throwaway SIM card," said Harper.

"Charger?"

Harper put his hand into his coat pocket and pulled out a black charger with its lead rolled up. Shepherd laughed. "I was joking, I've got all the chargers I need." He put the phone away. "Seriously, you're sure this secrecy is necessary? I'd never heard of you being involved in anything shady."

"That's because I keep below the radar whenever I can," said Harper. "The guys who drive the Rollers and the Ferraris and who swan around the nightclubs and restaurants, they're the ones who get on the most-wanted lists. I'm a nobody, Spider, and I plan to stay that way. For as long as possible." He stubbed the cigarette out on the sole of his shoe and then slipped the butt into the pocket of his parka. He realised Shepherd was watching. "DNA," Harper said.

"Are you serious?"

"Dead right I'm serious," said Harper. "At the moment, I'm not in the system. But once they have your DNA, they have you for ever. And then it's game over."

"Who's 'they' exactly?"

"Your mob, for a start. And the cops. And the government. I'll make you a bet, Spider. Within our lifetimes they'll make DNA sampling compulsory. They want everyone in the world to be in a mass database so that they can track and identify us all. And they'll have us chipped, too."

"Chipped?"

"A GPS-enabled microchip, under the skin. Then they'll know who you are and what you are. Trust me, Spider. It's coming. All I'm doing is delaying the inevitable."

"And why would they do that?"

"Control. So that we all became good little consumers."

Shepherd laughed. "You're starting to sound paranoid."

"Really? Most criminals get caught in the act, or they get grassed up, right?"

"Sure."

"But how else do you catch people?" Shepherd opened his mouth to speak but Harper beat him to it.

"I'll tell you. DNA. And mobile phones. The cops use phones to show where you were at such and such a time. Which is why they want the chip out of the phones and under your skin. I tell you, mate, that's where we're heading. Everyone's DNA on record, a chip under your skin, and then they can see everything you do. They'll do away with money, too. All your assets will be recorded on the chip and if you don't toe the line your chip will be wiped and you'll be a non-person."

"I'm starting to wish I hadn't asked."

Harper leaned closer to him. "Listen, Spider, do you think we could get away with slotting Khan if the cops were able to pinpoint his location and then identify everyone who came near him? That information plus the time of death makes it an open and shut case. That's what they want, and eventually that's what they'll get." He sat back again. "But until then, I stay off the grid and squirrel away my assets as best I can. At least in Thailand the authorities pretty much leave you alone. Do you know what Thailand means?"

"Land of the free," said Shepherd.

"Yeah. Land of the free. And they are free, pretty much. Much more free than people are here. I don't understand how we let things get as bad as they are." He clapped his hands together. "Anyway, enough of my bellyaching. Let's find this Khan and give him what he deserves."

"Where are you staying?" asked Shepherd.

Harper nodded over at the north side of the park. "I'm in a B&B in Bayswater," he said. "One of the few places left that doesn't ask for a credit card." He stood up and flipped the hood of the parka up over his head. "It's good to see you, Spider. The circumstances are shit but I wish I'd kept in touch."

"Me too," said Shepherd. He stood up and the two men shook hands, then Shepherd grinned, pulled the man towards him and hugged him, patting him on the back between the shoulder blades. "You be careful," he said.

"You too, mate."

Shepherd called Jimmy Sharpe's number as he walked across the park. It had been almost six months since he had seen his former colleague but he needed someone he could trust and Razor Sharpe had never let him down. "Please tell me you're in London," said Shepherd as soon as Sharpe answered.

"I'm in New Scotland Yard as we speak," said Sharpe in his gruff Glaswegian accent. "Being briefed on a group of Romanian ATM fiddlers."

"Now how the hell are you going to blend in with a group of Romanian gypsies?"

"You can't call them gypsies," said Sharpe. "That's racist."

"You've been on another racism and diversity course, haven't you?" Shepherd laughed.

"My sixth," said Sharpe.

"Is it sinking in yet?"

"You know me, Spider, I treat everyone the same no matter what their colour or where they're from. If you're bad you go to jail, if you're good I'll do what I can to help you. But I have to say, these Romanians are a right shower of shits. They're bringing in hundreds of child pickpockets because they know that even if we catch them red handed we can't do a thing to them. Now they're using the kids to work the ATM skimmers. The adults stay in the background, organising and taking the money, while ten-year-old kids do the criminal work. And they're all EU now so we can't even deport them."

"So what's the strategy?"

"Following the little fish upstream, see if we can get the godfathers. But you know as well as I do that the sentences the judges hand out are a joke these days. Anyway, enough of my trials and tribulations, what do you need?"

"Why do you think I need anything?"

"Because the only time I ever hear from you is when you want something," said Sharpe. "No offence."

"None taken, mate. Any chance of a quick chat?"

"It'll have to be near me," said Sharpe. "We're out and about all this evening and into the early hours."

"I can get to the Feathers." The Feathers was the closest pub to New Scotland Yard, a regular hangout for off-duty officers, or at least the ones that still drank.

"Text me when you get there and I'll pop down," said Sharpe.

Shepherd ended the call and as soon as he left the park he flagged down a black cab. The traffic was light and in less than half an hour the cabby dropped him in front of the pub. Shepherd paid the driver and sent Sharpe a text telling him he'd arrived. As he walked into the pub, Shepherd received a text back. "Mine's a pint of Foster's."

Shepherd was sitting at a corner table with a pint of lager and a Jamesons with ice and soda when Sharpe walked in. He was wearing a heavy black leather coat over a black pullover and black jeans and clearly hadn't shaved in a few days. The two men shook hands. Sharpe was in his fifties, his hair was greying but the beard growth was almost pure white. He'd grown his hair long and combed it back and was only a week or so away from a ponytail.

"You look tired," said Shepherd as Sharpe sat down and picked up his pint.

"I've been on this case for over a week and it's doing my head in," said Sharpe. "They're real lowlifes and I've got to blend. They drink in some very dodgy dives."

"I'm assuming you're not trying to pass yourself off as a Romanian?"

Sharpe laughed. "Nah, I'm a Scottish gangster in the market for swiped debit cards," he said. "I keep upping the ante and I'm working my way up to the top guys." He took a long pull on his pint and then smacked his lips. "First of the day."

"They're OK with you drinking on duty?"

"On this one I'm on duty twenty-four hours a day," said Sharpe. "And the guys I'm dealing with, if they don't smell alcohol on my breath they'll assume something's wrong." He looked around the pub and shook his head sadly. "Back in the day this would have been full of coppers," he said. "Some of them in uniform. Now most of them are scared to show their faces here. God forbid a copper should enjoy a drink or two." He chuckled. "My old boss in my first CID job, up in Strathclyde, kept a bottle of malt in his bottom drawer and every time we had a result it would come out and it'd be drinks all round. You get caught with a can of lager over there and you'd be out on your ear. I tell you, I'm glad I'm getting near retirement." He took another long pull on his lager.

"You'll never retire, Razor. And they'll never sack you. You're too valuable a resource."

"Aye, well, maybe I'll go freelance for your mob," he said.

"They'd have you like a shot," said Shepherd.

"Even the fragrant Miss Button?"

Shepherd grinned. "Well, her not so much, maybe, but there'd be plenty of departments would jump at you. Surveillance is always recruiting."

"I'm too old to be a pavement artist," said Sharpe. "And like you I get a kick out of being undercover."

"A kick? I don't do undercover for kicks, Razor. Behave."

"You say that, but we both know that you get a buzz from it," said Sharpe, jabbing his finger at Shepherd. "The adrenalin rush, the endolphin thing."

"Endorphins," said Shepherd. "And I don't get a buzz. It's a job. And it's a bloody scary one at times."

"And you like that. We both do. If you didn't, you'd have taken a desk job at Five a long time ago." He leaned towards Shepherd and lowered his voice. "Come on, admit it. Telling lies to get close to someone and then turning them over, you get a kick out of that. Getting a complete stranger to trust you, when everything you're telling them is a lie, there's not many people who get the chance to do that, legally."

"It's my job, and I'm good at it, but that doesn't mean I enjoy lying to people," said Shepherd. "I do get a kick out of putting away bad guys, though. I can't deny that."

Sharpe took another pull on his pint. "So what is it you want?"

"You know I got shot, back when I was in Afghanistan? Well, the Pakistan-Afghanistan border to be accurate."

"I've seen the scar," said Sharpe.

"I nearly bought it," said Shepherd. "Closest I ever came. A young SAS captain died during the same operation. Died in my arms."

Sharpe said nothing and sat watching Shepherd, his face impassive.

"His name was Harry Todd," continued Shepherd. "Typical Rupert, wet behind the ears but thought he knew everything." Shepherd shrugged. "Afghanistan was a baptism of fire for him. He fucked up and three Paras were killed." He stopped talking and stared at the floor as the memories flooded back.

"Fucked up how?"

"He thought he had this SEP. A Surrendered Enemy Personnel. Basically a Taliban fighter who wanted to change sides. The story was that this muj wanted to bring in his mates and they needed an escort. Todd got a hard-on for the guy and sent him out with three

Paras. We found them dead a few hours later. Two of them shot in the back of the head, one shot as he was running away. And no sign of the muj."

"It was a trap?"

Shepherd nodded. "Yeah. It was a trap. The muj — his name was Ahmad Khan — had set the whole thing up. Told Todd what he wanted to hear and Todd sent three Paras to their deaths."

"I hope he was out on his arse," said Sharpe.

"Nah, he wasn't RTU'd."

"RTU?"

"Returned to unit," said Shepherd. "That's generally what happens when someone screws up. But they let Todd stay on." He shrugged. "As it turned out, it would have been better for him if he had been RTU'd."

Sharpe sipped his lager and waited for Shepherd to continue.

"Some time later Todd found out where Khan was. He'd been seen at an al-Qaeda place over the border in Afghanistan, a staging post for money they'd been collecting from opium farmers and the like. Todd put together a team and we went out on a search and destroy mission." He drained his glass, then took a deep breath. It wasn't a memory that he enjoyed reliving. "We flew in by helicopter, six of us including the captain. Four-man perimeter while me and Todd set explosives and blew the place. The concussion killed everyone inside so we set fire to the place and exited. That was when Khan started firing. Killed the captain and caught me in the shoulder." He shook his head, trying to blot out the memory of the captain dying in his arms. "Khan did a runner and the guys got me to the chopper."

"That was why you left the SAS, right?"

"It was part of it," said Shepherd.

"So what's the problem now?" asked Sharpe.

Shepherd sighed. "I need another drink," he said, and stood up.

Sharpe finished his lager and held out his empty glass. "Amen to that."

Shepherd went over to the bar and returned with fresh drinks. He sat down and stretched out his legs. "The thing is, it looks like Khan is in the UK. I don't know how he managed it but he's here."

"Probably got asylum," said Sharpe. "He's not the first and he won't be the last. Remember we let Robert Mugabe's chief torturer claim asylum here not so long ago?"

Shepherd nodded. "It's a crazy system, there's no doubt about that," he said. "In the old days any Afghan threatened by the Taliban could claim asylum if he got to the UK. Then after the Coalition invaded Afghanistan, the Taliban could maintain that their lives were at risk so they could claim asylum. Now that the Taliban is regaining control, we're back to stage one. It's crazy."

"If it was me, I'd put them all up against a wall and shoot them," said Sharpe.

"Afghans?"

Sharpe grinned. "The bloody politicians who got us into this state," he said. "You explain to me why we've got Taliban, former or otherwise, living here?"

"Ours not to reason why, Razor. You know that. We're just instruments of the state."

"And what do you want from me?" asked Sharpe.

"I need you to have a root around the PNC for Ahmad Khan," said Shepherd. "And run the name by the intelligence guys."

"I'd have thought your mob would have had more intel on him," said Sharpe. "You've got access to the PNC, right?"

"Sure. But every time Five accesses it the request is flagged and I don't want a trail."

"But you're happy for my name to be flagged?"

"No, I know you're smart enough to get in and out without anyone knowing you were there."

"You know that's a sackable offence now?" said Sharpe. "The days of pulling up reg numbers for mates are long gone."

"Yeah, and I know how you always play by the rules, Razor," said Shepherd, his voice loaded with sarcasm.

"So this isn't official?"

"If it was official, Razor, why would I be plying you with drink and asking for a favour?"

Sharpe nodded thoughtfully. "I'll sniff around. But that won't be any help if he's here illegally. In fact, if he's got into the country under a false name and is living below the radar . . ." He shrugged and left the sentence unfinished.

"If it was easy, I wouldn't be asking you, would I?"

Sharpe grinned. "Don't try manipulating me, Spider. I've known you too long."

"I'm serious, this is a tough one. But I need to find him."

"Because?"

"Because?"

"He's the guy that shot you, right? I'm assuming you don't want to shake him by the hand and tell him that bygones are bygones."

"Best you don't know."

"Best I do, actually," said Sharpe. "If something happens to this Khan character I don't want my name in the frame."

"That's why it needs to be done on the QT," said Shepherd.

Sharpe held Shepherd's look and Shepherd could see the concern in his friend's eyes. "Revenge can get nasty, Spider," he said quietly.

"He shot me. He killed my captain, shot him in the head and he died in my arms. And he shot three Paras in the back."

"It was war, right?"

"Even in a war situation you don't shoot people in the back. There are rules. Some of them are in the Geneva Convention and some of them aren't written down, but there are rules." He took another sip of his drink. "He shot them in the back, Razor. Two of them while they were sitting in a Land Rover, the other one when he was running away. And now he's in the UK. That can't be right."

Sharpe nodded slowly. "Yeah, the days of the Queensberry Rules are long gone," he said. "OK, I won't ask you what you're going to do because it's best I don't know. Just be careful, yeah?"

"Always," said Shepherd.

Sharpe reached over and clinked his pint glass against Shepherd's whiskey and soda. Then he raised his glass in the air. "To crime!" he said.

Shepherd laughed and repeated the toast and then the two men drank.

"There's something else," said Shepherd as he put down his glass.

"There usually is," growled Sharpe.

"I need you to check up on the guy who gave me the info on Khan. A former Para by the name of Alex Harper. Everyone calls him Lex. He was a Para with me in Afghanistan. He was my spotter for a while."

"Spotter?"

"I did a bit of sniping and you always need a spotter, someone who watches your back, helps ID targets, checks the wind and stuff. Sniping's a two-man game and Lex was my number two. Bloody good, he was. Pulled my nuts out of the fire a few times."

"I'm sensing a but, here."

Shepherd laughed. "Yeah, a lot's changed in ten years, that's for sure," he said. "He's left the army and lives out in Thailand now."

"Ah, the Land of Smiles," said Sharpe.

"Yeah, well, turns out it's a small world. He knows the Moore brothers and he's in the same line of work."

"Armed robbery?"

Shepherd nodded. "Yeah, he left the army and did a few banks. I think in his mind he was a sort of Robin

Hood, told me that it was a way of getting back at the banks because of what they did to the country."

"That's logical for you."

"In a crazy way he made sense," said Shepherd. "The banks screwed the economy, the MoD has to get rid of men to save money, Lex loses his job, so Lex hits back at the banks." He shrugged. "Sort of made sense at the time."

"He hurt anyone?"

"Doesn't seem to have done," said Shepherd. "You know that the key to successful blagging is shock and awe. It's a bit like being an armed cop — if you get to the stage where you actually have to pull the trigger, you've pretty much failed." He swirled his whiskey and soda around his glass. "Anyway, he's moved on now. Drugs. The big league."

Sharpe grimaced. "That's not good," he said.

"You're telling me."

"You need to watch yourself, Spider. Seriously."

"I know, I know."

"I mean it. If you get caught in bed with a drugs dealer your feet won't touch the ground."

Shepherd put up his hand dismissively. "I'm not stupid, Razor."

"Never said you were, but you sometimes have a blind spot where friends are concerned. You can cut people too much slack, you know? I get that he was a Para, I get that he saved your bacon in Afghanistan." He realised what he had said and laughed. "Ha ha, bacon in a Muslim country. Not much chance of that."

"Very funny, Razor. Hilarious. I sense another racism and diversity course on the horizon."

"OK, dietary humour aside, people change. And if you get caught passing confidential information to a drugs dealer, you're screwed and you're screwed big-time."

"I hear you. I'll be careful. And whatever happens, you know your name won't be mentioned."

"Just be careful," said Sharpe. "So what do you need?"

"Lex is clever, he knows how to keep off the grid. There's nothing on him on the Five databases, I've already checked, but I don't want to go on to the PNC, so can you do that for me? Then maybe reach out to Intel and to Drugs? See what, if anything, is known. He was in Spain for a while, but now he's based in Thailand. He's super-careful about CCTV and communications, so he might have been lucky."

"I'll check," said Sharpe.

Shepherd took his wallet and slipped a piece of paper across the table. "I got some basic info from his army record," he said.

Sharpe picked up the piece of paper, folded it, and slid it into his pocket. "This Lex was a friend of the Paras who were killed?"

Shepherd nodded. "Yeah. In fact, if I hadn't warned him not to go with them, he'd probably be dead now too."

"So he's out for revenge, too?"

Shepherd nodded again. "Yeah."

"So why not just let him have what intel we get and leave it up to him? Keep yourself out of it."

Shepherd sighed. "It's not as easy as that."

"It never is," said Sharpe.

AFGHANISTAN, 2002

Little Lailuna loved to sing, but singing was forbidden by the Taliban. Afghanis had kept caged birds from time immemorial but they were now banned, for the beauty of their song and of their plumage was considered too distracting for those whose lives should be devoted to the serious study of the Quran. The flying of kites, which had always drawn watching crowds as they swooped and soared against the backdrop of the azure sky and the snow-capped peaks of the Hindu Kush, was also outlawed, as were films, magazines containing pictures, and music, singing and dancing.

Little Lailuna didn't know that as she sang for her classmates. She was only five years old, and she loved to sing. She didn't know that Taliban patrols attacked and beat women and even girls as young as nine years old for not wearing the chadri — the Afghan burqa. Nor did she know that high-heeled shoes were also forbidden as "no man should hear a woman's footsteps lest it excite him". Or that women were forbidden to speak loudly "lest a strange man should hear their voice", and they were banned from leaving their houses unless accompanied by a male blood relative.

72

She was so lost in her song that Lailuna didn't hear the Taliban militants pull up outside the school building in a Toyota Landcruiser. Lailuna was singing to her classmates, her back to the dusty street. She saw their smiles fade and she faltered and stopped as she saw them back away from her. She turned around and her eyes widened as she saw the four tall, bearded men in the black robes and turbans of the Taliban glowering at her. They were carrying canes. She shot a glance at her teacher, who was now ghost white and visibly trembling. Still Lailuna did not understand. "Shall I finish my song?" she asked, hesitantly.

One of the Taliban swung back his bamboo cane and began lashing out at her, striking her on the legs and back. She fell to the floor crying, but still the cane whistled down, again and again. She curled up into a ball, still sobbing, and through her tears saw her teacher kicked, punched, dragged away and thrown into the back of the Toyota.

The men returned to herd Lailuna and her classmates out of the building with more kicks and blows. Then they took a can of petrol, splashed it around the classroom and set fire to it, and as the building burned, they told Lailuna and the other girls to go home and never return, that the school was finished. Then the Taliban jumped into the Toyota and drove off with Lailuna's teacher in the back. The teacher was never seen again. Lailuna ran home and hid in the dark corner beneath the stairs. She was still there when her father, Ahmad Khan, returned several hours later, and it was some time before he was able to persuade her to tell him what had happened. He sat with her throughout the night as she tossed and turned in the grip of nightmares.

Ahmad Khan had been born the son of a poor farmer from Nangahar province in the far east of Afghanistan. The remote and lawless lands straddling the border were ruled by warlords and tribal headmen, and neither the Afghani nor the Pakistani governments had more than minimal control or influence over them. Khan's father grew opium poppies in the arid, stony soil, the only cash crop that would produce enough income to feed his family. Khan's father was a devout Muslim, a haji who had scraped and saved for over twenty years to raise the money for his pilgrimage to Mecca, one of the five pillars of his faith that was required of all Muslims at some point in their lives.

Khan had suffered an eye infection as a child which went untreated because there was no doctor in the village and richer men than his father could not afford the cost of the doctor in Jalalabad, fifty miles away. For a while it looked as if he would lose his sight, but in time he recovered, though his left eye, while still functioning, was left with a strange milky-white pupil instead of its previous hazel colour. When they saw him, some of their more superstitious neighbours muttered about "the evil eye", and ushered their children away from him. From then on Khan was something of an outsider even in his own community, feared more than liked.

His two younger brothers worked the fields but Khan's father had always had greater ambitions for his

74

eldest son. His dream was that Khan would one day become a mullah or imam — a leader of the faith — or a hafiz — devoting himself to memorising the entire Quran. With that in mind, his father had enrolled him in a madrassa across the border in Peshawar. But Khan was more interested fighting than studying, and when he turned nineteen he recrossed the border to join the mujahedin fighting the Russians in the dying days of the war against the Soviets. Most Afghan men were good shots, but Khan was exceptional, a lethal sniper at long range and equally deadly with an AK-47 or an RPG.

Eventually the Soviets withdrew after their final humiliation at the hands of the mujahedin and Khan returned to the family farm and reconciled with his father. He shared the work in the poppy fields and married the wife his father had chosen for him, the young, doe-eyed daughter of a cousin, named Bahara — "the bringer of spring". For a while, Khan remained aloof from the fighting that again engulfed the country as the rival mujahedin factions plunged Afghanistan into civil war.

Time after time, rival warlords either stole his opium crop or demanded tribute for leaving it unmolested. So when Mullah Omar, "The Commander of the Faithful", pledged that his new movement would eliminate corruption and the rule of the warlords, and bring peace and order to Afghanistan, Khan was one of the first to enlist in the cause — known as the Taliban.

He rose rapidly through the ranks and was a commander by the time that the Taliban liberated

Kandahar province, and was one of those who hanged the principal warlord from the barrel of one of his own tanks. Herat followed next and within two years Kabul had also fallen to the Taliban, with Mullah Omar taking power and renaming the country "the Islamic Emirate of Afghanistan".

Khan returned home to his wife, but although several years had passed since their marriage, still they had not been blessed with a child. He had almost despaired, believing that Bahara must be barren, but at last she told him she was pregnant, and in time she gave birth to a daughter. Born during the full moon, she was christened Lailuna — bright moonlight. Three years later came a double tragedy. Pregnant again, Bahara died in childbirth and her baby, the son they had both dreamed of, died with her.

That was why Lailuna was everything to him now, all that he had. She was the sun, the moon, the stars in the winter sky, the blossom on the mulberry trees in spring, and when she sang, her voice was as sweet to him as the song of the mountain nightingale, whose beautiful call was always the first, long-awaited harbinger of summer.

Khan's father grumbled that raising children was women's work and urged him to marry again, but Khan refused. When he was away, he left Lailuna in the care of his sister, but whenever he was at home, his daughter was at his side. Few Afghan girls were educated, least of all in the frontier territories, but Khan defied his father's opposition to the idea and sent her to a small school in the nearest town. Funded by foreign charities, it was run by an Afghan emigrée who had returned to

76

her native land after living abroad for twenty years. There Lailuna blossomed. If Khan's Taliban comrades disapproved of his actions in seeking an education for his daughter, they kept their opinions to themselves, for he was a great warrior, feared and respected by all.

When the Americans invaded the country, Khan again took up arms, fighting shoulder to shoulder with the Taliban against Americans, Britons and the new Afghan army, using the same guerrilla warfare tactics with which the mujahedin had brought the Soviets to their knees.

But the freedoms that Mullah Omar had promised never materialised. A new breed of Taliban commander emerged, hard-eyed fanatics determined to impose their own interpretation of the Prophet's teachings on the areas they controlled. Khan watched with mounting unease as the soldier-monks of the Taliban clamped down on almost all sources of recreation and pleasure.

Lailuna was never the same after she had been beaten by the Taliban. She would start at any sudden noise and tense at the sound of any approaching vehicle. Her ready smile no longer sprang to her lips, the songs that had gladdened both their hearts had now been silenced and she barely left the house at all. Khan longed for his daughter to change, trying to coax her out of the dark place to which she had retreated, but the old Lailuna now seemed beyond his reach.

Khan's burning anger at the men who had done this to his daughter remained, hardening into a cold, implacable hatred. He knew now that as long as she remained in Afghanistan there would be reminders of what had happened. As the weeks passed, he decided that he had no choice other than to seek a new life in the West. That was the only way that he and his beloved daughter had any sort of future together. So he cradled her on his lap and made his plans.

Jimmy Sharpe called back two days later. It was early morning and still dark and Shepherd had to grope around to find his vibrating phone. It took him a few seconds to remember that he was in his bedroom in Hereford. He squinted at the screen of the Nokia. It was five o'clock in the morning. "Bloody hell, Razor, you're up early."

"Chance'd be a fine thing," growled the Scotsman. "I've just got in and I'm knackered."

"The Romanians?"

"They're like bloody vampires, they only come out at night. They're going to be the death of me."

"Just don't let them bite you in the neck."

Sharpe chuckled. "Yeah, well, should be done and dusted in a few days. I met one of the godfathers last night and I'm back to see him later this week. I'll be going in with a mic so with any luck we'll be able to hang him out to dry." He began to cough and couldn't speak for a few seconds.

"Are you OK, Razor?"

"They smoke like chimneys and it's doing my lungs in," said Sharpe. "Isn't there something about smoking being illegal in a place of work? I should sue the Met for putting my health at risk."

"You know what, the way things are you'd probably get a six-figure settlement. You should talk to your Fed rep."

Sharpe laughed. "Yeah, I'll put in a memo, see what happens. OK, so this Ahmad Khan. Turns out it's a fairly common name, at least out in that part of the world. There's a dozen or so on the PNC but none match the age range of the guy you're looking at. Half of them were born here, two are in the nick and the others, like I said, just aren't your guy."

"That's a pity."

"Yeah, well, nothing in life is ever easy, is it? Now, I've got a pal in the Border Force and he ran the name for me and there have only been eight Ahmad Khans who have arrived in this country in the past three years. Now two of those match the approximate age of your guy, but they both left before their visas expired."

"That's a bugger," said Shepherd.

"Yeah, it means that if he is here he's here as an illegal or he's here under an assumed name. You know how it works, they get on a plane to the UK using whatever passport they can, then they destroy it en route and claim asylum when they land. He could have claimed to be an Iraqi or Iranian or a bloody Syrian. The checks are minimal once they've said the magic word 'asylum'. And the only name and date of birth on file are the ones they give the immigration officer. My mate was telling me that every week they get grown men, clearly twenty-up, arriving at Heathrow without any paperwork claiming to be unaccompanied minors from Somalia. It's as plain as the nose on their face that they're not kids, but there's nothing they can do. They know that so-called orphans get fast-tracked to a passport. Once they've got that they magically discover their families and they come over too. And my guy reckons that half the so-called Afghans who get asylum here are actually Pakistanis. Can you believe that? They throw away any ID they've got when they get here and we can't even tell what country they're from."

"Yeah, the system's flawed," said Shepherd.

"Flawed? It's broken to bits, totally unfit for purpose, as the politicians love to say. The thing is, your Ahmad Khan could have got here without any paperwork at all and provided he's played the system right he could be living here with his family under a totally different name with a British passport that's as real as yours and mine."

"Thanks for checking, anyway, Razor."

"You know what you might think of trying," said Sharpe. "Facial recognition. He's side-on pretty much in that picture but the facial recognition systems are getting more sophisticated every year. If he did go through the system he'll have been photographed and fingerprinted. You should be able to run his picture through their database. My mate says he can't do it, he's just a foot soldier, but he says it can be done. Might be worth thinking about."

"Cheers, Razor."

"And your mate the Para. Alex Harper. Not much on him, either. Drugs aren't aware of him but he's in the frame for a few armed robberies, 2007 and 2008, but the only case against him was dropped when a witness recanted her evidence. They did a building society in Leicester and escaped on bikes, one of them smashed into a bus and ended up doing six years, he's only just been released. He was a Para too and they tried everything to get him to turn over his mates but he kept quiet and did his time."

"Six years doesn't seem long for armed robbery?"

"He was firing blanks," said Sharpe. "To be fair, he didn't fire at all. They didn't have to, they went in mob-handed brandishing AK-47s and the staff and customers pissed themselves, and not in a good way. Anyway, when they examined the gun of the guy they caught they discovered there were only blanks in the clip. The judge still gave him ten years but he was as good as gold behind bars so they let him out early this year."

"And what was the story about Harper?"

"Different robbery. Birmingham. About three months prior to the Leicester job. Harper was wearing a balaclava but one of the cashiers said she'd never forget his eyes. And she remembered a mole on his nose. The MO was the same as the Leicester job, motorbikes and AK-47s, so a very enterprising detective got hold of the arrested guy's service record and ran the pictures of the guys in his unit past the cashier. She picked out Alex Harper. By then he'd scarpered. But then the cashier contacted the cops and said that she wasn't sure after all. It was about that time that she started driving a new car and all her credit card bills were paid off. Cops couldn't prove anything, but that was the last time Harper appeared in the system. He's never been fingerprinted and his DNA isn't in the system. Far as intel goes, looks like he's in Spain now, on the Costa del Crime. But he's not wanted. You said he was in Thailand, but that intel's not in the system."

"Thanks, Razor. I owe you."

"Yes, you do. But you can do me a favour."

"Sure."

"Watch yourself with this Harper character. He's obviously not your run-of-the-mill crim, I'll give you that, but the job you're in now, you've got to be careful who you associate with."

"I hear you."

"I can tell my advice is going in one ear and out of the other," said Sharpe. "Anyway, I'm off to bed. You got anything interesting on?"

"Just my boxers."

"I meant job-wise, idiot."

"Yeah, there's something on, Charlie has summoned me to Thames House later today."

"Give her my love."

"I'll definitely do that," said Shepherd, and ended the call. He put the phone down on the bedside table before rolling over and trying unsuccessfully to get back to sleep. His mind kept racing, filled with jerky images of his time in Afghanistan: the searing heat, the foul smells, the firefights, the explosions, the mortar fire, the rattle of Kalashnikov fire, the adrenalin rush of being under fire. He tossed and turned for more than an hour, then he rolled out of bed, pulled on a tracksuit and went downstairs. His boots and his rucksack were in the cupboard under the stairs. Shepherd always ran with the rucksack, which he had filled with house bricks wrapped in newspapers. He laced up his boots, swung the rucksack on to his back and let himself out of the kitchen door.

He ran for the best part of an hour, most of that time at full pelt, and he was bathed in sweat by the time he got back to the house. His au pair, Katra, was in the kitchen making coffee. She was wearing a grey sweatshirt a couple of sizes too big for her and jeans that seemed to be a couple of sizes too small. She had her blond hair tied back in a ponytail and the sleeves of her sweatshirt pulled up to her elbows. "You're up early," she said.

"Couldn't sleep," he said. "I'm heading to London after breakfast," he added, tossing the rucksack back under the stairs and slipping off his muddy boots. "I'm not sure when I'll be back, I think they have a job for me."

"You know Liam's back for half term in two weeks?" she asked, giving him a mug of coffee.

"I'd forgotten," he said. "I'll Skype him this evening. I'm going to go by train, so I'll need a lift to the station."

"Egg and bacon? And toast?"

"You read my mind," said Shepherd, taking his coffee with him upstairs.

He sat on his bed and phoned Lex Harper on the Samsung phone that he'd given him. "Just wanted to update you on my progress," said Shepherd.

"Which is zero, right?"

"How did you know?" asked Shepherd.

"I can hear it in your voice. I knew it wasn't going to be easy."

"Yeah, well, I've tried the obvious things and drawn a blank, so it looks as if he's here under a different name."

"Mate, I bet he's here as an illegal. Probably got asylum under that different name." Harper cursed. "So near and so bloody far," he said. "Looks like I'll just have to keep pounding the streets of West London looking for him. Not much of a plan, is it?"

"I'm in the office later today," said Shepherd. "There's a guy there I can ask, he'll do some digging for me on the QT. What about you, are you OK hanging around?"

"I'm not going anywhere," said Harper. "I'm staying right here until we get this bastard."

Thames House had been the home of MI5 since 1994. It was an imposing grey Portland stone edifice on the south side of Horseferry Road, with statues of St George and Britannia on the frontage glaring across the road at Nobel House, the former headquarters of ICI, which was built at the same time and to virtually the same design. A flag fluttered on the roof of the building with MI5's crest and motto — Regnum Defende, Defend the Realm. As well as being home to the Security Service, Thames House also contained the Northern Ireland Office and the Joint Terrorism Analysis Centre. Because of the undercover nature of his work, Shepherd rarely visited the building, but Charlotte Button had asked him in for a meeting first thing on Monday morning. Security was tight and Shepherd had to show his MI5 ID, press his right thumb against a fingerprint detector and pass through a metal detector before he was allowed to use the lift to the fourth floor.

Button was waiting for him in a windowless meeting room. There was a pine table with six high-backed leather chairs around it, and the wall opposite the door was filled with a whiteboard. There were a dozen or so photographs and notes written in black and red ink on the whiteboard and a pale green file and a large manila envelope on the table.

"Spider, punctual as always," said Button. She was wearing a dark blue linen jacket over a cream dress and had her chestnut hair clipped up at the back. She air-kissed him and patted him on the left arm, just above the elbow. He caught the fragrance of her perfume, floral with a hint of orange. "I've got you a coffee," she said, pointing at a white mug next to a plate of chocolate biscuits.

Shepherd grinned. "Good to see that the cutbacks haven't hit the catering budget," he said, sitting down.

"A few years ago I would have been able to offer you Kit Kats," she said. She sat down opposite him and reached for a cup and saucer. She stirred her tea and smiled at him. "No lasting effects from the taser?" she asked.

"A couple of burn marks," he said. "But it could have been a lot worse. I could have gone up like a Roman candle."

"Ready to get back in the saddle?"

Shepherd looked over at the whiteboard, wondering what she had planned for him. "Sure."

Button opened the file and took out a photograph of a large, heavy-set man in a dark suit. He was in his late fifties with a squarish, unsmiling face and receding hair cut close to the scalp. "Peter Grechko," she said. "One of the Russian oligarchs who now makes London his home. He's one of the world's richest men, up there with Roman Abramovich, Boris Berezovsky and Abram Reznikov."

Shepherd nodded and took the photograph from her. "I've heard of him. He tried to buy Liverpool but missed out and now he's hoping to buy Manchester City, right?"

"Among other things," said Button. "Did you hear about the attempt on his life? A sniper took a shot at him two days ago as he was leaving Stamford Bridge. He'd been watching Chelsea play. A bodyguard was wounded but Grechko was unscathed."

Shepherd frowned. "That's news to me."

"Hardly surprising," said Button. "He owns a chain of provincial newspapers and several news magazines and is close to the owners of several national newspapers. Skis with the younger Murdochs and lives down the road from the owner of the *Daily Express*."

"Who needs a D notice when you've got friends in high places?" said Shepherd, handing back the photograph.

"His friends go higher than that," said Button. "He's very close to the prime minister. He's been on Grechko's yacht, several times. As have several members of the cabinet and half a dozen peers, Labour and Conservative. Mr Grechko is on the board of several charities patronised by the PM's wife and made a substantial donation to his old college."

"I think I can see where this is going," said Shepherd.

"I'm sure you can," said Button. "The PM's office has asked us to make sure that nothing happens to Mr Grechko while he is on British soil. He has his own security team, of course, but I need you to go in and oversee it."

"I'm sure they're thrilled about that idea."

"It's not up to them," said Button. "The PM's office wants Mr Grechko looked after and that's what's going to happen."

"And Mr Grechko's happy with that?"

"It was his idea, apparently," said Button. "He was at Chequers over the weekend and asked for help then." She stood up and walked over to the whiteboard. She beckoned Shepherd to join him. "This is Grechko's security team," she said. At the top of the board was a head-and-shoulders photograph of a man with a squarish face and a thick brow. There was a scar on his left cheek as if a broken bottle had been thrust into the flesh and twisted, and he had a neck so thick that his head seemed to merge seamlessly into his shoulders. Button tapped the photograph with her pen. "Dmitry Popov has been Grechko's head of security for the past eight years," she said. "He's a former senior Moscow police officer and his previous job was on Putin's security team."

"*The* Putin? The Russian president?"

"The very same. But Putin regularly shuffles his protection teams to keep them on their toes and when Popov found himself demoted, Grechko moved in and made him an offer he couldn't refuse."

"What's with the scar?"

"It happened during his military service, apparently," said Button. "Make no mistake, Spider, his nose is going to be well out of joint when he hears that you'll be overseeing Grechko's security. He's bound to see it as a slap in the face, so watch him."

"Understood," said Shepherd. "What's he being told?"

"The truth, pretty much. That Grechko has asked the government for help and that you're being assigned to oversee Grechko's security while he's in the UK."

"And who am I?"

"The legend we've put together has you as Tony Ryan, part of the Met's SO1 Specialist Protection Unit. You've heard of them?"

"Sure," said Shepherd. "They look after the PM and former PMs and anyone considered to be under threat from terrorists in the UK and overseas. They look after foreign dignitaries, too. And the likes of Salman Rushdie."

"Got it in one," said Button. "Grechko has been told by the PM's office to expect you. We're keeping Five's involvement out of it. I'll be liaising with Grechko but I'll be doing it as Charlotte Button of the Home Office."

"And I'll be a career cop?"

"We think that's best," said Button. She nodded at the table. "There's a file there with the complete legend but it's pretty straightforward, a few years on the beat, ten years with SO19 as a firearms officer and five years with SO1."

"Did I guard Tony Blair?"

"Did you want to?"

Shepherd laughed. "That's one man I definitely wouldn't take a bullet for. What's the position over weapons?"

"Grechko's men aren't permitted to carry guns on British soil. We suspect that they do, and the word from the PM's office is that if you do see them with arms, turn a blind eye."

"And what's my position?"

"As an SO1 officer you're authorised to carry a concealed weapon, and the Russians will know that. That's how it'll be sold to Popov and the rest of the team, they need you there because you're licensed to bear arms. I'll talk to the armourer and get the paperwork done today. Someone can bring it out to you tomorrow. Any preferences?"

"A regular Glock'll be fine."

"Holster?"

"Shoulder, nothing fancy. It's not as if I'll be entering any quick-draw contests."

Below the photograph of the head of security were photographs of eight men, most of them shaven headed and all of them with hard faces, set like stone as they stared at the camera.

"These are the core of Grechko's personal security team," said Button. "Alexei Dudko, Boris Volkov, Grigory Sokolov, Ivan Koshechkin, Vlad Molchanov, Konstantin Serov, Leo Tarasov and Mikhail Ulyashin." She tapped the final photograph. "Ulyashin is the one hit by the sniper. He's out of hospital and will be returning to the team later this week."

"Two teams of four working twelve-hour shifts? That's tight."

"I think they were on three-man teams plus a driver," said Button. There were three more photographs at the side of the board. "These are the drivers. Roman Khorkov, Yulian Chayka and Nikolay Eristov. They're all former Russian police drivers, they joined with Popov." Along the bottom of the whiteboard were another six photographs. "Since the sniping attack, Grechko has increased his security staff, hiring these six men. Well, five men and a woman as it happens."

"All Russian?"

"Three of the new intake are Ukrainian," said Button. "Max Barsky, Thomas Lisko and the one woman on the team, Alina Podolski. I've got CVs of all the members of the team in the file."

"And what's my brief, Charlie?"

"Your brief is to make sure that nothing happens to Peter Grechko while he's in the UK," said Button. "You do that by sticking close to him whenever he's in a vulnerable situation, and by doing whatever you deem necessary to beef up his security."

"And presumably you're working on tracking down the sniper?"

"The Met's on that case," said Button. "It's being treated as a police matter."

"Good luck with that," said Shepherd. He walked over to the table, sat down and picked up the file. "What do you think?" he asked. "Who do you think took a pot shot at Grechko?"

"There are actually two questions there," said Button, joining him at the table. "The man who pulled the trigger was almost certainly paid to do it, so we're looking for a professional. And the way the world works, he could be from anywhere. Just because Grechko's a Russian, it doesn't mean the sniper is. He could be home grown, he could be American — hell, he could be Chinese." She picked up her cup and sipped her tea. "The bigger question is who paid for the hit. And the answer to that probably does lie in Russia."

"A business dispute?"

Button shook her head. "Grechko says not. He thinks the government's behind it."

"The Russian government?"

"That's what he thinks. And there have been a number of high-profile Russians murdered in the UK over the last few years. Some make the papers, and some don't. Alexander Perepilichniy collapsed outside his home in Weybridge. He was only forty-four and toxicology reports were inconclusive, but it looks like he was poisoned. He was linked to an investigation into corrupt tax officials in Russia. We had another Russian businessman narrowly escape death when he was gunned down in broad daylight in Canary Wharf. Guy called Gorbuntsov. Shot six times by a man we think is a Romanian hitman. Gorbuntsov is convinced that Kremlin insiders ordered the hit. And of course we're all too familiar with Alexander Litvinenko, the former KGB officer who died in a London hospital not long after being poisoned with radioactive material."

"Polonium 210," said Shepherd.

"Exactly. And almost certainly administered by a KGB officer who then fled to Moscow. Litvinenko publicly accused Putin of being responsible for his death. And there's plenty of evidence to suggest that the Russian government has been the prime mover in a lot more Russian deaths in the UK."

"Killing their own citizens? Nice."

"They're not the only country doing that, unfortunately. The Iraqis did it during Saddam's era, the Libyans have been doing it for years, ditto the Chinese."

Shepherd smiled thinly. "And let's not forget our dear cousins across the pond. The Americans lead the world in assassinations at the moment."

"Well, to be fair, pretty much all the American killings take place on enemy territory," said Button. "And they tend to use the military, which at least gives it some degree of legality. What's been happening with the Russians is far more sinister. Another oligarch, Boris Berezovsky, was found dead in his bathroom in Ascot and we still don't know exactly what killed him. But we do know he was one of Putin's fiercest critics and he was supposed to be a key witness at Litvinenko's inquest. He had a full complement of bodyguards but they still got to him."

His eyes narrowed as he looked at Button. "What about us, Charlie?"

"Us?"

"Us Brits. Do we have an assassination policy?"

"The UK's policy is that we don't carry out assassinations," said Button.

"I know that's the official policy, but is there a section somewhere within MI5 or MI6 that kills people, in the way that the Yanks do it?"

"If there is, I'm not aware of it," said Button levelly.

"That's a politician's answer," said Shepherd.

"No, it's a truthful answer. But you have to bear in mind that if there was such a section and I was aware of it, I wouldn't be able to tell you."

Shepherd grinned. "Yeah, I'd realised that."

"Let me ask you a question, Spider."

"I'm listening."

"Suppose there was a section that did carry out judicial killings. Would you be prepared to work for it?"

"Are we talking hypothetically, Charlie?"

She studied him with unblinking eyes. "Of course."

Shepherd looked back at her, trying to work out whether she was making him a serious offer or whether the conversation was, as she said, hypothetical. "It would depend," he said eventually.

"On what?"

"On the nature of the targets," he said.

"I'm not sure that if there was such a section its operatives would be given the freedom to pick and choose their assignments," she said.

"That's the problem," said Shepherd. "I've killed, of course I have. That goes with the turf when you're in the SAS, but that was mainly in war zones and it was kill or be killed. Assassination is a whole different thing. It takes a particular kind of mindset to kill a human being who isn't a clear threat."

Button sipped her tea. "You were a sniper, weren't you?"

"That was one of my areas of expertise," he said. "And I had my fair share of kills in Afghanistan. But again that was a war zone. Could I shoot targets solely because some politician had decided that they deserve to die? I'm not sure that I could."

"Because?"

"Because I don't trust politicians, of any persuasion. I don't trust their judgement and I don't trust their motivation. If an officer identified a target, I'd take that target out without questioning the order. But if a politician told me to assassinate someone, I'd want to know why and if there wasn't a bloody good reason then I'd tell them to go stuff themselves."

"I can understand that," she said. "But as I said, you wouldn't get the choice."

"We are still talking hypothetically?" said Shepherd.

Button laughed. "Of course. So this sniper, the man who tried to kill Grechko. What sort of person would he be?"

"Like you said, a professional. Almost certainly former military. Of course, if it was a government-sanctioned operation he might still be in the army. So he'd either be doing it because it was his job, or because he was being paid a lot of money."

"Could you kill for money?"

Shepherd frowned. "Of course not."

"Because?"

"Because I've got a conscience. Because I've got a moral compass. Taking a life is no small thing, Charlie. And no matter what the circumstances, it stays with you for ever."

Button nodded slowly. "So we're looking for a what? A sociopath? Someone with no feelings, no emotions?"

"Or someone who's used to obeying orders. I thought the Met was looking for the sniper?"

"They are. But we've got better lines of communication with the FSB so we'll make use of them. We've put in a request for information of snipers, military and freelance."

The Moscow-based Federal Security Service of the Russian Federation was Russia's main domestic security agency, the equivalent of MI5 and the successor to the KGB. Like MI5, it was responsible for counter-intelligence, internal and border security, counter-terrorism, and surveillance. "Are they likely to help if it is the Russian government who's behind it?" asked Shepherd.

She smiled. "Good point," she said. "In a way it's a test. We'll see just how cooperative they are. Or aren't."

Shepherd sipped his coffee. "If it is the Russian government that tried to kill Grechko, why would they use a sniper? It's very in your face." He grinned. "No pun intended. I mean, don't they usually use more subterfuge? Remember the Bulgarians with that poisoned umbrella thing? And they got that Alexander Litvinenko guy by putting Polonium-210 in his food."

"Litvinenko was working for MI5 at the time," said Button. "He'd been given political asylum and he was active in Russian politics, helping dissident factions. I don't think there's any doubt that it was a political assassination."

"So why not try something like that with Grechko? Why use a sniper?"

"Because Grechko has always been well protected," said Button. "Strangers don't get near him, his food is tasted, his rooms and vehicles are constantly checked. With a man like Grechko, it would have to be done at a distance. You're going to have to bear that in mind when you're with him. The sniper tried once and he's still out there. He could well try again."

"Where is he now?"

"At his house in The Bishops Avenue. Near Hampstead. He's staying there until we get his security arrangements sorted out. But I warn you, he's intent on doing a fair bit of travelling over the next few months. I'm hoping that you'll be able to dissuade him from that, at least until we've identified and apprehended the sniper." She pushed a manila envelope across the table to him. "That's the details of your legend. Also the keys to the flat you used in Hampstead, when you were using the John Whitehill legend last year. The flat is pretty much as it was, though it's been used a couple of times since you were there. It's already been dressed but it's doubtful that you'll be taking anyone back there." She pointed at the envelope. "There's a passport, driving licence and warrant card in the name of Tony Ryan, plus credit cards and an organ donor card, which is a nice touch. Plus keys to the flat. And a SIM card on a Met account, so put that in any phone you want."

"What about a vehicle?" asked Shepherd, slipping the envelope into his pocket.

"Talk to the car pool. Something in character but bearing in mind the case I'd feel happier if you were in something with ballistic protection."

"You think I might be a target?"

"Better safe than sorry," said Button. "And I want you in a vest at all times. Since the sniper, all Grechko's bodyguards have been wearing vests and I want you in one, too." Shepherd sipped his coffee and grimaced. "Is the coffee not great or is it the job you're not happy with?" asked Button.

Shepherd put down his mug. "The coffee's fine."

"But you're not happy about the job?"

"If you think this is the best use of my talents then who am I to argue," he said.

"But?" said Button. "I'm sensing a definite but here."

"He's a Russian, Charlie. If he was a Russian journalist or a political exile then maybe I'd have some sympathy or empathy or whatever, but he's a bloody oligarch and you don't get to make a billion dollars from scratch without treading on a few toes."

"He deserves to be shot, is that what you're saying?"

"Of course not," said Shepherd, brusquely. "But this isn't his country for a start. He chose to be here. If he's worried about his safety here then he's perfectly capable of going somewhere else."

"Which would be an admission that we can't protect him."

"But why are we protecting him, that's the question, isn't it? Because he's a friend of the PM's. How much do you think he's given them in political donations?"

Button smiled and nodded to concede the point. "Actually, he's an equal opportunity donor," she said. "He gave a million pounds to all three political parties."

"Hedging his bets? So no matter who runs the country, they're beholden to him?" Shepherd sighed. "Don't you feel sometimes that we're behaving like a Third World banana republic, selling ourselves to the highest bidder?"

"I hear what you're saying, Spider, but you have to realise that men like Peter Grechko are now world citizens. The normal rules don't apply to them. And wherever they settle, there's a trickle-down factor that only benefits their host country. If they start to believe that the UK isn't a safe place for them, we stand to lose billions. And let's not forget that a killer is a killer, no matter who his target is."

Shepherd held up his hand. "You're right, of course. But if the sniper is a hired hand, even if we do catch him, there's no reason to think that'll be the end of it. Whoever is footing the bill can just find someone else."

"Let's worry about that down the line," said Button. She finished her tea and flashed him an encouraging smile. "First let's make sure that Peter Grechko has whatever protection he needs. And don't forget, I want you wearing a vest at all times."

"When do I start?"

"No time like the present," she said. "Assuming you can pick up the gun and the car tomorrow, you might as well go around and introduce yourself and get the lie of the land."

"And this is full-time, right?"

"Pretty much," said Button. "Certainly I want you by his side whenever he leaves the house. My understanding is that his home is secure, so providing he's there you can take a break. We can't afford anything to go wrong, Spider. If anything happens to Grechko on our watch, our lives won't be worth living."

Shepherd said goodbye to Button, but when he reached the lifts he went up and not down. He got out on the sixth floor and walked along to the office of Amar Singh. Singh was in his early thirties and one of MI5's top technical experts. Shepherd had worked with him at the Serious Organised Crime Agency and they had both moved with Charlotte Button to MI5.

Singh grinned when he saw Shepherd at his door. He hurried from around his desk and hugged him hard. "Long time no see, Spider," he said. He was in his mid-thirties, wearing an expensive Hugo Boss suit. Shepherd could never work out how Singh managed to spend so much on his clothes when he was the father of three young children. "Didn't expect to see you here."

"Special occasion," said Shepherd, dropping down on to a chair. There was a framed photograph of Singh and his family on the desk — his arms protectively around his pretty long-haired wife Mishti and equally gorgeous daughters. The youngest was just over a year old but already had her mother's smouldering eyes, of a brown so dark that they were almost black. "Charlie wanted to brief me *in situ*. So what's the latest in ballistic protection?"

"Human or vehicle?"

"Both," said Shepherd.

"We've got some new lightweight vests that are the bee's knees," said Singh. "We've got them from a company in Israel. They use fabrics infused with nanoparticles, putting them in multiple layers with the weaves in different directions. They stay soft and pliable until the moment of impact, at which point they go harder than Kevlar. The material is so soft the vest can be extended down the upper arms and down to the groin area. They actually look like a thick T-shirt and are as easy to put on and take off."

"Sounds perfect," said Shepherd. "Do they come in blue?"

Singh laughed and scribbled on his notepad. "White only," he said. "They're not for general release just yet but I'll get you a couple. What are you, a thirty-eight?"

"Closer to forty these days," said Shepherd. "They do work, right?"

Singh laughed again. "It's the high cost that's holding them back," he said. "They're ten times the price of a Kevlar vest at the moment. Our purchasing department is waiting for the cost to come down before placing a major order. What I have is a few samples. I've seen them in operation, and they're really something. They'll stop any handgun round at any range, and they'll stop a round from an AK-47 at about fifty feet up. That's not to say you won't get bruised, but the round won't penetrate. As soon as the round hits the fibres they harden, almost instantaneously. But with a high-powered round that means the vest will impact a couple of inches. The skin won't be broken but it'll hurt like hell. They have the facility of adding ceramic plates, if you want, of course."

"The vest will be fine," said Shepherd. "And Button wants me to have a bulletproof car."

"Of course she does," said Singh. "You're one of our most valued employees. What's the legend?"

"Police, close protection squad. I'm thinking a four-by-four."

"What do you drive these days? BMW X5?"

"Yeah. But mine's back in Hereford."

"We've got several in the pool and I'm pretty sure that one of them is already fully armoured."

"Not sure that I need bomb-proofing," said Shepherd. "Just the glass and ballistic protection in the doors."

"When do you need it by?"

"Today?"

Singh chuckled. "Tomorrow morning?"

"Can you have it dropped off? I'll be in Hampstead."

"Should be able to do that," said Singh. "Are you on your old mobile?"

"Yeah, but I'll be picking up a new one for this job. The legend is Tony Ryan."

Singh made a note on his pad. Shepherd gave him the address of the Hampstead flat and Singh wrote that down, too.

"What about the car? Registered to Tony Ryan?"

"Better make it a Met car," said Shepherd. "As far as anyone knows I'm on secondment from the Met so that'll add to the legend."

"Not a problem," said Singh. "Might cut down on the parking tickets, too."

"Good point. Can you get a resident's permit for the car, too, I'll have to leave it on the street when I'm in Hampstead."

Singh made another note on his pad.

"And I need a favour," said Shepherd. He reached into his jacket and pulled out the newspaper cutting that Harper had given him. He gave it to Singh and then sat quietly as he read it through. When Singh looked up again, Shepherd leaned across and tapped the face of the man he was sure was Ahmad Khan. "I need to identify this man."

Singh frowned as he reread the story and caption. "He's not mentioned in the article."

"He's not mentioned anywhere," said Shepherd. "I'm fairly certain his name is Ahmad Khan and he's from Afghanistan. But he could be in the UK under any name or nationality." He gestured at the cutting. "That was blind luck, he was in the wrong place at the wrong time. Though as he's walking along the pavement, it could well be that he lives in that area of London."

"If he's hiding, he could be long gone by now."

102

"I doubt that he'd be reading the local paper," said Shepherd. "But the problem is, I have no idea what name he's using. So here's my question, starting with what I've got — which is that — how do I identify him?"

"You've checked the name you have?"

Shepherd nodded. "He's not on the PNC and he wasn't issued a visa. Of course, he could be in the country completely illegally and not using any paperwork at all."

Singh nodded thoughtfully. "That's doubtful," he said. "Even illegals try to get something, a driving licence or an NHS number, something that they can show to the cops."

"The thing is, this guy being who he is, I think he'll be better organised."

"What do you think he is?"

Shepherd flashed him a tight smile. "I think he's al-Qaeda," he said.

Singh held up the cutting. "Then put this in the system and red-flag it, put everyone on it."

"It's not as simple as that."

"It never is with you."

"At this stage, all I want to do is to confirm my suspicions. I haven't seen this guy face to face for more than ten years. The eye's a giveaway, but I'm sure he's not the only Afghan with a dodgy eye. And I don't want to be responsible for ruining someone's life on a hunch."

Singh put down the cutting and sat back in his chair, his eyes fixed on Shepherd's face. "Why do I get the feeling there's something you're not telling me?" he said quietly.

"That's why this comes under the heading of a favour," said Shepherd.

"He's definitely al-Qaeda?"

"The last time I saw him was in Pakistan, outside of an al-Qaeda money house. And he shot me. He killed a young SAS captain."

Singh whistled softly. "I'm starting to wish I hadn't asked."

"Maybe we could both forget we had this conversation," said Shepherd. He leaned forward to grab the cutting but Singh held it out of his reach. "I'm serious, Amar, I shouldn't have asked you."

"What else are friends for?" said Singh. "You want to know if it's definitely him, right?"

"Exactly."

"OK. That I can probably help you with. But as to what happens after that, I definitely don't want to know."

"That'd probably be best," said Shepherd.

"And it goes without saying that mum's the word."

"My lips are sealed," said Shepherd.

Singh grinned. "Then let's have a go," he said. "Did you run the photograph through the Border Force's computer?"

"No. Just the name."

"They've started taking photographs and fingerprints of anyone applying for a visa, so I'll run the picture through their database." He wrinkled his nose as he studied the cutting. "What I'll do is scan the picture first and see if we can clean it up, improve the resolution. I can also run a cross-check with the DVLC database and the Identity and Passport Service which will ID him if he has a British passport or driving licence. Don't suppose you've got a photograph or a date of birth?"

Shepherd shook his head. "That picture is all I've got."

"I can pass it through the PNC, which will flag him if he's ever been arrested here, and there's our own naughty-boys database. And the facial recognition systems at all the airports, of course. Assuming he flew into the country."

"Any idea how long it'll take?"

Singh wrinkled his nose. "Increasing the resolution will take the best part of a day. That's computerised, there's no way of speeding that up. The cross-checking should be a few hours at most for the databases — the airports will take longer because it involves CCTV. Are you in a hurry?"

"The sooner the better, obviously. I really appreciate this, Amar."

Singh held up his hand. "It's no biggie," he said. "It'll be a useful test of our facial recognition systems, anyway. We're always looking for ways to tweak it." He looked at his watch. "OK, you need to let me get started on your car. I'll have it and the vests at your place tomorrow."

"Maybe liaise with the armoury, they're giving me a Glock."

"Two birds with one stone."

★　★　★

Shepherd woke early, and it took a few seconds lying in the darkness before he remembered where he was. And who he was. He was Tony Ryan, a Metropolitan Police firearms officer, and he was lying in his one-bedroom flat in Hampstead. As flats went it was just about OK, with a bedroom just large enough to take a double bed, a sitting room with a sofa, an armchair, a coffee table and a thirty-two-inch television. The last time he'd used the flat he'd been a journalist and they'd given him the full Sky package, and he was pleased to see that hadn't changed. When he'd been passing himself off as freelance journalist John Whitehill the flat had been full of art books and news magazines. Whoever had dressed the flat for his Tony Ryan legend had gone much more butch, with photographs of Shepherd with various weapons on the walls and military books lining the shelves. The contents of the wardrobe had changed; Whitehill's corduroy jackets and check shirts had gone, replaced with dark suits, white shirts and ties for work, and polo shirts and chinos for casual wear. There was no bath in the bathroom, but there was a power shower which more than made up for it, and he wasn't in the least inconvenienced by the tiny kitchen as cooking was never high up on his agenda.

The one really good thing about the flat was its proximity to Hampstead Heath. Its near-800 acres of woods and hills were the perfect setting for a run. He'd left his rucksack and boots in Hereford but there were still some of his old clothes from the last time he'd stayed in the flat, tucked away in carrier bags at the bottom of the wardrobe. He found an old pair of trainers, baggy tracksuit bottoms and a T-shirt that had once been white but was now a shabby grey. He pulled them on, let himself out of the flat and went for a run, arriving at the Heath just as dawn broke. There were already plenty of other joggers around, and a fair number of dog-walkers. Shepherd ran a mile at a medium pace to loosen up, then stepped up a gear and ran close to his maximum pace for another mile. He had soon worked up a sweat despite the chill in the air. He dropped to the ground and did fifty sit-ups and fifty press-ups before resuming his run, another two miles at full speed. The lack of a rucksack full of newspaper-wrapped bricks and his old army boots meant that he could run faster than usual. He overtook a tight group of young runners in spandex shorts, tight vests and headbands, then ran up a long slope, maintaining the same pace, enjoying the feel of his muscles starting to burn. At the top of the slope he dropped and did another set of sit-ups and press-ups, and then he headed home.

He arrived back at the flat an hour after he'd left. He shaved and showered and changed into one of the dark blue suits that the dresser had left, along with a white shirt and a tie of red and dark blue stripes. There was a choice of three pairs of shoes, all black and all with laces, and he choose the pair that looked most comfortable. He had just made himself a bacon sandwich when his Tony Ryan mobile phone rang. It was Mark Whitehouse, one of the MI5 armourers. "Delivery for Mr Ryan," said the armourer. "And I have a very nice X5 for you."

"Where are you?" asked Shepherd.

"Just turning into your street," said Whitehouse. "Where do you want it?"

"Anywhere you can find a spot," said Shepherd. "Parking's tight here at the best of times."

Shepherd managed to bolt down his bacon sandwich before his door entryphone buzzed. He pressed the button to open the door downstairs. Whitehouse was with one of the men from the car pool. He introduced himself as Ian McAdam and handed Shepherd the keys to the X5 and asked him to sign a form on a clipboard. "All yours," said McAdam. "There's a number in the glove compartment to call if you have any problems but she's only got twenty thousand miles on the clock and we've never had any problems with her." He was in his twenties, with gelled hair and a small gold earring in his left ear. He nodded at Whitehouse. "I'll wait down with the car — I saw a traffic warden down the road."

McAdam headed down the stairs. "I'm running him back to Thames House," said Whitehouse. He was in his sixties, a former soldier who had been wounded in the Falklands War and who had gone on to serve as one of MI5's armourers for almost twenty years. He had thinning grey hair and a shabby brown suit. Shepherd realised that he wasn't wearing his trademark thick-lensed glasses. "You lost the spectacles, Mark?"

Whitehouse grinned. "Just had them lasered," he said. "Brilliant, it is. I can read a book without glasses for the first time in I don't know how long, and driving is so much easier." He was carrying a metal case and he swung it on to Shepherd's coffee table.

108

"It's a fourth-generation Glock 17, but there's not much I can tell you that you don't know already," he said. He checked the barrel was clear and handed the gun butt-first to Shepherd. Shepherd checked the action and nodded his approval. "Three clips, they hold seventeen rounds as you know, but I've put fifteen in each to keep the pressure off the spring." Shepherd took one of the clips and slotted it home. "Miss Button said we didn't need to go heavy on the ammo, is forty-five rounds enough?"

"More than enough," said Shepherd.

"And she said a shoulder holster. You prefer leather to nylon, right?"

"You know me too well," said Shepherd. Whitehouse grinned and handed Shepherd a dark brown leather shoulder holster. The leather had been recently oiled and it glistened as Shepherd stroked the leather. Whitehouse handed over two leather holsters designed to hold the clips. "If you want the spares on your belt," he said. He reached into the case and brought out two plastic-wrapped vests. "And these are courtesy of Mr Singh," he said.

Shepherd took the packages and ripped one open. He held out a white vest, about the thickness of a pullover. It had sleeves that reached to just above the elbows. He held it against his chest and smiled at the look of contempt on the armourer's face. "You're not convinced?" he said.

"Mr Singh swears by them," said Whitehouse.

"But you're not convinced?"

"You know where you are with Kevlar and ceramic plates." He reached over and rubbed the vest that Shepherd was holding. "This feels like wool." He wrinkled his nose. "I just don't get it."

"He says it changes its structure when the bullet hits," said Shepherd. "Nanotechnology."

"I'll believe it when I see it," said Whitehouse.

"I could put it on now and you could take a shot at me." He grinned at the look of surprise on the armourer's face. "Joke," he said.

"I'm glad to hear that," said Whitehouse. "But I have to say I'd feel a lot happier if I'd had the chance to run a few tests myself. I look at them and I ask myself if they would really stop a bullet."

"According to Amar they'll stop any handgun at close range and an AK-47 from fifty feet," said Shepherd. "But like you, I'll believe it when I see it." He grinned. "Hopefully it won't come to that."

"And let's not forget that if the person who's shooting at you knows what they're doing, they'll probably go for a head shot anyway."

Shepherd laughed. "Yeah, that's the truth." He put the vest down and picked up the Glock again. "You took a bullet, in the Falklands?"

"Two," said the armourer. "One in the calf, one grazed my head. According to the lads the second one didn't count, it was just a flesh wound. But an inch to the left and I wouldn't be here now."

"What happened?"

"I'm not a great one for war stories, Spider."

Shepherd rubbed his shoulder. "I've just been thinking about the time I got shot, that's all. You never forget it, right?"

"Every time I get into the shower I see the scar," said Whitehouse. "The scar in my head is hidden by my hair, but you can see that the hair around it is greyer than the rest. But yeah, you never forget."

"How bad was it?"

"The wounds? Not too bad. There were plenty that got worse — two hundred and fifty-five of our guys didn't come back. But the Falklands was nothing like what you went through in Afghanistan. We didn't have IEDs or ambushes or men pretending to be women, or suicide bombers. At least we were fighting soldiers, even if a lot of them were kids."

"Do you know who shot you?"

Whitehouse shrugged. "Could have been any one of half a dozen," he said. "We were coming down this hill towards where the Argies were dug in. It was all about speed, back then, they knew we had to retake the Islands within weeks or we never would. There was no wait and see, it was full steam ahead, lads, and to hell with the bullets. This was the second hill we'd taken and it went pretty much the same way. Their lads were dug in and firing up the hill, we came charging down with as much firepower as we could muster. Then once we got to within about fifty yards of their position they'd just throw down their weapons and surrender. It was weird, Spider. They knew the Geneva Convention meant that you can't shoot an unarmed man. So as soon as they knew they were beaten they threw their guns down. So you had the ridiculous situation where they would shoot the guy next to you, killing him stone dead, but then they'd drop their gun and you can't fire back. Bloody stupid, if you ask me. Anyway, I got hit in the leg but that didn't stop me. Then a round went under my helmet, grazed my head and exited at the back. Hurt like hell but no real damage. There was a lad next to me, only just turned twenty, took a bullet in the face. Just blew his face away. Will Dunbar, his name was. I'd given him some smokes the night before and we'd had a bit of a chinwag. I saw the guy who shot him. He was a young lad, probably a teenager. As soon as Will went down the lad chucked his rifle and put up his hands." Whitehouse held up his hand, the thumb and first finger half an inch apart. "I came this close to slotting him, I swear to God. I had a bead on his chest, my finger was tightening on the trigger, there was blood trickling down my neck and I had the full adrenalin rush. Then my sarge starts screaming at me to lower my weapon, that it was over. I was still going to fire but the sarge pushed the barrel down. I tell you, it was the hardest thing I've had to do because that kid deserved to die. No question. He shot Will in the face and because it was war that was OK. Then he drops his gun and I have to round him up with the rest of them and he's now back in Argentina probably with a bloody medal."

"It's even weirder out in Afghanistan and Iraq," said Shepherd. "Over there they don't have uniforms, they use women and kids as suicide bombers and they fire missiles from mosques. Yet we carry on following the rules of war that are supposed to apply to soldiers in uniform. It's like fighting with one arm behind your back."

"Lions led by bloody donkeys," said Whitehouse. "They should just have let your lot run things out there. Done it as Special Ops instead of putting bodies on the ground."

"I'm not sure that would have been any better," said Shepherd. "You can't defeat an enemy that fights like that. The Yanks should have learned that from Vietnam. And if not from that, the fact that the Russians had to leave Afghanistan with their tail between their legs should have shown them which way the wind was blowing."

"Shouldn't have been there in the first place, is that what you mean?"

Shepherd shrugged. "It's not my call, Mark. I went to Afghanistan because I was told to go. I was eight years old when the Falklands War broke out, but looking back, I can see why we were there. The Argentines invaded British territory. End of. We had every right to do what was necessary to take it back. But you look at Afghanistan and Iraq and you have to ask yourself why British troops were ever sent."

"You know why. Because Tony Blair was Bush's lapdog. Did what his master told him to." The armourer shrugged. "You're right. At least I knew what I was fighting for."

Shepherd put down the Glock. "If you got the chance to take that shot, to shoot the guy who killed Will, would you do it?"

Whitehouse tilted his head to one side as he looked at Shepherd. "That's one hell of a hypothetical question," he said. "Where's that come from?"

"Just wondered, that's all."

"It was a long time ago," said Whitehouse. He closed his metal case and snapped the locks shut. "More than thirty years."

"Time heals all wounds?"

"I often wish I'd told the sergeant to go to hell and had just pulled the trigger," said Whitehouse. "That was the time for the bastard to get what he deserved. In the heat of battle. That is one of the great regrets of my life. I went to Will's funeral and met his mum and his dad and his sister and it fair broke my heart when they asked me what had happened. I had to tell them, right? I had to tell them that Will was shot and that the guy who shot him went unpunished. They wanted to know why he wasn't at least put on trial and you have to explain that it was war. But then if it was war why wasn't I allowed to shoot him?" He grimaced at the memory. "I'll never forget the way his mum burst into tears and his father tried to comfort her, all the time looking at me with the unspoken question in his eyes. Why? Why didn't I do something?"

"Like you said, he'd surrendered. That changes everything."

"Yes, but it shouldn't. You can't be a killer one second and a prisoner of war the next. That's just not right. But if you're asking me if I'd slot him now, then no, I wouldn't. He'd be in his fifties now, he's probably a father himself, maybe a grandfather. He wouldn't be the same man who'd killed Will all those years ago." He rubbed the back of his neck. "Now, if Will had been my son, then it might be different. You've got a kid, right?"

Shepherd nodded. "Yeah, Liam. He's sixteen this year."

"Will was only a few years older. See now, that I would never forgive. If someone killed one of my kids I'd never forgive or forget, I'd slot them no matter how much time had passed."

"Yeah, amen to that," said Shepherd.

Whitehouse stood up. "Well, better be going." He held out his hand and the two men shook. "I'm not sure what's on your mind, Spider, but you take care. There's an old Chinese proverb. A man setting out for revenge needs to dig two graves."

Shepherd nodded. "I'll bear that in mind," he said.

After the armourer had left, Shepherd made himself a mug of coffee and phoned Charlotte Button. "I've got my car, gun and vests," he said.

"And Grechko is expecting you, so you're good to go. He's at home all day and says he'll see you after dinner. You're to liaise with Dmitry Popov."

"I'll Popov and see him," said Shepherd.

"Just be aware that the Russians aren't renowned for their sense of humour," said Button. "Popov's nose will be out of joint, so bear that in mind."

"I'll treat him with kid gloves," said Shepherd. "But at the end of the day I'll be the one carrying the gun."

"Please don't shoot any of Grechko's bodyguards," said Button, only half joking. "I really couldn't bear the paperwork."

★ ★ ★

115

The Bishops Avenue was a ten-minute drive from Shepherd's Hampstead flat. The tree-lined road ran from the north side of Hampstead Heath to East Finchley. Houses on the road had never been cheap but in recent years prices had gone stratospheric and it was now commonly known as Billionaires' Row. There were just sixty-six houses on the road, each standing on a two — to three-acre plot. As and when older properties came on the market they were snapped up, demolished, and replaced with multimillion-pound mansions, with the result that only the word's richest families could afford to live there.

The president of Kazakhstan had paid £50 million for his mansion in 2008 but many in the street were now valued at double that figure. Ten of the houses were owned by the Saudi royal family with a collective value of almost a billion pounds, and the Sultan of Brunei's residence there was rumoured to have solid gold toilets and baths.

The houses that Shepherd drove by were a strange mix. There were designs based on traditional Greek and Roman styles with towering columns and triangular pediments, but there were also huge modern cubes of steel and glass and massive country houses that would have been more at home on a Scottish grouse moor. Most were hidden by high walls and electric gates and all had the warning signs of private security firms predominantly displayed.

Shepherd had often driven down the street and was always struck by the thought that the mansions resembled prisons. He couldn't imagine a more soulless

116

place to live. The residents usually flew in by private jet and were taken to their luxurious mansions by limousine to be protected by high walls and guards. There would be no popping around to a neighbour's for a chat. In fact no one ever walked down The Bishops Avenue and if anyone did decide to take a stroll they'd be under CCTV and human scrutiny every step of the way.

Grechko's mansion was about halfway down the avenue. It was fronted by a brick wall that was a good ten feet high and there was a black metal wheeled gate. He pulled up and sounded his horn. The gate steadfastly refused to move and he blipped the horn again. There was a loud clicking sound and then the gate slowly rattled back, revealing a drive a hundred metres long leading to a sandstone mansion with half a dozen towering chimneys. There were tennis courts to the left of the house and a double-door garage to the right.

As the gate withdrew, Shepherd edged the car forward. He had barely moved a dozen feet when a large man in a black suit appeared in front of the car holding up his hand. "Turn off the engine!" he shouted.

Shepherd wound down the window. "Tony Ryan," he said. "Dmitry Popov is expecting me."

"Turn off the engine and get out of the car!" the man shouted again. He was short, probably not much more than five foot seven, but he was broad shouldered and had bulging biceps that strained at the arms of his suit. He was wearing impenetrable Oakley wraparound sunglasses and had a Bluetooth earpiece in his left ear.

Shepherd recognised him as Timofei Domashevich, one of the recruits to the security team. From his attitude it looked as if he had something to prove.

Shepherd pulled his Tony Ryan warrant card from his jacket pocket and held it out. "I'm a cop," he said. "I'm here to see Dmitry Popov." The gate started to rattle closed behind him.

A hand grabbed at the handle of the X5 and yanked the door open. "Out!" said a second man. He was tall, a good foot taller than the first man, and wearing a similar suit, shades and earpiece. It was Konstantin Serov. According to the file he'd read, Serov had been with Grechko for almost ten years. Shepherd realised there was no point in arguing. He put his warrant card away and released his seat belt. He stepped down out of the four-by-four but his feet had hardly touched the ground before the man had spun Shepherd around and pushed him against the car. "Hey, go easy!" shouted Shepherd, but as he put his hands on the roof to steady himself the bodyguard roughly kicked his legs apart.

A third bodyguard appeared on the other side of the car. It was Alina Podolski, the only female member of the security team. Like the other two bodyguards she was wearing a black suit but her white shirt was tieless and open at the neck. She stood watching him with amused pale blue eyes, her arms folded. She had short blond hair with a fringe that reached down past her eyebrows and her red lipstick matched the colour of her nails.

Shepherd flashed her a tight smile as hands roughly patted him down. He decided not to tell them that he was armed, he figured they might as well discover it for themselves. A few seconds later a hand patted the Glock in its holster. Serov shouted something that sounded like *"pistolet"* which Shepherd assumed was Russian for "gun". He held the Glock in the air and waved it around for the rest of the bodyguards to see.

"I'm a cop," said Shepherd, but a hand hit him in the middle of the back and pushed him against the car.

Another man was rooting through the back of the X5 while a fifth bodyguard had appeared with a mirror on the end of a metal pole and was using it to examine the underside of the car. It was Max Barsky, the youngest member of the security team and one of the new arrivals. He was tall and thin and his suit was slightly too small for him so that his white socks were clearly visible below the hems of his trousers. He was wearing Ray-Bans that were too big for his face, giving him the look of an ungainly stick insect.

Another man patted him down again, paying particular attention to his legs. They didn't seem to notice the vest that he'd put on underneath the shirt. "OK, turn around," said the man. Shepherd did as he was told. It was Boris Volkov, tall and skinny with a shaved head, his eyes hidden behind impenetrable Oakleys. A former Moscow policeman, according to the file that Shepherd had committed to memory. "Boris Volkov," said Shepherd.

Volkov frowned and put his face closer to Shepherd's. Shepherd could smell garlic on the man's breath. "You know me?"

"I'm here to see Dmitry Popov," said Shepherd. "But you know that, of course." He held out his hand. "Now stop pissing around and give me back my wallet and my gun."

"No one gets in with a gun," said Volkov, his English heavily accented.

"You realise I'm a cop, right?" said Shepherd.

Serov ejected the clip from Shepherd's Glock.

"You break it, you pay for it," said Shepherd. Serov ignored him and slotted the clip back in.

To the side of the gate was a brick gatehouse with a thick-glassed window and above it a white metal CCTV camera. Shepherd realised that someone was watching him from the gatehouse, a big man with a weightlifter's build and the standard wraparound Oakley sunglasses. It was Dmitry Popov. He was standing with his arms folded, and Shepherd nodded, acknowledging his presence. His ears were slightly pointed, giving him the look of an oversized elf.

Popov turned away from the window and a few seconds later stepped through the doorway. Serov held out the Glock. "*Pistolet*," he said.

Popov took it from Serov and looked at the gun as if it had just appeared from a cow's backside. "Plastic," he said. "I never liked plastic guns." He jutted his chin at Shepherd, emphasising the ugly scar on his left cheek. It looked as if someone had taken a broken bottle and ground it into the flesh. "Guns are not allowed on the premises." Like the rest of the bodyguards he had a Bluetooth earpiece in his left ear.

"I'm an SFO, a specialist firearms officer, and I'm authorised to carry my weapon anywhere in the British Isles," said Shepherd.

"This is private property," said Popov. He took Shepherd's wallet and flicked through it. He paid particular attention to the warrant card.

"How about you and I have a quiet word," said Shepherd, gesturing at the guardhouse.

Popov nodded, turned his back on Shepherd and walked inside. Shepherd followed him. The door opened into a small room with two plastic chairs facing the window. There was a line of grey metal lockers on one wall and a whiteboard on which were written various car registration numbers, times and dates.

Another door led into a windowless office in which there was a desk with a computer terminal and behind it another whiteboard. Under the whiteboard was a line of charging transceivers. Popov walked behind the desk, placed the Glock and the wallet next to the terminal and sat down. He waved Shepherd to a chair on the other side of the desk. Shepherd sat down and crossed his legs. He said nothing as Popov picked up the wallet, opened it and scrutinised the warrant card again before going through the rest of the cards. He tossed the wallet towards Shepherd and it thudded on to the desk, but Shepherd ignored it. Popov picked up the Glock, ejected the clip and checked there wasn't a round in the breech. "You like the Glock?" he said.

"It does the job," said Shepherd.

Popov reinserted the clip and leaned over to put the gun next to the wallet.

Still Shepherd said nothing. Popov leaned back and put his hands behind his bull neck. He stared at Shepherd with pale blue eyes. "You said you wanted a word," he said eventually.

"Are you done?" said Shepherd.

"Done?" repeated Popov.

"Done. Finished. Have you finished showing me how on top of things you are? Because I'm assuming that's what that little charade out there was all about."

Popov put down his hands and leaned forward, putting his elbows on the desk. He opened his mouth to speak but Shepherd beat him to it.

"First let me say that I understand what happened out there," said Shepherd. "You wanted to demonstrate that security here is good, and I got that message loud and clear. There's a few things we need to put right but I can see that you're on top of things."

Popov inclined his head slightly to acknowledge the compliment but his face remained impassive.

"And I understand your need to let everyone see that you're the top dog here. Having me brought in like this, it suggests that you've somehow failed, so by giving me a hard time, you show everyone that you're still in control. I understand that, which is why I'll let today pass." Shepherd smiled thinly. "But make no mistake, Dmitry, if you ever disrespect me like that again, I'll destroy you."

Popov's eyes hardened but still his face remained neutral.

"I'm sure you've got the right working visa but I can have the immigration authorities all over you. I gather you're in the UK more than ninety days a year so I'll have you audited by the Inland Revenue — they'll squeeze you so hard that your eyes will pop. I'll make a call to a contact of mine who works for Homeland Security in the States and I'll have you put on the no-fly list which means your flying days will be pretty much over. And that's before I get through telling your boss what a liability you are." He smiled easily. "But I'm sure it's not going to come that. We both need the same thing, Dmitry. We want to make sure that nothing happens to your boss. So no more pissing around, OK? We work together, we help each other, we make each other look good."

Popov nodded slowly. "I understand."

Shepherd smiled. "Just so we're clear, I'm running the show while I'm here. It has to be that way, I don't have time to run everything by you or to waste time massaging your ego. I'll be respectful and I'll include you as much as I can, and wherever possible I'll make suggestions rather than issue orders, but at the end of the day I'm in charge. If something does happen and I tell you to jump, I need you to jump. On the plus side, if this does turn to shit it'll be down to me and everyone will know that." He leaned over, picked up the Glock, and slid it into his holster, still smiling.

Popov stared at him for several seconds and then forced a smile. "Agreed," he said. "And I apologise for the over-enthusiasm of my team." He held out his hand and Shepherd reached over and shook it. Popov squeezed hard as they shook, but not hard enough to hurt.

"Dmitry, mate, if our roles had been reversed I would have done exactly the same to you," said Shepherd. "Except I'd have had them gloved up and giving you an internal examination." He stood up and pocketed his wallet. "Right, why don't you give me the tour?"

Peter Grechko's mansion was the biggest home that Shepherd had ever seen. He'd been in five-star hotels that were smaller and less luxurious and it took the best part of an hour for Popov to give him the lie of the land. Popov took Shepherd into the house through the garage. They had driven towards the garage doors in Shepherd's X5 but as they rolled up it became clear that the garage was actually the entrance to the lower levels of the house. The ramp curved around and opened into an underground parking area large enough for a dozen cars. They climbed out and Popov took Shepherd over to a lift. The lift doors opened as they approached. There was a keypad to the right of the door and Popov tapped out a four-digit code and touched his thumb to a small sensor on the keypad before pressing the button for the second floor. Shepherd frowned at the buttons. "There are five floors?" he said.

"Three are underground," said Popov. "The control centre is on Basement One, where we are now, with the car parking area and storage rooms. Basement Two has the recreational areas, including the cinema, games room, billiards room and bowling alley. Basement Three has the pool and the boss's gym, the wine cellar, more storage. Our gym is on Basement One. You're welcome to use it."

"I'm not a great one for gyms," said Shepherd.

"You keep fit, though," said Popov.

"I run," said Shepherd. He gestured at the scanner. "So you know who is where at any point, right?"

"We know which doors have been accessed and by who. And the transceivers we carry have GPS so have real-time locations for all the security staff. I'll fix you up with a transceiver and get you a security code once we've done the tour."

They arrived at the top floor and Popov walked Shepherd though the two wings, either side of a large hallway from which a huge marble staircase swept down to the ground floor. There were ten bedrooms in each wing, each exquisitely furnished and each with a massive en suite bathroom. The bedrooms all had double-height ceilings but they were individually designed in a range of styles and colours, any one of which could have been featured in a glossy magazine. None of them appeared to have been slept in.

"Where does Mr Grechko sleep?" asked Shepherd.

"Since the shooting he has slept in a room on Basement Two," said Popov. "He says he feels safer there."

"Understandable," said Shepherd. He was looking out of the window of a room decorated in Japanese style with a low bed and rosewood furniture. There was a collection of Japanese pottery that looked as if it had just come from a museum and several Japanese swords in display cases. "But the house isn't overlooked." He

125

tapped the window. "And this is bulletproof glass, right?"

Popov nodded. "I explained that but he insisted on going below ground."

Shepherd turned to face him. "He's scared?"

"You've never met him, have you?" Shepherd shook his head. "Mr Grechko doesn't scare easily," said Popov. "But after the sniper he sent his wife to France." He grinned. "Shopping."

"Shopping?"

"Mrs Grechko likes to shop."

"And he has two sons, right?"

"Sixteen and fourteen. They are with their mother. The former Mrs Grechko. Mr Grechko owns a large estate on Cyprus and Mrs Grechko knows that she is to stay there with the boys until this is resolved."

"And what about security in Cyprus?"

"Mrs Grechko has her own security, but they have all been with the family for many years. Totally trustworthy."

Shepherd nodded. "Before the attack, he had a lot of guests?"

Popov shook his head. "Mr Grechko rarely entertained here," he said.

"But all these rooms?"

The bodyguard shrugged. "The new Mrs Grechko likes nice things," he said. He grinned. "I'll show you her dressing rooms."

"Rooms?"

Popov's grin widened. "Oh yes," he said. "Rooms." He led Shepherd down a corridor lined with a thick

126

green carpet, with small chandeliers hanging every ten feet or so. At the end of the corridor were two gilt doors. Popov threw them open. "The shoe room," he said. He wasn't joking. The room was filled with rack upon rack of shoes, most of which hadn't been worn. Popov pressed a button and the racks began to move to the side. More shoes appeared. And more.

Shepherd began to laugh and Popov laughed with him. "Are you serious?" said Shepherd.

"If she sees a style she likes, she buys them in every colour," said Popov. "At the last count she had close to one thousand pairs." He pressed the button and the racks stopped moving. At the end of the room were two more double gilt doors and Popov pushed them open. "The handbag room," he said. The room was smaller than the previous one and lined with display cases containing handbags of every conceivable design and colour. Shepherd recognised many of the brands — Gucci, Chanel, Prada, Louis Vuitton.

"Are you married, Tony?"

"I was. She died." Even though the Tony Ryan legend was a work of fantasy, legends always worked best when they bore some resemblance to reality.

"Sorry about that. I was going to say wives go crazy over this room. Mrs Grechko, when she goes into a handbag shop, if she sees something she likes she orders dozens and gives them to all her friends." He pointed to a bright green Prada bag. "She gave me one of those for my wife last Christmas."

"That's generous," said Shepherd.

"It means nothing to her," said Popov. "She doesn't even ask the price when she buys something. In most of the shops she doesn't even have to hand over a credit card. She points out what she wants and they deliver and the bill goes to Mr Grechko."

The next room was the evening wear room with rows and rows of gowns and dresses. There was a huge gilt mirror on a stand in the middle of the room and two winged leather armchairs. Popov pointed at one of the chairs. "Sometimes Mr Grechko sits here while she tries on dresses. If I'm lucky I get to watch, too. Have you seen Mrs Grechko?"

"I've seen photographs."

"She is beautiful. Seriously beautiful. Eight years ago she was Miss Ukraine but if anything she is even more beautiful now."

"Mr Grechko is a lucky man."

"Mr Grechko is a very rich man," said Popov. "I don't think luck has much to do with it." He took Shepherd through to the next room. It was the casual wear room and there were countless shirts, jeans and dresses on hangers and on shelves. There was another large free-standing gilt mirror and two leather armchairs. The room was the size of a regular high street clothing store; all that was missing was a cash register.

The next room was what Popov called the underwear room, and it was filled with underwear, lingerie and swimwear, and was a riot of colour. Shepherd realised the clothing rooms pretty much occupied the whole top floor of a wing that was running parallel to the main house. There were no windows but if there had been they would have been overlooking the tennis courts. The next room also didn't have windows. It was a complete beauty and hairdressing salon with a mirrored wall that made it look twice its size. "Mrs Grechko has her two hairdressers and a make-up girl," said Popov. "They're with her in France."

"When they are here, where do Mr and Mrs Grechko sleep?" asked Shepherd.

"The master bedroom suite," said Popov. "It's in the opposite wing, along with the children's bedrooms and the bedrooms of the children's nannies. I can't show you those quarters without Mr Grechko's permission."

"Nannies? They're a bit old for nannies, aren't they?"

"The boys are accustomed to servants," said Popov. "They are in Cyprus with them now. Four women, all from Russia."

"And where is Mr Grechko at the moment?" asked Shepherd.

"In his gym," said Popov. "I'll show you the ground floor and then we'll do the basement floors."

The rooms on the ground floor were even bigger and more opulent than the bedrooms. There were two enormous sitting rooms, one with a Victorian cast-iron fireplace that was taller than Shepherd, and another in a minimalist style dominated by a circular fireplace under a stainless-steel hood. There was a library lined with leather-bound books, two dining rooms each with tables large enough to accommodate two dozen diners, a room with two grand pianos in it, and two fully equipped kitchens. In one of the kitchens a pretty brunette in chef's whites was preparing Beef Wellingtons. Popov introduced her as Sheena Edmonds, one of Grechko's three personal chefs. She grinned at Shepherd. "Let me know if you need feeding at any point," she said. "Mr Grechko's here on his own at the moment so I'm not exactly rushed off my feet."

"Sheena's club sandwiches are the best I've ever eaten," said Popov. He patted his waistline. "And I have to force myself not to eat too many of her cheeseburgers."

Popov showed Shepherd a pantry the size of a small supermarket, and a cold storage and freezer filled with enough meat to feed an army.

Just outside the kitchen was another lift, and Popov used it to take them down to the first basement level. Shepherd watched as Popov tapped in the four-digit code and touched his thumb against the sensor. The Russian saw him and gestured at the keypad. "Every member of staff has their own code," he said. "The code has to match the thumbprint. That way we know exactly who goes where." He nodded up at the roof of the lift, where a small shiny black dome showed their reflections. "Plus we have CCTV in all the lifts and hallways."

"But not in the rooms?"

"Mr and Mrs Grechko like their privacy," said Popov. "But we do have CCTV in the boys' quarters, and in the kitchens. And all around the exterior of the house."

The lift doors opened and Popov took Shepherd through into the main car parking area. "This is where we park our cars," said Popov. There were two black Range Rovers and two Mercedes SUVs, and half a dozen saloons. He nodded at a steel shutter. "This is where Mr Grechko keeps his vehicles." He pressed a red button and the shutter slowly rattled up to reveal several dozen immaculate cars, most of them classics. There were three bright red Ferraris, a yellow Lamborghini, a Maserati, two Bentleys, and a number of vintage cars with huge grilles and sweeping mudguards. "Mr Grechko likes cars almost as much as Mrs Grechko likes shoes and handbags," said Popov with a sly smile.

"Does he go out in them?"

Popov nodded. "Every now and again. Sometimes takes a run out to a pub with Mrs Grechko. When he does go out there's always one of our vehicles with him."

"And what about maintaining the cars?"

"You're thinking bombs?" said Popov.

"Considering all the options," said Shepherd.

"There are two mechanics but they've both been with Mr Grechko for five years. A father and son." He pointed at a small cubicle next to a ramp and a workshop. "They're usually in there drinking tea."

"If Mr Grechko does decide to go out, no matter in which vehicle, I need advance notice," said Shepherd.

"No problem," said Popov. "We have a full briefing every day at seven hundred hours. I detail any travel arrangements, visitors, deliveries and so on then." He pressed the button to close the shutters and they rattled back into place.

Popov took Shepherd down a corridor and showed him a door marked "security centre". Popov gestured at the sign. "This is where we coordinate security," he said. "I'll bring you back at the end, it'll make more sense that way." On the opposite side of the corridor were six identical doors, numbered one to six. "Our people have the option of living in or getting a place outside," said Popov. "I'm here most of the time but the guys work twelve-hour shifts, six days a week, according to the contract but with the option of doing a seventh as overtime." He opened the door to number six. It was a cube about ten feet by ten feet with a single bed, a built-in wardrobe and desk, a small television and Blu-Ray player. "These are just crash-rooms," said Popov. "There are showers down the corridor. You're welcome to any free room whenever you want, first come, first served."

"Do all the guys live in?" asked Shepherd.

Popov closed the door. "Some do, some don't. It's up to them. There are more permanent rooms on the level below this, more like small apartments with their own bathrooms. Why, do you need a place?"

Shepherd shook his head. "I've got a flat not far away," he said.

"There are seven of the guys living in, plus me," said Popov. "It's the cheaper option but some of the guys like their own space."

"I guess they're not allowed to bring girls back," said Shepherd.

"No one is allowed in unless . . ." began Popov, but then he realised Shepherd was joking. He wagged his finger at him. "English humour," he said. He took him back down the corridor and along to another area of the car park where there was a room marked drivers. Popov opened it. There were two cheap plastic sofas and a small table around which three middle-aged men in grey suits were playing cards. They had the guilty look of schoolboys caught doing something they shouldn't have been. Shepherd realised there was a handful of banknotes in the middle of the table and that the men were gambling.

If Popov noticed the money, he didn't mention it. "These are Mr Grechko's regular drivers," he said. He introduced them from left to right. "Roman Khorkov, Yulian Chayka, and Nikolay Eristov." The three men hadn't been in the file that Shepherd had seen and he made a mental note to check up on them when he got the chance. "There are two more drivers but they are with Mrs Grechko."

Chayka said something in Russian to Popov and the other two drivers laughed. Popov replied, also in Russian, and the three drivers nodded. "He was asking if you were the latest member of my team," explained Popov. "I told them that you're here to advise on security."

Shepherd had the feeling that there was more to it than that but decided not to press it.

At one side of the car park was a glass wall beyond which was a room full of exercise equipment, including treadmills, exercise bikes and weights. "You said you were a runner but if you want to work out, the gym is always open," said Popov.

There were two men in the gym, both of them big with thick forearms emphasised by their sweat-stained vests and slightly bowed legs. One of them was lying on his back lifting a heavy barbell while the other stood over him, his hands out ready to grab the bar if his colleague began to struggle. The guy doing the spotting noticed Popov. It was Konstantin Serov, one of the bodyguards who had been at the front gate. He took the barbell from the man on the bench and slotted it on to the rack. The man on the bench sat up, his face bathed in sweat. Leo Tarasov. Serov was a former mixed martial arts champion; Tarasov had been in the Russian navy but had been court-martialled after punching a fellow sailor unconscious.

Popov pushed open a glass door and introduced Shepherd to the two men. They both shook hands with Shepherd. Serov said something in Russian to Popov and Popov replied. Tarasov said something and all three men laughed. Shepherd looked over at Popov and Popov put up a hand. "They were asking if you worked out and I said you were a runner," said Popov.

"And what was so funny?"

"Leo said that running could come in handy. It was a joke."

Shepherd nodded at Tarasov. The man's forearms were about twice the size of Shepherd's and he had a neck so thick that Shepherd doubted he could get his hands around it if he tried. "You speak English, Leo?"

The Russian nodded. "Sure."

"You look strong," said Shepherd. "What can you bench-press? Three hundred and fifty?"

134

"Three eighty kilos," said Tarasov, nodding.

"That's impressive," said Shepherd. "How are you on pull-ups?"

"Pull-ups?" Tarasov frowned. "What are pull-ups?"

Popov said something to Tarasov in Russian and pointed at a Nautilus Gravitron machine. It had been specifically designed for chin-ups, pull-ups and vertical dips, with numerous bars and handholds at various sites. "Sure," said Tarasov. "Pull-ups." He raised his right arm, bent it at the elbow and flexed his bicep. It was the size and shape of a rugby ball.

"How many can you do? I bet you can do a lot."

Tarasov frowned. "Fifteen. Twenty."

Shepherd could tell from the uncertainty in the man's voice that pull-ups didn't form part of his regular exercise regime. He grinned. "I bet I can do more than you," he said. Shepherd knew that he was taking a risk, but it was clear from Tarasov's build that he was better suited to lifting heavy weights with his legs than he was to lifting his own body weight with his arms. It was all down to power-weight ratios and Shepherd was pretty sure that while he didn't have the muscles of the big Russian, he did have the advantage when it came to stamina.

"A bet?" said Tarasov. "For money?"

"Sure," said Shepherd. "That'll make it interesting. For every pull-up I do more than you, you give me ten pounds. Or for every one you do more than me, I'll give you ten pounds."

Tarasov frowned in confusion so Popov explained in Russian. Tarasov nodded enthusiastically. "Deal," he said.

Shepherd waved at the machine. "Why don't you go first?"

Tarasov nodded and then began flexing his arms and wiggling his fingers. He walked up and down, his face impassive.

"Leo is strong," said Popov.

"I can see that," said Shepherd.

"How many can you do?"

Shepherd shrugged. "I'm not sure, it's been a while."

Tarasov bounced up and down on the balls of his feet and then got into position. He grunted, then jumped up and grabbed the bar above his head. He grunted again and began to lift his chin towards the bar.

"Wait a minute," said Shepherd, holding up his hand. "What are you doing?

Tarasov let go and dropped down on the floor. "What's wrong?"

"That wasn't a pull-up. That was a chin-up."

Tarasov looked over at Popov. Popov nodded. "He's right," he said. "With a pull-up, you have the palms facing away as you do the lift. Your palms were facing you. That's a chin-up." Tarasov still didn't understand so Popov explained again in Russian and demonstrated the different grips with his hands.

Tarasov looked a little less confident now. With the palms facing away, pull-ups were more to do with using the back muscles than the biceps. He took several deep

136

breaths and psyched himself up with a few deep grunts, then he stood under the overhead grips, jumped up and grabbed them. He began lifting himself. In a smooth motion until his chin was just above the bar. He grinned and let himself down in another smooth motion. He had a steady rhythm, and grunted at the top of each lift. He pumped the first five quickly but then began to slow down. By the time he'd reached eight his face was red and he was bathed in sweat. The muscles in his arms were pumped up and he was gripping the bars so tightly his knuckles had turned white. After the tenth pull-up he hung for several seconds before starting the eleventh. Shepherd knew that meant he didn't have many left in him. Once you lost the rhythm the muscles became much less efficient. Tarasov's grunts had become more like bellows and his whole body shook as he strained to lift his body weight. He made the eleventh, but on the twelfth barely managed to get his chin above the bar. He dropped down too quickly and grunted in pain as he stressed his elbows. He growled as he strained to make a thirteenth lift but all his strength had gone. His growl turned into a howl of rage and then he let go and dropped back to the floor, his chest heaving.

"Twelve," said Popov.

"I can do more than twelve," sneered Tarasov.

"Not today you can't," said Popov.

Tarasov ran his right hand up and down his left bicep and glared at it as if it had failed him.

"Your turn," Popov said to Shepherd.

Shepherd took off his jacket and draped it over a bench. He took his gun out of its holster and placed it on a bench, then rolled up his shirtsleeves and took off his shoes. He tucked his tie into his shirt, flexed his fingers, took a couple of slow, deep breaths, then stood under the bar, rotating his shoulders. Pull-ups were about muscle strength, but they were also about stamina and determination. Once the muscles started to burn the brain instinctively tried to get the body to stop what it was doing so that it wouldn't get damaged. The trick was to override the brain's instructions and to keep on going. Shepherd smiled to himself, knowing that was easier said than done.

He took another deep breath and then jumped up to grab the bar, making sure that his grip locked it in close to his fingers. He crossed his legs at the ankles, took a big breath, squeezed his glutes and pulled himself up in one smooth motion, leading with his chest and keeping his shoulders back. He kept his eyes fixed on the bar, ignoring the pain in his arms and back. As soon as his chin crested the bar he began to exhale, and kept breathing all the way down.

As soon as his arms were fully extended he took another deep breath and hauled himself up. He stayed focused on the bar but he could feel Popov, Tarasov and Serov watching his every move. He ignored them and concentrated on maintaining his rhythm. Up. Down. Up. Down. He did the first five in exactly five seconds. The muscles in his back and shoulders were burning but he ignored the pain. Up. Down. Up. Down. Breathing in at the bottom, breathing out at the top.

The second five were a little slower than the first, but he still had a comfortable rhythm. His brain was telling him to stop but he kept his rhythm and powered through another five.

Shepherd heard Popov laugh. "Fifteen!" he said. Shepherd stayed focused. He was tired now and his biceps felt as if they were on fire but he ignored the pain. It was the brain trying to fool him, he knew that. His muscles still had maybe half their energy reserves left but the brain was trying to get him to pack it in before he did himself serious damage. It was the same with running — if you ran hard and fast you hit a wall where you thought you couldn't go any farther but if you forced yourself on your brain would eventually realise that it wasn't fooling anyone and stop complaining. Sixteen. Seventeen. Eighteen. His arms felt like lead but he knew he had more left, it was just a question of forcing his brain to issue the necessary instructions. He took a deep breath, squeezed his glutes hard to lock his legs and forced himself up, staring at the bar all the time. His chin crested the bar and he exhaled.

"Nineteen!" said Popov.

Someone grunted contemptuously, probably Tarasov, but all Shepherd's energy was focused on the bar. He lowered himself down. Every fibre of his being wanted to let go of the bar and drop to the floor but he was determined to do at least another one. It wasn't about beating Tarasov — he'd already done that — it was about proving to himself that he could do twenty. He took two deep breaths, ignored the burning pain in his arms and back and forced himself up. He began to groan through gritted teeth and almost stopped short of the bar but then he kicked out with his legs and managed to gain another couple of inches. He held his chin above the bar for a full two seconds and then dropped down.

Popov clapped him on the back. "Twenty!" he said. "You're the man."

Serov patted Shepherd on the shoulder and even Tarasov flashed him a thumbs-up. "I'll pay you later," said Tarasov.

Popov pointed at him. "Sixty pounds," he said. "Don't you forget."

"I won't," said Tarasov. He turned and walked over to a set of free weights and picked up two twenty-kilo dumb-bells. And began pumping them into the air.

Shepherd pulled out his tie, put on his shoes and rolled down his shirtsleeves before holstering his Glock and pulling on his jacket. Popov was still chuckling and he put his arm around Shepherd's shoulder as he guided him out of the gym. "You're stronger than you look," said the Russian.

"I've been told that before," said Shepherd. He pointed at an unmarked door. "What's in there?"

"The gun range."

"The gun range? You've got guns?"

"Airguns," said Popov. "Mr Grechko's children used to like playing with them."

"But you're not armed, are you?"

Popov looked offended. "Of course not," he said. "Handguns are illegal in this country."

140

"I just thought maybe you'd been given special permission."

Popov shook his head. "I think Mr Grechko asked but permission was refused." He pushed open the door. The room was about fifteen feet wide and sixty feet long. The walls and ceiling were soundproofed and there was a wall of sandbags at the far end, reaching from the floor to the ceiling. There were three targets in front of the sandbags, figures of terrorists holding AK-47s. By the door was a bench from where the guns could be fired, and there was a wire system that allowed the targets to be run back and forth.

"This is pretty elaborate for airguns," said Shepherd.

Popov walked over to a metal cabinet with a keypad on the door. He tapped out a four-digit code and pressed his thumb against a sensor. The door opened and Popov stepped to the side to show Shepherd a dozen air rifles and half a dozen pistols of various shapes and sizes. All of them seemed to be air-operated. The bigger ones would provide quite a kick but you would have to be very lucky — or unlucky, depending on your point of view — to kill anyone with them. Popov closed the door of the cabinet.

"So what's the story with the kids?" asked Shepherd.

"They spend most of their time with Mrs Grechko, when they're not at school," said Popov. "The first Mrs Grechko. She has a Cypriot passport. So does Mr Grechko and the children. He invested a lot of money in Cyprus many years ago and they were all given passports."

"And they're on good terms?"

Popov frowned, not understanding. "Good terms?"

"The divorce was amicable? Friendly? They're not fighting?"

"Mr Grechko is a very generous man," he said. "Mrs Grechko wants for nothing. They both love their sons. They have nothing to fight about." He walked out of the gun range with Shepherd and pushed open another door marked fire exit. It led to a concrete stairwell. "This is one of the three stairways that serve as emergency exits in the event of a fire. Also covered by CCTV. There are no locks or keypads on the doors on the outside for obvious reasons, but every inch is covered by CCTV. Once inside the stairwell, you need a thumbprint and code to exit at any level other than the ground floor. So again, we know who is where at any point just by tracking what doors they've opened."

He walked down the stairs and pushed open a door that led to the second basement level. They stepped into a wood-panelled corridor with recessed lighting. "This is where the family comes for fun," said Popov. He showed Shepherd a full-size bowling alley with two lanes, a billiards room with two tables, a games room packed with video arcade games, pinball machines and two pool tables. He pushed open red double doors that opened into a plush red-velvet-lined cinema with twenty large La-Z-Boy reclining chairs and sofas facing a screen as big as Shepherd had ever seen. "Now this I like," said Shepherd.

"Mr Grechko likes to watch movies," said Popov. "He gets to see a lot of them before they are released. He owns a movie studio in Los Angeles."

He closed the doors to the cinema and pushed open another door that led to the concrete stairwell. They went down to the third basement level.

Popov nodded at a pair of teak double doors with the omnipresent keypad. "That's Mr Grechko's gym," he said. "He has two personal trainers and a Thai man who teaches him Muay Thai. You can box, Tony?"

"Not really," said Shepherd. "I'm more of a lover than a fighter."

"Pity, if you were any good we could have a bet as to whether you could beat our Thai boxer."

"Is he good?"

"Hard as nails," said Popov. "Half my size but I wouldn't go into the ring with him."

"How often do the trainers come?"

"Monday and Thursday. They take it in turns. The boxer is here on Saturdays if Mr Grechko is home." From the other side of the doors they heard a loud grunt. Popov grinned. "That's Mr Grechko," he said. "He's doing weight training today. He can bench-press more than Leo."

Popov gestured at frosted double doors at the far end of a tiled corridor. "And that's the pool. That's out of bounds when Mrs Grechko and the kids are here, but when she's away Mr Grechko allows us to use the pool. Absolutely no smoking or drinking."

"No problem, Dmitry, I won't be doing either." He looked up at the ceiling and caught their reflection in yet another black plastic dome. "You're constantly monitoring the CCTV?"

"In the security centre on Basement One," said Popov. "We'll go there now." He took Shepherd along to a lift and they went up two floors. Popov pressed his thumb against the scanner and tapped in his four-digit code on the keypad outside the security centre. The lock clicked and he pushed open the door. There was a large room with three high-backed chairs facing a dozen large LCD screens. Each of the screens was filled with nine camera views from around the mansion and the grounds.

Only one of the chairs was occupied, by a thin man in his twenties who was trying in vain to disguise a receding hairline with a waxed comb-over. Shepherd recognised him from his file picture but said nothing as Popov introduced him as Vlad Molchanov. Molchanov was holding an iPad and he switched it off and placed it on a desk as Popov walked over to the screens. "As you can see we have eleven screens each with nine cameras," he said. "Ninety-nine in all." He pointed at the largest of the screens, which showed a view of the main gate. "This screen we use for anything of interest, to get a better view. The screens on the left are pre-programmed with the cameras we want to be watching all the time. The grounds, the corridors, the garage. The screens on the right take feeds from the rest of the cameras in a pre-programmed order but that can be overridden if any movement is spotted. The motion detectors take precedence over the timer so if something moves, we see it on one of these screens straightaway."

"What about recordings?"

"It all goes straight on to hard discs, but the discs are recycled every seven days," said Popov.

"OK, as of today let's stop doing any recycling. Keep everything." There was a row of transceivers in charging docks on a table against one wall. "How does the communication system work?" he asked.

"We all speak on the same channel. Channel One. If I need a personal chat we move to another frequency."

"Are the conversations recorded?" Popov shook his head. "And you allow conversations in Russian?"

"Of course."

"OK, well, from now on I want all chatter to be in English. All of it. I have to know what's going on at all times."

"I'll make sure that happens," said the Russian. He waved Shepherd to a chair and they both sat down. "This is Vlad Molchanov, he's usually in here."

Molchanov leaned over and shook hands with Shepherd. His grip was weak and clammy and Shepherd had to resist the urge to wipe his hand on his trousers.

Popov opened a door to reveal a larger room with a table surrounded by a dozen high-backed chairs. In one corner there was a kitchen area.

"What time can I see Mr Grechko?"

There was a bank of clocks up on the wall above the screens showing the time in six different cities, from Los Angeles to Sydney. "He's in the gym for another half-hour, then he has a massage and then he will shower and rest. He is eating at six and can see you for half an hour before that."

"Very good of him," said Shepherd. "It'll give me time to do a walk-around outside. Now, what's happening with the guy who was shot? Ulyashin?"

"Mikhail's coming back tomorrow," said Popov. "He's using crutches but we can put him in here, he'll be fine."

"If it's OK with you I'd like to take a run out to where the shooting happened. You can talk me through it."

"No problem," said Popov. "Mr Grechko is here all day tomorrow."

"Can you fix it so that everything is pretty much the same as when you were shot at? Same guys, same car."

"We can do that," said Popov. "But why?"

"I want to get a feel for what happened," said Shepherd. "It'll give me an idea of what we're up against."

Shepherd and Popov walked around the outside of the house and then around the extensive grounds, which included an orchard, a large terrace and barbecue pit, a basketball court and a kennels where three large Dobermans watched Shepherd with suspicion through a chain-link fence. "We let the dogs out at night," said Popov. "Be careful when they are around, their bites are much worse than their bark." One of the dogs bared its teeth at Shepherd as if to prove his point. "They are trained in German," said Popov, "but they won't obey strangers."

"No problem," said Shepherd. "I have my gun."

146

Popov turned to look at him and then he smiled when he realised that Shepherd was joking. "English humour," said the Russian.

"I hope so," said Shepherd. He had a Bluetooth earpiece in his left ear and a transceiver clipped to his belt in the small of his back. Popov had also scanned the thumb of his right hand and had him set up his own four-digit security code for the keypads.

Popov showed Shepherd several sensors in the ground that picked up vibrations and sound. "We had these installed after the sniping incident," Popov explained. "They are fed to a console in the security centre but at the moment they're oversensitive and of course the dogs keep setting them off."

"You'd be better off with movement-activated security lights," said Shepherd. "Though again the dogs will set them off. What about your people? Do they patrol?"

Popov nodded. "We make that random," he said. "But there's always at least one of us somewhere in the grounds. Day and night." He looked at his watch, a rugged stainless-steel Omega. "Mr Grechko will be ready for you now." He took Shepherd in through one of the back entrances. Again it took a thumb-print and a four-digit code for them to gain access before they headed along a hallway to the library. Grechko was already sitting behind a large desk. He stood up and walked towards Shepherd, his arm outstretched. He was a big man with hair so black that it could only have been dyed, with a square chin, a snub nose and thick eyebrows that had grown together so that they formed a single line across his forehead. "Welcome to my home," he said, offering a big hand with manicured nails, a diamond-encrusted Chopard watch on his wrist. He was wearing black trousers and a white silk shirt open to reveal a thick gold chain around his neck and greying chest hair that seemed to confirm that the hair on his head was indeed dyed.

There were two sofas at the far end of the library and he headed for them. As they sat down facing each other across a coffee table piled high with glossy books about antiques, Dmitry slipped out, pulling the double doors closed behind him. The walls were lined with books, thousands of them pristine and, by the look of it, unopened. There were stepladders on rails that ran the length of the walls, allowing access to the top shelves, and there were leather-bound books in display cases that were probably first editions. Grechko didn't look like a reader, though. He sat with his arms outstretched along the back of the sofa and crossed his legs. The soles of his shoes were totally unmarked, as if he only ever wore them indoors. "So what do you think of my security?" asked the Russian.

Shepherd wasn't sure whether he meant the people on his team or the physical security arrangements, but either way he had no intention of badmouthing Popov to his boss. "Everything's professional," he said.

"Do I need more people?" asked Grechko. "I can bring in extra staff if necessary."

"I think manpower-wise you're probably OK," Shepherd said. "And you've done everything that needs to be done here. But I'd like to make some changes to the way you move around away from the house."

"What do you mean?"

"The fact that a sniper was able to get you in his sights shows that you are predictable," said Shepherd. "Getting a sniper into position takes a lot of planning. You have to know where the target will be at a particular time, and that can only happen if the target is following a set timetable. You should never use the same route consecutively, you should vary entrances and exits when you visit a location, and you shouldn't have any regular meetings. For instance, Dmitry tells me that on the first Friday of every month you go to The Ivy."

Grechko nodded. "There are six of us. Good friends. If we are in London, we meet. Is that a problem?"

"The problem is that if you are predictable, you are vulnerable. I bet you have the same table each time, right?"

"Of course. They know us there."

"Exactly. You're known. So suppose I book the same table the day before the first Friday of the month. And suppose I take with me an explosive device. Nothing special, just a few ounces of C4 and some nuts and bolts for shrapnel. And a simple timer, set for twenty-four hours. And I fix the device to the underside of the table." He smiled at Grechko. "Bang!" He mimed the explosion with his hands.

Grechko flashed him a tight smile. "You realise that every time I go to The Ivy I'm now going to be looking under the table?"

"If you continue being predictable, that wouldn't be a bad thing to do," said Shepherd. "Same goes for your route. When you drive from here to The Ivy, do you go the same way each time?"

Grechko nodded.

"So I get a car and fill it full of explosives made from ammonium nitrate and fuel oil and I park it on the route. Detonated via a mobile phone. I wait until your car drives by and . . ." He mimed an explosion again. "Bang!"

"I understand," said Grechko.

"But it doesn't have to be as dramatic as that," said Shepherd. "Do you eat the same food? Drink the same wine?"

"I am a big fan of their steak. And they have a Château Neuf du Pape that is out of this world."

"So I get a job in the kitchen and on the day you're in I poison the steaks or the wine. It's not an easy thing to do, but it's happened in the past. The CIA and Mossad are especially good with poisons." He shrugged. "I'm not saying that you have to be paranoid, but you have to be careful. The only way that a sniper can take a shot at you is if you are predictable. Instead of meeting at the same restaurant, vary it. And leave it until the day before you decide where to go. I'll talk to Dmitry about varying your routes. But a lot of it you can do yourself. If you have to meet your lawyer, meet him in a hotel rather than his office. Or have him come to you. If you're out socialising, vary the location and, if you can, vary your entry and exit."

"You talk a lot of sense, Tony."

"It's my job, Mr Grechko." Shepherd nodded at a large framed photograph of the Russian with his wife and sons. "Do you mind me asking about the security arrangements you have in place for your family while they're away?"

"My family?"

"Your ex-wife and sons are in Cyprus, right?"

"We have a villa there. The villa has a full staff and I sent a driver and two of Dmitry's best men with them."

"Do you think that's enough?"

Grechko frowned. "You think that someone would hurt my family?" He smiled and shook his head. "You do not understand Russians, Tony. Those dogs in the Kremlin would kill me, they'd lock me in a dungeon and throw away the key, they would steal all my money if they could get their hands on it, but they would not dream of hurting my family. That is not the Russian way, Tony. It never has been and it never will be."

"I'll take your word for that," said Shepherd.

"You can," said Grechko. "No matter how much I hated someone, I would not attack their family. It's just not something I would do and nor would any other Russian. Men do not attack women and children, Tony. And if you are worried about my ex-wife's security you can check it for yourself in two days. I'm flying out there. You should come."

"I will do, Mr Grechko. I'll be with you now whenever you leave the house. And what about the present Mrs Grechko? She is in France?"

"Nadya has her own security. She will be safer away from me for the time being, that's what I told her. Who's to say that she won't be standing next to me if the sniper should try again."

Shepherd stood and turned to go. "Then I'll say good evening and go through tomorrow's schedule with Dmitry."

"And you'll be coming along with my security team?"

"Every time you leave the building, yes."

Grechko jutted his chin out. "Good," he said. "I can see you are a professional, Tony. I like to work with professionals."

"As do I, Mr Grechko."

Shepherd left Grechko's house at just after ten o'clock and drove back to his Hampstead flat. On the back seat of his car he had a transceiver and the Bluetooth earpiece was in his jacket pocket. Popov had also taken a print of his thumb and given him a four-digit keypad code for the security system. He phoned Button on hands-free as he drove and updated her on his progress. "What do you think?" she asked.

"His house is a fortress," said Shepherd. "I don't think he'll have any problems while he's there. Fully alarmed and with CCTV everywhere, and most of the time he's underground."

"Underground? How does that work?"

"His house is like the Tardis," said Shepherd. "I mean, it's big enough but there's even more of it below ground. But the house isn't overlooked anyway so no sniper's going to get him while he's at home. The problem is, he does put himself about and while he's outside he's vulnerable."

"Well, make sure he stays inside as much as possible."

Shepherd laughed. "He's an oligarch, I don't think anyone tells him what to do. But I'll give it my best shot. One thing's for sure, we're flying to Cyprus the day after tomorrow."

"That doesn't sound such a great idea," said Button.

"He's got a private jet so we're flexible about the take-off time, and his plane is at RAF Northolt so security there is tight."

"And what about Cyprus? What's the story there?"

"He says it's not generally known that he's flying out there, he'll be taking security with him obviously, and there's security on the ground. It'll be OK. Can you speak to Europol and get me cleared to keep my gun while I'm there?"

"I will, but I'm not happy about this," said Button.

"The gun?"

"The gun's fine. It's Grechko flying around the world while there's an assassin after him that worries me."

"I'm not thrilled about the idea, but he's probably safer in Cyprus than he is in London. Plus if anything happens to him when he's there, it's not really our problem."

"I do hope you're joking."

"I am."

"Because if anything happens to Grechko while he's in our care, we'll be the ones carrying the can. And by 'we' I mean 'you', of course."

"Message received loud and clear, ma'am," said Shepherd, and he ended the call just as he drove into Hampstead High Street. He found a parking space in the road close to his flat. He popped into a corner shop and picked up a bottle of milk, a loaf of bread and a packet of Birds Eye fish fingers before heading for the flat. He did a quick U-turn and looked at a mobile phone shop window display to check that no one was following him, more out of habit than because he seriously thought he was under surveillance, and then he walked home. He let himself in, tapped in the alarm code and went through to the kitchen and switched on the kettle. He'd left Harper's Samsung phone in the cutlery drawer and he took it out and checked the screen. There had been no texts or calls while he'd been away.

He called Harper's number and he answered almost immediately. "Where are you?" asked Shepherd. He walked through to the bedroom and sat on his bed.

"In the hotel," said Harper. "It's doing my head in. There's no hot water after nine and the guy above me is watching some foreign channel with the volume full on. I might look for somewhere else tomorrow. It's finding a place that'll take cash that's the problem."

"Why don't I help?" said Shepherd, bending down to untie his boots. "You can use my credit card to book somewhere."

"Yeah, but then if it turns to shit there's a clear link between you and me," said Harper. "Also, in a fleapit like this no one looks at me twice."

"You really are serious about keeping below the radar."

"I have to be, mate," said Harper. "So what's happening with Khan?"

"I'm on the case," said Shepherd, slipping off his boots. "They can try some face recognition software but it'll take time. What about you? What are you up to?"

"I'm staking out the mosques."

"You're what?"

"I'm checking out the mosques in West London. There aren't too many and he's got to be going to one of them, right? He's a Muslim and Muslims pray five times a day."

"Yeah, but they don't have to pray at mosques. They can do it home, they just need to be facing Mecca."

"They're happier in mosques, you know that. And in that newspaper photograph he was happy enough walking around. I figure he'll use a mosque fairly close to his home, so assuming he's living in West London there aren't too many options."

"It could be that he was just passing through when that photograph was taken."

"It could be. But he was holding a carrier bag so it looks to me like he'd just popped out for a bit of shopping. I don't think he was too far from home when that picture was taken."

"Be careful, Lex. You're playing with fire."

"Even if he saw me, I doubt he'd recognise me," said Harper. "I don't think he ever got a good look at me in Afghanistan. I saw him in the camp but he's got no reason to remember me."

"That's not what I meant," said Shepherd. "Most of the mosques are under constant MI5 surveillance. Especially those that are in any way connected with fundamentalism. They've got agents inside the mosques but they've got people on the outside watching as well."

"I'm not going inside," said Harper. "Give me some credit."

"Lex, they're not just watching for Islamic fundamentalists. They're also looking for the right-wing nutters who go around leaving pigs' heads on the doorstep. If you start hanging around outside any mosque, alarm bells will ring."

Shepherd waited for Harper to reply, but there was only silence.

"You see what I'm saying?" said Shepherd eventually.

"Yeah. I hadn't thought of that," said Harper. "I was too busy watching out for Khan to think that someone might have been watching me. Shit. If I have been spotted, what will they be doing?"

156

"They'll have a tail on you, to find out who you are and what you're up to."

"I'm pretty much sure I've not been followed."

"If they're good, you wouldn't see them," said Shepherd.

"It's not the end of the world," said Harper. "I'm not registered under my own name and the passport I came in on isn't in my name either. But you're right, I need to be careful."

"You might be OK," said Shepherd. "But better safe than sorry. How are you on counter-surveillance?"

"I look over my shoulder from time to time."

Shepherd laughed. "Yeah, that'll do it. I tell you what, stay put and I'll take a look tomorrow. You can take a walk around and I'll see if there's anyone on you. I'm free in the afternoon so I'll fix something up and give you a call. But in the meantime, stay away from the mosques."

Shepherd ended the call, lay back on the bed and stared up at the ceiling. He was as keen as Harper to track down Ahmad Khan, but it had to be done properly. There was no point in finding him if they exposed themselves at the same time. But the question that was troubling Shepherd was what had to be done once they'd found Khan.

AFGHANISTAN 2002

Ahmad Khan left Lailuna with his sister and went to meet his Taliban comrades. He knew that many of them were privately as unhappy as him with the extremism of some of their leaders. Sitting around a campfire sipping cups of hot sweet tea, he told them what he proposed to do, knowing that he was putting his life in their hands.

"You all know me," he said. "We have fought together side by side, some of us for many years. We have defended our country and our faith. We have fought the Russians, the Americans, the British, and we have crossed the border to fight the Pakistanis when they attacked our brothers there and, when there were no *faranji* to fight, we have fought among ourselves. But now I am growing weary of war. Have I, have we all, not earned the right to live in peace? Soon it will be time to go home, cultivate our land, raise our families and live our lives."

There were nods and murmurs of agreement from his men. And when it came time to leave the campfire, his men had agreed to his plan. He left them and made off as if heading for his home, but after nightfall he made his way down from the mountains, walking westwards throughout the night and the day that followed. A few miles outside Jalalabad he stopped and lay up in the cover of some trees, observing an American Forward Operating Base. He knew its location because he and his comrades had mortared it on several occasions. He watched and waited, less concerned by the comings and goings of military patrols than the whereabouts of Afghan civilians. Among them, he knew, were Taliban spies and informers, and he could not afford to be seen by them. In late afternoon, he saw his chance. The road leading to the base was largely deserted and a convoy of American vehicles returning from patrol had created a cloud of dust that hung in the air like fog.

Holding his AK-74 rifle by the end of the barrel, and with both arms spread wide to show he posed no threat, he walked slowly towards the gates, calling out that he wanted to speak to an officer. The guards ordered him to stop and open his jacket to prove he was not wearing a suicide vest and he had to lie flat in the dirt while they searched him and took his weapon. When they were satisfied that he wasn't a threat he was allowed into the base under guard and taken to see the commanding officer.

The officer heard him out in silence, asked a few less than penetrating questions and then left the room to confer over a secure link with his superiors at Bagram. Through the half-open door, Khan could hear the murmur of the officer's voice and then his returning footsteps. The officer tossed him a can of Coke, cool from the fridge, winked and said, "Welcome aboard."

Khan was given back his AK-74, though the magazines and spare ammunition were kept in a locked box carried by his American escort. He was flown to Bagram by helicopter that night, and debriefed by an African-American intelligence officer with the Defense Intelligence Agency. "*Salaam alaikum*, Khan," the officer said, touching his hand to his heart in the Afghan way, as Khan was shown into his office. "I'm Joshua." Khan suspected that it was not his real name, but the officer seemed open and honest, he met Khan's gaze when he spoke to him, and he treated him with respect.

Khan first laid out his terms. "I'm willing to come over to your side," he said. "I'll tell you everything I know, the names of my comrades and the senior Taliban commanders I know, the tactics they use, the places where their weapons and explosives are hidden, the locations of their safe houses, and how they're financed. I can tell you about the money house across the border in Pakistan where the money from drug smuggling, protection rackets and the stolen bribes you pay to buy the loyalties of warlords is stored and distributed to Taliban fighters and their allies. I can tell you the names of a few of the spies and sleepers within the Afghan regular army and I'll even spy for you if you want."

"And what's your angle?" Joshua said. "What do you want in return for all of this?"

"Do you have children?" Khan said.

"Why do you ask?"

"Because if you have children, you will understand. I want a new life for my daughter in the West. Afghanistan is not safe for her. The Taliban have beaten her and I fear that one day they will return to kill her."

"And presumably you want to go to the West with her?"

"*Insh'allah*, yes. But you must promise me that even if I am killed, you will still arrange for my daughter to leave this country."

He waited in silence as Joshua weighed his words. "Deal," he said at last, and held out his hand. "Shake on it."

160

For the next forty-eight hours, Khan told and retold his story, as Joshua interrogated him, probing and cross-examining him like a courtroom lawyer, never satisfied until he had teased out the last detail of everything Khan said, and, where possible, had cross-checked it against other information that he already possessed. He also brought in a succession of his colleagues for whom Khan had to repeat his story over and over again.

When Joshua at last pronounced himself satisfied, Khan added one final piece of information. "I think my men are also ready to come over," he said. "They are disenchanted with some of our leaders and tired of the endless fighting. There's been no peace in Afghanistan for thirty years. They're proud men and they won't surrender to you, but if you give them a way to save face and hold out the prospect of peace to them, if not immediately, then at least soon, I think they will take it."

He explained his planned rendezvous with his comrades and showed Joshua the place on a map. "The Brits are responsible for that area," Joshua said, "and they've an FOB a few miles from there. I'll introduce you to a British contact and he can make the arrangements to bring your guys in."

Khan was unconvinced by Joshua's insistence on involving the British. He realised that Joshua didn't completely trust Khan so he was letting the British handle the surrender. That way, if anything went wrong, it would be the British and not the Americans who would take the blame.

"One other thing," Joshua said. "There is another agent in the same area. I don't know his identity but he's being run by the Brits, and if his own cover is threatened and he has any inkling that you are also an agent, he might betray you to save himself."

"Is there nothing else you can tell me about him?"

"There is one thing. I've heard the Brits talk about him when we've been exchanging intelligence, and they used a code name for him that apparently he chose himself: 'Abu Qartoob'. Do you know what it means?"

"It means Father of the Earlobe," said Khan. "Afghans and Arabs don't always see eye to eye, but we do have our sense of humour in common, and it is quite strange and very dark. You have heard of Abu Hamza, for instance? Well, his name translates as 'Father of the Five'. Know why?"

Joshua shook his head.

"It's because he blew off one of his hands in an explosion, so he now has only five fingers." He studied Joshua for a moment. "I told you our sense of humour was strange."

"So this Abu Qartoob is likely to have a physical distinguishing mark too: big earlobes, or no earlobes at all, or something?"

"Possibly. I shall watch out for such a man."

Joshua completed briefing Khan on codes, systems for contacting Joshua or another American agent-handler, dead drops in which messages could be left, and emergency procedures, and then stood up. "Give me a few moments to brief the Brit guy," he said, "and then I'll introduce you."

"Who is he?"

"Captain Harry Todd. He's a British Army officer serving a three-year tour with the SAS, but he's been detached from his SAS squadron to the Intelligence Clearing Centre, where we collect and evaluate all the intelligence from human and electronic sources." While Joshua went in search of Todd, another American handler entered the room and began chatting to Khan.

Joshua returned half an hour later with the English officer. Todd's long, floppy blond hair and pink, fresh-faced complexion gave him an air of boyish innocence. "I'm Harry," Todd said, extending his hand. "It sounds like you have an interesting story to tell."

"*Salaam alaikum*, Harry, I hope you'll find it worthwhile," Khan said. He repeated his account to Todd, noting to himself that the Englishman asked far fewer questions about it than Joshua, and those that he did ask were less perceptive and incisive. After they had talked for some time, Todd nodded slowly. "Right," he said. "I'm convinced, let's go and get them." He glanced at Joshua. "If you've finished with Khan, I'll take him back to our section and arrange for some transport up to our FOB."

Joshua reached into a desk drawer and handed a bundle of dollars to Khan.

"What's this?" Khan said.

"Payment."

Khan shook his head. "I don't need your money. That's not why I'm doing this."

Joshua spread his hands wide. "I understand that," he said. "But everyone needs money. Take it for your daughter, if not for yourself."

Khan hesitated, then shrugged, took the dollars and stuffed them into the money belt that he wore around his waist. Most men in Afghanistan kept their cash and valuables in money belts, pockets were not to be trusted.

Khan followed Todd out of the American section of the base and into the British area. The British section appeared chaotic compared with the order and efficiency of the American operation, with its banks of computers, new-looking desks and equipment. Todd's desk was covered with stacks of papers and files and there were more piled on top of the filing cabinet behind him, and a row of Post-it notes stuck to the edge of his desk heightened the impression of disorganisation. "I hope you take better care of your informants than you do of your documents," Khan said with a smile that belied his unease.

"Don't worry," Todd said. "Every document is locked away before I leave this office and every room is checked by the guards during the night. If there's so much as a scrap of paper on show when they do so, I'll be up on a charge." He smiled confidently. "You're in safe hands, I promise you."

His words would have been more reassuring, Khan thought to himself, had Todd not left all his documents on open display while he'd been spending more than an hour talking to him in the American section. But Khan knew that he had no choice other than to trust the

British officer. Todd and Joshua were Khan's only hope of escaping Afghanistan with his daughter.

The Bentley pulled up in front of the West Stand of Stamford Bridge stadium, home to Chelsea Football Club. It was just after ten o'clock in the morning and the street was pretty much deserted. They were well away from the main entrances where every match day more than forty thousand fans would pour in to cheer on their team. Popov gestured at a blue door, from which led a small flight of stairs to the left, and to the right a concrete wheelchair ramp. "That leads to the lift that goes straight up to Mr Abramovich's private box." Two CCTV cameras covered the door and there was an intercom set into the wall to the left of the door.

"It doesn't look very VIP," said Shepherd. He was sitting in the back of the Bentley, directly behind Popov. Ulyashin was sitting next to him with his aluminium crutches between his legs, and Serov was squashed up against the other door, behind the driver. Shepherd could feel the transceiver pressing against the small of his back and he was having trouble getting used to the Bluetooth earpiece.

"It's not advertised," said Popov. "But it means high-profile visitors can get in and out without being snapped by the paparazzi."

"But it's generally known that Mr Grechko would use it?"

Popov nodded. "More for convenience than because he wants to avoid publicity. Mrs Grechko likes to have her photograph taken."

"I bet she does," said Shepherd. "And this was where the car was parked, when it happened?"

"For sure," said Popov. He said something to Chayka in Russian and the driver grunted and nodded. "Absolutely sure," said Popov.

"And you came out of the door, with Mr Grechko?"

"Me and Leo and Mikhail were with him in the box. We came down in the lift together after I confirmed that the cars were here."

"Cars?

"The Bentley and one of the SUVs. Alexei and Boris were in the SUV with Nikolay driving."

"So there were two cars?"

Popov nodded.

"Dmitry, I said I wanted everything to be the same."

Popov frowned, not understanding the point Shepherd was making.

Shepherd sighed and reached for the door handle. "OK, run through it with me." He climbed out and then helped Ulyashin out with his crutches. His leg had a plastic protector around the dressing which reached from his ankle up to his knee and he had put an old sock over his foot. Popov got out of the front passenger seat and slammed the door behind him.

Popov, Tarasov and Shepherd walked up the steps to the door. Ulyashin looked at the steps, thought better of it and walked around and up the wheelchair ramp.

"So in what order did you come out of the door?" asked Shepherd.

"I came out first," said Popov. "I had a quick look around to check that we were clear and then Leo joined

166

me. Once we were in place Leo moved down the steps and Mr Grechko came out."

"Show me," said Shepherd. "Let's pretend I'm Mr Grechko."

Tarasov walked slowly down the steps, his arms swinging by his side. "So at this point I'm at the door, you're to my left and Leo is in front of me," said Shepherd. "Then what?"

"Then Mikhail came out."

"And did what? Stayed behind me?"

Popov nodded.

"And what about the men in the SUV? Alexei and Boris?"

"They stayed there. Watching from the car."

Shepherd was about to point out that a bodyguard's place was next to his principal, not sitting in a car watching what was going on, but he bit his tongue. He had meant what he'd said about not embarrassing the man in front of his colleagues. "OK, and what was the plan? Leo's on the step, you're on my left and Mikhail is behind me."

"Leo moves down to the car and opens the rear door. I go down and stand to the front of the car, next to Leo. You — Mr Grechko — walks down the stairs and gets into the car. Mikhail covers his rear, Leo gets in next to you, I get in the front and Mikhail goes back to the SUV."

The SUV which isn't there, thought Shepherd, but again he didn't say anything. Nor did he point out that in a situation like Stamford Bridge there was safety in numbers and the safest option would have been to have brought Grechko out of one of the main exits. The isolated VIP entrance was a gift to any attacker.

Shepherd looked around. A good sniper, a really good one, could make a near-guaranteed kill shot at a mile or more, but that would be exceptional. Shepherd had honed his sniping skills in the deserts of Afghanistan, which is where an Australian sniper had a GPS-confirmed shot of more than three thousand yards and where Craig Harrison, a corporal with the Blues and Royals, shot and killed two Taliban machine-gunners at a range of two thousand seven hundred yards. But such distances really were the exception, and most snipers weren't comfortable beyond half a mile. And at anything above half a mile the wind made a big difference, and calculating the distance the round would fall became crucial. The problem was that the stadium was in a built-up area of West London and was overlooked by all manner of residential and office buildings. From where he was standing Shepherd could see at least a dozen vantage points that would be perfect for a sniper, from open windows to office block roofs to cranes high above building projects.

"Did the police do this with you?" Shepherd asked Popov. "Did they do a run-through like this?"

Popov shook his head. "Mr Grechko didn't want to talk to the police," he said. "He said the British police are useless when it comes to things like this. He said the British police couldn't find their own arses if they used both hands." He laughed, and then repeated what he'd said in Russian for the benefit of Tarasov and Ulyashin.

"Yeah, he might be right," said Shepherd. "Which direction did the shot come from?"

"Difficult to say," said Popov. "We didn't hear the shot."

"It was a single shot?"

"The only round that we know about is the one that struck Mikhail."

"But it's possible that there were more?"

Popov shrugged. "Like I said, we didn't hear the sound of a shot."

Shepherd nodded. That meant that the sniper was too far away to be heard or used a suppressor. Spider wasn't a big fan of suppressors, because while they cut down on the noise they also affected the performance of the round.

"OK, walk me through it," said Shepherd.

Popov spoke to Tarasov in Russian and the big man moved down the steps, his legs swinging from side to side. As he headed for the rear door of the Bentley, Popov moved down the steps. Shepherd stood where he was and looked around. With the two bodyguards at the bottom of the steps, he was totally exposed. If the sniper was going to take the shot, the obvious time would have been when the target was on the steps, not when he was getting into the car.

Tarasov opened the rear door of the Bentley and turned to look at Shepherd. He was standing on the wrong side, Shepherd knew, he should have been standing at the rear of the car and not close to the front passenger door. Popov was standing behind Tarasov, watching Shepherd as he walked down the stairs. The fact that the two men were at the front of the car meant that Shepherd was vulnerable to an attack from the rear.

Behind him, Ulyashin cursed as his crutch skidded across the concrete. "And the guys in the SUV stayed where they were?" asked Shepherd.

Popov nodded. Again Shepherd bit his tongue. Grechko had been at his most vulnerable when he moved down the steps and at that point he should have been surrounded by his team. As he moved down the steps, Ulyashin continued to have problems using the crutches and he cursed again, in Russian.

Shepherd reached the door of the Bentley and turned to look at Ulyashin, who had only just reached the bottom of the steps.

"So when did he get hit?" asked Shepherd.

"Just as Mr Grechko got to the car. Where you are standing now."

"And Mikhail?"

"He was moving back to the SUV."

"Mikhail, where did the bullet hit you?"

Ulyashin frowned. "The leg." He said something to Popov in Russian. Popov didn't reply, he just waved away whatever Ulyashin had said.

"The front of the leg or the back?"

"The back," said Ulyashin.

"The calf," said Popov. "The bullet went in the back and blew a chunk out of the front."

Shepherd nodded thoughtfully. The fact that the round hadn't taken off the man's leg suggested that it was fired from far away, possibly a mile, so that by the time it reached its target it had lost most of its momentum. "Mikhail, think carefully, where exactly were you standing when the round hit?"

Ulyashin frowned. "Round?" he repeated.

"Bullet," said Shepherd.

"*Pulya*," translated Popov.

"Ah, *pulya*." Ulyashin nodded and stood with his legs apart at the rear of the Bentley, facing towards Shepherd.

"See that?" said Shepherd. "If he was standing there, he'd have been shielded by the SUV, right? So the sniper can only have been down there." He pointed down the road. In the distance was a crane and beyond it an apartment block and several office towers. "There are plenty of buildings he could have taken a shot from. Or he could have done it from a vehicle."

Popov nodded slowly. "Mr Grechko was lucky."

"Yes, he was, wasn't he? OK, I've seen enough, you guys can head back to the house."

"You're not coming with us?"

"I'll catch a black cab," said Shepherd. "I've got something to do but I'll be back at the house in a few hours. Mr Grechko's not going anywhere, is he?"

"There's nothing on the schedule — you know that."

"Exactly. If anything changes then call me ASAP, otherwise I'll see you back at the house."

"Is there a problem?"

Shepherd shook his head. "It's all good, Dmitry," he said.

Shepherd caught a black cab and had it drop him outside the Whiteley's shopping centre in Queensway. He paid the driver, went inside and walked along to Costa Coffee, where he bought himself a cappuccino and found a quiet seat by the window before using the Samsung mobile to phone Harper. "Are you ready for a spot of cleaning?" asked Shepherd.

"Sure," said Harper. "What do you want me to do?"

"You're close to Queensway, right?"

"Just around the corner."

"OK, here's the deal. I know you hate tube stations but I need you to go to Queensway tube station. Keep your head down and your hood up and the CCTV cameras won't get your face. Buy yourself a one-day travel card from a machine. Don't worry, the machines don't have CCTV. The only line that uses Queensway is the Central Line. Go straight down the escalator to the eastbound platform. Wait for the first train and look as if you're going to get on, then take a seat on the platform. Don't make a thing about looking around but be aware if anyone does the same."

"Got you," said Harper.

"Then get up and make a thing about looking at the map. Put on a bit of a show as if you've realised that you're on the wrong platform and walk across to the westbound. Do the same there. Make it look as if you're getting on the next train and then change your mind and sit down."

172

"So I'll spot if there's a tail."

"Either that or they'll get on the train so that they don't show out. If they do board, they'll call in a watcher at the entrance. The thing is, don't make it too obvious. Just act a bit confused, as if you're not sure what you're doing. Then look at your watch as if you're late for something, and head back up the escalator and out into the street."

"Then what?"

"I'll have watched you go in and out. If you've been tailed I should have spotted it. I'll phone you as soon as you're back in the street."

"Sounds like a plan," said Harper.

"Now this is important, Lex. Don't look for me, but if you do see me just blank me. No reaction at all. And don't look for a tail. Even on the tube platform. No looking around. If someone stays on the platform you'll see them, you don't need to look at them. That's how it works on the tube, no one makes eye contact."

"I'll be keeping my head down, that's for sure. When are we going to do this?"

Shepherd looked at his watch. It was just after eleven o'clock in the morning. "The sooner the better."

"I can be at the tube station in twenty minutes."

"Perfect." Shepherd ended the call and spent ten minutes drinking his coffee before walking back down Queensway. He arrived opposite the tube station at 11.15 and spent the last few minutes window-shopping. He spotted Harper walking from the direction of Hyde Park, his hands in his parka and his head down. Shepherd took his mobile and started speaking into it as he walked slowly along the pavement. There didn't seem to be anyone interested in what Harper was doing, but if MI5 were watching him that was to be expected. The surveillance teams of the Security Service were among the best in the world. They had honed their skills during the Cold War and against the IRA and were at any one time following hundreds of potential Islamic terrorists.

As Harper disappeared inside the station, Shepherd continued to pretend to talk on his phone as he watched to see who else went inside. A man in a grey suit with a briefcase, two students with backpacks and beanie hats, an old lady in a cheap coat with what looked like a dead fox around her neck, a woman with a pushchair, a very fat man in an anorak and stretch pants, a girl with a Hello Kitty suitcase, three Japanese teenagers with spiky hair and chains hanging off their tight jeans, a curly-haired man in a London Underground jacket, a Sikh man with a blue turban and a violin case.

Shepherd took his phone away from his ear but kept it in his hand as he walked slowly along the pavement. If the followers were good they'd have left one watcher in the ticket hall, just in case Harper did what Shepherd had suggested and doubled back. Sending Harper into the tube station would also have confused any vehicles or cyclists being used as part of a surveillance team. Normal protocol would be to send any vehicles to the next stations along the line or to put them on stand-by. Queensway was a busy road with no places to stop. A black cab disgorged a businessman with a leather briefcase and then it went on its way, its yellow light on. A white van went by. There were two men in it, one of them eating a Cornish pasty and reading a copy of the *Sun*.

A bike courier, a woman in black spandex leggings and a tight fluorescent jacket, had stopped outside the station and was talking into a mobile phone clipped to her collar. She wheeled her bike along the pavement and then padlocked it and went inside a money exchange shop. An ambulance turned into Queensway from the Hyde Park end and its siren kicked into life as it sped down towards Whiteley's. Heads turned to watch it go. Shepherd ignored it and concentrated on any passers-by who were more interested in the tube station. Two pensioners, a man and a woman, walked arm in arm into the ticket hall, wearing matching raincoats.

The woman with the pushchair reappeared, looking flustered, but then she looked around and saw a man in a long leather jacket walking down the road towards her, waving. She kissed him on the cheek and they walked back into the ticket hall together. The bike courier reappeared from the currency exchange shop, unlocked her bike and rode off towards Hyde Park.

Harper emerged from the tube station. Shepherd called him on his mobile. "Looking good," he said. "Turn left and head down Queensway to Whiteley's. On the way stop at a shop window, any one, it doesn't matter. Walk past, stop, then walk back and stare in the window for about thirty seconds."

"Got you," said Harper, and he began to walk down the busy road, his parka hood still up.

"Go into Whiteley's, there's an escalator up to the first floor," continued Shepherd. "Take it but then come straight back down on the down escalator. Then just head up to Hyde Park and I'll see you there. Don't look around, you don't have to worry about spotting a tail, that's down to me."

Harper put his phone into his pocket and slouched off down the road. Shepherd was standing on the opposite side of the road, looking into the window of a shop that sold London souvenirs and T-shirts. He turned, his phone still held against his ear as he carried out an imaginary conversation. If Harper was being followed, a professional would almost certainly be on the opposite side of the road, though if there were multiple followers they would use both sides. If the surveillance was top notch, they might even have someone ahead of Harper. The fact that Harper had gone into the tube station meant that there were unlikely to be vehicles or cyclists in the area as they would have moved towards the next stations on the Central Line.

Shepherd continued to talk into his phone as he watched Harper head down Queensway. He waited until Harper was about a hundred yards away before he started walking after him. Harper did his U-turn in front of a Chinese restaurant with a dozen dark-brown ducks hanging from their feet in the window. Shepherd didn't see anyone falter on either side of the street.

When Harper began walking again, no one stopped to allow him to get ahead, which was a good sign.

Shepherd walked quickly, jogged across the road, and by the time Harper walked into the Whiteley's shopping centre, Shepherd was only twenty feet behind him. As Harper walked towards the escalator, Shepherd turned towards a shop selling leather jackets and used the reflection to watch Harper go up the escalator. Shepherd's photographic memory enabled him to effortlessly remember every person who followed Harper up the escalator, and not one of them followed him back down when he made the downward journey a few seconds later. Nor did anyone follow Harper out of the shopping centre.

Shepherd crossed Queensway and followed Harper back up to Hyde Park. As Harper entered the park Shepherd stayed on the pavement, pretending to make a call on his mobile. Over the next five minutes a dozen or so people walked into the park, but it was clear that none was involved in surveillance. Shepherd put his phone away and walked over to the bench where Harper was sitting and smoking a cigarette. "Clean as a whistle," said Shepherd, sitting down next to him.

"I've never understood what that meant," said Harper. "People are always blowing in whistles so they're not especially clean, are they?"

"I think it goes back to the days of steam engines," said Shepherd. "They were made of brass and were always well polished."

Harper grinned. "You and your trick memory," he said.

"Yeah, but just because I remember it doesn't mean it's true," said Shepherd. "Anyway, there's no one following you. Not today, anyway."

"What do you mean?"

"You could be marked for occasional surveillance. If they've nothing else on. High-priority targets are followed twenty-four-seven but there are plenty of low-priority targets who get followed as and when."

"Shit. So we have to go through this every day?"

Shepherd shook his head. "I think you're OK. If they had spotted you at a mosque they'd be all over you for the first few days just in case you were an imminent threat. But from now on, no more hanging around outside mosques."

"But walking around Fulham and Hammersmith is OK, right?"

Shepherd shrugged. "I don't see why not."

"Thought I might visit a few of the Asian shops, check out the restaurants from that part of the world."

"Afghan cuisine?"

"You'd be surprised, mate," said Harper.

"Seriously, Lex, keep your head down. Let my guy do his thing first. Let's work the databases before we start prowling the streets."

Harper flicked ash on to the grass. "You're right," he said.

"I know I'm right. It's what I do for a living."

Harper shivered. "Why's it so bloody cold?" he asked.

"The weather's been funny all year," said Shepherd. "We had snow right through March."

"So much for global warming."

"They call it climate change now," said Shepherd. "And there's no doubt that there's something funny going on with our weather."

"Yeah, well, I'll be glad to get back to Thailand." He winked at Shepherd. "You should come."

"Yeah, maybe. How is it these days?"

"Full of Brits," Harper said. "And the Russians are moving in big-time. They pretty much run Phuket already and they're taking over Pattaya."

"How so?"

"Russian mafia, mate. They're vicious bastards. They've even got clubs with Russian go-go dancers and the cops just let them get on with it." He grinned. "The best police force money can buy. But they're moving into property, big-time. Drugs. Counterfeit medicines, counterfeit anything. The Thais are terrified of them. Get into an argument with a Russkie and . . ." He made a gun with his hand. "Bang, bang."

"But not a problem for you, right?"

"I get on with everyone, mate. You know that. But it's changed a lot since you were there."

"Everything changes," said Shepherd. "The weather, people, places. Nothing stays the same."

"More's the pity."

Shepherd nodded. "Life does seem to get more complicated, doesn't it? Back in Afghanistan, everything was black and white, pretty much. We were the good guys, the Taliban were the bad guys. They tried to kill us and we tried to kill them. You knew where you stood. Now we've got a Taliban killer living in London and

I'm protecting a Russian mobster from a professional hitman."

Harper turned to look at him. "Seriously?"

"Can't talk about it," said Shepherd. "Well, I can, but then I'd have to kill you." He looked at his watch. "I've got to go. Duty calls."

Shepherd got back to his Hampstead flat at just after eight o'clock in the evening. He put the kettle on and had a quick shower while it boiled. Grechko was staying in all night and it was clear that security was tight at the mansion so there was nothing to be gained by Shepherd sleeping on the premises. He changed into a clean polo shirt and chinos, made himself a coffee and then called Charlotte Button. He apologised for calling so late but she cut him short. "I'm always on duty, you know that," she said. "And I guess it's difficult to call when his security team are around."

"I wanted a chat about the attack on Grechko," he said. "It wasn't investigated by the cops, was it?"

"They weren't informed until well after the event," said Button. "They drove the bodyguard who was hit to a private hospital and Grechko called the PM before the police were informed. To be honest it wouldn't have made any difference, the sniper was a pro so he would have been long gone."

"Yeah, that's what I wanted to talk to you about," said Shepherd. "I was out there for a look-see with his security team."

"And?"

"And there's something not right. If as you said the guy is a pro, then I don't see how he could have missed Grechko. As he came out of the stadium, he was a sitting duck."

"Snipers sometimes miss," said Button. "You must know that, what with your sniping experience and all that."

"Except he didn't miss, he hit a bodyguard in the leg. The bullet wasn't recovered, was it?"

"The bullet went in and out. There was a search of the area carried out, but it was two days after and it didn't turn up."

"That's a pity. It might have given us a better idea of the type of weapon used. I'm not sure if it was a long-distance shot or not. There were plenty of vantage points within a mile, but it could have been done from a parked vehicle and that would have been a much closer shot."

"Why do you think that?"

"The bodyguards didn't hear a shot so that suggests that the gun was some distance away. But it could have had a suppressor on it, and then I started thinking about that sniper in Baltimore, the one who made his shots from the boot of a car."

"Why does it matter where he was?" asked Button.

"If he was a mile away then it's understandable that he might have missed. There'd be big variations on air speed from high up to low down, plus updraughts from the stadium. It'd be a complicated shot so a miss wouldn't be unexpected. But the thing is, professional killers don't usually make shots when there's a chance they might miss. Makes them look less than professional. But if he was closer then he shouldn't have missed."

"Where are you going with this?" asked Button.

"The stadium was behind them and there were two cars in the road. The bullet hit the bodyguard in the back of the leg, so the cars being where they were, the sniper could only have fired from one direction. When he fired, Grechko was getting into the car and the bodyguard was in the way."

"So it was an accident. Grechko was lucky."

"If the sniper had made the shot earlier, the bodyguard wouldn't have been in the way."

"What are you saying?"

Shepherd sighed. "I'm not sure. There's just something not right about this. He hit the bodyguard in the leg. Are we supposed to believe that he was trying for a kill shot at Grechko and he missed by, what, five or six feet? And why did he wait until the bodyguard was between him and the target when if he'd fired earlier, he'd have had a clear shot?"

"Are you saying that the sniper deliberately missed?"

"Either that or he wanted to shoot the bodyguard. He hit the target he was aiming for."

"For what reason?"

"That's the question, isn't it? And I'm afraid I don't have the answer. But what's the alternative, the world's worst sniper is on Grechko's case?"

"What do his security team think?"

"To be honest, I don't think thinking is in their skill set. They're not the brightest and I'm having to put a lot of work into getting them up to speed on the personal protection front. Look, how do we move forward on this? Presumably someone is trying to catch the sniper, right?"

"We're liaising with the Russian intelligence services and cross-referencing names with the immigration people," said Button. "We're on the case."

"Because I really don't want to spend the rest of my life babysitting a Russian oligarch," he said.

"You won't, I promise," said Button, and she ended the call.

Shepherd finished his coffee and then picked up his laptop and placed it on the coffee table. He booted it up and launched Skype. He smiled when he saw that Liam was online. He started a call and after a few rings Liam answered and his face filled the screen. "Hi, Dad," he said. He was growing his hair long and he flicked it out of his eyes.

"Hey. Please tell me you're doing homework on the computer and not playing around on Facebook or Twitter or whatever."

"Sure, if that'll make you happy," said Liam. He grinned. "Only joking, Dad. We do a lot of our maths homework online now, I was just finishing it."

"Good lad. Everything OK?"

"Sure. I've got a match on Saturday against a team from Rugby. That's ironic, isn't it? Football against Rugby?"

"Good luck with it."

"Is there any chance you could get to see it?" asked Liam.

"I'd love to, Liam, but I've got a job in London. I've got to be there every day."

Shepherd's stomach lurched when he saw the look of disappointment on Liam's face. "Soon as the job's done, I'll come and see you."

"It's OK, Dad. No problem."

"I've got to be here twenty-four-seven pretty much," said Shepherd.

"Really, it's OK. Hey, there's something I want to ask you."

"Sure. Go ahead."

"What would you think if I wanted to join the army?"

Shepherd laughed. "You're only sixteen."

Liam raised his eyebrows and looked at him with the withering contempt that had become a feature over the past year or so. "I know that," he said. "I meant when I finish school."

"I was sort of hoping you'd go to university."

"You didn't go."

"I went. I just didn't finish."

"You studied economics at Manchester University. But you never sat your finals because you joined the army."

Shepherd couldn't help but smile. Liam would make a great interrogator. "Things were different when I was a teenager," said Shepherd. "These days employers expect you to have a degree."

"OK, I could sign up after I go to university. In fact the army will pay for me to get my degree." He looked excited and he was nodding as he spoke, trying to encourage Shepherd to agree with him.

"What's brought this on?" said Shepherd. "You've never mentioned this before."

"We had a careers talk today from a captain in the Royal Marines and it got me thinking, that's all."

"Why was a Royal Marines captain talking at your school?"

"He's an old boy. But he was there as part of our careers talks. We've had all sorts of people in, trying to persuade us that they've got the best job in the world."

"You know that the Marines are part of the navy, not the army."

Liam rolled his eyes again. "Yes, Dad, I'm not a complete moron."

"No, I'm just saying, a military career is one way to go, but you need to give some thought to what branch of the service you want to go into. But it's a tough life, Liam. It's bloody hard work."

"But it's fun, right? And you get to travel."

"Most of the travel these days is to Afghanistan and Iraq," said Shepherd. "And trust me, there's not much fun in those places."

"But what else am I going to do, Dad? Sit in an office? Or more likely sit on the dole. At least in the army I get to have a career."

"It's not as secure as it used to be. They're letting a lot of people go."

Liam pulled a face. "I thought you'd be more enthusiastic."

"Like I said, you're only sixteen. You've plenty of time ahead of you."

"Not that much time, Dad. I have to start deciding about university next year. And the more I think about it, the more I like the idea of being in the army. Maybe flying helicopters."

"Again, they're cutting back on the number of helicopters."

"God, you're being so negative." Liam threw up his hands and sat back. "I knew it'd be a waste of time talking to you."

Shepherd took a deep breath. He always found it difficult talking to his son over Skype. "I'm not trying to be negative," he said. "I just don't think you want to rush into something like this."

"I'm not rushing, I'm considering my options. That's what the careers teacher says we should be doing. Dad, you were a soldier. Why are you so against me doing the same?"

"I think you need to go to university. It was different when I was a kid, not everyone went. It wasn't unusual to start work at eighteen. Hell, some of my friends started work at sixteen. But these days a degree is the norm and you'll be left behind if you don't have one."

"But having a degree doesn't mean you'll get a job. There are plenty of graduates on the dole."

Shepherd nodded. His son was right, of course. But with all that was happening to the country's armed forces, he didn't think a military career would be a smart move for Liam. And like any father, he didn't like the idea of his son being in the firing line. "This

186

captain, what did he say that made it sound so attractive?"

Liam wrinkled his nose. "He said it was a worthwhile career. That you were doing something for the country. Something to be proud of. Most people work for themselves, they do a boring nine-to-five job just to have money. But if you're serving your country you're doing something important."

"Well, that's certainly true," said Shepherd.

"He said that every day was different, that you never got into a routine. That the job challenged you and stretched you."

"Again, that's true. But there's a lot of waiting around. But he's right, every day is different."

"And you get to travel."

"You don't need to be in the army to travel," said Shepherd. "But OK, if you're really interested then I can put you in touch with people in different branches of the services. And next time we're in Hereford you can come into Stirling Lines and talk to some of the guys there."

"I don't want to be in the SAS, Dad."

"Why do you say that?"

"I don't think I'd be good enough."

"Rubbish," said Shepherd. "If you want to be a soldier I'll make sure you're the best darn soldier there is."

Liam laughed. "I'm not running around with a rucksack full of bricks on my back," he said.

"It builds stamina," said Shepherd. "But seriously, if you're thinking about it then let's go and talk to some people, see what your options are. But I want you going to university first. That way if the army thing doesn't work out you've got something to fall back on."

"That's cool," said Liam. He looked at his watch. "I've got to go, Dad. I've got to finish this maths."

"You take care," said Shepherd. "And good luck with the match."

He ended the call and closed his laptop. He lay back on the sofa, picked up the television remote and flicked through the channels, looking for something to watch. Part of him was pleased that Liam wanted to follow in his footsteps, but he was very aware of what his mother would have said if she had been alive. Sue had been no great fan of the army and there was no way that she would have agreed to Liam signing up. The Royal Marines captain had been right about military service — it was worthwhile and it was exciting, and Shepherd had relished the buzz he'd always had in combat, the knowledge that it was kill or be killed and that every breath could be your last. But it was one thing to experience the adrenalin rush for yourself and quite another to know that your child was in mortal danger. Shepherd wasn't sure how he'd be able to cope with the knowledge that his son was in a combat zone and that at any moment there could be a knock on his door and two men in uniform would be there to break the bad news. He shuddered. For the first time in his life he had an inkling of what it must have been like for Sue when he was away. Time and time again she'd begged him to quit the SAS and get a job where he'd be closer to home and where she wouldn't be lying awake at night fearing the worst. He'd told her that it was just a job and that it was no more dangerous than driving a cab or stocking shelves in a supermarket. That had been a lie, of course, and she'd known it. Shepherd had loved being in the SAS, though it was only once he'd left that he was able to admit to himself that he had been addicted to the adrenalin rush of putting his life on the line. He closed his eyes. "I'm sorry, Sue," he whispered.

In Monte Carlo on the weekend of the Monaco Grand Prix even the super-rich sometimes struggled to find a berth for their yachts in Port Hercules, the tiny principality's main harbour. First priority was notionally given to citizens and permanent residents of Monaco, and there were such long waiting lists that applications from non-residents were supposedly not even considered, yet somehow Russian oligarchs and other billionaires always found a way to secure a berth for their yachts, while the eye-watering cost of such rentals, like the revenues from the casino, disappeared into the capacious pockets of officials serving "His Serene Highness, the Prince of Monaco".

The marinas were packed with scores of super-yachts, moored at right angles to the quayside. The multi-millionaire and billionaire owners and their privileged friends and guests had watched the race from the decks in the afternoon and now, as night was falling, the after-race parties were beginning on almost all of them. Like Hollywood stars at Oscar night parties, the grand prix drivers could pick and choose from dozens of invitations, and their diminutive figures, head and shoulders shorter than the tall, willowy models clustered around them, strolled the decks of many of the super-yachts like deities. On others there were gangsters, money launderers and traffickers in everything from guns and drugs to women rubbing shoulders with an array of fixers, wheelers, dealers, tax exiles, princes and titled paupers, descendants of obscure European royal houses. Monaco had not changed an iota since the 1920s, when Somerset Maugham witheringly dismissed it as "a sunny place for shady people".

One of the largest yachts of all, its name picked out in Cyrillic script, was moored to a small pontoon covered with an awning and separating the yacht from the quay. The yacht was decked out with bunting, flags and lights, Eurotrash music was playing and beautiful young women and rather older and less beautiful men were drinking, dancing and partying. Others paired up and disappeared together below decks.

There was a small marquee at the quay end of the jetty and inside it, a security team was very carefully screening the invitations of the guests — most of them yet more beautiful young women — as they arrived, and confiscating any cameras or mobile phones. Those would not be returned to the guests until they left. The owner valued his privacy and could afford to ensure that it was maintained. The covered walkway had its own security system, and as the guests walked through it, they were scanned by concealed machines to ensure that they were not carrying anything that the security guards had missed. Cocaine or ecstasy were fine, but knives, guns or other weapons were not. The yacht owner, Oleg Zakharov, was a Russian oligarch and billionaire, and like most of his kind he had attracted more than his fair share of enemies over the years.

Those monitoring the security system could see the guests' bodies under their clothes — one of the perks of the job for the two men monitoring the screens, who got to see some of the most beautiful women they'd ever come across stark naked. As usual, Zakharov himself had joined them, moistening his lips with his tongue as he leaned over the screen, seeing what would be available for his pleasure later that night.

The man they called Monotok had already been to Genoa to visit the shipyard where Zakharov's yacht was built. Posing as the fixer and right-hand man of yet another Russian billionaire looking for a super-yacht, he was given a tour of the yard and shown a model of Zakharov's yacht. The Genoese boat-builders were so proud of it that they even showed him the plans. If not quite the biggest yacht in the world — an American software billionaire had one a few feet longer, they said, grinding their teeth — it was "definitely the most beautiful and luxurious". Monotok had smiled and nodded sympathetically, keeping them talking, and then sending them off in search of more information while he memorised the lay-out of the yacht and took a few discreet photographs with his iPhone while they were distracted.

Getting the yacht's schedule had been harder, but he had that and a copy of Zakharov's diary showing him when he'd be on board. Even as he toured the boatyard he had decided that Monte Carlo was the place to strike. After he left the boatyard, he went to a workshop, once a manufacturer of beautifully crafted sextants but now specialising in making one-off gadgets for rich men. Monotok commissioned an extending climbing-pole, sketching what he wanted on a piece of paper. He told the technician who took his order that he was going rock and ice climbing in the Alps and would be using the pole to bridge crevasses and "unclimbable" sections of rock face. The device was a telescoping aluminium tube made up of six sections, four inches at its widest and tapering down to half that in the final section. Pressing a lever broke the seal on a small gas bottle and the released gas caused the pole to extend swiftly and silently to its full length. A four-pronged grapple covered with sprayed-on rubber was fixed to the top, and when extended, each section also had a couple of narrow footholds along its sides that sprang out as it extended and retracted when it was collapsed again.

From a diving shop he bought a neoprene scuba drysuit that clamped tight around his neck, wrists and ankles, giving a watertight seal, but leaving his hands, feet and face exposed. In the prolonged immersion in the sea that he was planning, they would get very cold, so he also bought gloves, boots and a hood, as well as a spear gun and a diving knife.

On the night of the grand prix, he waited for nightfall and then made his way down through the Japanese Gardens, near Larvotto Beach, a mile east of the marina. He climbed down the short, rocky cliff and slipped into the sea, then swam and finned his way along to the marina, using a slow but powerful stroke. He moved along the lines of yachts, a dark shape barely distinguishable from the darkness of the sea itself, and eventually slipped under the pontoon, next to Zakharov's super-yacht.

He watched and waited for several hours while the party was still in full swing on the yacht. All the security was focused on those walking on to the yacht from the jetty, and there was only the most cursory surveillance of the yacht itself and even less of its seaward side. Eventually, in the early hours, the music and noise from the yacht died down and the cabin lights were extinguished one by one. There were still two bored security men standing on the quayside, but the yacht itself was quiet.

He finned his way across to the seaward side of the yacht. He popped the seal on the gas bottle to extend the climbing pole and hooked the rubber grapple over the deck rail of the yacht, then removed his fins, attached them to his belt with a karabiner, and then began to climb the pole. Monotok's heart was not even beating fast as he swung himself over the rail and began to pad silently along the deck, the spear gun on a strap over his shoulder and the knife held ready in his hand. The spear gun made little noise but it could not be guaranteed to kill instantly, and it would be a last resort, to be used only if a target was too far from him to be dealt with by a swift, silent kill with the knife. But the spear gun and the knife were there only in case something went wrong and he was discovered. If all went to plan only one man would die, and that would be Zakharov. And Monotok wouldn't be using the spear or the knife to take the oligarch's life.

As he reached the midpoint of the deck in the shadow of the main mast, he heard a noise from the far side of the yacht. He froze and turned to look down the deck. One of the beautiful young women, out of her head on cocaine and alcohol and barely aware of what was happening, had been pinned to the deck and was being screwed by one of the crewmen, while a line of four or five others waited their turn, all eyes fixed on her naked body, oblivious to the black-clad figure ghosting between the shadows on the other side of the yacht.

As Monotok watched, the crewman got up, wiped himself down with the woman's torn and discarded designer silk blouse and was at once replaced by the next man in the queue. As the crewman lowered himself on to the woman, her head rolled sideways, her blond hair matted and her vacant, drugged eyes staring straight at Monotok. She looked no more than sixteen or seventeen, but Monotok merely made certain that she had not registered his presence before moving on along the deck. He was coldly indifferent to what was happening to her, and even grateful for the distraction she was providing for the crew and security men awaiting their turn.

The lay-out of the yacht imprinted on his mind, he moved along the deck until he reached an open hatch, and then went down the companionway. Below decks, he made his way to the main stateroom in the stern.

After listening for a couple of minutes, he eased open the door. It wasn't locked; on his own yacht, surrounded by his security team, Zakharov obviously felt he had nothing to fear. The room was littered with empty champagne bottles and discarded clothes. Lines of cocaine were still laid out on the glass-topped dressing table, with a bag of the white powder spilling across the glass, and there seemed to be powdery traces of cocaine on every flat surface.

Zakharov had passed out and lay snoring, naked on the silk sheets of the super-king-size bed while three naked young women lay around the cabin, two on the bed, the other sprawled across the floor. Monotok knew that Zakharov always plied his women with gamma-hydroxybutyrate, GHB, the date rape drug. That way they neither remembered nor complained about whatever he did to them. They were close to unconsciousness and would be feeling no pain.

Monotok leaned his spear gun by the door and slid his knife back into its scabbard. He reached for a waterproof pouch on his belt and quietly popped it open. He took out a syringe, eased off the cap and bent down over the woman on the floor. He didn't bother looking for a vein, the liquid Valium was just as effective when it was injected into muscle. With this combined with the GHB already in their bloodstream, the girls would be out for hours. He put the empty syringe back into the pouch and repeated the process with the two girls on the bed before lifting them up and placing them on the floor.

He took four lengths of cord from the pouch and used it to carefully tie Zakharov's wrists and ankles to the bed, then took out a roll of duct tape and used his teeth to bite off a piece. He climbed on to the bed and straddled Zakharov, shoving the tape over his mouth and winding it around his face several times. Only then did Zakharov start to wake up, but it was too late. He was bound and gagged. As the oligarch struggled, Monotok walked slowly around the bed, tightening the cords, until Zakharov was spreadeagled like a stranded starfish.

Monotok sat down on the edge of the bed and stared down at Zakharov. "Do you know me, Oleg?" he asked in Russian. "Do you have any idea who I am?"

Zakharov tried to speak but the duct tape made it impossible.

Monotok smiled and patted him on the cheek. "You don't need to say anything, my fat little friend," he said. "In fact, I don't want you to say anything. There is nothing you can say that will be of any interest to me. And you will only embarrass yourself by threatening me or offering me money or begging me to spare your life. All I need you to do is to nod or shake your head." His massive hand reached for Zakharov's throat and gave it a little squeeze. "Now, do you understand me?"

Monotok released his grip on the man's throat and he nodded, quickly. Monotok smiled and patted him on the cheek again. "That's a good little fat man," he said. "So, do you recognise me?"

Zakharov shook his head.

"And does the name Kirill Luchenko mean anything to you?"

Zakharov shook his head again.

"Well, by the time I have finished that name will mean something to you. What about my father? Mark Luchenko?"

Another shake of his head. More frantic this time.

"Or my mother? Misha?"

Zakharov stared fearfully at Monotok, and then shook his head.

Monotok smiled sadly. "How quickly you forget," he said. "That's what I don't understand. I've killed a lot of people and in most cases I never got to know their names. I was in Chechnya, killing for our masters. And there wasn't time to ask for names. But when I did know their names, I remembered. I still remember. I don't see how you can take a life and not show the respect to at least remember the life you have taken." He patted Zakharov on the cheek again. "You will remember me, my little fat friend. But not for long. I'm going to explain to you who my parents were and who I am and how what you did made me the man I am. You will understand who I am and why I am going to kill you. Then I will take your life. But at least I will do you the courtesy of remembering your name. So now, let's get started. I'm going to tell you a story, about a nine-year-old boy."

Monotok spoke for the next ten minutes, his voice barely above a whisper. From time to time he patted Zakharov's face and once he gripped his cheek tightly between his thumb and forefinger. As he spoke,

Zakharov struggled to free himself, but his efforts were futile. Eventually he gave up and tears rolled down his cheeks. When Monotok finished talking and pulled out the syringe, Zakharov's bowels emptied and he soiled the bed.

Monotok reached over with his left hand and squeezed the oligarch's throat until his face went purple and his heels were drumming on the mattress. When Zakharov's veins were fully engorged, Monotok plunged the needle into the carotid artery and injected the entire contents of the syringe, then released his grip on Zakharov's throat. The girls had been injected with concentrated Valium, ensuring a deep dreamless sleep. But the syringe Monotok used on Zakharov contained a concentrated cocaine solution. Zakharov died quickly, but painfully, his eyes filled with a mixture of fear and hatred.

Once Zakharov had stopped breathing, Monotok pulled off the duct tape and undid the cords around his wrists and ankles. He picked up his spear gun, slipped out of the cabin and moved back along the deck, silently passing the point where the crewmen were still taking turns with the now unconscious young woman. He climbed back down to the water, collapsed the pole and swam away into the night.

Shepherd arrived at Grechko's house at 6.30. He wound down the window of his X5 and waved at the CCTV camera and the metal gate immediately rolled back. Max Barsky, the young Ukrainian, was in the gatehouse, and he waved through the window as Shepherd drove by.

The doors to the garage were already up and Shepherd drove down to the car parking area. He left the X5 next to Grechko's Bentley, which they would be using to drive to Northolt airfield. He took with him a kitbag containing his running gear — most of his day was spent in the control centre and he had decided that he was going to start exercising every day. The gym was available twenty-four hours a day but he had never been a fan of exercise equipment or weights.

He walked over to the control centre, pressed his thumb against the sensor and tapped in his four-digit code before pushing the door open. Mikhail Ulyashin was sitting in front of the screens, his aluminium crutches next to him on the floor. Ulyashin nodded and pointed at the connecting door. Shepherd pushed it open. Alina Podolski was making coffee and she looked over at Shepherd and raised one eyebrow. "Splash of milk and no sugar," he said in answer to her unspoken question. He dropped his bag by the wall and sat down at the end of the table, facing Popov. Alexei Dudko, Boris Volkov and Grigory Sokolov were already seated. Dudko was munching on a banana and Sokolov was eating a yoghurt with a plastic spoon.

Podolski put mugs down in front of Popov and Shepherd and then went back to the coffee maker for her own cup. She sat down. Like the rest of the bodyguards she had a small notepad and a pen in front of her.

"Right," said Popov, removing his Oakleys. "We might as well get started. We're looking at wheels up at three o'clock this afternoon, a flight time of just under five hours, wheels down in Cyprus at nine p.m. Mr Grechko will be staying at the villa of his friend, Georgy Malykhin. Mr Malykhin's car will be at the airport to meet us, along with two other vehicles."

Shepherd raised his hand. "This is the first I've heard of this," he said. "I thought Mr Grechko was staying with his ex-wife."

Popov shook his head. "Mr Grechko never stays with Mrs Grechko," he said. "He will be visiting her and the children tomorrow. But tonight he stays with Mr Malykhin."

"He's stayed there before?" asked Shepherd.

"Many times," said Popov. "There is no reason to worry, Tony. Mr Malykhin's security arrangements are on a par with ours. His villa is secluded and has full CCTV and alarms, and he has a security team of twelve."

"I need CVs of all the team this morning."

"You shall have them," said Popov.

"And the transport arrangements? We'll be using his vehicles?"

"He has armoured Mercs," said Popov. "Everything will be fine, we have done this many times."

Shepherd was about to argue but he remembered his promise not to embarrass Popov in front of his team so he sat back, folded his arms and said nothing. Popov continued his security briefing and his team made copious notes.

200

Shepherd waited until the briefing was over and the team had left before taking his coffee over to Popov and sitting down next to him. "I should have mentioned the sleeping arrangements to you earlier," said the Russian. "My apologies."

"No problem, Dmitry," said Shepherd. "Just make sure I get the CVs. Now what about the pilot?"

"He's been with Mr Grechko for eight years. As his co-pilot. Both are former Russian Air Force pilots."

"And who else will be on board?"

"Two stewardesses. They have been with us for three years. I personally checked both of them out when we hired them."

"And the plane has stayed at RAF Northolt?"

Popov nodded. "I sent Leo out last night to check the plane out and he will stay with it until we arrive."

"And it will be just the six of us flying out with him?"

"Six will be enough. We will have Mr Malykhin's people with us at all times in Cyprus and the driver who will be in Mr Grechko's car is one we have used many times before."

Shepherd nodded, impressed. It sounded as if Popov had covered all the bases. "Just one more thing," he said. "Can we vary the route this time? Travel a route that we haven't used before?"

"Of course," said Popov.

Shepherd went for a run at ten o'clock in the morning. He changed into his sweatshirt, tracksuit bottoms and trainers and did a couple of laps of the grounds. It felt strange running without his usual rucksack of bricks and army boots and he barely worked up a sweat. Running on the flat in running shoes was no challenge at all. He jogged towards the gates and waved at Barsky. Barsky waved back and the gate opened. He headed south down The Bishops Avenue and waited for a gap in the traffic on Hampstead Lane before jogging across to the Heath. He spent the next hour alternating between running full pelt across the grass and doing fast press-ups and sit-ups. It was a far more efficient cardiovascular workout than he would ever get in the gym, and his sweatshirt had earned its name by the time he jogged back through the gate.

He showered and changed back into his suit and tie before heading to the kitchen, where an amiable chef — a portly Italian lady — made him a chicken salad sandwich and coffee. Popov joined him just as Shepherd was tucking into the second half of his sandwich. The chef made a big fuss of Popov and insisted that he try a seafood spaghetti dish that she was planning to serve when they returned from Cyprus. She busied herself over the stove as Popov went through the CVs of the security team they would be working with in Cyprus. Most were Russian but there were two Latvians and a Ukrainian. All had worked with Malykhin for at least a year.

They were interrupted by the chef serving Popov a plate piled high with spaghetti, lobster, oysters, prawns and squid in a steaming spicy spaghetti sauce. She saw Shepherd's eyes light up and gave him a small helping too. It was pretty much the best pasta Shepherd had ever tasted. "Maria used to work with Raymond Blanc until Mr Grechko doubled her salary," said Popov. "It's the best thing he ever did." He patted his stomach. "I've put on five kilos since she came to work here."

"You have not," laughed the chef, flicking a tea towel at him, her eyes sparkling with amusement. She nodded. "What do you think? Mr Grechko will be having guests for lunch and they like seafood. It's not too spicy?"

"It's heavenly, Maria," said Popov, twisting his fork around in the spaghetti. "To die for."

The chef blushed with pleasure. Popov finished his briefing in between mouthfuls of seafood and pasta.

"What about this Mr Malykhin?" asked Shepherd. "Has anyone ever tried to hurt him?"

"He's very low profile and has always backed the right horses in the Kremlin," said Popov. "He's clever, is Mr Malykhin. He never badmouths Putin. Never badmouths anyone, in fact. And he's in Moscow as much as he is in Cyprus. What causes resentment is when they relocate to London or New York as if they are too good for Mother Russia."

"Is that what Mr Grechko has done?" asked Shepherd, lowering his voice so that Maria wouldn't hear him. "Caused resentment?"

Popov shrugged but didn't answer.

"Dmitry, I'm here to help," said Shepherd. "I can only do that if I have all the facts."

"It's not for me to say," said the Russian.

"You're not talking out of school, it's information I need to do my job properly," said Shepherd. "Someone tried to kill your boss. We need to know if the attack was political, personal, or connected to his business."

"Personal?"

"It's not unknown for wives to see killing as an alternative to divorce," said Shepherd.

Popov looked shocked, but then a smile spread slowly across his face. "Mrs Grechko? You think Mrs Grechko would want Mr Grechko dead?" He shook his head. "He is the father of her children and he is very generous to her."

"What about the new Mrs Grechko? Does she have a pre-nup?"

Popov's smile widened. "Mr Grechko loves her. She gets whatever she wants. Believe me, she would gain nothing if he were to die."

"So you think it's political?"

"I'm not a detective, Tony. I'm a bodyguard. I prevent crimes, I don't solve them."

Shepherd nodded. "Fair point."

The Russian leaned over towards Shepherd. "But there's an expression I heard. Tall poppies. Have you heard that?"

"Sure. It's the tall poppies that get cut down,"

"Well, Mr Grechko is a tall poppy, that's all I'll say." He shoved the last forkful of pasta into his mouth. "One of the tallest."

They left the house at just after one o'clock. There were three vehicles; Grechko was in his Bentley with Shepherd and Popov, with Dudko and Volkov in a

Range Rover in front and Sokolov and Podolski bringing up the rear in a BMW.

RAF Northolt was just six miles north of Heathrow Airport, but whereas Heathrow was one of the world's busiest airports, Northolt was a lot more selective. It had a single runway which was used only by the RAF and by wealthy individuals who were able to pay the exorbitant landing and handling fees.

Security was as tight as would be expected at a military airport. Their vehicles and IDs were carefully checked at the gate before they were allowed in. They drove over to a hangar where Leo Tarasov was waiting beside a gleaming Gulfstream G550, which Shepherd figured had cost somewhere between sixty and seventy million dollars. It was a sleek, white hawk with two massive Rolls-Royce turbofan engines by the tail and it looked brand new. The captain, who seemed to be barely out of his twenties, was standing at the top of the stairs wearing a white short-sleeved shirt with black and gold epaulettes and he saluted Grechko before disappearing into the cockpit. Two very pretty stewardesses gave Grechko beaming smiles and led him into the plane.

Popov spoke to Tarasov in Russian and slapped him on the back. Tarasov climbed into the Range Rover and all three vehicles drove away from the hangar.

The bodyguards filed up the steps into the plane. As he stepped inside, Shepherd's estimate of the value of the plane went up another five million dollars. The interior had been panelled in white oak and the seats were of the finest leather. The carpet was plush with a warm, golden glow, and the seats were so far apart that the cabin felt airy and spacious.

Grechko flopped down into a large beige armchair in the centre of the cabin, and before his backside hit the leather the stewardesses were at his side, one offering him a glass of champagne and the other a hot towel.

Podolski and Dudko sat immediately behind Grechko. Volkov made himself comfortable on a black leather sofa that ran along one side of the fuselage while Sokolov strapped himself into a seat opposite a computer workstation.

Popov took Shepherd to the rear of the plane where there was a separate seating area with two large beige seats the size of armchairs either side of a walnut coffee table. The seats could be swung around 360 degrees, and when side-on to the table could be lowered into flat beds.

"Do you travel much in jets, Tony?" asked Popov.

"Usually sat in the back, in economy," said Shepherd. "This is another world, isn't it?"

"This is nothing," said Popov. "He's having a bigger one fitted out at the moment. Mrs Grechko found out that Abramovich has a Boeing A340 with a gym, Turkish bath and Jacuzzi. Two hundred million dollars."

"So she wants one?"

Popov grinned. "No, she's insisting that Mr Grechko buys her something bigger. And has it outfitted exactly the way she wants it. The price tag is looking to be two hundred and twenty-five million dollars."

Shepherd shook his head as he tried to work out how many lifetimes he would have to work to be able to afford his own jet.

"She is getting him to commission a bigger yacht too. It has to be at least ten feet longer than Abramovich's. They get very competitive, the wives."

One of the stewardesses asked them whether they wanted tea or coffee. Popov asked for a black tea and Shepherd a cappuccino. The drinks arrived just as the captain announced that they were ready to leave.

Grechko spent most of the flight studying share prices and currency movements on a forty-two-inch screen that somehow managed to fold out from the ceiling. Most of the bodyguards catnapped but Sokolov watched movie after movie at the workstation.

Popov stretched out his legs and sighed. "It's hard to go back to commercial flights after this," he said.

"I bet," said Shepherd. "Was it like this with Putin?"

Popov sat up quickly as if he'd been stung, then a smile slowly spread across his face. "Of course, you would have been briefed on me," he said.

"Just the bare minimum," said Shepherd. "That your last job was with the Russian president, that's all."

"Three years," said Popov, relaxing back into his seat. "But I was one of hundreds, and I was never in the inner circle. He has a group of a dozen that he's known since his KGB days, and then another fifty or so trusted men who have all been with him for at least ten years. The rest are brought in for a few years, three at most. It keeps them on their toes. You never know how long you're going to be there, and mistakes aren't tolerated."

"Hard work?"

Popov chuckled. "The man has a lot of enemies."

"Can't have been an easy job."

The Russian shrugged. "No, but it looks good on the CV. It's the equivalent of being a butler to your Queen. Once that's on your CV you can work anywhere."

"Mr Grechko seems to think that it might be someone in the Kremlin who wants him dead."

Popov shrugged but didn't say anything.

Shepherd lowered his voice to a whisper. "What do you think, Dmitry?"

For several seconds Popov didn't say anything and Shepherd was starting to think that the Russian was deliberately ignoring him, but then Popov leaned towards Shepherd. "I saw your face when we were outside the stadium, looking at the angles the sniper could have used. And I could see that you were thinking the same as me."

"Which was?"

"Which was that any decent sniper would have made that shot. Certainly a sniper in the pay of the Kremlin would not have missed."

"Which means what, Dmitry?"

Popov shrugged his massive shoulders. "Let's just say that the fact that Mr Grechko has been targeted for assassination will probably help his application for a British passport, don't you think? You Brits do love to welcome asylum seekers, don't you?" He tapped the side of his nose. "Mr Grechko is a very clever man. Cunning, you might say."

There were more than two dozen private jets parked at the general aviation terminal at Larnaca International Airport, many of them with Russian registrations. They came to a halt next to a Learjet and the pilot switched off the engines. The steps were folded down and a few minutes later two uniformed officials entered the cabin. One went to talk to the captain in the cockpit. Popov approached the second official and handed him the passports of everyone on board.

The official sat down and took a metal stamp from his pocket, and an inkpad. He opened the inkpad, removed a pen from his pocket and put on a pair of wire-framed reading glasses. One of the stewardesses handed Grechko a glass of champagne as the immigration officer methodically worked his way through the passports, checking the details against a printed list and carefully stamping them and then scribbling a signature over the stamp.

The first official came out of the cockpit and walked around the cabin, opening several cupboards before disappearing into the toilet for several minutes. Shepherd figured he was a customs officer but his search appeared cursory at best.

It took the immigration officer fifteen minutes to deal with the passports, after which he handed them to Popov, nodded unsmilingly at Grechko, and left the plane with the customs officer in tow.

Grechko stood up, stretched, and waited for Popov and Shepherd to go ahead of him. Popov went down the steps first, scanning the immediate area for possible threats before checking out the buildings overlooking the plane. Shepherd did the same as the two men walked down the steps to a line of waiting cars. There were two Mercedes SUVs either side of a pale blue Rolls-Royce, which from the way it was so low on its suspension was clearly heavily armoured. It was a clear night, the sky overhead full of stars, the moon a pale sliver off to their right.

Malykhin's bodyguards were all out of their vehicles and standing around the convoy. Only two, the ones by the Rolls-Royce, were looking at the plane, the rest were checking out the surroundings. Shepherd noted their professionalism and began to relax a little.

Popov walked across the tarmac and hugged one of the bodyguards, a tall sandy-haired bruiser of a man with mirrored sunglasses. He introduced him to Shepherd as Vassi Kozlov, Malykhin's head of security. Shepherd and Kozlov shook hands as Popov turned back to the plane. "You speak Russian?" asked Kozlov in heavily accented English.

"Sadly not."

Kozlov said something in Russian to Popov and both men laughed.

"I hope that wasn't about my mother," said Shepherd.

"He said you've got the eyes of a killer," said Popov. "And he's not wrong."

Podolski came out behind Grechko and they moved down the steps together, sticking close until Grechko had slid into the back seat of the Rolls-Royce. The two stewardesses came down the steps carrying Grechko's

Louis Vuitton luggage, which they loaded into the boot of the Rolls-Royce.

One of the bodyguards was already in the front passenger seat and Shepherd could see that three of them weren't going to sit in the back of the Rolls-Royce so he looked at Popov expectantly. "Why don't you ride up front with Vassi?" said Popov. Shepherd saw Dudko and Volkov head up the stairs and back into the plane.

Shepherd walked with Kozlov to the Mercedes at the front of the convoy. One of the bodyguards was already sitting next to the driver. Kozlov opened the door and motioned for Shepherd to get in. As he slid inside another bodyguard opened the rear door on the other side and climbed in, leaving Shepherd in the middle. Kozlov got in and slammed the door. He and the other bodyguard were both big shouldered, and despite the size of the SUV Shepherd had very little room to move.

As the doors slammed shut, Shepherd looked back at the plane. Dudko and Volkov were coming down the steps, each carrying two heavy aluminium suitcases. They took them to the Mercedes at the rear of the convoy and loaded them into the boot before getting into the back. Shepherd frowned. He hadn't seen them on the plane, nor had he seen them being taken on board at Northolt.

They drove out of the airport and on to the main road. The drivers were clearly professional, staying close enough so that no cars could infiltrate the convoy but leaving enough room to manoeuvre if there was a problem. There was little traffic around so everyone was relaxed.

"So, Dmitry says you are a policeman, Tony," said Kozlov in almost impenetrable accented English.

Shepherd nodded. "Executive protection," he said. "My unit looks after diplomats and visiting dignitaries as well as local politicians."

"And you have a gun?"

Shepherd thought that his Glock had remained hidden in its shoulder holster but Kozlov had obviously spotted it. "Cleared through Europol," he said.

"But before you were a policeman you were a soldier, correct? Special forces?"

Shepherd frowned. "Why do you say that?"

Kozlov patted him on the knee. "Do not worry, Tony. Your secret is safe with me."

"I'm a policeman," said Shepherd, sticking with his legend. "Always have been. I've done some training with the SAS, but that's it."

The Russian winked and patted him on the knee again. "There are many former SAS on the island, did you know that, Tony?"

"I didn't."

"Men like Mr Grechko and Malykhin, they prefer to have Russian security. For some, there is nothing better than a SAS man. Many of them work on the island. I know many Russian special forces men and they are giants. Big men with big muscles." He grinned and tapped his finger against his temple. "Not so smart, but big and strong. But the SAS, they're not giants. They are not big men, nor do they have big muscles. How tall are you, Tony? Five ten?"

"Five eleven," said Shepherd.

Kozlov nodded. "Five eleven," he repeated. "Now the Spetsnaz, that's what they call their special forces, are all well over six feet. Six six. Six seven. If you tried to join the Spetsnaz, they would laugh at you." He put his lips close to Shepherd's ear. "But the SAS men I know, they are all five ten, five eleven. And they look ordinary. Nothing special. But they are fit, as fit as thieves."

Shepherd tried not to smile but he failed. "It's as thick as thieves," he said.

The Russian frowned. "That doesn't make any sense at all," he said. "Why would thieves be thick? A thief needs to be fit."

"I guess they do, but it means that thieves stick close together."

Kozlov shook his head. "That still doesn't make sense. But you know what I mean, Tony? You look like the SAS men that I see in Cyprus. Hard bodies but not big, cold eyes but not crazy, and there's a calmness about you."

"A calmness?"

"I don't explain myself well," said Kozlov. "My English is not so good. But the men of the Spetsnaz they are not calm. They always look as if they are about to start killing, they just need an excuse." He patted him on the leg again. "So come on, we are friends. You can tell me. You are SAS?"

Shepherd shook his head. "Just a policeman."

"But a British policeman with a gun?"

"A lot of British policemen have guns," said Shepherd.

"Yes, I hear that London is a very dangerous city these days," said Kozlov. "Especially if you are Russian." He laughed and slapped Shepherd's leg. "But don't worry, here in Cyprus you will be safe."

Malykhin's villa was a forty-five-minute drive from the airport. It was perched on a rocky outcrop overlooking the Mediterranean and the last mile was a narrow two-lane road that for much of the time had a sheer drop to the sea below. Off in the distance navigation lights bobbed up and down and high overhead another jet was heading to the airport. There was a ten-foot-high stone wall running around the estate, dotted with CCTV cameras, and two metal gates that swung open as the convoy approached. There was a watchtower to the right of the gates where a man was talking into a walkie-talkie. The entire wall was illuminated with spotlights and Shepherd could see that it was topped with decorative ironwork that also functioned as effectively as razor wire.

The villa was almost as large as Grechko's mansion but was far less symmetrical, as if it had been added to over the years with little thought given to its overall style. The central part had the look of a Greek temple with columns and architraves, but a wing had been added on to the left which had floor-to-ceiling windows overlooking an infinity pool, and there was another wing to the right that appeared to be Spanish, with verandas and a terrace overlooking the sea. There were lanterns hung around the verandas and cast-iron street lamps around the edge of the terrace. The entire villa was illuminated with spotlights buried in the gardens.

In front of the main entrance was a massive fountain depicting three dolphins frolicking in the surf, with plumes of water spouting from their blowholes. Two bodyguards in dark suits and sunglasses were waiting when the convoy pulled up next to the fountain. Shepherd had to smile at the bodyguards wearing their ubiquitous shades. They might look good but in the dark the eyes needed as much light as they could get for night vision to function efficiently.

Popov got out of the Rolls-Royce and hurried around to open the passenger door for Grechko. Kozlov and Shepherd joined him as Grechko climbed out.

The front door of the villa opened and Georgy Malykhin hurried out, wearing a gleaming white suit and white patent leather shoes. He was a short, squat man, a bald Danny de Vito, who barely reached Grechko's shoulder. He hugged the bigger man, said something in Russian, and then hugged him again before standing on tiptoe and kissing him on both cheeks. The two men walked into the villa. Shepherd looked at Popov. "Now what?" Two liveried maids hurried over to the Rolls-Royce to retrieve Grechko's luggage.

"They're in for the night," said Popov. "Mr Malykhin has a Michelin-starred chef and one of the best wine cellars in the world." He looked at his watch. "And the entertainment will be arriving in an hour or so."

"The entertainment?"

Popov grinned. "Mr Malykhin has an eye for the ladies. And Mr Grechko isn't one to turn down the hospitality of a friend." The two maids disappeared inside with Grechko's bags and the door slammed shut.

"You're talking hookers?" said Shepherd. "Are you serious?"

"I think high-class ladies of the night would be more the way they would see it, but yes, money will most certainly be changing hands."

"Dmitry, have you gone crazy? You're bringing a group of strangers into a secure location at a time when the principal's life is under threat."

"They are girls, Tony. Young and pretty girls." He slapped Shepherd on the back, hard enough to rattle his teeth. "If it makes you happier, you can frisk them."

Malykhin's security centre was a series of rooms in an annexe at the back of the villa. There was a control room similar to the one in The Bishops Avenue mansion with CCTV screens and a rack of charging transceivers, a room with sofas, easy chairs and a big-screen TV, and a small kitchen and bathroom. There were two men sitting with their feet on a coffee table playing a shoot-'em-up video game. They stopped playing when Popov walked in and there were several minutes of backslapping and Russian banter before Popov introduced Shepherd.

One of the bodyguards made coffee and for the next hour the four men sat talking about weapons, women and sport. Most of the conversation was in Russian but Popov was good at translating most of what was said. Eventually a transceiver crackled and Popov grinned over at Shepherd. "The girls are here," he said.

216

The four men went outside as a minibus pulled up, driven by an old man in a flat cap. A side door opened and half a dozen girls tottered out in impossibly high heels and short skirts. Shepherd doubted that any of them were out of their teens but none of them appeared to be under-age. They all had long hair, three were blondes, two were brunettes and one was a natural redhead, and they had the look of catwalk models. One of the blondes lit a joint, took a drag, and passed it to the redhead.

Kozlov opened the front door and waved for the girls to enter. The driver of the minibus slammed the door shut and drove off down the hill. "Sure you don't want to pat them down?" Popov asked Shepherd.

Shepherd nodded at the skimpy tops and tight skirts the girls were wearing. "I guess we know they're not carrying concealed weapons," he said.

Popov laughed and put his arm around Shepherd's shoulders. "My friend, most of them are regulars here. And the first time they come, Vassi has them checked out."

"Medically?"

Shepherd was joking but Popov took the question seriously. "Full blood work, a criminal record check and details of their ID card or passport."

The girls disappeared inside and the door closed.

"Before you ask, the CCTV cameras are shut down in main rooms while the guests are there," said Popov.

"I understand now why he doesn't stay with his ex-wife," said Shepherd. He looked at his watch.

"Look, I'm going to stay outside for the next couple of hours. What about you?"

"I'll get some sleep then I'll take over from you. I'll talk to the guys to make sure the rear is covered." He patted him on the shoulder. "You can relax, Tony, we're regular visitors here."

Popov walked away, leaving Shepherd listening to the clicking and whirring of insects around him. He looked up at the hillside above the villa, wishing that he was as confident as the Russian. The problem with the isolated villa was that there were dozens of vantage points where a sniper could get a clear view. For all he knew there could be a scope centred on his chest at that very moment. At that instant his phone vibrated and he jumped, then shook his head at his skittishness. He took out his phone to see that he'd received a text message from Amar Singh. "Call me," it said. Shepherd figured it could only be good news.

He looked around to check that there was no one in earshot and then called Singh. "I've got your man," said Singh.

"Are you serious?"

"I wouldn't be joking, not after all the time and trouble I've been to," said Singh. "Do you want the name or not?"

"Amar, I'm gobsmacked," said Shepherd.

"Like I said, it wasn't easy," said Singh. "The facial recognition took for ever but once I had a usable picture I was able to get a match through the Passport Agency."

"You mean the Border Agency?"

"I mean the Passport Agency. Your man is a British citizen, has been since 2003. He has a British passport and, as it happens, a UK driving licence."

"That can't be," said Shepherd.

"Thanks for the vote of confidence," said Singh.

"No, I mean the guy's a Taliban fighter, or at least he was ten years ago. I don't see how that could possibly have him fast-tracked to a British passport."

"Well, it's happened. His name is Farzad Sajadi."

"The driving licence has his address, right?"

"Sure." Singh read out the address, along with the date of birth. "That's strange, I hadn't noticed that," he said.

"Noticed what?"

"The passport and the driving licence were issued on the same day. That's one hell of a coincidence."

"That's practically impossible, right?" said Shepherd.

"Unless there's something funny going on."

"Any details about where and when he got citizenship?"

"Nothing," said Singh. "Which is also a bit strange. There's usually a huge paper trail that goes along with asylum applications. But all I've got is the passport and driving licence. I can start digging for utilities, mobile phones and credit cards, but for that I'll need a case file."

"We're not at the case-building stage yet," said Shepherd. And he knew that he never would be.

"So I'll wait to hear from you?" said Singh.

"Amar, I owe you, big-time. If you ever need a favour, just ask."

Singh laughed. "Funny you should offer. I've got a nephew who's crazy about the SAS. Reads everything he can about them, loves the Andy McNab books, plays special forces video games all the time. Is there any chance you get take him to Hereford some time?"

"It'd be a pleasure, no problem at all," said Shepherd. "I'm back and forth all the time and I'd be more than happy to show him around, let him fire off a few rounds, the works."

"That'd be brilliant," said Singh.

"In fact I'm going to be taking my boy around over the next few weeks. He's thinking about joining the army so I want to let him know what he's letting himself in for. I could take your nephew along with us. I'll let you know when we're going." He thanked Singh again and ended the call, then tapped out Jimmy Sharpe's number.

Sharpe answered the phone with a weary sigh. "Another favour?" he said.

"I was just going to ask if you fancied a drink one night this week," said Shepherd.

"Don't mind if I do, especially if you're paying."

"And I wouldn't mind you checking out another name for me. Farzad Sajadi." Shepherd spelled it out for him and gave him the man's date of birth and the address that Singh had given him.

"Is this connected to that Khan guy?"

"I think they might be one and the same," said Shepherd. "He's got a passport and a driving licence in that name."

"Fake?"

"Doesn't look like it, no. But there's something not right. He was a bloody Taliban fighter, how can he have a British passport?"

Sharpe laughed. "You don't get it, do you? When the Taliban were killing off the Afghanistan population, any Afghan who got into the UK could claim asylum. But once we and the Yanks invaded, the Taliban became the endangered species so they can claim that Afghanistan isn't safe for them. Any of them that could make it to the UK would be pretty much guaranteed asylum. So we've got the crazy situation in London now where in the same street you've got a Taliban murderer living a few doors down from a guy whose family was killed by the Taliban. But we treat them exactly the same. The same happened in Iraq. The first wave of asylum seekers were people who'd been persecuted by Saddam Hussein. Then we invaded and the worm turned and all the Iraqis who'd backed Saddam found they were being persecuted so it was their turn to run. It's Alice in Wonderland."

"But I don't see how they could have given asylum to Khan. He shot an SAS captain. Hell, Razor, he shot me."

"Yeah, well, presumably he didn't tell the immigration tribunal that. It's much more likely that he told them he was a poor farmer who was threatened with beheading because he didn't give all his money to the Taliban."

"Can you find out, Razor? Run his name and date of birth through the PNC but also see if you can find out anything about his immigration status?"

"You're not asking much, are you?"

"Pretty please."

Sharpe laughed. "Yeah, don't worry, I'm on it. Now what about that drink? You around tonight?"

"I'm in Cyprus. Taking care of a Russian guy who as we speak is being taken care of by some of the fittest hookers I've seen in a long time."

"You get all the best jobs," said Sharpe. "I'll call you if I get anything." Shepherd cut the connection. As he turned around he was startled to see Podolski walking towards him, holding a pack of cigarettes in one hand and a lighter in the other.

"Sorry, didn't mean to alarm you," she said, taking out a cigarette and slipping it between her lips. She offered him the pack but he shook his head.

"I didn't realise you were a smoker," he said.

She lit her cigarette and blew smoke before shrugging. "I don't get the chance, much," she said. "Can't smoke in buildings or cars or planes. And when I'm outside I'm usually working." She looked at the burning cigarette in her hand. "This is my first since last night."

"So you're not addicted?"

She laughed and tossed her hair. "I just like smoking. Same as I enjoy a glass of wine or a joint." She saw the look of surprise on his face and smiled slyly. "I forgot you were a policeman. You won't arrest me, will you?"

"We're in Cyprus," said Shepherd. "I can't arrest you here."

"But you can carry your gun."

"Ah, because Cyprus is in the EU so Europol can arrange it. What about you, Alina? Were you a cop?" Having seen her file he knew her work history by heart. She had graduated from the Petro Sahaidachny Ground Forces Academy before spending six years with the Ukrainian armed forces. She'd seen action too, with two tours in Iraq, and in 2004 she'd been wounded when Ukraine's peacekeeping contingent was almost overwhelmed by Mahdi militants.

"I was a soldier," she said. "Ukrainian army. But this pays better."

"How did you get the job?"

She shrugged. "Friend of a friend. I heard they were looking for Russian speakers at short notice and I was between jobs." She took a long drag on her cigarette and then carefully blew the smoke away from him. "To be honest, I normally get to work with the wives."

"Because the wives prefer female bodyguards?"

She flicked the hair away from her eyes. "Because the wives don't want me working with their husbands," she said.

"I can see why you'd be a worry," said Shepherd.

"How sexist is that?" she said, her eyes flashing. "Would anyone assume that you were going to screw Mrs Grechko's wife just because you've got a dick? You're either professional or you're not, it's got nothing to do with what sex you are."

Shepherd raised his hands. "I'm sorry," he said. "I was clumsily trying to pay you a compliment."

She tilted her head on one side, then slowly smiled. "OK, I suppose that was a compliment, in a way."

"What's it like, taking care of the wives?" he asked.

"There's a lot of shopping involved," she said. "And they always insist that I help carry the bags, even when I explain that bodyguards have to keep their hands free."

"At least you don't get the sort of nonsense we've got here tonight," said Shepherd.

"Don't you believe it," said Podolski. "The wives aren't stupid. They know what their husbands get up to and what's sauce for the goose . . ." She shrugged. "They deserve each other."

"You've got a pretty low opinion of our principals?"

She looked up at the bedroom windows and scowled. "He's on his second wife and yet he's up there rutting like a pig," she said. "And the wives? Have you seen the way they spend? The last woman I was with, when she went to the Louis Vuitton store in Bond Street they would close it for her so she could walk around. If she saw a bag she liked, she'd buy fifty and have them sent to her friends. Never to the staff, of course. We were invisible unless she needed us to fetch and carry. She would buy dresses by the dozen and wear them once." She turned back to Shepherd. "You've seen Mrs Grechko's dressing rooms? Do you think she'll ever wear half the shoes that she owns?" She took a final drag on her cigarette and flicked it away. "More money than sense," she said. "My father would have to work for a year to afford a single pair of her shoes."

"Life's not fair, that's for sure," said Shepherd.

"You think that woman has worked a day in her life?" she continued. "She opens her legs, that's all the work she has ever done. And she lives like a princess."

"Yeah, but is she happy?" asked Shepherd.

Podolski opened her mouth to reply and then realised he was joking. She laughed and tossed her head, flicking her hair to the side. "I moan too much," she said.

Shepherd shrugged. "No, I take your point," he said. "There is something very wrong with a world that allows one man to have so much, when children are dying because they don't have enough to eat. His house, it's just . . ."

"So big?"

"So big. And tacky. And unnecessary. Rooms that no one ever uses."

"It's for show," said Podolski. "All of this is. The houses, the clothes, the yachts, the planes. None of it is really necessary." She laughed again. "We're starting to sound like couple of communists, aren't we?"

"God forbid," said Shepherd.

She looked at her watch. "I'm going to get a bite to eat. There's a chef in the kitchen who'll cook anything we want, pretty much, Dmitry says. Do you want anything?"

"I'm good," said Shepherd. The stewardesses on the private jet had kept everyone supplied with smoked salmon, caviar and little sandwiches with the crusts cut off throughout the flight, along with endless cups of coffee.

Podolski winked and walked back to the villa. Shepherd was fairly sure that she was swinging her hips for his benefit, and when she looked over her shoulder as she stepped on to the terrace his suspicions were confirmed.

The hookers left at six o'clock in the morning. One of them must have called the driver because he was in front of the villa in his minibus when the front door opened and they tottered out into the early morning light. They all looked the worse for wear with smudged make-up, their clothes in disarray and messy hair. The redhead looked as if she had been crying and they were all suffering from too much drugs or alcohol or both. One of the blondes grinned lopsidedly at Shepherd, waggled her fingers at him then stumbled and fell to her knees. Two of the girls helped her up and on to the minibus.

Shepherd and Popov watched as the girls piled on to the vehicle. "Does this happen a lot?" Shepherd asked.

Popov shrugged. "Rich men have appetites," he said.

The driver slammed the door shut and climbed back into the driver's seat.

Shepherd shrugged. "Yeah, but this is . . ."

"Not how we'd spend our evenings if we were billionaires?" Popov finished for him. The two men laughed and Popov slapped him on the back. "Seriously, Tony, this is nothing compared to what some of them get up to."

"I bet," said Shepherd.

"No, really. Rape, assaults, and worse. If you're in the business for a while you'll hear some serious horror stories. Especially for the guys doing protection work for the Arabs. Compared with them, Mr Grechko is a pussycat, believe me."

The minibus drove out through the gates and they began to close. Popov and Shepherd headed back inside the villa. Shepherd had caught a few hours' sleep on one of the sofas in the bodyguards' room during the early hours and he managed to grab another hour's sleep after the girls left. Popov gave him a travel pack with a razor, shaving cream, toothbrush and toothpaste and he shaved and showered before joining Popov and the rest of the team in the kitchen for eggs and steak cooked by a young American chef, a twenty-something Texan with his hair clipped back in a ponytail who made the bodyguards laugh with his attempts to speak Russian. While his Russian skills might have been wanting, there was no mistaking his talent in the kitchen — the steak he cooked was just about the best that Shepherd had ever tasted. "Flown in every day from Japan," the chef explained to Shepherd after he'd complimented him on the food. "It's Matsusaka beef, which I reckon is better than Kobe because of its intense fat-to-meat ratio. They only raise female cows and they feed them on beer, give them regular massages and play them soothing music." The chef had laughed when Shepherd had asked him how much it cost per pound. "You really don't want to know," he said.

The cars were lined up outside the villa at nine o'clock in the same order in which they'd arrived the previous evening. Grechko and Malykhin appeared at 9.30 with Kozlov. Grechko had changed into a dark suit and Malykhin was wearing a yellow linen jacket and baggy white linen trousers that rippled in the warm wind blowing in off the sea. As a butler in a black suit put Grechko's luggage into the back of the Rolls-Royce, Grechko and Malykhin hugged and once again Malykhin stood on tiptoe to kiss his friend on the cheeks.

Shepherd and Popov stood by the Rolls-Royce and watched. "Malykhin's not coming with us?" asked Shepherd.

"No, Mrs Grechko isn't a fan of his, I think she's heard about his parties. And Mr Grechko wants to keep his business private."

Kozlov strode over, grinning. He hugged Popov and then put his hands on Shepherd's shoulders. "You be careful, SAS man," he said, and then hugged him tightly enough to force the air from his lungs.

"SAS?" said Popov as Kozlov walked back to the villa.

"It's his little joke."

"He thinks you are special forces?"

Shepherd shrugged. "Like I said, it's his joke."

"He might be right, I suppose. You did a lot of pull-ups."

"It takes more than pull-ups to get into the SAS."

Popov rubbed his chin thoughtfully. "But I suppose if you were in the SAS, you wouldn't be able to tell me, would you?"

"I suppose not," said Shepherd.

Popov laughed and slapped him in the middle of the back. "Then we shall never know," he said. "Come on, you and I will ride with Mr Grechko. You can have the front seat."

Shepherd got into the front of the Rolls-Royce and nodded at the driver. "Tony," he said, offering his hand.

The driver held out his hand but didn't smile. "Olav," he said, and shook.

Podolski and Sokolov got into the front Mercedes SUV and Dudko and Volkov got into the car at the rear. The convoy headed out.

Grechko and Popov talked in Russian as they drove towards Nicosia. Shepherd concentrated on what was going on outside, his eyes constantly flicking to the wing mirrors. Several times they were overtaken by motorcyclists and each time it happened Shepherd tensed, even though Popov had said that the Rolls-Royce was fully armoured.

They drove through the city, which Shepherd knew was the most dangerous part of the journey as the crowded streets gave them little room for manoeuvre. The two men in the back stopped talking and in the rear-view mirror Shepherd could see that Popov was in full attention mode, his head swivelling from side to side, constantly checking with the teams in the front and rear cars. The drivers were good, as good as the ones Grechko had back in London. They drove smoothly and confidently without giving other vehicles the chance to cut in.

Their first visit was to a glass tower block topped with the logo of the Bank of Cyprus. A uniformed security guard waved them through to an underground car park where another guard waved them into three spaces close to a lift. The bodyguards climbed out of the vehicles as soon as they came to a halt. Podolski and Sokolov moved to either side of the Rolls-Royce while Dudko and Volkov stayed by their car, their eyes scanning the car park from behind their sunglasses.

When Popov was satisfied that the area was secure he opened the rear passenger door of the Rolls-Royce so that Grechko could get out. As Grechko strode over to the lift, Dudko and Volkov went around to the boot of their car and took out two of the aluminium suitcases. They followed Grechko to the lift, where a grey-haired man in a suit was waiting. He shook hands with Grechko and ushered him into the lift. Dudko and Volkov followed him with their suitcases. Shepherd moved to step into the lift but Popov stopped him. "Mr Grechko would prefer to keep his business private," he said.

"I have to know that he's secure," said Shepherd.

Popov shook his head. "This is Cyprus," he said. "It's not your problem."

"Dmitry . . ."

Popov shook his head again. "No arguments, Tony. I'm sorry." He nodded at the grey-haired man, who pressed the button to close the doors. Shepherd gritted his teeth in frustration but realised there was nothing he could do.

"Was it something you said?" asked Podolski. She had come up behind him, as silent as a cat. Shepherd shrugged but didn't say anything. She laughed and patted him on the shoulder. "Don't take it personally," she said, and walked back to the cars.

After half an hour Shepherd heard Popov in his earpiece, asking whether the area was secure.

"Secure," said Shepherd.

A few minutes later the lift door opened and Popov stepped out. Grechko stayed in the lift with Dudko and Volkov until Popov had checked the area, then they all moved to the cars. Dudko and Volkov were still carrying their suitcases but Shepherd got the feeling that they were heavier.

Grechko got back into the Rolls-Royce while Dudko and Volkov took the cases over to their SUV.

Shepherd and Popov climbed into the car with Grechko and the convoy moved off. They visited two more banks and the procedure was pretty much the same as it had been with the Bank of Cyprus.

At the second bank, Grechko went inside with Popov, though only Volkov accompanied them, carrying a single suitcase. After half an hour they reappeared, and this time there was no doubt that the suitcase had gained weight.

They spent even less time inside the third bank, and when they reappeared Volkov was carrying the suitcase and a small attaché case.

"That's the work part done," Popov said to Shepherd as Grechko climbed into the back of the Rolls-Royce. Volkov put the suitcase and attaché case into the SUV and climbed into the back. "Now it's family time and then back to the airport."

They drove out of Nicosia and through the countryside. The sun was blindingly bright and the sky a perfect blue, a far cry from the leaden skies they had left behind in London. They headed inland, towards a line of hills covered in stunted trees, driving through villages that looked as if they had remained unchanged for hundreds of years. Shepherd saw stone houses with flat roofs, shaded by olive trees, with old men sitting on wooden benches, smoking cigarettes and gossiping. They drove by farms with dust-covered farm equipment and cars with mud-splattered windscreens and balding tyres but saw no one working in the fields. There was hardly any traffic on the roads, but three times huge modern double-height coaches powered past them, brightly painted and covered in Cyrillic script. "Russian holidaymakers," said Grechko after the third one went by. "It's a big holiday place for us now."

"Even after what they did to the banks?" asked Shepherd.

"More so," said Grechko. "The prices of land and houses are tumbling, and a lot of Russians are buying now. They'll never trust their money to a European bank again but they'll buy property." He looked over at Popov. "You should buy something here, Dmitry. All that money I pay you."

Popov laughed but said nothing.

They reached Mrs Grechko's estate, a sprawling winery in the foothills of a mountain range. There was a fresh breeze that took some of the heat out of the sun, but Shepherd still had to shade his eyes with his hand as he peered through the car window. They drove through a stone arch and along a single-track road that cut through acres of tended vines. The house was smaller than Shepherd had expected, a two-storey grey stone farmhouse with a black roof and white shutters on the windows. There was a barn to the left built of matching stone and more buildings behind the house.

As the cars approached the house, two men in casual dress appeared at the door. The dark glasses and the way they stood with their arms folded gave away their profession. The two SUVs peeled off and parked next to a double garage to the right of the house while the Rolls-Royce pulled up in front of the house. Shepherd and Popov were out as soon as the car stopped, but even a cursory look around showed that the house was well protected. There was a bodyguard by the gate who had a rifle slung across his back and there was another man in sunglasses sitting under an umbrella at a table outside one of the outbuildings.

The two men at the front door nodded to Popov and one of them shouted something in Russian. Popov laughed and waved, then opened the door for Grechko. As Grechko headed for the front door two teenage boys came rushing out shouting "Papa! Papa!" and Grechko hugged and kissed them in turn. They were big, strong boys, good looking with thick chestnut hair and the same strong chins as their father. He put his arms around them and they walked inside.

Shepherd moved to follow them but Popov put a hand on his shoulder. "This is family time, we stay away," said Popov. "Mrs Grechko is never happy seeing us around, we remind her too much of London." He shrugged. "She's a nice lady." He gestured at the garage, where Podolski, Sokolov, Dudko and Volkov were waiting. "There's a rec room behind the garage with a kitchen and a bathroom if you need to freshen up. There's a couple of couches too if you want to grab some sleep."

"Coffee would be good," said Shepherd as they started walking towards the garage.

"Coffee's easy, and Mrs Grechko's chef is a Russian who cooks like a dream. I'll get her to bring us some *kalduny*."

"*Kalduny?*"

"Stuffed dumplings. Seriously, to die for. Do you like Russian food?"

Shepherd opened his mouth to say that his au pair was Slovenian and a great cook but he stopped himself just in time. Tony Ryan didn't have a son or an au pair. He was finding himself so at ease in Popov's company that he had almost slipped out of character. "I tried goulash once."

Popov nodded. "She does a great goulash, too."

They went over to join the team and filed into the rec room. Podolski offered to make coffee for everyone and she busied herself in the kitchen. Dudko flopped down on one of the sofas and was asleep within seconds. There was a pool table at the far end of the room and Sokolov and Volkov began to play. Shepherd felt uneasy, he never liked hanging around doing nothing. What he really wanted to do was to go for a long run but that was out of the question. He took off his jacket and draped it over the back of a chair before sitting down.

The hours dragged. At just after noon Shepherd watched through the window as two maids carried a table out into the garden at the side of the house, draped it with a cloth and then set it for lunch. At 12.30 Grechko appeared with his ex-wife. Mrs Grechko was in her late forties and not at all what Shepherd had expected. She was tall, only a few inches shorter than her husband, with shoulder-length blond hair and a model's cheekbones. She had a ramrod-straight back, even when she sat drinking wine with her husband and listening to her sons talk to him. Whenever Grechko spoke to his sons, Mrs Grechko would look at him with a slight smile on her face. She had clearly never stopped loving him and Shepherd couldn't help but wonder why Grechko had walked away from her.

After lunch Grechko took off his jacket and kicked a football around with his sons before they all went for a walk through the vineyard, shadowed at some distance by two of the bodyguards. Grechko slipped an arm around his ex-wife's waist as they walked and she rested her head against his shoulder.

Popov came over to join Shepherd at the window. "She still loves him," said Shepherd.

"And he loves her," said Popov.

"So why . . .?"

"Why aren't they together?" Popov shrugged. "He's a billionaire, billionaires have trophy wives."

"That's the rule, is it?"

Popov nodded. "They all do. But I agree with you, Tony. He had the perfect wife. She will love him for ever."

"And the new Mrs Grechko?"

Popov chuckled and looked around to make sure that there was no one within earshot. "She will love him so long as he has money. Which will be for ever, of course."

The Gulfstream touched down at RAF Northolt at ten o'clock at night. The Bentley and two Range Rovers were already waiting at the hangar. The drivers were in their vehicles but Tarasov, Gunter and Serov were already out, watching the jet as it came to a halt and the pilot turned off the engines.

As soon as the steps were lowered, Popov and Shepherd left the plane and looked around. "All good," said Shepherd.

Popov waved at Sokolov and Grechko came down the steps with Sokolov and Podolski. He settled into the back of the Bentley as Dudko and Volkov came down the steps with the suitcases. They loaded them into the boot of the Bentley and then climbed into the Range Rover.

"No passport checks, or customs?" Shepherd asked Popov.

Popov shrugged but didn't say anything.

"So no one checks what's in the suitcases?" said Shepherd.

Popov clapped Shepherd on the back. "Relax, Tony. You're a cop, not a customs officer."

"I'm serious, we fly in from overseas and no one checks?"

"This is England, things are more relaxed here, especially for men like Mr Grechko," said Popov. "We submit a passenger and crew manifest to the National Border Targeting Centre at Manchester and they liaise with Heathrow, who also cover Northolt. They decide whether or not to send someone out, and as it's Mr Grechko, they tend not to bother." He put his hand on Shepherd's shoulder. "Don't worry, it's not drugs."

"Cash?"

"You remember when the EU stole all that money from depositors as part of the bailout of the banks in Cyprus?"

Shepherd nodded. "Sure."

"When Cyprus froze all its bank accounts early this year, most of the big deposits belonged to Russians. That was always the plan, the EU wanted to punish the Russians. Well, we flew in three days before it was announced." He grinned and tapped the side of his nose.

"Grechko was tipped off?"

"A few of the oligarchs were, yes. I can't tell you how Mr Grechko knew, but I do know that one of his English friends phoned him and two hours later we were on a plane heading to Cyprus. Mr Grechko moved most of the money out of his accounts but he also put a lot of cash into safe deposit boxes. His wife has access to the money but he brings it back into the UK, too." He patted him on the shoulder again. "So don't worry,

Mr Grechko is only bringing back what is rightfully his."

"Yeah, well, the Cypriots might see it differently."

Popov shrugged carelessly. "The bank manager's fine. You have to remember this was theft, Tony. A lot of Russians lost a lot of money, and it wasn't their fault that the banks in Europe got into trouble."

"Including you?"

"Me? Of course not. But I have a lot of friends who work in Cyprus and they are very unhappy. They lost fortunes. Small fortunes, but fortunes nonetheless." He nudged Shepherd towards the Bentley. "You should ride up front. And please, treat what I have said as confidential."

"Of course," said Shepherd.

They climbed into the Bentley and the three vehicles moved off. It took them less than an hour to drive to Grechko's mansion. Grechko said he was going to bed and left Popov and Shepherd in the hallway under a massive crystal chandelier. "Are you going home?" Popov asked Shepherd.

Shepherd looked at his watch. He was dog tired and couldn't be bothered driving back to his flat. "I'll crash here tonight," he said.

"Excellent," said Popov. "We're effectively off duty so we can sample a bottle of vodka that I've been wanting to try. I shall get it from the freezer." He slapped Shepherd on the back. "You check that all's OK outside and I'll get some snacks and see you in the recreation room."

As Popov headed for the kitchen, Shepherd walked out of the house and down to the guardhouse. Lisko was there and he waved to Shepherd through the bullet- and bomb-proof glass. Shepherd smiled and flashed him a thumbs-up. He looked back at the house. There were no lights on the upper floor, Grechko was still sleeping below ground. It seemed an overreaction as the house wasn't overlooked so there was no way a sniper could strike from outside the grounds. His phone rang as he walked back up the driveway. It was Jimmy Sharpe. "Still in Cyprus pimping for that Russian mobster?" asked Sharpe.

"Back in London, and I never said he was a mobster."

"He's a Russian with money, that makes him a mobster," said Sharpe. "None of them have clean money, you know that."

"I couldn't possibly comment," said Shepherd.

"Yeah, well, at least you can take me for that drink."

"Happy to," said Shepherd.

"Because I've got some intel for you on Farzad Sajadi. He's known, but minor stuff. He was stopped for driving without insurance three years ago and has been done for speeding a couple of times. Never went to court or anything, just points and fines. Nothing major. Same address as you gave me. He has a four-year-old Honda CRV."

"And you checked with Immigration?"

"He's not known to them. Not under that name. And I got them to check under Khan using that date of birth. Nothing."

"That's not possible," said Shepherd. "He had to have got into the country in the first place."

"He could have used any name for that. Or no name at all — he could have come in the back of a lorry from Calais."

"Sure, but at some point the name Khan or Sajadi must have come up during the asylum process."

"You'd have thought so, but he's not on the Border Agency database and there's no record of an immigration tribunal ever looking at either name. You're sure the passport is kosher?"

"The guy who checked for me would have known if there was anything wrong with it," said Shepherd. "The passport's real and so is the driving licence. And presumably the traffic cops found nothing untoward."

"Other than the fact he wasn't insured and is a bit heavy on the accelerator, he seems a fine upstanding citizen. He's not even claiming benefits."

"He's got a job?"

"That I don't know, but I ran a check with DWP and they're not paying him. He's responsible for his own council tax, too. Like I said, he's an upstanding citizen."

"What about finding out where he works?"

"I can't do that without speaking to him, and that's probably not a good idea, is it?"

"Yeah, you're right. Let me have the car registration, will you?"

Sharpe gave him the number and Shepherd promised to call him back about the drink. He looked at the clock on the screen of his phone. It was almost eleven o'clock. He was walking towards the house when Alina Podolski drove out of the garage on a bright green Kawasaki trail bike. She was wearing a black helmet and she flicked up the visor and grinned at him. "You not going home, Tony?"

"I'm dog tired. What about you? You don't sleep on the premises?"

She laughed, flashing perfect white teeth. "What, sleep down there with farting and belching men, you must be joking. I've got a flat in Camden."

"Yeah, Camden's nice."

"Where do you stay?"

"Not far. Near the Heath." He pointed off to the west. "That way."

"You run on the Heath?"

"How do you know that?"

She brushed a stray lock of hair behind her ear. "I saw you running before. You were heading to the Heath, right? I pegged you for a runner. You've got a runner's build."

"Yeah, I do some training there."

"We should run together some time," she said. She jerked a thumb at the house. "The guys, they're all gym rats. I prefer my exercise outside with the wind in my hair."

"Bring your gear in whenever you want," said Shepherd. "I'm always up for a run." She waved and drove towards the gate, which was already opening for her. As she turned into the road she beeped her horn and accelerated. Shepherd watched her go. She wasn't heading towards Camden, he realised. She was going in the opposite direction.

He heard excited barking from the kennels and realised the Dobermans were about to be released for the night, so he hurried inside.

Shepherd was up at six the next day. He had brought an overnight bag with a washbag and several changes of clothes, so he showered and shaved and put on a clean shirt before heading to the control room. As he was checking the overnight log, one of Grechko's male chefs turned up with a tray of bacon and egg rolls, freshly made porridge and a large bowl of fruit salad. He ate with Dudko, Volkov and Sokolov, and they were just finishing when Popov arrived. Popov grabbed a breakfast roll and poured himself a coffee. He sat down at the table. "We can do the morning briefing now if you want," he said to Shepherd, and Shepherd nodded. "Basically Mr Grechko's in for the day. He's taken to heart what you said about getting people to come to him, so he was going to see his designers today in Mayfair but they've agreed to come here."

"Designers?"

"Mr Grechko has commissioned a new boat and a new jet and the designers are being briefed on his specifications. They were with Mrs Grechko in France last week but everything has to be cleared through him first." He grinned. "I was talking to one of our guys over there and apparently there's a problem with having chandeliers on planes. Who knew?"

They all laughed and Shepherd sipped his coffee. He was warming to Popov. He ran a tight ship but he had an easy way with his men, working them hard but letting them have enough fun to stop them getting bored. And he had the same sarcastic sense of humour as policemen the world over.

"So, we have the designers arriving at ten. He was due to see his bankers at Canary Wharf for lunch but they have agreed to come here, though considering the vintages in Mr Grechko's wine cellar I don't think they needed much persuading. And he was due to go to Claridge's for dinner with friends but he's asked them to come here for eight."

"The friends?"

"Three. He's known them all for ten years or more. They've been to the house before."

"Do they have security?"

Popov shook his head. "One is a writer, one is an actor who's going to be starring in a movie Mr Grechko's production company is due to film in Canada, and his accountant is coming."

"We'll be checking their vehicles?"

"Of course. But as I said, they have all been here before, they're trusted friends."

"Sounds good," said Shepherd. "I think I'll probably pop off home this afternoon, then. If you need me, I'm at the other end of the phone."

Popov grinned. "We'll try to get by without you, Tony," he said. "It'll be a struggle but hopefully we'll manage. You enjoy your day off."

★ ★ ★

Shepherd and Popov were at the entrance to the house when the designers arrived, a middle-aged blond woman with the chiselled looks of a former model, a plump Asian girl with a briefcase and a long plastic tube on a shoulder strap, and an effeminate man in tight Versace jeans who kept batting his eyelids at Popov.

As Popov ushered the team into the house, Shepherd gave the driver and his car the once-over. "Anywhere I can get a coffee, pal?" asked the driver, a fifty-something man in a grey suit and a yellowish pallor that suggested liver problems.

Shepherd called Volkov over and asked him to take the driver to the kitchen and to stay with him. He was uneasy whenever outsiders were in the house, but the design team were harmless and the driver didn't have the look of a professional assassin.

The meeting lasted just over an hour and a half and then they left, with the male member of the design team blowing Popov an exaggerated kiss through the car window before they disappeared through the gate.

Half an hour later, a black top-of-the-range Mercedes prowled through the gates and disgorged two fifty-something men in Savile Row suits. They adjusted their silk ties and expensive shirt cuffs and blinked in the sunlight like vampires emerging from their coffins before following Popov inside. The Mercedes headed back to the gate.

Shepherd waited until the gate had closed before walking over to the garage. He pressed his thumb against the sensor and tapped out his four-digit code.

He walked inside and down the ramp to the car parking area. He waved up at a CCTV camera, knowing that Molchanov would be watching him in the control centre. He climbed into his X5 and drove out.

He parked in an underground car park in Park Lane and put on a black raincoat before walking outside. The sky was a leaden grey and it looked as if it wouldn't take much for the heavens to open. He was ten minutes early but Harper was already sitting at a table at the café overlooking the Serpentine, smoking a cigarette, his face half hidden by the hood of his parka. "How's it going, mate?" he asked.

"All good," said Shepherd. He gestured at the empty coffee cup in front of Harper. "Another?"

"Yeah, go on," said Harper. Shepherd went over to the counter and returned with two cappuccinos. He sat down next to Harper and looked out over the water. Half a dozen swans were trying to persuade people to part with chunks of their cakes and sandwiches. "They're keeping you busy?" asked Harper, flicking ash on to the ground.

"As always."

"I suppose if I asked what you're working on you'd say that you could tell me but then you'd have to kill me?"

"It's not like that," said Shepherd. "Most of what I do is more like police work than spook stuff."

"But classified?"

"Sure, but then pretty much everything I work on is."

"Terrorists?"

"Mainly. But big-time crims, too."

"Drug dealers?" asked Harper, with a sly smile.

"Some," said Shepherd. "But most of the resources are now targeted at home-grown Muslim terrorists, for obvious reasons. Back in the old days it was old Cold War stuff, then the IRA, but when the Soviet Union imploded and the peace process kicked in, they had nothing to do for a while. That's when they started looking at organised crime, but that went on to the backburner after 9/11."

"Yeah, well, it's an ill wind, they say."

Shepherd nodded. "From your standpoint, sure."

"You checked up on me, right?" Shepherd didn't say anything and Harper grinned mischievously. "What, do you think you can go rooting around the PNC for me and that I wouldn't find out?"

"It wasn't me," said Shepherd.

"Whoever it was they were clever enough not to leave their fingerprints," said Harper. "They went in under the log-in of a young PC who obviously thought he could leave his terminal unattended while he went for a coffee."

"You've got someone in the Met on your payroll?" said Shepherd.

Harper faked indignation. "How dare you suggest that I would do anything as illegal as paying a member of Her Majesty's Constabulary for information!"

"No offence," said Shepherd.

Harper grinned and took a long pull on his cigarette. "Well, come on, tell me what you found out about me."

"Not much, as it happens."

Harper's grin widened. "Told you," he said.

"You've done a good job of staying below the radar. The consensus seems to be that you're in Spain."

"Yeah, well, as long as they think that, I'm a happy bunny."

"How did you find me, Lex?"

"It wasn't difficult. For a start you weren't hiding, plus I knew you back in Afghanistan, I knew your name and your date of birth and that you were married to Sue and that you had a kid, Liam." His face fell. "Shit, sorry."

"Sorry?"

"About the wife. The car crash. I only just found out. Sorry."

"It was a long time ago."

"I know, but I'm sorry. I never met her, but you were always talking about her." He sipped his coffee and then wiped the foam from his upper lip with his sleeve. "Always nagging you to leave the Regiment, remember?"

Shepherd chuckled. "Yeah. She got what she wanted after I got shot. I left a few months later. Out of the frying pan into the fire, as it happens."

"Yeah?"

Shepherd nodded. "Yeah. They never had me walking a beat, they put me straight into an undercover unit and the work was every bit as dangerous as Afghanistan. High-level crims, drug dealers, hitmen, gangsters. She was soon nagging me to leave the cops."

"To join Five?"

Shepherd shook his head. "Nah, I moved to SOCA, but that was after she died."

"SOCA? Now that was a great idea, wasn't it? The British FBI? They couldn't find their arse with both hands."

"You've come up against them, have you?"

"There's half a dozen of them in Pattaya but they don't know me. I've sat opposite two of them in a go-go bar and they've looked straight through me."

"How come?"

"Because they're tossers. Like your mate, what was his name, Razor? In and out of the massage parlours like bloody yo-yos. If ever they started to get busy about me I've more than enough to get them pulled back to the UK. SOCA was never going to work. You can't shove cops, customs officers and taxmen into the same organisation and expect them to work together. They form their own little kingdoms and start plotting against each other."

Shepherd raised his eyebrows. "You seem to know a lot about SOCA."

"I know a lot about a lot, mate. Knowledge is power. End of." He took a long pull on his cigarette. "Still, if they were any good they'd have been giving me a hard time, wouldn't they, so thank heaven for small mercies. I just hope this new mob, the National Crime Agency, isn't much better. Doubt it will be. It's like renaming the *Titanic* just before the iceberg hits."

"How did you get my number, Lex? And how did you know I worked for Five? Because that sort of info wouldn't be accessible by your average cop."

Lex smiled as he blew a plume of smoke at the floor and watched it disperse. "You think because your phone's unlisted that it's not listed somewhere? Come on, you're in the business. If a phone's got a contract then there's a trail. The only safe phone is a public landline and the powers that be are doing all they can to cut down on those. They want everyone on mobiles because they can track them."

Shepherd nodded but didn't say anything. Harper was right, of course. Mobile phones had made the job of surveillance much easier. If you had a target's phone number you could follow the phone around the world, listen to every phone call made and see every text. And with the latest technology, all that could be achieved even if the phone was switched off.

"I tell you, mate, Big Brother is already here."

Shepherd turned to look at him. "You still haven't answered my question, Lex."

"How did I get your number? And your address in Hereford? I paid for it. Cold hard cash and a lot of it. There's a whole industry out there geared up to providing information. And a lot of the guys doing it are former cops and former spooks. They still have access. But don't worry, all they could find out was that you worked for MI5, their database is as secure as it gets. I don't ask how they get their intel, and they don't say. The money does the talking."

"OK, so here's the big question. If you've got access to all that information, how come you needed me to check up on Khan? You found me, why couldn't you find him?"

Harper nodded as he drew on his cigarette and held the smoke deep in his lungs before exhaling. "Because you're in the system. You've got a passport and credit cards and a driving licence and you pay your council tax like a good citizen. And like I said, I already had your basic details. Easy peasy. But Khan was a whole different kettle of fish."

"You tried under his real name?"

"Real name doesn't really apply, does it? We knew him as Ahmad Khan in Afghanistan but who's to say that's his real name? A guy can use any name he wants out there, most births aren't even registered. That's why when they do come over here they get to stay. You can have finger-prints, DNA, iris scans, the works, but they're no bloody use if you've nothing to compare them with." He dropped what was left of his cigarette on the floor, stamped on it, then picked up the flattened butt and put it into his pocket. He leaned across the table. "So, time to shit or get off the pot, Spider. Did you find him?"

Shepherd nodded. "Yeah, I found him."

Harper grinned. "I knew you would. Hammersmith? Near the court?"

"Yeah."

"Family?"

"Not that I know of. He's not known as Ahmad Khan any more. Now he's got a British passport under the name Farzad Sajadi."

"That's interesting."

"What's your plan, Lex? What do you want to do?"

"What do you want to do?" Lex's eyes bored into Shepherd's. The two men stared at each other for several seconds. It was Spider who looked away first.

There was something different about Lex's eyes, a coldness that hadn't been there when he'd been Shepherd's spotter in Afghanistan. The relationship between a sniper and a spotter was as tight as any relationship could be. It was all about trust. A sniper had to concentrate on his target with every fibre of his being, and that meant the spotter had to be watching his back. A sniper had to be able to trust his spotter completely, and in Afghanistan Spider had trusted Harper, literally, with his life. But the Lex Harper sitting next to him on the bench in Hyde Park wasn't the same man who'd partnered him in Afghanistan. But then Shepherd had changed, too. Everyone changed. Time and events made sure of that.

Shepherd rubbed his right shoulder as he thought back to the day that Khan had shot him. He had nearly died that day in 2002. And the officer he was with, Captain Harry Todd, had died as he lay in Shepherd's arms, shot in the head and throat. He shuddered as the memories flooded back. Khan had shot Todd twice but either of the wounds would have been fatal. And if the round that had slammed into Shepherd's shoulder had been an inch to the left, Shepherd would have died too.

"Spider?" Harper was looking at him with concern in his eyes.

"Yeah, sorry," said Shepherd. He shook his head to clear his thoughts.

"You thinking about Captain Todd?"

"Yeah."

"That bastard Khan ambushed him. And you. You weren't even shooting when you came out of that building, you were no threat to him."

"What do you want to do, Lex?"

Harper leaned towards Shepherd. "Remember what the captain wanted? That French phrase?"

"*Droit de seigneur?*"

That's the one. The right to be in at the kill. That's what I want, Spider. I want to see the bastard die."

"You're talking about murder."

Harper shook his head fiercely. "I'm talking about justice, and you more than anyone should know how important that is. He killed the captain. He shot three of my mates in the back. And he damn near killed you."

Shepherd nodded. Everything Harper said was true. But that didn't make what he was suggesting the right thing to do.

"Well?" said Harper.

"You're up for this?"

"Damn right," said Harper. "Are you?"

Shepherd closed his eyes. His brain kicked into overdrive, pulling out images from his almost perfect memory. The blood trickling down Todd's face. More blood frothing from the wound in his throat. The way the life had faded from the captain's eyes and his body had shaken and then gone still. Then the nightmare journey back to the helicopter, Shepherd lying on a makeshift stretcher being dragged behind a moped, bouncing and banging across the rough terrain, every movement sending bolts of pain through his shoulder as the blood seeped into the trauma bandage covering the gaping wound, the wound that he saw every morning in the bathroom mirror. He opened his eyes and smiled thinly at Harper. "Yeah," he said. "I'm up for it. But first we have to make sure."

"Make sure?"

"We need to know it's definitely him."

"You said you'd ID'd him."

"I said I've identified the guy in the picture. But we need to be one hundred per cent sure that it's Khan."

"An Afghan with a milky eye and a straggly beard? How many of them do you think there are in the world?"

"To be honest Lex, I don't know. And neither do you. We need to get a close look at him. And I'll get Jock along. Jock got up close and personal with Khan so I want to know what he thinks."

"How the hell is Jock?"

"Haven't seen him since Afghanistan. The Regiment'll know where he is. Soon as I've got Jock on board, we'll go take a look at Khan."

Shepherd drove back to Hampstead and found a parking space fairly close to his flat in a side road off Hampstead High Street. The cramped one-bedroom flat was on the second floor of a block built during the sixties to fill the gap left when two mews houses were demolished by a stray German bomb during the Second World War. Shepherd let himself in, tapped in the burglar alarm code and made himself a cup of coffee before phoning Major Gannon. The call went through to voicemail but Shepherd didn't leave a message. He was taking his first sip of coffee when the phone rang. "Sorry, Spider, I was in the range — how's things?"

"All good, boss," said Shepherd. "You?"

"Helping train a group of SFOs," said the Major. "Slow going."

Specialist Firearms Officers had originally been confined to specialist units that were used only in emergency situations, but recently they had become a familiar sight on the streets of British cities. While public opinion would have preferred to have kept the traditional bobby armed only with a stick and a whistle, times were changing, and the armed units were the only defence against criminals armed with guns and knives. Most of the country's police forces now sent their SFOs to the SAS for training.

"I had a run-in with armed cops a while back," said Shepherd. "Found myself on the receiving end of a taser."

The Major laughed. "And how was it?"

"Hurt like hell," said Shepherd. "And as I was covered in petrol at the time, it could have been lethal."

"Better than a bullet," said the Major.

"No argument there," said Shepherd. "Boss, I need a favour. Jock McIntyre. Any idea where he is?"

"Now there's a blast from the past," said the Major. "It's been a couple of years since I've seen him. I was in Iraq with him five or six years ago and I used him in the Increment a few times." The Increment was one of the government's best-kept secrets, an ad hoc group of special forces soldiers used on operations considered too dangerous for the country's security services, MI5 and MI6. The Major had headed the unit for several years. "I haven't heard from him for at least three years."

"He's left the Regiment?"

"Yes, he had a couple of close calls during the last tour and he started drinking more than was good for him. I had him in for a couple of chats and we put him through a detox programme but it didn't do much good. He'd put in the years so he left with a decent pension but he wasn't happy about going."

"He wasn't dishonourably discharged?"

"Hell no, he was always professional in the field. It was just when he got back to Hereford that he had problems. He'd have a few too many drinks in the pub and then get into fights with the local yobs. You know what it's like here, Spider. There's always some tough guy who wants to prove he can take on the SAS. Most of the guys just walk away but Jock seemed to welcome the attention. It got so that we had to ban him from the local pubs."

"Can you find out where he is? I need to get in touch."

"Something I can help with?"

"It's personal, boss."

"Personal is sometimes when you need the most help, Spider. You were there when I needed you, I'm here for you if you need me."

"I appreciate that, boss," said Shepherd. "But it's no biggie, seriously." Shepherd wasn't happy about lying to the Major but the fewer people who knew what he was planning, the better.

"No problem," said the Major. "I'll take a walk over to the admin office and pull his file. OK to call you on this number?"

"Yeah, I'm at home," said Shepherd.

"Hereford?"

Shepherd laughed. "Sorry, no. London. I've been in this flat so long it's starting to feel like home."

The Major ended the call and Shepherd went through to the pokey kitchen and opened the fridge. There were a couple of Marks and Spencer salads, a pack of cheese slices and a pack of yoghurts. Shepherd wasn't a great food shopper and tended to eat out more often than not when he was away from Hereford. He pulled out the salads but both were a week past their sell-by date and he tossed them into the bin by the cooker. There was half a pack of Hovis bread that was just within its sell-by date so he made a couple of slices of cheese on toast and took them and a cup of Nescafé back into the sitting room. He had barely flopped down on to the sofa when his phone rang. It was the Major and he had an address in Reading and a phone number for Jock McIntyre. "I think the number's out of date," said the Major. "There's a note in the file saying that someone from the SAS Association tried to get in touch last year but didn't get any reply." The SAS Association looked after former members of the Regiment who had fallen on hard times and paid out more than £120,000 a year in financial support. "According to the file he's

256

separated from his wife and working as a security guard."

"A security guard? Jock?"

"He's not the Jock you remember, Spider. Look, if you do see him, get him to get in touch with me, will you?"

"Will do, boss." Shepherd ended the call, finished his sandwich, and then tapped out McIntyre's number. It went straight through to voicemail.

The Major hadn't given Shepherd a work address for McIntyre so Shepherd's only option was to try catching the man at home. He figured it would take just over an hour to drive to Reading. It wasn't a town that he was familiar with but the Major had given him the postcode and the X5 had satnav. He looked at his watch. It was three o'clock in the afternoon. There was probably no good time to get there — there was no guarantee that McIntyre was still at the address, and if he did still live there he could be working days or nights.

He locked up the flat and walked downstairs. He'd parked a short walk away and within minutes he was driving west, the destination programmed into the car's satnav. The navigation system took him to a street of run-down terraced houses close to the town centre. The houses were on three floors, with a large bay window on the ground floor, two smaller windows on the first floor, and a single arched gable window set into the roof. Most appeared to have been converted into flats and had multiple doorbells by the front door.

Shepherd parked on the opposite side of the street and walked over to McIntyre's address. He was in Flat

3 but Shepherd couldn't work out whether that was the top-floor or the ground-floor flat. He pressed the bell and waited. There was a small speaker below the three bell buttons but it remained resolutely silent. He pushed again, and then a third time. He was just about to turn away when the door opened. A large black woman in a bright green African-style dress and a matching headscarf started to back through the door, pulling a double stroller. Shepherd helped keep the door open as she manoeuvred the stroller on to the pavement. "Thank you," she said. Two small boys looked up at Shepherd with matching grins. They couldn't have been more than eighteen months old, still at the stage where every stranger was a source of amusement. He couldn't help smile back at their cheery faces and one of them put a hand to his mouth and blew Shepherd a kiss.

"No problem," said Shepherd. "You don't happen to know Jock McIntyre, do you?"

"The Scottish man?" said the woman, pulling the door shut. "He drinks a lot, and he scares my children sometimes."

"I'm told he lives in Flat 3."

"That's right, the top," said the woman. "He lives above me. The one good thing is he's quiet. I never hear him when he's home."

"But he's not in now?"

"I don't think so. Did you ring the bell?" She was clutching a leather handbag to her ample chest as if she feared he might try to take it from her.

258

Shepherd nodded. "I'll come back later." He turned to go.

"Is he your friend?"

"Sure."

She looked at him earnestly. "You should tell him not to drink so much. Sometimes he falls over on the stairs. He's going to hurt himself. Alcohol is a bad thing."

"I'll tell him," said Shepherd. He went back to the car as the woman manoeuvred the pushchair down the street.

Shepherd was about to get into the car when he saw a small shop down the road, so he wandered down and bought a bottle of water, a box of Jaffa Cakes and a copy of the *Daily Mail*. Back in the car, he reclined the front seat, nibbled on the Jaffa Cakes and read the paper.

It had been dark for almost an hour when McIntyre came walking down the road from the direction of the station. He was carrying a backpack slung over one shoulder and was walking slowly, as if every step was an effort. It was a far cry from when Shepherd had seen him in Afghanistan, where McIntyre had no problem running with thirty kilos of equipment on his back plus a loaded weapon and ammo. He had been one of the fittest men in the Regiment and one of the few who could give Shepherd a run for his money in the stamina stakes.

He had his head down and his shoulders were hunched as if he had the cares of the world pressing down on him. His sandy hair had greyed over the years and there was a grey pallor to his skin as if all the colour had been drained out of him.

Shepherd tossed his paper on to the passenger seat and climbed out of the car. McIntyre didn't look up as Shepherd crossed the road, a sure sign that the man had lost his edge.

"Jock?"

McIntyre carried on walking as if he hadn't heard.

Shepherd jogged the last few steps. "Hey, Jock!"

McIntyre looked up, his brow furrowed into a deep frown. "Yeah, what?" His eyes were red and watery and there were broken veins peppered across his nose and cheeks. He blinked as if he was having trouble focusing, and then his face cracked into a lopsided grin. "Bloody hell, Spider Shepherd."

"One and the same," said Shepherd.

"What the hell are you doing in this neck of the woods?" He shook his head in amazement.

"Just dropped by to see how you were doing," said Shepherd.

"All the better for seeing you, my old mucker," said McIntyre. He grabbed Shepherd and gave him a fierce bear hug, then patted him on the back with both hands. Shepherd could smell stale sweat and booze and it was obvious that under the heavy coat McIntyre was carrying a lot more weight than the last time they'd met. McIntyre put his hands on Shepherd's shoulders and studied his face with eyes that were bloodshot from too little sleep or too much alcohol or most likely a combination of the two. "Bloody hell, you're a sight for sore eyes," he said. "How long's it been?"

"Last time I saw you was November 2002, when I was leaving Afghanistan," said Shepherd.

"Aye, but I didn't know that you'd be leaving the Regiment," said McIntyre. "That bloody wife of yours finally got her way, didn't she? Nagged and nagged until you left. How the hell is Sue? She was a fit one, all right. You did well bagging her. We always thought she was too good for you."

Shepherd forced a smile. "She died, Jock. Back in 2004. Car accident."

McIntyre's face fell. "God, I'm sorry." He gripped Shepherd's shoulders tightly. "Me and my big bloody mouth."

"You weren't to know, Jock."

"And your boy? I'm scared to ask."

"Liam's fine. Away at boarding school at the moment."

"Boarding school? Hell, you win the lottery, did you?" He gestured over to the BMW. "And a bloody Beamer? Life must be good, huh?"

"Boarding school isn't that expensive and the car's from the office pool," said Shepherd. "What about you, Jock? How's life?"

"Life's shit," said McIntyre. "But it's better than the alternative. Anyway, let's not stand out in the street like this. Come in — I don't have Jamesons but I've got some Johnnie Walker."

Shepherd nodded. What he had to say to McIntyre was better done in private than sitting in a pub or coffee shop. McIntyre slapped him on the back. "Hell, it's good to see you, Spider. Ten years goes by in a flash, doesn't it. Seems like only yesterday we were in Afghanistan." He shoved his hand into his trouser pocket and pulled out two Yale keys on a keyring with a small black and white plastic football on it. "Do you see much of the old guys?"

"Some," said Shepherd. "Let's get that drink and I'll tell you."

McIntyre slotted the key into the lock and took Shepherd through into the hallway. The walls were dirty and scuffed and the carpet had worn through in places. A bare bulb hung from the ceiling. "Top floor, I'm afraid, but it keeps me fit," said McIntyre.

He headed up to the first floor. The door there looked as if it had been kicked in at some point and it had been reinforced with strips of metal. There were two locks, one at eye level and one at knee level. "I met your neighbour," said Shepherd, nodding at the door.

"The Kenyan bird?" said McIntyre. "She's a sweetie, isn't she? Cooks amazing curries. I can smell them upstairs. Her kids are always crying, though. Does my head in sometimes."

There was no carpet at all on the final flight of stairs, which had been painted purple but that had worn away to bare wood in places. There was another bare bulb hanging from the ceiling. Shepherd followed McIntyre up the stairs, where he used the second key to open a white-painted door. "Home sweet home," he said, tossing his backpack on to the floor by a pile of unopened mail and circulars.

It was just about the most depressing room that Shepherd had ever been in. It was the attic of the house and the only light came from the single gable window. There were several damp patches in the corners, the plaster wet and speckled with black mould. There was a single bed pushed against the wall opposite the door. There was no headboard, just a pillow and a grubby duvet. Under one of the eaves there was a built-in kitchen unit with a microwave and a single hotplate, and there was a battered kettle on top of a small fridge that rattled and hummed as if nearing the end of its useful life. A plastic accordion door led to a poky bathroom. Shepherd caught a glimpse of a stained toilet and a tiny plastic shower cubicle. His nose wrinkled at the foul smell coming from the toilet.

"Aye, there've been problems with the drains," said McIntyre. "I think the Kenyan bird has been trying to flush her Pampers. Still, this is only temporary, I'm going to be moving to a new place soon." He went over to a wall cupboard and took out a half-full bottle of Johnnie Walker Red Label and two glasses. "I don't have soda water," he said apologetically. "But there's tap water."

"Neat is fine," said Shepherd, looking around for somewhere to sit. There was a single wooden chair next to a small table under the window but there were three crusty saucepans stacked on it and the table was littered with KFC and pizza boxes. There was a scuffed leather armchair with stuffing bursting from the sides but it was covered in dirty clothing, including several pairs of soiled underwear.

"I know it's a mess, it's the maid's day off," said McIntyre, handing a glass to Shepherd. "Good to see you, Spider." The two men clinked glasses. McIntyre waved at the bed. "Sit yourself down there," he said. As Shepherd perched on the end of the bed, McIntyre shoved the dirty saucepans off the wooden chair and they clattered on to the stained carpet, which had possibly once been beige or yellow but now was the colour of a smoker's fingers and there was barely a square foot that wasn't peppered with cigarette burns. The ceiling had once been white but years of smoking tenants had turned it the same shade as the carpet. It was presumably from the previous tenant because there were no signs of McIntyre being a smoker.

McIntyre took a gulp of whisky and then poured more into his glass. He raised it in salute. "You know, you're the first visitor I've had in here," he said, sitting on the wooden chair.

"How long have you lived here?" asked Shepherd.

McIntyre screwed up his face as if he'd been given a difficult mathematical problem to solve. "Six months," he said eventually. "Seven, maybe. It's just somewhere to sleep."

"What happened to your marriage, Jock? You and Emma seemed a great couple. Two kids — they're in their twenties now, right?"

"Haven't seen the kids for four years," said McIntyre. He smiled tightly. "Had a bit of a falling-out with Emma. Can't go near her at the moment."

"Can't go near her? What do you mean?"

"Restraining order. Bloody cops." He shrugged and drained his glass before refilling it again. "She'll come around eventually. Till death do us part, right?" He grimaced. "Sorry. Stupid thing to say."

Shepherd waved away the man's apology. "Where are you working, Jock?"

"I'm looking after an office building near the station," said McIntyre. "Days mainly but I get overtime overnight a couple of days a week. It's quiet at night so I can catch forty winks." He raised his glass to Shepherd. "At least no one's shooting at me and I don't have to keep looking out for IEDs."

"I thought there was plenty of work out in Iraq, private security and that," said Shepherd.

"Not any more," said McIntyre. "At least not for the likes of you and me. They do it on the cheap now, the days of a thousand dollars a day are long gone. Used to be you got great food and business-class flights back and forth and plenty of leeway to do what needed to be done, but that's all gone. There are guys out there now earning a hundred and fifty bucks a day, Spider. That's close to minimum wage. And it's as dangerous as it ever was. More so. What they've done is to privatise casualties. Whereas it used to be the army that took the hits, now it's the contractors. And when you do get hurt, you're sent back home and left to your own devices. You have to take out your own insurance and that costs an arm and a leg." He laughed harshly, the sound of a wounded animal. "No pun intended. I wouldn't go back to Iraq if they got down on bended knee and begged me." He raised his glass but his hand was unsteady and whisky slopped on to the carpet. "So what brings you to Reading? I'm guessing it's not a social visit." He sipped his whisky and scrutinised Shepherd over the rim of his glass.

Shepherd met McIntyre's gaze and forced a smile. McIntyre was a mess, he looked as if he was close to a breakdown. There was a tenseness about his movements and a small twitch to the side of his right eye that made it look as if he was winking. His nails were bitten to the quick and his skin had a yellowish pallor, a sign that all the alcohol he was drinking was taking its toll on his liver. Shepherd had half a mind to walk out.

"Come on, Spider. Spit it out. It's got be something important to get you out here."

Shepherd nodded as he held his glass with both hands. "Remember Ahmad Khan?"

"The muj that shot you and the captain? Like it was yesterday. One of the biggest regrets of my life is that we didn't slot that bastard in Pakistan."

Shepherd reached inside his jacket and pulled out the newspaper cutting that Harper had given him. McIntyre put his glass on the table next to a Domino's pizza box and walked unsteadily over to Shepherd. He took the cutting from him and peered at it, then walked back to the table and began rooting through the fast food boxes, muttering to himself. Eventually he found a pair of reading glasses and he perched them on the end of his nose and stared at the cutting again. "What the hell is he doing in the UK?" he said.

"You think it's him?"

"Of course I think it's him. And so do you. You wouldn't be here if you didn't."

"I'm not sure," said Shepherd.

"Come on, how many Afghans with straggly beards and one milky eye do you see in London?"

"I don't know, to be honest," said Shepherd. "There are thousands of Afghans in London, and a lot of them have beards. I don't know how common that eye thing is."

"We were in Afghanistan and he was the only one I saw with an eye like that."

Shepherd nodded. That was true. It was a very distinctive blemish, one that Shepherd had never seen elsewhere.

McIntyre paced up and down the tidy room as he reread the newspaper cutting. "How the hell does this happen?" he muttered. "How does a Taliban murderer end up living here?"

"That's a good question," said Shepherd. "But a better question is what are we going to do about it?"

McIntyre took off his glasses. "You know what we're going to do about it. We're going to slot him, like we should have done in Pakistan."

"One step at a time, Jock," said Shepherd. "First we've got to be sure it's him."

McIntyre gave the cutting back to Shepherd. "Then we slot him, right?"

Shepherd pocketed the cutting. "One bridge at a time," he said.

McIntyre put his spectacles back on the table and picked up his glass of whisky. He raised it in salute. "We're going to give that bastard what he deserves."

"No offence, Jock, but you need to lay off the booze."

"Sure, sure."

"I'm serious. We're going to need clear heads to pull this off."

McIntyre nodded. "No worries. I can take it or leave it." He saw the look of disbelief on Shepherd's face and he grinned. "Spider, I drink because I'm bored, end of."

"That's good to hear," said Shepherd. "How about we start by pouring that in the sink?"

McIntyre held up the glass. "Now that'd be a waste of perfectly good whisky, wouldn't it?"

"Clear heads," repeated Shepherd. "Starting now."

McIntyre sighed, then walked over to the sink and emptied the glass. Then he fetched the bottle and poured the contents away. "Happy now?" he said, tossing the empty bottle.

"Happier," said Shepherd.

McIntyre gestured at the glass in Shepherd's hand. "The no-drinking rule applies to you as well, right?"

Shepherd laughed. "Fair comment," he said. "I'll stay off the booze as long as you do." He looked at the whisky in his glass, then quickly drank it. He grinned at McIntyre. "Starting now."

AFGHANISTAN, 2002

Ahmad Khan and Captain Todd flew to the Jalalabad base on a Blackhawk helicopter and then drove the final thirty miles to the SAS Forward Operating Base in a convoy of armoured Land Rovers as soon as it was light. It was "bandit country" and all the occupants of the Land Rovers, including Khan, were armed. Khan had a scarf around his head and face, concealing his identity from any Taliban spies who might be watching from the shadows.

He looked around him with interest as they approached the Forward Operating Base. The road that led up to the gates was studded with huge concrete blocks, forcing any vehicle to slow down and weave from side to side as it approached, preventing suicide bombers from driving a truck packed with explosives straight into the gates.

The base was small, surrounded by razor-wire fences and berms bulldozed out of the stony soil, providing blast protection and cover for those inside. From what he could see, it looked much less well equipped than the American bases. Beyond the berms, Khan could just glimpse the tops of rows of shipping containers and tents and a heavily sandbagged, mud-brick building, the only permanent structure on the site. Around them were sandbagged emplacements from which protruded the barrels of General Purpose Machine Guns, and the much thicker firing tubes of mortars.

Bulldozers had flattened everything within half a mile of the perimeter in all directions, removing any cover for insurgents and giving the defenders of the base a clear field of fire. The cleared ground included the flattened rubble of a series of buildings, and as they passed them, Khan wondered whether they had merely been sheds or barns, or had once been people's houses.

When they reached the gates, the British soldiers travelling with them were waved through after a brief check of their ID, but when Todd and Khan tried to follow them, the two armed guards blocked their way. Khan could see the looks of contempt aimed at his black dishdasha and AK-47, but he kept his expression neutral and looked away as Todd first talked and then argued with them, his voice rising as he became increasingly frustrated.

As the captain argued with the guards, two soldiers walked over. They were not dressed like the other British soldiers he had seen, but wore shorts and sun-faded T-shirts. They were no taller than he was and did not appear particularly powerfully built, but from their lean, muscled physiques and air of relaxed self-confidence, Khan suspected they were special forces.

He heard the bigger of the two men refer to the other as "Spider", presumably a nickname. Spider looked at Khan's weapon, and then nudged his colleague. "Clock that, Geordie?" he said beneath his breath. The AK-74's orange plastic stock and magazine made it very distinctive, and Khan could tell from their expressions that they knew that this newer, improved version of the AK-47 was rare enough in the Taliban's armoury for it only to be issued to its commanders and its most elite troops.

Todd was still arguing with the guards. "I'll have you on a charge for this, I'm warning you!" he said.

"What's the problem, Captain?" the one called Geordie said.

"This guard is refusing to let us into the compound," Todd said, brushing his hair back from his eyes.

Geordie's face broke into a grin. "That's probably because you've got an armed and unknown Afghan with you," he said. Khan noticed that he didn't call the officer "Sir", even though Todd was a captain and the other man was obviously from the ranks.

"This man is Ahmad Khan, a Surrendered Enemy Personnel," Todd said.

"Well, that doesn't carry too much weight in these parts," Geordie said. "I can tell you from my own experience that SEPs are like junkies — they're only with you long enough to get their next fix — cash, weapons, whatever — and then they're gone again. With respect, Captain, no experienced guy would trust an SEP as far as he could throw him."

Todd glared at him. "This man has vital intelligence I need to put before the boss and I am not going to exclude him from the compound just because of your prejudice against SEPs and perhaps Afghans in general."

The soldier called Spider glanced from one to the other and then made a calming gesture to both of them with his hands. "It's not about prejudice," he said. "It's based on bitter experience. We've had more than our fair share of green on blue attacks out here." He pointed at Khan's rifle. "One: He's carrying a loaded AK-74. Only the top guys in the Taliban carry them. So he's not some tribesman picking up a few extra dollars for fighting the *faranji* invaders, he's one of their leaders. Two: This is a secure compound. Not even a

Brit would get in here without being vetted or vouched for, and yet you're trying to bring an armed Taliban fighter in here."

"The thing is, Captain," Geordie said, emphasising his point by jabbing his finger towards him, "you're not only jeopardising the safety of everyone here, but you'd better watch your own back, because I'd take odds that he'd rub you out if he thought he could get away with it."

"Your comments are noted," Todd said, struggling to keep his anger under control. "Now step aside, the OC needs to hear what he has to say."

The two guards — both paratroopers — stood their ground, with their weapons ready to fire.

"With the greatest of respect, Captain, they're not going to let you in while your SEP has a loaded weapon," Spider said. "But if he unloads his weapon and leaves the magazine and his ammunition belt with the guards, he can probably be allowed into the compound. He can pick them up again on his way out."

Khan glanced at Todd, then shrugged and began unloading his rifle, but no Afghan man, let alone a warrior, would willingly be deprived of his weapon and he glared at the two SAS men as he did so.

"Do you speak English?" Geordie asked Khan as he handed his ammunition belt and magazine to one of the guards.

"Enough," Khan said.

"What's your name?"

"Ahmad Khan."

"Well, Ahmad Khan, you'd better be on your best behaviour while you're here, because we'll be watching you."

Khan smiled. He was on their ground, not his, but he was not going to be bullied or intimidated by them. "Do I scare you, soldier?" he said. "Is that it? Yes, I can see the fear in your eyes." He smiled again as Geordie's fists clenched despite himself.

"You don't scare me, mate," he said. "I've slotted more than my fair share of guys like you."

Khan's smile did not waver. "Tread carefully, my friend. We Afghans are a proud people. We don't give in to threats, nor tolerate insults to our honour."

"Leave it, Geordie," Spider said at last, breaking the growing silence and putting a hand on Geordie's shoulder. "He can't hurt anyone now." He nodded to Todd. "Morning prayers are about to start," he said, puzzling Khan, for he had seen no sign that any of the troops he had met were religious men.

"He means our morning briefing," Todd said, seeing his baffled expression. "I'm afraid you won't be able to accompany me — security, need to know, and all that stuff — but make yourself as comfortable as you can," he said with a rueful smile, gesturing at a makeshift waiting area near the gates consisting of tattered deckchairs and upturned ammunition boxes, "and I'll be back as soon as possible."

Todd whistled to a soldier who'd been doing his morning run. "Corporal, look after our Afghan friend for a few minutes, would you?" He caught Khan's look and gave a sheepish grin. "Sorry, camp regulations: no unescorted visitors." He turned and hurried after Spider and Geordie into the mud-brick building.

Ignoring the soldier, Khan squatted down in the dust in the pool of shade cast by a shipping container, and settled himself for a long wait. About an hour later he saw Todd emerge from the building with a face like thunder and stride off across the compound to a group of soldiers clustering around a tent as they prepared themselves for a patrol. Khan watched as Todd moved from group to group and had a long conversation with two of their sergeants, but when he at last turned and walked back towards Khan, he was accompanied by three of the soldiers and had a smile back on his face.

"OK," he said to Khan. "It's on, though I've had a hell of a job convincing them. I'm afraid that some of my colleagues just don't trust you — I can't entirely blame them, because there have been some unfortunate incidents in the past — but if this all goes smoothly, that should not be an issue in the future." He paused, checking Khan's expression before he continued. "These three men will be your escort," he said, gesturing to the soldiers.

"You are not coming with me?" Khan said. He kept his voice even but Todd read the message in his eyes and flushed with embarrassment. "I'm afraid the boss has vetoed me going with you, but these Paras are good guys and can handle themselves if there's any trouble. Though obviously I'm not expecting there to be any," he added hastily as he saw Khan's expression. "The RV with your fighters is in an area that has been pacified by us and is peaceful, at least during daylight hours.

So one vehicle and three men should be all we'll need."

Khan looked at the faces of the Paras that Todd had assembled and was immediately struck by how young and fresh faced they looked, compared to his own battle-hardened men. "*Insh'allah* there will not be," he said. He wondered again whether the trust and loyalty his men felt for him personally and the dislike they felt for their other commanders would be enough to outweigh their tribal loyalty to the Taliban. He glanced at his wristwatch. Russian-made and taken from the wrist of a dead Soviet soldier many years before. It still kept perfect time. "The rendezvous is in four hours," he said. "And it is always wise to be the first to arrive, so we need to leave as soon as your men are ready."

Todd sent the three Paras off to collect their kit and then turned back to Khan. "You won't let me down, will you?" he said. "I've staked my own reputation, such as it is, on this."

"I have my own reasons — and, with respect, they are far more powerful than yours — for wanting this to succeed. My daughter's future, perhaps even her life, depends on it." He held Todd's gaze and the Englishman was the first to look away.

The Paras loaded their gear into a Land Rover with a General Purpose Machine Gun mounted on the bonnet. Each of the three men was also armed with an M16 rifle. Khan's AK-74 and his magazines and ammunition were given back to him and he cradled the weapon in his lap as he sat in the back alongside one of the Paras. As they drove out of the compound, Khan saw Spider and Geordie standing off to one side, watching him. The expressions on their faces showed that they did not trust him an inch.

"It's him," said McIntyre. "It's definitely him. No question." Shepherd, McIntyre and Harper were sitting in Shepherd's X5 in the street opposite the house occupied by the man they used to know as Ahmad Khan. McIntyre was in the back of the car, directly behind Shepherd.

"What do you think, Lex?" asked Shepherd, moving to the side to give him a better view.

"The eye's the giveaway," said Harper. "The beard's shorter and he's older but then we're all getting older, aren't we?"

"I'd be happier seeing him in Afghan dress," said Shepherd. "The Western clothing is throwing me off." Khan was wearing baggy brown corduroy trousers and what appeared to be carpet slippers, and a green quilted jerkin over a dark brown pullover. On his head was a knitted skullcap. "But the way he moves, the way he carries himself, it all feels right." Khan had left a terraced house in the Hammersmith street and was walking purposefully away from them, his arms swinging freely at his sides.

"Yeah, if he had an AK-74 slung over his shoulder then we'd know for sure," said Harper. "Can we get closer?"

"If he recognises any of us then we'll blow it," said Shepherd.

276

"Why would he recognise us?" asked Harper. "It's been more than ten years and we probably all look the same to him."

"He got up close and personal with me," said Shepherd. "And you tend to remember the people you've shot. I know I do."

"I don't know why we're even discussing this," said McIntyre. "It's him. Even without the eye I'd know him anywhere."

"Yeah, I think you're right," said Shepherd. He shook his head. "No, I don't think. I know. It's him."

"Yeah, that milky eye nails it," said Harper.

"So what do we do?" asked McIntyre.

"We take it one step at a time," said Shepherd.

"Sod that," said Harper. "Let's just slot the bastard. He's due, Spider. He's overdue. After what he did to you and the captain."

"Have you got a gun on you, Lex?" asked Shepherd. "This isn't Afghanistan. Everything we do from now on has be planned out in advance and executed flawlessly otherwise we'll all end up behind bars."

The man disappeared around a corner. "So what do you want to do?" asked Harper.

"We need intel," said Shepherd. "We need to see who he's living with." He gestured at the house. "That's one house, it's not been subdivided into flats. So he probably lives with someone. His family maybe. We need to find out where he works. What his movements are."

"Here's what I don't get," said Jock. "The last time we saw him he was taking pot shots at us in Pakistan. How does he end up here?"

"That's a good question," said Shepherd. "He was involved in that money-clearing house that was channelling funds for al-Qaeda. Maybe he pocketed some of the cash himself and used it to buy his way into the country."

Harper nodded in agreement. "Ten grand will buy you a genuine UK passport," he said.

"A fake, you mean?" said McIntyre.

"No, the real thing," said Harper. "There's a whole industry geared up for it. They use genuine citizens who don't need a passport. They effectively buy up the identity and apply for a passport using a different photograph."

"Sounds like the voice of experience," said Shepherd.

"I've got three, under different names," said Harper. "A British one, an Irish one and a German one. All kosher. The only drawback is facial recognition. If you're on two different databases under different names then facial recognition will catch you out. But if Khan's new identity is the only one in the system then he can stay here for ever without being found out."

"What do you need three passports for?" asked McIntyre.

"It's a long story," said Harper. He sat back in his seat and pulled out his cigarettes. He showed the pack to Shepherd. "OK if I smoke?"

"Sure, it's not my car," said Shepherd. "Just crack the window open."

Harper opened the window a few inches and lit a cigarette. He offered the pack to McIntyre but he shook his head.

"Assuming it is him, what then?" asked Harper.

"We slot him," said McIntyre quickly. "Maybe kick the shit out of him first."

"Spider?"

Shepherd sighed. In his heart he knew that he had already decided what he was going to do, but he was finding it difficult to say the words out loud. Ahmad Khan deserved to die for what he had done back in Afghanistan, but deserving to die and committing a cold-blooded murder were two very different things.

"Spider?" repeated Harper.

Images flashed through Shepherd's mind. The gaping wound in Captain Todd's throat and the frothy blood that oozed from between his lips. The splintered skull and the mangled brain tissue beneath it. The look of panic in the young captain's eyes before the life had drained from them. "Yeah, it has to be done," said Shepherd quietly.

"Then how?" asked Harper.

"How?" repeated Shepherd.

"Ways and means," said Harper. "We're going to need guns, right? Unless you're planning something more creative." He laughed. "I'm sure you MI5 guys have all sorts of tricks up your sleeves."

"MI5 doesn't kill people," said Shepherd. "We don't have a licence to kill. It's not like the movies."

"Just because you don't have a licence to kill doesn't mean it doesn't happen," said Harper. "It'll be handled by a department you'll never hear about. Remember that scientist, the one involved in the weapons of mass destruction nonsense. Are you telling me that MI5 didn't top him and try to make it look like suicide? And that guy who fastened himself up in a kitbag in the bath?"

"Don't tell me you're one of those conspiracy theory nutters," said Shepherd.

"I'm just saying, governments have people killed, it happens all the time. You know that the Libyans used to do it, and the Russians, right? And Saddam Hussein used to kill off his enemies all around the world."

"We're not Libya, Russia or Iraq," said Shepherd. "Our government wouldn't get away with killing people."

"Israel, then," said Harper. "Are you saying that you don't think Mossad knocks off enemies of Israel?"

"Israel's different," said Shepherd. "They're a law unto themselves."

"America, then? What was the killing of Bin Laden if it wasn't state-sponsored assassination?"

"That's different," said Shepherd. "That was a military operation."

"Because the assassins wore uniforms and flew in army choppers?" said Harper. "They broke into a guy's house and shot him in front of his family. How is that not an assassination?"

Shepherd threw up his hands. He could feel that he was losing the argument though he had no idea why he was suddenly trying to defend MI5. "You're comparing apples and oranges," he said. "I'm just saying that MI5 doesn't have a department that kills people."

"And I'm telling you it does, it's just that you don't know about it," said Harper. "But we're getting away from the point. Assuming you don't have a mysterious Q to give us some state-of-the-art assassin's stuff, we're going to need guns, right?"

"I know a few Regiment guys who have a little something tucked away for a rainy day," said McIntyre.

"Yeah, well, more fool them," said Shepherd. "The days of being able to keep a few souvenirs in the attic are well gone. Several guys have been sent down for keeping guns they shouldn't have." He looked across at Harper. "What are you thinking?"

"I know people who can get us guns here. Shorts and longs. Pretty much whatever we want."

"Untraceable?"

"Sure. They'll want cash, obviously."

"Let me think about it," said Shepherd. He started the engine and edged the car into the traffic.

"I wish we could just go and slot the bastard now," said McIntyre. He punched the back of Shepherd's seat. "That raghead bastard has it coming."

"One step at a time, Jock," said Shepherd. "Like I said, we need to get a bit more intel."

"Intel?" repeated Harper. "What bloody intel do we need? We know it's him and we know where he lives."

"Yeah, but we can hardly gun him down in the street, can we?" said Shepherd. "We need to know where he goes, what he does. Who he lives with. Where he works."

"You think he works?" said Harper. "I don't think you'll find many jobs for Taliban warlords down at the Jobcentre."

"He's not on benefits, I know that much," said Shepherd. "So he must be getting money from somewhere. He must be paying for that house himself. Plus he's got a car. A white CRV. If he wasn't working, he wouldn't need a car."

"Speak of the devil," said McIntyre. He pointed at a white CRV parked across the road from where they were. "Is that it?"

Shepherd looked over at the SUV. The registration number matched the number that Sharpe had given him. "That's it," he said. He indicated right and headed east, towards Paddington station.

"So what's the plan?" asked Harper.

"Like I keep saying, we gather intel."

"And we'll need guns," said Harper.

"Intel first," said Shepherd.

"Then guns," said Harper, rubbing his hands together. "Then we slot the bastard."

Shepherd dropped McIntyre at Paddington station from where he could catch a train to Reading. "He's changed," said Harper as they watched McIntyre walk into the station. His shoulders sagged and he had his head down as he trudged along with the evening commuters

"We've all changed, Lex. It's called getting older."

"He's lost his edge, and you know it," said Harper. "He's put on a couple of stone and you can smell the drink on him."

"He's stopped drinking," said Shepherd.

"You believe that?"

"That's what he says. Do you want me to drop you at Bayswater?"

"Aye, might as well." Harper lit another cigarette.

"You never smoked in Afghanistan, did you?" asked Shepherd.

"Nah. The guys I was doing the blagging with were all smokers so I thought if I can't beat them, join them." He blew smoke through the open window. "You think you can rely on Jock?"

"Jock's sound," said Shepherd.

"What about getting Jimbo? Jimbo Shortt?"

Shepherd nodded. "Yeah, I was thinking that myself."

"And Geordie. Geordie'll want to be on board for this. The two of them saved your life, remember." He chuckled. "Yeah, of course you remember. You remember everything."

"Geordie's dead, mate. Died in Iraq a few years back. Sniper."

"Shit."

"Yeah. You can say that again."

"It's funny how quickly you lose touch with people. In the army you're as tight as tight can be, you know? Then you hand in your papers and that's it, you never see your muckers again." He blew more smoke through the window. "You keep in touch with your SAS mates?"

"Some," said Shepherd. "But you're right, once you leave you're not part of it any more. The guys who are still in don't treat you the same, and the ones that leave tend not to look back." He looked across at Harper. "Look, I don't mean to get all emotional, but I'm sorry we lost touch."

"It doesn't matter, mate. We're good."

"No, I mean it, Lex. We were tight in Afghanistan, we got each other out of no end of scrapes. I should have made more of an effort to stay in touch."

"I'm a big boy, Spider. And it's not as if I called you, is it?"

"I wished you had, Lex. I wished you'd called me when you were having problems. I could have pulled some strings."

"And saved me from a life of crime, is that what you mean?" He grinned. "I chose this life of crime, and I've no regrets. None at all."

Shepherd stared at Harper, trying to work out whether the man was telling the truth.

"I'm not lying, Spider. I got the life I wanted. Sun, sea, sand, all the birds I want, good muckers around me, and enough excitement if and when I need it."

"So long as you don't get caught."

"Sure. And how safe is your job? Who's to say you won't get a knife in the back or a bullet in the face this time next week? Nothing lasts for ever, Spider. And really, I'm happy with the life I've got. You staying in touch wouldn't have changed that." He laughed. "I might even have tempted you over to the dark side. You'd make a bloody good villain."

Shepherd smiled and nodded. "You're not the first person to have said that."

"I'm serious," said Harper. "You were a cop and now you're a . . . what, a spy?"

"I'm not a spy, Lex. I'm an MI5 officer. But the work I do is pretty much policing."

"And you're on the side of the good guys, I get it. But what does MI5 really do? Protect the country's citizens, or its ruling class?"

Shepherd grinned. "Bloody hell, when did you go all political?"

"I can see what's going on in the world, mate," said Harper, earnestly. "I can see how the rich are getting richer and the poor are getting poorer, how multinational companies pay almost no tax and bankers can screw up our economy and still get seven-figure bonuses. And the cops and MI5 are helping to keep that system in place."

"There's a bit more to it than that, Lex."

"Really? So what case are you working on now?"

Shepherd sighed. "I can't tell you," he said. That was true. All of Shepherd's work was covered by the Official Secrets Act and it was an offence to discuss his work with outsiders. But it was also true that protecting Peter Grechko was less about making the UK a safer place than it was about doing a favour for the prime minister's office.

"You mean you could tell me but then you'd have to kill me?" said Harper, and he laughed.

"I keep telling you, I'm not James Bond," said Shepherd.

Harper took a long pull on his cigarette before blowing smoke out of the window. "Let me tell you how I see the world, Spider," he said. "The bankers have damn near destroyed the West. They've plunged millions into poverty and saddled us with debts that our grandchildren will be paying off."

"Not you, though," interrupted Shepherd. "I'm sure you're not paying taxes on your ill-gotten gains."

Harper ignored Shepherd and stared out of the window as he continued to speak. "They stole billions, mate. Billions. So how can anyone complain if I and a few mates go into one of their branches and take some of that for ourselves? It's not as if anyone gets hurt. And the money we take is insured. All we're doing, on a very small scale, is redressing the balance. What's wrong with that?"

"It's theft," said Shepherd. "You're taking something that doesn't belong to you and that's against the law." He chuckled. "Hell, Lex, my boy knew the difference between right and wrong when he was four years old."

"Because you taught him," said Harper. "But if I had kids, I'd be giving them a different definition of right and wrong."

"And what about drugs?" said Shepherd.

Harper turned to look at him. "What do you mean?"

"You'd tell your kids that drugs are a good thing, right?"

"I'd tell them what I believe, that drugs are no more dangerous than alcohol or cars."

"Cars?"

"More people die in car accidents every year than they do from drug overdoses. Yet you don't hear anyone saying we should ban cars. Alcohol causes way, way more damage than drugs. Yet you can buy it in supermarkets. So you tell me why drugs are singled out the way they are. Your rich banker can sit on a cellar with a thousand bottles of wine and all's well with the world. But you get caught with half an ounce of cocaine and you're banged up. Our hospitals are full of people dying from alcohol abuse, and half of all the people in jail have alcohol problems."

"There are plenty of people behind bars because of drugs."

"You see, that's where you're wrong, mate," said Harper. "They're in prison because the powers that be have decided that drugs are illegal. So you get sent to prison for possession of drugs or for selling them. If drugs were legal, none of those people would be in prison."

"See, that's not true," said Shepherd. "Look at all the violent crimes caused by drugs."

Harper shook his head. "It's not the drugs that cause the crime, it's the drugs trade. It's because drugs are illegal that the trade is controlled by gangsters. They shoot each other over turf wars and get violent with anyone who owes them money. But it's not the drugs that make people violent. You can't say that about alcohol. Drunks punch and knife each other every day of the week. Hospital A&E departments are full of people affected by alcohol, and like I said, most car crashes involve booze. But people on drugs generally

287

don't drive and generally don't fight each other. You smoke some dope and you chill, you pop a few tabs of ecstasy and you love your neighbour, you don't want to punch him in the face. Even coke is about enjoying yourself. Mate, if drugs were legalised tomorrow the world would be a much happier and safer place." He took another pull on his cigarette, blew smoke through the window, and then held the still-smouldering butt under Shepherd's nose. "And what about these?" he asked. "Biggest self-administered killers on the planet, cigarettes. And no sign of them being made illegal." He flicked ash out of the window. "It's Prohibition, mate. Pure and simple. And one day that's how it'll be seen."

"You think so?"

Harper nodded. "I'm sure so. People want drugs, and eventually they'll get a government that gives them what they want. That's how democracy works, right?"

Shepherd chuckled. "I have to say I don't think I know how democracy works these days," he said. He tapped his fingers on the steering wheel. "Do you want me to drop you in Bayswater?. I'm guessing you don't want to go back on the tube, what with your thing about CCTV."

"Anywhere near Queensway'll be fine," said Harper.

Shepherd put the car into gear and edged into the traffic. "What Jock was saying, about souvenired weapons, it's not a bad idea."

Harper frowned. "I told you, I can get whatever we need here. Untraceable and no comebacks."

"I believe you. But maybe traceable is what we need." He braked to allow a black cab to perform a tight U-turn in front of them. "Khan is from Afghanistan. If we use guns from Afghanistan and they do get traced, the Afghan connection would muddy the waters, wouldn't it."

"Using SAS guns would muddy the waters? You'll need to explain that to me."

The black cab tooted its horn and continued on its way. Shepherd accelerated, heading west. "Not SAS guns, you plonker. Taliban weapons, if we can get any. I'm sure lots of the guys brought guns over and have them tucked away. And with the clampdown on illegally held guns at the moment, they'd probably be happy enough to get rid of them."

"Do you know anyone?"

"I think I might know someone who has a little something tucked away for a rainy day, yes."

Shepherd parked his X5 next to a meter and fed it with a couple of one-pound coins. He took out his mobile phone as he walked towards the entrance of the park and tapped out Amar Singh's number. He explained what he wanted — a GPS tracking device that he could leave on a car for a few days.

"Not a problem, Spider. Can you drop by today, I'll have one waiting for you."

Shepherd looked at his watch. It was just after three and he'd almost certainly get stuck in rush-hour traffic. "Can you wait for me, if I try to get there before six?"

"I'm on a late one tonight so no rush," said Singh. "We're working on CCTV links to a lock-up in Bradford that's got some very interesting stuff in it."

Shepherd stood to the side to allow two large women with a golden retriever and a liver-and-white cocker spaniel exit the park. It was a sunny day but there was a chill in the air and he was wearing an overcoat over his suit.

The park was in North London, edged with trees and overlooked by a terrace of Edwardian brick mansion blocks. To the right was a line of tennis courts and to the far left, behind a building housing showers and changing rooms, was a running track and an outdoor gym. There was a children's playground beyond the running track but most of the park was given over to a huge field where dogs could be exercised and where during the summer weekends pub teams played cricket. Around the field ran a tarmac path with wooden benches every fifty yards or so.

A middle-aged man in a camouflage-pattern T-shirt and baggy khaki cargo pants was shouting at a group of eight women, who were all attempting to do push-ups with varying degrees of success. One of the women, rolls of fat outlined by a too-tight lilac jumpsuit, was merely lying face down and moaning. The man went over to stand by her and shouted for her to put some effort into it. The woman grunted in pain and managed one press-up before collapsing back into the grass. The man bent down, patted her on the shoulder and whispered what Shepherd assumed were words of encouragement before standing up and shouting again.

As Shepherd watched the man put the women through a series of star jumps, sit-ups and jogging, all the time shouting at them like an ill-tempered sergeant major, he couldn't help but smile. It had been several years since Shepherd had seen Jim "Jimbo" Shortt, but the man had barely changed. Like most former SAS he was wiry and toned rather than muscle-bound, and had the sort of face that could easily be lost in a crowd. His only distinguishing feature was his sweeping Mexican-style moustache, now starting to show touches of grey. As Shortt shouted at the women to lie flat on their backs he looked over at Shepherd. The two men locked eyes and Shortt gave him a small nod of recognition. Shepherd grinned and went to sit down on a bench.

Shortt spent the next half an hour putting the women through their paces, never pushing them so hard that they gave up, but never letting them off easily, and by the time the session had finished the women were all exhausted and drenched with sweat. The large woman in the lilac jumpsuit grabbed Shortt and gave him a hug and a kiss on both cheeks before heading over to the changing rooms.

Shortt jogged over to where Shepherd was sitting and Shepherd stood up to greet him. "Fuck me, Spider Shepherd," said Shortt. "What brings you to my neck of the woods?"

"Good to see you, Jimbo," said Shepherd. The two men hugged and slapped each other on the back. "When the hell did you get into shouting at women?"

"They call it Boot Camp," said Shortt. He gestured at the camouflage T-shirt he was wearing. "You don't think I'd wear this by choice? Mainly housewives who don't get any other exercise. I tell them, sign up for my

Boot Camp and you'll drop a kilo a week, guaranteed. I'll give them their money back if they don't."

"A rucksack full of bricks, can't beat it," said Shepherd.

Shortt laughed. "These girls haven't exercised for years, you have to break them in gently." He leaned towards Shepherd. "Do you have any idea what those housewives are paying me?" Shepherd shook his head. "Thirty quid for a ninety-minute session," said Shortt. "And there are eight of them there. I've got another ten doing the evening session. That's more than five hundred quid for three hours a day. There's guys out in Iraq right now earning less than that a week. And no one's shooting at me here." He grinned. "And I do one-on-one training for a hundred and twenty quid an hour, Spider. That's serious money. For hanging out in a gym."

"Can't argue with that," said Shepherd.

"You should give it a go," said Shortt, patting him on the back. "I've just signed a deal with a model agency to put some of their models through their paces. I could put some very fit birds your way."

Shepherd laughed and held up his hands in surrender. "I've got a job, Jimbo," he said.

"Where are you these days? Still with SOCA?"

The two men sat down on the bench. "Nah, I moved on."

"Secret squirrel?"

"Why do you say that?" asked Shepherd.

"Just figured you'd end up with the spooks," said Shortt. "Anti-terrorism's where it's at these days and you're a good fit — SAS background plus police experience. Is the pay good?"

"I'm not getting nine hundred quid a day, that's true," laughed Shepherd.

"Then think about giving this a go," said Shortt. "The personal trainer business is booming, everyone's health conscious these days."

"You're the second person to suggest a career change this week," said Shepherd.

"Yeah? Who was the first?"

"Remember Lex, that Para who was my spotter out in Afghanistan? Scottish lad. Keen as mustard?"

Shortt nodded. "Yeah, thought he was putting in for selection?"

"Change of plan. He's self-employed these days." Shepherd reached into his jacket pocket and slipped the newspaper cutting to Shortt. "Recognise this guy?"

"Ahmad fucking Khan," said Shortt as soon as he glanced at the photograph in the article. He looked at the name of the newspaper at the top of the cutting, and the date. "He's in England? How the hell is he in England?"

"We're not sure."

"He's a Taliban killer. He shot those three Paras in the back and he killed Captain Todd."

Shepherd forced a smile. "I was there, remember."

"Damn right you were there." He bent his head down and read the article. "It doesn't mention him," he said when he'd finished.

"He was just caught in the picture," said Shepherd. "Wrong place, wrong time. But I've tracked him down.

I know what name he's using and I know where he lives."

"And now you're going to slot the bastard?" Shepherd nodded. Shortt handed back the cutting. "Count me in," he said.

"I thought you'd say that."

"And that's why Lex is around, right? What about Jock?"

"Jock's on board," said Shepherd.

"The four musketeers," said Shortt. "Pity we lost Geordie. Geordie would have loved a chance to take a crack at Khan."

Shepherd nodded. Geordie Mitchell had been the sixth man on the mission to destroy the al-Qaeda money house in Pakistan, the operation that had ended with the death of Captain Harry Todd and Shepherd taking a bullet in the shoulder. Mitchell had died a few years earlier in Iraq, killed by a sniper in the same way that Ahmad Khan had killed Harry Todd. "Do you have much in the way of souvenirs, Jimbo?"

Shortt arched his eyebrows. "What are you suggesting, Spider? Don't you know that it's a criminal offence to own unlicensed weapons?"

"I do indeed," said Shepherd. "But I also know that every time you flew back from Afghanistan you had a rucksack full of souvenirs."

"Yeah, those were the days," said Shortt. "I made a packet selling stuff back at Stirling Lines. They were queuing up to buy AK-47s and Makarovs."

"But you kept some for yourself, right?"

"I couldn't possibly comment," said Shortt, rubbing his moustache.

"Here's the thing. We want to use Afghan guns for this. That way if the guns are ever traced, it'll look as if it was someone from Afghanistan who'd done the dirty deed."

"There'd be a certain justice in that, wouldn't there? He comes over here to make a new life, and guns from his past take that life away." He grinned. "That's practically poetic, Spider."

"So you'll help?"

"Bloody right I will."

Shepherd got to Thames House at 6.30. Amar Singh was still in his office, tapping on a computer terminal as he carried out a conversation via a Bluetooth headset. He waved Shepherd to a chair as he continued to talk about video feeds and IR cameras. Eventually he finished, took off his headset and shook hands with Shepherd. He reached down and pulled open a drawer. "OK, here it is, and I have to say it's a nice bit of kit."

He handed Shepherd an iPad and Shepherd frowned. "It's an iPad?"

"Top of the range," said Singh. He gave Shepherd a small metal box, the size of a cigarette packet. "That's magnetic so you put it under the wheel arch or on the chassis, anywhere that it's out of sight. You can hide it inside the car but if you do it's important that you put it against metal. It's the attachment that activates it. As it is, you can keep it for a year or two and it won't lose its charge. As soon as it's put up against metal it activates and the battery is good for about a week."

Shepherd switched on the iPad. It had all the normal apps but there was one called Tracker. He held the iPad out and Singh nodded. "That's it," he said. "It'll give you a location on a map or Google Earth and it's accurate to within six feet or so. The iPad needs a mobile phone connection but you should have that all the time, it's done through a monthly account."

"You're a star, Amar, thanks."

"No sweat. As far as I'm concerned it's out on a test, just let me have it back when you're done."

Shepherd's phone rang. He apologised to Singh and took out his phone, but grimaced when he saw who was calling. Charlotte Button. He considered letting the call go through to voicemail but the fact that she was calling him suggested that she knew he was in the building. He tried to keep his voice as cheerful as he could when he answered.

"A little bird tells me you're in Thames House," she said.

"I'm with Amar," he said.

"Problem?"

"Just picking up a bit of kit," he said.

"Swing by my office on your way out, would you? There's something I need to run by you."

She ended the call and Shepherd put his phone away. He picked up the iPad and the transmitter and put them into his backpack. "I should have them back in a couple of days," he said.

"No rush, they're as cheap as chips," said Singh. "It's funny, ten years ago a device like that would have cost ten grand or more. Now the whole set-up is less than a grand and most of that is for the iPad. How's the vest, by the way?"

"Difficult to say, no one's taken a shot at me yet."

Singh grinned. "I meant comfort-wise."

"Yeah, good. Most of the time I'm not even aware that it's on."

"No itching, no discomfort?"

"I've started wearing a regular cotton vest under it, and it's fine."

Shepherd shook hands with Singh then walked to the lift and took it to Button's floor. She was sitting at her desk studying a whiteboard on which were stuck a dozen surveillance photographs of Asian teenagers. She waved a hand as he looked at the pictures. "Nothing to do with you, Spider," she said. "This is up in Bradford. They're planning a Mumbai-type massacre. They seem serious, too." She nodded at a chair and Shepherd sat down, placing the backpack on the floor and hoping that she wouldn't ask about what he'd been doing with Amar Singh. "But that's not what I needed to see you about. There's a problem over Grechko."

"Problem?"

"Well, let's call it a complication," said Button.

Shepherd used his satnav to find Shortt's house, a neat three-bedroom semi-detached in Wembley, about half a mile from the stadium. There was a Jaguar parked in the driveway so Shepherd left his X5 in the street. It was just after ten o'clock in the morning. Shepherd had already checked in with Popov and Grechko wasn't planning to leave the house until early evening, so he'd said that he would take the morning off. Shepherd had picked up Harper in Bayswater. As always he was wearing his parka with the hood up.

Shortt opened the front door wearing a polo shirt and pale blue jeans. He grinned when he saw Harper and stepped forward to hug him. "Bloody hell, what's it been? Twelve years?"

"More," said Harper. "You're looking good, Jimbo."

"Clean living," said Shortt. "What's with the parka? The mod look coming back, is it?"

Harper grinned and flipped the hood back as he walked into the hallway. Shepherd followed him. "Where's the family?" he asked.

"The wife's playing golf and the kids are at school," said Shortt, closing the front door.

"Golf?"

Shortt shrugged. "I know. Why ruin a perfectly good walk by walloping a little ball with a piece of metal on the end of a stick? But she's bloody good at it. Her handicap's two. Her instructor reckons she'll be scratch within the year."

"Good for her," said Shepherd, following Shortt through to the kitchen. He was carrying a black nylon holdall.

"Coffee?" asked Shortt. "I've just made a pot."

Shepherd and Harper nodded and sat down at the kitchen table as Shortt prepared three mugs of coffee. Shepherd opened his holdall and took out the iPad and

298

transmitter that Singh had given him. Harper looked at the transmitter with interest. "See, I knew you had a Q," he said.

Shepherd laughed. "We don't call him Q. His name's Amar."

Shortt put the coffee on the table and sat down. "So what's the story?" he asked.

"We need intel," said Shepherd. "Khan knows me so I have to keep well away. We need to get that transmitter on to his car, under a wheel arch, then follow him at a distance. Lex doesn't have a car and neither does Jock, so it's down to you with Lex's help."

"I can do that," said Shortt.

"The Jag's a bit high profile," said Shepherd.

"I'll swap with the wife," said Jimbo. "She's got a Vauxhall Astra."

"Best to attach it in the early hours of the morning," said Shepherd. "The range is limitless, pretty much. It tracks through the phone network so you can be anywhere in the world and pick up the location."

"Nice," said Harper. "Think you could get me one?"

Shepherd laughed. "No, and I'll need that one back when we're done."

He reached into the holdall and took out a clipboard with a questionnaire and a laminated card clipped to it. He passed it across the table to Shortt. "We need to know what his personal situation is. It could be that he lives alone but, assuming he doesn't, we need to know who he lives with, where he works, where he goes." He tapped the laminated card. "This is a council ID, no photograph but it looks like the real thing. Are you up for ringing the doorbell and seeing if you can get them to answer a few questions? You tell them that the council's doing a residents' survey to know what resources the area needs."

Shortt nodded. "I can do that." He grinned. "I was always good at the secret squirrel stuff." He looked over at Harper. "Did Spider ever tell you about my little adventure during Selection?"

Harper shook his head.

"I was told to go into a pub in the St Paul's district of Bristol with a gun. I was the only white face in a pub full of Afro-Caribbean blokes. My sole task was to stay there for an hour without anyone detecting the weapon. Sounds easy, doesn't it? But the problem was that the pub was the headquarters for the local pimps and drug dealers, and any unfamiliar face was instantly suspect. As soon as I stepped through the door, one of the players whispered to this very good-looking woman who made straight for me. She said, 'Hi, handsome, want to buy me a drink?' and was all over me, and her hands were everywhere — and I mean everywhere!" He grinned. "Perks of the job, you might say. Of course, she didn't really fancy me, she was just patting me down to check if I was carrying a weapon or wearing a wire."

"She didn't find the gun?"

"I'd tucked it between my legs. If she'd felt it I'd have just told her she was giving me a hard-on. But I tell you, by the time I walked out of that pub I had them eating out of my hands." He picked up the clipboard. "After that, this'll be a piece of cake."

300

"Any chance of you doing this tomorrow?" asked Shepherd.

"I don't see why not," said Shortt. "I can rejig my schedule easy enough." He looked over at Harper. "Where are you staying?"

"Bayswater," said Harper.

"I'll pick you up five-ish, so we can get there nice and early," said Shortt.

Shepherd finished his coffee and put down his mug. "And the guns? Are they here?"

Shortt stood up, opened a cupboard and took out a pole with a hook on the end. He saw the look of confusion on Shepherd and Harper's faces. "Attic," he said.

The three men went upstairs and Shortt used the hook to pull open a trapdoor and release a folding metal ladder. He propped the pole up against the wall, went up the ladder and flicked a switch. A fluorescent light flickered into life as Shepherd climbed up behind him. The attic had been lined with plywood and the floor was bare boards. There were half a dozen cardboard boxes and a metal trunk against one wall and a battered chest of drawers against another.

"Give me a hand to move this," said Shortt, taking one end of the chest of drawers. Shepherd took the other and together they dragged it into the centre of the attic as Harper came up the ladder. Shortt pulled open one of the drawers and took out a screwdriver. The sheet of plywood behind the chest of drawers was held against the rafters by six screws and Shortt undid them

301

one at a time. He passed them to Shepherd and pulled the sheet away and propped it against the wall.

Shepherd whistled softly as he saw what had been concealed behind the panel. There was an AK-47 with a foldable stock and below it an AK-74. And beneath the two carbines were two pistols. Standing upright was a Lee Enfield bolt-action rifle that must have been more than sixty years old. Shepherd took it out and held it up to his shoulder. "How the hell did you get this?"

"Took it off a dead muj," said Shortt. "He didn't have any use for it, seeing how he was dead and all."

"I meant how did you get it back to the UK?"

Shortt shrugged. "What can I say? They didn't do much in the way of checks back then. I could probably have bought a tank back, bit by bit."

Harper took out the AK-47 and nodded admiringly at it. "Now this brings back memories," he said.

"Have you got ammo?" asked Shepherd.

"Not for the AKs or the Enfield. But I've kept a few rounds for the pistols. Used to take them to a quarry in Wales to fire off a few now and again. And I keep them clean and oiled."

Shepherd put the rifle back in its hiding place and picked up one of the pistols. It looked clean and serviceable. He checked the action and nodded approvingly. "Looks fine, Jimbo. But what about the ammo?"

"It's old, no argument there. Can't guarantee it hasn't gone off." He laughed. "No pun intended."

"I can get ammo, no problem," said Harper. "For the AKs, too, if you want?"

"Just the pistols," said Shepherd. He gave the gun back to Shortt. "You might think of giving them a really good clean just in case there's DNA anywhere."

"I've cleaned them already," said Shortt.

"The DNA tests they have these days are really sensitive," said Shepherd. "They can get a full profile from the merest smear of sweat. In the grip or inside the chamber. Just a touch. Before we use them you need to put on gloves and wipe every surface, inside and out. Did you ever strip them down?"

"Sure, a couple of times."

"Then your DNA will be all over the mechanism. A lot of gangbangers forget that. They wipe down the grips and the barrel but forget that their DNA's all over the inside of the gun. And on the clip, too. You'd be amazed at the number of guys in prison who wiped down the gun but left their prints on the clip. And on the ammo."

"Understood," said Shortt. He put the gun back in its hiding place and replaced the wooden panel. "To be honest, I've been thinking of getting rid of them for a while now. Guns and kids aren't a good mix." He nodded at Shepherd and Harper and they pushed the chest of drawers back in front of the panel.

"Who else knows about them?" asked Shepherd.

"As of today, just us," said Shortt. "The missus doesn't even know they're there. I just wanted a few souvenirs, you know? Didn't you bring something for a rainy day?"

Shepherd shook his head. "Sue wouldn't have stood for it," he said. "But to be honest, I was never a great one for souvenirs."

"Probably because of your trick memory," said Shortt. "You remember everything. But for me, holding one of those guns brings it all back."

The three men went downstairs to the kitchen. Shortt took a bottle of Bell's whisky from a cupboard and showed it to Shepherd. "Just a small one," said Shepherd. "With soda. I'm driving."

"I'll take ice with mine," said Harper.

Shortt made a whisky and soda for Shepherd in a tall glass, and poured himself and Harper equal measures of whisky before dropping in a couple of ice cubes. They clinked glasses and drank.

"You're sure about this?" said Shortt, sitting down at the table.

Shepherd joined him. "About Khan? Sure."

"You don't sound convinced."

"He's convinced," said Harper, swirling his ice cubes around with his finger.

"It needs to be done," said Shepherd. "It's the right thing to do. But it's . . ." He struggled to find the right words.

"The wrong thing to do?" Shortt finished for him.

Shepherd nodded. "Yeah. It's not the doing of it, it's making sure that there are no repercussions. This won't be the first time I've done something like this, so it's not about having a conscience or anything. It's about doing it right."

"We've all got a lot to lose, Spider. The last thing I want to do at my age is to go to prison. And the job you've got." He shrugged. "If they get you, they'll throw away the key."

"I know."

"So that's why I'm asking if you're sure."

"We're sure," said Harper. He drained his glass. "We're damn sure."

Shepherd stared at his glass. "This isn't about what he did to me," he said quietly. "It's not even about the fact he killed Captain Todd. That was combat. OK, the captain and I weren't a threat to him, but we were the enemy and we could have shot back. It's what he did to those three Paras that I can't forgive. They were shot in the back, Jimbo. He pretended to be on our side, he said he'd bring in the rest of his men, and he waited until they were out in the desert and he shot them in the back." He shook his head and drained his glass, then slammed it down on the table. "That was nothing to do with war," he said. "That was terrorism. If a man picks up a gun and fights another man, that's combat and may the best man win. But lying and cheating and shooting soldiers in the back, that's something else."

Shortt poured more whisky into Shepherd's glass and added soda water. "We'll get the bastard, don't worry about that."

Shepherd nodded. "I know," he said. "But we have to make sure there's no comeback."

"There won't be," said Shortt. He grinned and clinked his glass against Shepherd's. "What can go wrong?" he said. "We're professionals."

Shepherd was back at Grechko's mansion by two o'clock in the afternoon. He hadn't eaten all day but Sheena the chef was in the kitchen and she happily made him one of her amazing club sandwiches, accompanied by a plateful of double-fried chips that were so good he had to force himself to refuse a second helping. He was finishing his coffee when he heard Dudko in his earpiece. Dudko had been manning the main gate all day.

"There's a Charlotte Button here, says she's got an appointment to see Mr Grechko. But she's not in the book."

"That's my fault, but she is expected," said Shepherd. "Check her ID and send her in. Vlad, where is Mr Grechko?"

Vlad Molchanov was in the control centre. "Library," said Molchanov.

Shepherd thanked Sheena and hurried out of the kitchen and down the corridor to the library. He knocked on the door.

"What?" snarled Grechko.

Shepherd pushed open the door. Grechko was sprawled on a sofa with the day's newspapers laid out over a coffee table. One of his secretaries was sitting at a side table with her pen poised over her notebook. "Charlotte Button's here, sir," said Shepherd. "She wanted a word with you, remember?"

Grechko growled and looked at his wristwatch, a diamond-encrusted Rolex. "What does she want?"

"She said she wanted to tell you herself, sir. Too important to talk about on the phone." Shepherd knew

306

exactly what she wanted but Button had made it clear that she wanted to be the one to have the conversation with Grechko.

Grechko chuckled. "That's right, you can't trust the phones here. MI5 spend more time eavesdropping on your citizens than the KGB ever did on ours." He tossed a copy of the *Financial Times* on to the table in front of him. "OK, show her into the piano room, I'll meet you there."

Shepherd closed the door quietly and walked across the hallway, his shoes squeaking on the Italian marble. He opened the front door just as a black Series 7 BMW purred down the driveway. It parked and Button climbed out. "I thought you'd have a driver," said Shepherd.

"Those days are long gone," said Button. She nodded at the house. "How is he today?"

"Same as always, alternating between that creepy smile and snarling like a bear with a sore head. I think he might be bipolar."

"A bipolar bear, now that would be something," said Button. She looked up at the house. "Now this certainly is something," she said.

"It's like a bloody hotel," said Shepherd. "And there's more of it underground than there is above. All the parking is down there and there's room for fifty cars on two levels. There's a gym for the staff and an even bigger one for Grechko and his family, a huge sauna, an indoor pool, a gun range, a cinema, a games room with pretty much every video arcade game ever made, and that's only the bits I've seen. I got the tour but I wasn't taken everywhere."

"A gun range?" said Button.

"Yeah. In a country where ownership of handguns is a criminal offence. Funny that. They say that it's only used for airguns but I've seen some of the targets and the holes are bloody big for pellets."

"Have you seen any of the bodyguards with guns?"

Shepherd shook his head. "To be honest the gun range is well soundproofed so I've never heard anything being fired. Just seems a funny thing to have in a private house, that's all. Dmitry showed me airguns and swore blind that's all they have, but I'd be very surprised if there weren't a few firearms in the house. Mind you, there's a full-size tenpin bowling alley and I've never seen that being used either."

He took her inside and down a wood-panelled hall to a set of double-height doors. He pushed them open to reveal a room the size of a basketball court with a Steinway piano at either end and a scattering of ornate sofas and easy chairs. "The piano room," said Shepherd.

"Does he play?"

"No, but the new Mrs Grechko does apparently. She's still in France."

There was a large fireplace in the centre of the room, and over it a gilt mirror with mermaids around the edge. There were two large chandeliers each with hundreds of small bulbs, and half a dozen oil paintings that looked as if they had just come from the National Gallery. "Does Mrs Grechko do the interior design?"

asked Button, sitting on one of the sofas and crossing her legs at the ankles.

"Have you seen the new Mrs Grechko?" asked Shepherd. "She's a twenty-two-year-old former Miss Ukraine, she doesn't do much of anything other than spend his money."

Button looked around the room. "Well, whoever did this seemed to be going for the Buckingham Palace look," she said.

"He has a team of people who do nothing else but design his homes, his yacht and his planes. They were discussing how big the chandeliers could be on his new jet before turbulence became a factor."

"Chandeliers? On a plane?"

"One of them is going to be above his Jacuzzi," said Shepherd. "I'm still trying to get to grips with the image of him sitting in a hot tub at thirty thousand feet."

The doors opened and Grechko strode in. Button didn't get up and the Russian made no move to greet her, he just walked over to the sofa facing her and sat down. He put his hands on his knees and looked at her expectantly. Shepherd went to stand by the fireplace.

"I'm sorry about coming to see you at such short notice, but we have come across evidence that suggests that the attack against you was perhaps not political."

Grechko sneered at Button with undisguised contempt. "Are you stupid?" he said. "How can it not be political? Those in power, those bastards in the Kremlin, they hate me because of what I have, of what I have achieved." He threw up his hands. "This is ridiculous. I will speak to your prime minister, it's as clear as the nose on your face that you have no idea what is going on. Perhaps you are in the wrong job, Miss Button."

"Of course, you are perfectly entitled to call the PM and I have no doubt he will listen to your concerns and then he will probably call the head of MI5 who will talk to my boss who will then call me into his office where I will tell him exactly what I'm telling you, because what I'm telling you is the truth. I'm not going to change that truth simply because it's not something you want to hear. All I ask is that you listen to me and then we can decide how to move forward. Believe me, Mr Grechko, all I want is to make sure that you come to no harm on British soil." She smiled reassuringly. "Or anywhere else, for that matter."

Grechko continued to glare at her for several seconds, then he flashed her an insincere smile. "I am not an unreasonable man," he said. "And I am not unaware that I am a guest in your country." He waved at the coffee table in front of her, a thick slab of crystal on gold legs. "Would you like tea? This is the time of day when you English drink tea, is it not?"

"I think we English will drink tea at any time of the day," she said.

"Excellent," said Grechko. He took a small remote control unit from his pocket and pushed a button. Within seconds the double doors to the room were opened by a butler in a crisp black suit. "Tea, for two," he said. "And those little sandwich things."

The butler, a grey-haired man in his fifties, nodded. "Yes, sir."

"Anything but Earl Grey," said Button.

"Earl Grey?" repeated the Russian, frowning.

"I've never liked Earl Grey tea," said Button with an apologetic smile.

Grechko pointed at the butler. "No Earl Grey tea," he said.

"Absolutely, sir," murmured the butler, and quietly closed the doors.

"He worked for Prince Charles for many years," said Grechko. "He served the Queen many times. Do you know how much the Royal Family pays its butlers?"

Button shook her head. "I don't. Sorry."

"Well, I do. A pittance. They treat their staff like serfs. I pay him five times what they paid him. Five times."

"I'm sure he appreciates working for you," she said.

The Russian's eyes narrowed as if he was trying to tell whether she was being serious or sarcastic, but then he smiled and chuckled. "He does," he said. He waved a shovel-like hand at Shepherd, who was still standing by the fireplace, his hands clasped behind his back. "And you, Tony, sit, please."

"I'm on duty, sir, and I'm supposed to be on my feet at all times," said Shepherd.

"Sit!" said Grechko. "I'm sure that I'm safe in my own home."

Shepherd nodded and sat down on the sofa next to Button. The Russian steepled his fingers under his chin and stared intently at Button, his brow furrowed. "So you have come here to tell me that the attack on me was not political, that someone other than the dogs in the Kremlin is after my blood?"

Button bent forward, maintaining eye contact. "The attack on you in London recently was clearly professional. But the assassin missed."

"Luckily for me," said Grechko with a tight smile.

"Indeed. And like you we put that down to good fortune. It was a difficult shot, even for a skilled marksman. But we hadn't realised that Oleg Zakharov was the target for another assassination attempt, earlier this year."

"Ah yes, poor Oleg. He was a good friend."

"A good friend who died recently, in Monte Carlo."

"A cocaine overdose." Grechko mimed sniffing the drug. "He also had a liking for drugs, I warned him many times to be careful." He frowned. "You think that it wasn't an accident?"

"Cocaine overdoses are somewhat unusual," said Button. "And if as you said he was a frequent user, the police might not look too closely at the death."

"Then if it was murder, it was those bastards in the Kremlin," spat Grechko. "They are filled with jealousy and hatred for what we have achieved." He threw up his massive hands. "If it was murder, then the death of Oleg proves that we are all targets."

"Targets, yes, I understand that, but not necessarily targets of the Russian state," said Button. "Mr Grechko, why didn't you mention to me that someone had tried to kill Mr Zakharov?"

"It was months ago. And it was in Prague."

"It was in Prague, yes. A sniper. He missed and a bodyguard was shot in the leg."

"Yes, Oleg told me he was lucky."

"I wish that you had told us this earlier."

"Why do you think it is important?"

"Because it suggests that a killer was also targeting Mr Zakharov."

"So? Doesn't that make it even more likely that what is happening is political?"

"We're not sure, but the fact that there were two failed assassination attempts is of some concern."

"Concern?" repeated Grechko. "You are concerned that he missed?"

"I am concerned that having missed Mr Zakharov, the same sniper also misses you."

"You are assuming that it was the same sniper, of course," said the Russian.

"I have checked and the ballistic evidence shows that the same weapon was used," said Button. "It's very unlikely that two snipers would use the same weapon. What I am having trouble understanding is why a sniper who failed once is then given a second chance. If I was hiring an assassin and he failed, I doubt that I would give him a second contract." She saw the look of surprise on Grechko's face and added quickly that she was talking hypothetically. Grechko folded his arms and lowered his chin as if deep in thought.

"Mr Grechko, since we last spoke I have widened my enquiries. You knew Sasha Czernik, is that correct?"

Grechko frowned. "Yes, he was a good friend. His heart attack came as a great shock."

"Did you know that a month before his heart attack, his security team found a bomb underneath his car?"

"Sasha had a lot of business rivals," said Grechko. "He was a Ukrainian, you know? And he refused to leave, said it was his homeland and that was where he wanted to be buried." Grechko flashed her a tight smile. "He didn't realise it would happen so quickly, of course. He was only forty-five." He shrugged. "I told him Kiev was a dangerous place, he should move to London or Paris. New York, even. He had enough money, he could buy citizenship anywhere. I told him he should speak to Murdoch, make an offer for some of his papers. Even in the age of the internet, the men who own the papers make the rules. Isn't that so?"

Button ignored the question. "The point I'm making is that someone tried to kill Mr Czernik. Is it possible that it was the same person who has tried to kill you and who took the life of Mr Zakharov? Can you think of anyone who might have a personal grudge against the three of you? Someone with a military background?"

Grechko shook his head. "I don't think you fully appreciate the position that men like us are in," he growled. "They want our companies or they want us dead. Or both." He looked up, his eyes blazing. "This is because we won't give them what they want."

"And what do they want, Mr Grechko?"

"They are like pigs at a trough," said the Russian. "All of them. Worse even than the grasping pigs in this country. They see what we have and they want it. In the past we've bought them mansions in London, we've put millions in Swiss bank accounts for them, we've bought businesses for them in Europe and America. Between us, we've given those robbers billions of dollars, Miss Button. And still they want more."

"And have you been directly threatened by politicians? Have they specifically said they will have you killed if you don't give them what they want?"

"They don't have to say that, we all know how Russia is ruled," said Grechko. "But now I am protected. And soon I will be a British citizen. Then I will be out of their reach and so will the companies I own."

The butler returned with a tray laden with a solid silver tea service and two plates of delicately cut sandwiches. The butler poured tea under the Russian's watchful eye, handed out cups and offered sandwiches before quietly slipping out through the double doors and pulling them closed behind him.

"Miss Button, I can assure you that if you are looking for the men who want my death, you need look no farther than the Kremlin." He looked at his watch pointedly. "Now if you will forgive me, I have a lot of work to do."

"I quite understand," said Button. She got to her feet and offered her hand but Grechko strode past her and out of the room. She looked at Shepherd and raised one eyebrow. "Nice," she said.

"He can be a charmer," said Shepherd.

He walked with her out of the piano room and along to the front door. "I really must get one of those remote control things," said Button. "You press a button and a butler magically appears."

"Not just the butler," said Shepherd. "It's programmed for all his staff. I think he'd have the bodyguards wearing them if he could but Popov spun him a line about them interfering with our transceivers."

"How are you getting on with Popov?"

"He's fine," said Shepherd. "He's a pro. And I think he realises that I'm on board to help and not to screw him over." He opened the front door for her.

"Security here does seem on the ball," said Button. "But I don't see the killer giving up. It's like the IRA said after they almost killed Margaret Thatcher in Brighton. They only need to be lucky once. We have to be lucky all the time."

"Is that true?" he asked as they reached the car. "About Grechko? Is he getting citizenship?"

"He's already entitled, the amount of money that he's invested in this country," said Button. "Under existing rules an investment of just a million pounds will get you British citizenship and Grechko has invested hundreds of millions here."

"And I suppose the fact that he's pally with the PM won't hurt."

"I can assume that'll get him fast-tracked," said Button. "But this isn't about his connections, it's purely financial. Let's face it, Spider, the trouble this country is in economically, we need all the investors like Grechko that we can get."

"Even though we know next to nothing about him?"

"He'll have to show that he doesn't have a criminal record," said Button.

Shepherd laughed. "Yeah, I'm sure that'll be a problem," he said. "I wonder how much a clean bill of health will cost?"

Button unlocked the car door and then turned to face him. "Is there a problem?"

Shepherd grimaced. "I don't like the man. I don't like the way he carries himself, I don't like the way he treats people. He's an arrogant bully, Charlie, and I don't think he got to where he is without riding roughshod over a lot of people. Maybe worse."

"Russia's a tough place," said Button. "You don't get to the top there by being a shrinking violet."

"I've got a bad feeling about him, that's all. We were in Cyprus and he was up to something, flying back and forth with suitcases filled with I don't know what."

"Contraband?"

"I don't know. Popov said it was cash. But who knows? You know, I can see that we need to protect him from assassination while he's on British soil, but I'd be a lot happier if he just went back to Russia. And I don't understand why we're offering guys like him the keys to our country. You know this road, half the houses are owned by Russians and most of the rest by Arabs. And at any one time most of the owners aren't even here." He shook his head. "I don't know why we don't just put a huge for sale sign up over our country and have done with it."

Button looked at him with narrowed eyes. "Are you OK?"

"I'm fine." He looked at his watch. "It's just a bit depressing seeing someone who has so much when you know that most of the population is struggling to just get by. I've got to go, Grechko is at the Mayfair Bar tonight so there's a lot to do."

"How much time off are you getting?"

"Why do you ask?"

"Because you look tired, Spider. Your eyes are so dark you look like a panda. Are you getting much sleep?"

Shepherd laughed despite himself. "I don't need mothering, Charlie."

"No, but you do need time off. There's no point in you being with Grechko twenty-four-seven if you're making yourself ill. I understand how stressful this is."

"So what are you suggesting? I take a break?"

"Let me see if I can get someone to share the workload," she said. "Babysitting Grechko is probably a two-man job until we get the guy that's after him."

"I might know someone," said Shepherd.

"I'm listening."

"Former Regiment guy. Jock McIntyre. He's left the SAS and is working security now but it wouldn't take much to get him to join me. I could probably get Grechko to pay his wages, too. But he'd need to know that he was on board with your approval because he only trusts his own people."

"Why did this McIntyre leave?"

"He's put in close to twenty years. Honourable discharge and all that. Bloody good operator, I was with him in Afghanistan."

"And he's up to speed on personal protection?"

"Like I said, he's working security at the moment. I can vouch for him." Shepherd knew that he wasn't actually lying to Button, but he was definitely stretching the truth. But she was right, he did need back-up, and it would be useful having McIntyre close by rather than having him running back and forth from Reading.

"Let me run a background check on him and I'll let you know. Have you got his date of birth?"

"I'll text you later today," said Shepherd.

Button nodded and climbed into the car. "You take care, Spider," she said. "And try at least to get a few early nights."

She closed the door and started the engine. Shepherd waved at the guard in the guardhouse and as the car purred down the driveway the massive black gates swung open.

As Shepherd walked back to the house, he phoned Jock McIntyre. "Jock, fancy a bit of real work?"

"What do you have in mind?"

"Helping me babysit that Russian I told you about. I can probably get you a couple of hundred quid a day. It means you can stay in London while we handle the other thing."

"I'm your man," said McIntyre. "Anything to get me out of this bloody office block. It's doing my head in."

"OK, first things first. I need your date of birth and your National Insurance number, they'll want to run a check on you. You haven't been in trouble, have you?"

McIntyre chuckled. "I've been as good as gold, mate."

"Terrific. Text me those numbers and make sure you've got a half-decent suit. I'll call you when it's sorted. You can live in, the security guys have their own quarters."

"This is getting better by the minute," said McIntyre.

Shepherd ended the call and weighed the phone in his hand as he headed around to the rear of the house. He hoped that he hadn't made a mistake in trusting McIntyre. But at least Shepherd would be able to keep an eye on him while he was based at Grechko's mansion. And he would be close at hand when the time came to move against Ahmad Khan.

Two days after Shepherd had given the iPad and tracking device to Shortt, he got a late night phone call from Harper. "All done," said Harper, "Are you up for a meet?"

"Tonight?" Shepherd looked at his watch. It was just after ten and he'd only just arrived back at his flat.

"Strike while the iron's hot," said Harper.

"Can't we at least meet in a pub?" said Shepherd. "This park thing is getting on my nerves."

"I can get a cab to yours if that's easier," said Harper. "Got anything decent to drink?"

"Few bottles of lager and a bottle of Jamesons."

"Jamesons will do. With ice. Text me the address and I'll come on over."

Shepherd's door entry system buzzed less than half an hour later and he pressed the button to open the downstairs door. Harper waited until he was in the flat before taking off his parka. He tossed it on a chair and pulled a face as he looked around. "Bloody hell, mate, they're clearly not paying you enough to be a spook."

"It's a cover flat," said Shepherd, pouring slugs of whiskey into two glasses.

Harper went over to look at the framed photographs of Shepherd. In a couple he was in police uniform, and in one he was in full CO19 gear. "Photoshop?" he said.

"Nah, I dressed up for that picture a few years ago," said Shepherd, dropping ice into the glasses and adding soda to his own.

Harper went over to study the contents of Shepherd's bookshelves. "So who are you? In case anyone asks?"

"Tony Ryan, Specialist Firearms Officer with the Met," said Shepherd, handing one of the glasses to Harper.

Harper raised it in salute. "Nice to meet you, Tony," he said, and drank half of it before dropping down on to the sofa. "So you have full ID, driving licence, passport, all in the name of this Ryan."

"Sure," said Shepherd, sitting down. "But before you even ask, the answer's no, I can't get paperwork for you."

"Wouldn't dream of asking," said Harper. "Besides, I've got my own people for that." He reached over to his parka and pulled a folded sheet of paper from the pocket. He gave it to Shepherd and leant back, stretching out his legs. "So, Ahmad Khan has a job. He works at an Asian supermarket in Shepherd's Bush. Big place, a lot of restaurants use it, cash and carry. Jimbo did a walk around and saw him stacking shelves and a while later he was manning one of the cash registers. He got there at eight in the morning and left at seven."

"He drove there?"

Harper nodded. "Parked around the back in a staff parking area. It's not overlooked so it'd be a perfect place to pick him up, either first thing when he arrives or later when he's leaving. We could be there with a van and he'd be in the back before he had any idea what was going on."

"What's his home situation?"

Harper grinned. "Yeah, Jimbo did his secret squirrel thing while Khan was at the supermarket." He nodded at the piece of paper. "The details are there. His daughter was at home and she was happy enough to talk to him. Her name's Najela and she's nineteen."

"Definitely the daughter?"

"That's what she said. And her English is good, Jimbo said. She's a student studying at a local college."

"What about her mother?"

"Just the two of them. Jimbo asked about the mother but all she said was that she was dead."

"And she's from Afghanistan?"

Harper nodded. "Kabul," she said. "She said her father was a teacher and left after he'd been persecuted by the Taliban."

"Well, that's a crock," said Shepherd.

"Khan isn't short of money. They're renting the house and have been for five years or so. Najela works part time at a Citizens Advice Bureau and she's a translator for the local council."

Shepherd nodded thoughtfully. "Anything else?"

"That's it, pretty much. Jimbo said he didn't want to push it too hard. So we do it, right? We pick him up and we slot him?"

Shepherd nodded. "We need ammo," he said.

"Ammo's not a problem," said Harper. "I know a man."

"It's got to be totally untraceable," said Shepherd. "There's no point in using weapons from Afghanistan if the ammo points to Brixton gangbangers."

"Give me some credit, Spider. I'm not a virgin at this."

"You know about the Makarov specs, right?"

"You mean 9.22 millimetre? Sure." He grinned. "I'm not the wet-behind-the-ears Para you knew back in Afghanistan. I've come on a bit since then."

"Apologies," said Shepherd. "But you're sure you can get it?"

"Russian stuff has been flooding into this country ever since the Soviet Union fell apart," said Harper. "Cheap, too. Your average gangbanger wants a nice shiny Glock or an Ingram or a Uzi. He thinks a Russian gun isn't as cool because he doesn't see them up on the big screen. Now your Bosnians and Serbs are quite happy to use a Russian gun, and London is full of them. Getting ammo will be a breeze. What about the longs? Do you want to use them?"

"AKs are noisy," said Shepherd. "We can make suppressors for the shorts but there's nothing you can do to quieten a Kalashnikov."

"We don't have to fire them. Just the look of an AK tends to make people do as they're told."

"The voice of experience?"

Harper laughed. "What can I say?"

"It seems like overkill," said Shepherd. "I assume we're doing this up close and personal. If we were planning a drive-by the AK would be the weapon of choice, but we're not."

"Four men, two guns, doesn't seem right, that's all."

"There's concealment, too. Even with the folding stock, the AK-47 is a big weapon. You could tuck it under an overcoat but even so it's bulky."

"Might be useful if armed cops show up."

Shepherd's eyes narrowed. "Please tell me you're joking."

Harper leaned over and slapped him on the shoulder. "Of course I am, you daft sod."

"Because we're not getting into a shoot-out with cops." He pointed a finger at Harper. "Any sign of cops and we run like the wind. Same with collateral damage — there isn't to be any. We don't hurt his family, we don't hurt passers-by, and we certainly don't hurt cops. I think we should pick him up, in a vehicle, and take him somewhere quiet. And we have to think about the body."

"We should bury him with a pig, or at least a pork chop in his mouth," said Harper.

"Behave, Lex. We need to bury it somewhere where it'll never be found."

"Sounds like a plan," said Harper.

"I'm serious, Lex."

"I know you are, mate. And I'm with you one hundred per cent. But let me make a suggestion. The two Russian shorts are perfect for the job. Like you said, they'll muddy the waters. But we need four guns. I'll pick up two more when I buy the ammo."

"They mustn't be traceable."

"They won't be. I know a gangbanger south of the river who does them on sale or return."

"That'll work. But make sure you don't get stitched up."

"I trust these guys, it'll be fine. Do you have a preference?"

"Go for revolvers, that way we're not picking up cartridges."

"Consider it done." He drained his glass, stood up and patted Shepherd on the shoulder. "I'll give you a call when it's done."

Shepherd looked up at him. "How are you fixed for cash?"

Harper chuckled. "You offering me a handout?"

"You've got a thing about ID so I'm assuming you don't use ATMs, or banks."

"I've got a few internet bank accounts but you're right, most ATMs these days have cameras. I use safety deposit boxes. And hawala."

"Are you serious?"

"About the safety deposit boxes? Sure. I've got three in London, packed with cash, gold and a passport or two." He took his pack of cigarettes out and slipped one in his mouth.

"You know what I mean. Hawala."

Harper tilted his head and lit the cigarette. He blew smoke before answering. "You don't have to be a

Muslim to use hawala," he said. "Plenty of places in Thailand that'll take my cash," he said. "I've got a mate who dropped off a million baht with a guy in Pattaya yesterday. Today I can pick it up in sterling at any one of half a dozen places close to my hotel in Bayswater. Don't even have to use ID if I don't want to."

"How does that work?"

"It's buyer's choice," said Harper. "If you want to use a driving licence or a passport as an ID to collect, that's OK. But you can use a number, too. Produce the number, get the money. No questions asked."

"And you've never been ripped off?"

"Other than the commission charge, nope. The hawala system is more reliable than the banking system. Quicker, too." He grinned. "So I've no problems with money, thanks for asking. And the guns and ammo, they're on me."

Shepherd's mobile rang and he picked it up. It was Button. "I've got to take this," he said, and hurried over to the kitchen.

"Sorry to bother you so late but I've just heard back about your friend," she said. "Interesting chap, this McIntyre." Shepherd could tell from her tone that there was more to come, so he didn't say anything. "You didn't mention his drinking," said Button eventually.

"Everyone drinks," said Shepherd.

"But not everyone gets into fights with civilians in pubs," said Button.

"Hereford's funny like that," said Shepherd. "The town's proud of its association with the SAS, but you get more than your fair share of local hard men trying to prove how hard they are. It happened to all of us at some point — you're having a quiet drink and some idiot on steroids will ask you if you're SAS and why you're not wearing your balaclava and did you come in through the window and all that nonsense, and you know it's leading up to the 'so how hard are you?' question and then fists start flying."

"And how do you handle that?"

"I never got to that stage," said Shepherd. "I always used to say I sold life insurance and if that didn't work I'd just walk away."

"Pity that Mr McIntyre didn't use the same technique," said Button. "He's been in a few scrapes, I see."

"He's a highly trained soldier who's seen action in some of the world's most dangerous places," said Shepherd. "Iraq, Afghanistan, Sierra Leone. You've got to expect him to blow off a little steam every now and again."

"And you said he was in the security business?" Shepherd winced in anticipation of what he knew was coming. "You failed to mention that he was a security guard and that he spends most of his time sitting at a reception desk in an office building in Reading."

"He's working. A job's a job."

"Look, I get that he's a friend, and I get that you served together in the SAS. But are you absolutely sure he's up for close personal protection with a man like Peter Grechko?"

"I'm sure," said Shepherd, but even as he said the words there was a nagging doubt at the back of his mind and he remembered the way that McIntyre's hand had shaken as he'd poured whisky in his miserable little room.

"He's to stay off the booze," said Button.

"He knows that."

"And he's to keep quiet about his SAS background, I don't want him getting all competitive with Grechko's people."

"No problem."

"And I need you to keep a close eye on him. He's your responsibility."

"He'll do just fine. And I'll feel happier with him around. I can rely on Jock one hundred per cent, which is something I can't say for Grechko's security team."

"What's the problem?" asked Button.

"They're clearly not happy about having an outsider telling them what to do," he said. "Let's just say that if Grechko is ever in the firing line, I'll be the one thrown in front of the bullet."

Button laughed. "Well, make sure you're wearing a vest," she said. "OK, I'll go with you on this. He's worked undercover before?"

"We all do undercover scenarios during selection," said Shepherd. "And he's been on undercover ops."

"Then I'll put together a legend and email it to you," she said. "We'll have him down as a security expert with a military background and I'll tell Grechko that we've used him before and that he's there as a back-up."

"As soon as you've done that, I'll take him over to the house," said Shepherd. "He can bunk down with

Grechko's team. He was one of the SAS's linguists and he speaks reasonable Russian so that'll be useful."

"Just make sure he knows he's to be on his best behaviour," said Button.

The line went dead. Shepherd went back into the sitting room. Harper was grinning like a naughty schoolboy. "What?" he said.

"Your voice changes," said Harper.

"What do you mean?"

"That was your boss, right? The woman?"

"Charlie, yeah."

Harper's grin widened. "Well, your voice changes when you talk to her. It goes softer. Lovey-dovey, in fact. It's like she gets you in touch with your feminine side."

"Bollocks," said Shepherd.

"Just saying, it's nice to see a softer, gentler Spider, that's all," said Harper.

"Carry on taking the piss like this and I'll show you my softer side all right," said Shepherd. "Charlie Button's my boss, end of." He could see from the look on Harper's face that he didn't believe him and that there was no point in trying to convince him otherwise. He sighed and poured another slug of Jamesons into his glass.

Harper spent the next day holed up in his hotel watching television and eating pizza delivered by Domino's. The Polish lady who cleaned the rooms seemed happy enough when he told her that he'd make his own bed and that he didn't need a change of towels.

He waited until it was dark before heading out and as always kept his head down and his parka hood up as he walked along the street. He let three black cabs go by him before holding up his arm and flagging down the fourth. He waited until he had climbed in the back before telling the driver where he wanted to go — a street close to Clapham railway station. It was starting to get dark and most vehicles had switched on their lights. He took out his cigarettes but then saw the no smoking sign on the glass panel behind the driver's head. He settled back in his seat as the cab crawled over the Thames.

The street lights were on when the cab dropped him off. He kept his head down as he walked along the street, his hands thrust deep in the pockets of his parka. It was a rough area, where the cops tended to drive by mob-handed in grey vans, and where street muggings happened so often that they weren't even mentioned in the local paper. A stabbing would be dismissed in a couple of paragraphs and the paper had long since given up printing police requests for witnesses as no one ever came forward.

There were two large black men in Puffa jackets standing in front of the house. It was in the middle of a run-down terrace and one of the few that hadn't been converted into flats. The two men were both wearing wraparound sunglasses and leather gloves and they stared at Harper with unsmiling faces as he walked along the pavement towards them. The bigger of the two men, his shaved head glistening in the light from a street lamp just feet away, clenched and unclenched his fists.

Harper kept his head down until he was right in front of them, then he looked up at the bigger man and grinned. "Bloody hell, T-Bone, you're not planning to stick one on me, are you?"

The big man's face creased into a grin. "Lex bloody Harper? Fuck me, a blast from the past." He stepped forward and grabbed Harper before hugging him to his massive chest. Harper gasped as the big man forced the air from his lungs.

"Steady, mate, don't break me," said Harper.

"Fuck me, you're a sight for sore eyes," said T-Bone, as he released him. "How long's it been? Three years? Four?" He put a hand around the back of his neck and squeezed.

"Four, I guess," said Harper. He shook hands with T-Bone, and then bumped shoulders.

T-Bone looked at his companion, who was watching them with amusement. "This here's Lex Harper, aka Harpic."

"You're the only one who calls me that," said Harper,

"Because you're clean round the bend," laughed T-Bone, thumping Harper on the shoulder. "This here's Jelly."

Jelly reached out with a hand the size of a small shovel and shook with Harper. "You buying?" asked Jelly as he bumped shoulders with Harper. He had his Puffa jacket open and a gold medallion the size of a saucer dangled in the middle of his chest from a thick gold chain. There were heavy gold rings, most of them sovereigns, on each of his fingers, though they looked to Harper to be more like makeshift knuckledusters than decoration.

T-Bone laughed. "Harpic here don't need to buy gear from us, he's big-time. He's a player. Isn't that right, Harpic? You're a player now." He gestured at Harper's parka and grinned at Jelly. "Don't let the homeless threads fool you. He's worth millions."

"Good to see my PR's doing a decent job," said Harper. "Actually I need something. Is Perry in?"

"Yeah, 'course," said T-Bone.

A black Golf drove down the road, rap music booming through its open windows. They all turned to look as the car drove by. There were four black teenagers in baseball caps but they were laughing and passing a joint around and T-Bone and Jelly relaxed.

"Everything OK?" asked Harper.

"We're having a bit of a turf war with some Somalians but it's all good," said T-Bone. He clapped Harper on the shoulder. "Come on, I'll take you in, but stay behind me and I'll pull Perry's chain."

He opened the front door and walked down a purple-painted hallway. He walked like a weightlifter on his way to attempt a personal best, his arms bent at the elbows and swinging in time with his steps. Harper followed. He could smell the distinctive aroma of smouldering marijuana and from upstairs came the pounding beat of a Bob Marley track.

T-Bone stopped at a door and pushed it open. From inside, Harper heard the rat-tat-tat of a video game being played at full volume. "Hey, Perry, remember that Scottish prick you keep talking about. What was his name? Your old mate. The one who went out to Spain?"

"Lex? Lex Harper."

"Yeah, Lex. Turns out he's a grass."

"What the fuck are you talking about?"

"He's spilling his guts to Five-O. He's a bloody supergrass."

"No fucking way."

"That's the word. I always knew he was a bad 'un." T-Bone slapped his hand against the wall.

"Lex Harper? A grass? You sure about this?"

"Sure enough to put a bullet in his head next time I see him." T-Bone stepped into the room. "Bloody grass."

The room went quiet as the video game was paused. "This is bullshit," said Perry Smith.

"You always said you never trusted him, remember?"

"T-Bone, what the fuck are you on?"

Harper heard footsteps and then T-Bone moved to the side so that Perry could see him. Perry flinched and took a step backwards, then burst into laughter, revealing a mouthful of gold teeth. "Lex, you bastard!" he shouted.

Harper pushed the hood of his parka down. "Long time, no see, mate," he said. The two men hugged, then Smith put his hands on Harper's shoulders and held him at arm's length as he stared at him, shaking his head in amazement. "What the hell are you doing here?"

"Just wanted to see the new pad. You're coming up in the world, aren't you? This is better than that rathole you used to have in Streatham."

The two men hugged again and Smith patted him on the back, hard. Smith grinned at T-Bone. "I knew you were pulling my chain, bastard," he said. "Lex here's one of the best." He released his grip on Harper and waved to one of three sofas around a square coffee table that was home to three tall bongs and a large silver bowl piled high with a white powder. Above the table was a white paper spherical lampshade that must have been three feet across.

A huge TV dominated one wall, with a heavily armed trooper in mid-flow, blowing apart two men holding rocket launchers. Harper laughed. "Still one for the video games, Perry?" he said as he sat down.

Perry laughed back. "It's training, innit?" He sat down next to Harper and pointed at the cocaine. "Help yourself." He flashed T-Bone a thumbs-up and the heavy headed back to the front door. "Hell, man, it's great to see you. When was the last time?"

"Brixton. Four years ago. The Fridge."

Smith laughed. "That's right. But it ain't the Fridge no more. Electric Brixton they call it now."

"Yeah? A rose by any other name, yeah?"

"You introduced me to the Dutchman there, remember? Seven years ago. Vouched for me and that. That made me a stack of money, man. That connection made me."

"Glad to have helped, Perry."

"I'm serious, man. You always looked out for me."

"And vice versa, mate."

There was a glossy magazine with a razor blade and a silver tube the size of a biro on it. Harper pulled it closer to him and used the blade to take a dollop of cocaine from the bowl. He used small, economical movements to divide the powder into four equal lines and then used the tube to snort up two of the lines. He felt the kick almost immediately and sat back, nodding his approval. "That's good," he said. A second wave coursed through his bloodstream stronger than the first. "Very good."

"Only the best for you, brother," said Smith. He pulled the magazine towards him and did the remaining two lines. "So where's your money these days? I've had to close down my Isle of Man accounts, and my Swiss accounts. And I hear the EU is after Jersey now."

Harper shrugged. "I'm spreading it around," he said. "I'm putting a lot in property owned by offshore companies. You can't trust the banks any more. And gold. Gold in safe deposit boxes is the way to go."

"Funny old world, innit? First cash was king, then they made us jump through hoops to get it in the banking system, and now we're trying to get out the banks."

Harper laughed. "Don't get me started, mate," he said. "I reckon it's a global conspiracy."

Smith piled more cocaine on to the magazine and split it into four lines. "So to what do I owe the pleasure?" he said. "I mean, always great to see you, Lex, but I'm assuming you want something."

Harper rubbed the bridge of his nose. He could feel his pulse racing as the cocaine coursed through his veins. He had a sudden urge to get up and walk around but he knew that was just the drug talking and he ignored it. "I've been away for a while and I need some chrome."

"Thought you always used Ks?"

Harper grinned. "That was back in the day. I need something small but with a kick. Can you help me out?"

"Open all hours," said Smith, leaning over the magazine and snorting up one of the lines. "You know me. You getting back into the blagging game?"

Harper shook his head. "Nah, this is personal."

Smith snorted a second line and then sat back, his eyes wide.

"T-Bone can sort you out, I can't keep it on the premises, Five-O keep kicking my door open. Looking for drugs, they say." Smith laughed and wiped the back of his nose with his hand.

"Do they ever find any?" asked Harper.

Smith waved at the remaining lines of cocaine. Harper grinned, reached for one of the tubes and snorted two lines, one up each nostril. "We're always clean as a whistle because we know when they're coming."

Harper took a deep breath and blinked a couple of times. It was very good coke. As good as anything he'd had before. "Where did you get this from?" he asked.

"The Serbs," Smith said. "They've got a deal going with one of the Colombian cartels." He laughed and squeezed Harper's knee, hard enough to hurt. "But if you want to place an order, Lex, you talk to me. You hear?"

"Loud and clear," said Harper. "But I was just asking. I don't do much coke, and definitely not out of South America. The DEA's all over that bit of the hemisphere and they're bad news."

"I only deal with the Serbs, and they're cool."

"Yeah, everybody's cool until the DEA starts offering deals," said Harper. "I'm sticking with dope these days, pretty much. That's practically legal now. And E. Can't go wrong with E."

"Coke's where the money is, though," said Smith. "Coke and crack." He stretched out his arms and arched his back. "Still in Spain?"

"Some of the time."

Smith laughed. "You always did play your cards close to your chest, man," he said, and squeezed his knee again. "You need any help with this personal matter then you call me, you hear me?"

"I hear you," said Harper. "But this one is complicated. There's a few other guys involved." He stood up and held out his arms. Smith stood up and the two men hugged.

Smith walked Harper to the front door and hugged him again before showing him out. Another heavy had joined Jelly on the doorstep and they both watched as T-Bone and Harper walked over to T-Bone's black Porsche SUV. "Nice motor," said Harper. T-Bone climbed in and Harper joined him. "I'm thinking of getting a Bentley. The convertible."

Harper laughed. "A black man in a Bentley? Why don't you just draw a target on your back?"

"They pull me over whatever I'm driving," said T-Bone, starting the engine. "But they never find nothing." He waved over at the two men outside the house and they nodded back. T-Bone drove to Streatham and parked in front of a row of six brick-built lock-up garages with metal doors and corrugated iron roofs in an alley a short distance from the town centre. He switched off the engine and the two men climbed out of the SUV and looked around. There was the hum of traffic in the distance but other than that it was quite. There was half a moon overhead but there were no street lights and it took Harper's eyes a while to get accustomed to the dark. T-Bone opened the back of the Porsche and took out a large black Magnalite torch. He switched it on but kept it pointing at the ground as he walked over to one of the lock-ups in the middle of the row. He pulled a set of keys from his Puffa jacket, selected one and used it to unlock the door. It went up and over but T-Bone raised it only a few feet before ducking under and waving at Harper to follow him.

There were four metal trunks lined up in the middle of the lock-up and a stack of wooden packing cases against the far wall. There was a cloying, damp smell mixed with an acrid tang that suggested an animal had been using the place as a toilet.

"Pull the door down," said T-Bone.

"You're not going to rape me, are you?" asked Harper.

338

"With your straggly white arse? You couldn't be farther from being my type if you'd been on a plane for twelve hours," said T-Bone. "Now stop pissing around and pull the door down so I can switch the light on."

Harper did as he was told and once the door hit the ground T-Bone flicked a switch and a solitary fluorescent light flickered into life. He switched off the torch and slid it into his pocket. "So what do you need, Harpic?"

"A couple of revolvers," said Harper. "Russian would be good. And if you really wanted to make my day, I'd love a couple of Makarovs. Failing that a revolver, but again I'd prefer Russian."

"Bloody hell, Harpic, when did you get so fussy?"

"It's a special situation. Can do?"

T-Bone frowned and shook his head. "Sorry. I don't have any Makarovs. I do have a few Russian pistols but they're semi-automatics."

"Nah, I need revolvers."

"I've got a couple of Colt KingCobras."

"How long are the barrels?"

"Six inches."

Harper pulled a face. "I'm looking for something to easily pull out of a pocket."

T-Bone nodded. "I've got some very nice Smith & Wessons, the Five Hundred short barrel. Four-inch barrel, only holds five rounds but it packs one hell of a punch. Five-hundred calibre, weighs almost three pounds."

"That's heavy," said Harper.

"Yeah, well, like I said, it packs a punch."

"Maybe something a bit more traditional."

T-Bone nodded and bent over one of the trunks. He released two catches and opened the lid to reveal several dozen packages in see-through Ziploc plastic bags. "How about a Smith & Wesson Model 629?" he said, rooting through the packages. "It's a .44 Magnum. It only holds six rounds but it has a three-inch barrel." He passed a package over to Harper and straightened up with a grunt. "I've got some Model 627s as well. They take eight rounds but the barrel is an inch longer."

Harper unzipped the bag and took out the gun. It was wrapped in oiled cloth and looked brand new. "It weighs forty-two ounces," said T-Bone. "You won't get much lighter than that, not without losing a lot of stopping power."

Harper weighed the gun in his palm. "This feels OK," he said. He looked down the sights and then flicked the cylinder open and closed. "Yeah, I like this. You've got two?"

T-Bone bent down, rooted through a package and pulled one out. "There you go."

"Price?"

"A grand and a half."

"For the pair?"

"Each."

"Three grand?"

"Maths is clearly your strong suit, yeah?"

"Three grand for two guns?"

"They're mint. Never been fired. They were stolen from a gun shop in LA last year. Absolutely untraceable. Take them away for three grand and if you don't fire them I'll pay you fifteen hundred to take them back."

"Rounds?"

"What do you want?"

"A box'll be fine."

"Box of twenty? You can have that for free. We got a deal?"

Harper nodded. "Yeah, we've got a deal." He put down the gun and took a envelope from the inside pocket of his parka. He rippled his finger over the fifty-pound notes it contained until he had counted out sixty of them. He handed them over to T-Bone. "I need something else, ammo-wise," he said. "I need rounds for a Makarov."

"You've got a thing for Russian guns?" said T-Bone, pocketing the cash.

"For this particular gun, yeah. I just need a box of ammo."

"Small gun, right? Nine-mill?" He closed the lid of the trunk and opened another. It was full of boxes of ammunition.

"It's more complicated than that," said Harper. "They talk about the Makarov being a nine-millimetre but the round is actually 9.22. The Russkies did that deliberately so the NATO forces couldn't use captured Soviet ammunition."

"Smart." T-Bone picked up a box of shells and tossed them to Harper.

"Paranoid, more like. Plus it meant they wouldn't be able to use any ammo they took from NATO soldiers. So six of one, really."

"But what you're saying is that it needs special ammo?" He closed the lid of the trunk.

"Yeah. Have you got any?"

T-Bone shook his head. "Nah, but I can probably get some. Let me make a call."

He took out his flashlight and switched it on, then switched off the fluorescent light. Harper pulled the door up and they both slipped underneath it and out into the alley. T-Bone locked the door. "You get in the car," he said to Harper. "I'll make that call."

T-Bone drove to Shepherd's Bush. The Porsche's satnav told them that they were arriving at their destination and Harper shook his head in disgust. "You've got to be careful with those things, T-Bone," he said. "The cops can use them to find out wherever you've been." They were heading for a supermarket with a large car park. The supermarket was open twenty-four hours a day but it was almost eleven o'clock and there were only a few cars there.

"Don't see how else I'd have found this place, it's well out of my comfort zone," said T-Bone.

"I'm just saying, it stores every location you've ever been to and the route you used." He gestured at the screen. "And here's the thing, it does that even if it's switched off."

"Bullshit," growled T-Bone.

342

"I kid you not. You think the thing's off but it's not. And it's all in there. Same as your mobile. Switching it off makes no difference. And the spooks, man, they can listen in to a phone even when it's off."

"Says who?"

"Says me, and I know people. People who know. The only way to silence a phone is to take out the battery. It used to be that you could get away with just changing SIM cards, but now it's the phone itself they use. Once they've got the IMEI number, they've got you."

"IMEI?"

"International Mobile Station Equipment Identity. Every phone has one. You can check yours by tapping in star hash zero six hash. Now in the good old days they tracked the IMSI number which is stored on the SIM. But now they go after the IMEI. And like I said, switching off the phone doesn't help."

"So what do you do, Harpic?"

"Me? I buy cheap phones and chuck them every couple of weeks."

They saw a grey Range Rover parked at the far end of the supermarket car park with its lights off. "That's them," said T-Bone.

"They've come all the way out here for a box of ammo?"

"We do a lot of business with them and I'm due a favour or two," said T-Bone. He brought the car to a halt about fifty feet away from the Range Rover.

"How much do I owe you?"

T-Bone laughed. "It's on me," he said. "I overcharged you on the guns." He switched off his lights.

"I know," said Harper. "But as I was paying with counterfeit notes, I figured what the hell."

T-Bone's hand was halfway inside his Puffa jacket when he realised that Harper was joking. "You stay here. They're not great with new faces." T-Bone climbed out of the SUV, flexed his shoulders, and walked slowly and purposefully over to the Range Rover.

Harper looked around. A young woman walked out of the store pushing a trolley laden with carrier bags. A bearded old man in a cheap cloth coat and a piece of rope for a belt spoke to her, presumably asking for a handout, but she hurried past. A white van pulled into the car park and stopped in a handicapped space. The fat man in blue overalls who climbed out of the van didn't appear to have any disabilities as he strode into the supermarket.

Harper looked back at the Range Rover. T-Bone was still walking slowly towards it, his hands swinging freely, his gloved hands clenching and unclenching like those of a cowboy preparing for a fast draw. For the first time the vulnerability of his situation struck home. He was in someone else's car, in a place he wasn't familiar with, while a drug-dealing gangster walked towards a car full of people he didn't know who were almost certainly armed. Harper trusted T-Bone but he didn't know the men in the Range Rover. Plus T-Bone had three thousand pounds in his pocket. Harper fumbled one of the packages out of his pocket. He unzipped the plastic bag and unwrapped the cloth to reveal the chromed revolver. The box of rounds was in his inside pocket and he pulled it open. The box was sealed and he used his teeth to rip off the plastic wrapping before pulling it open. He flicked out the cylinder and quickly slotted in six rounds. He clicked the cylinder back into place and slid the box back into his inside pocket. He sat with the gun between his legs, his finger outside the trigger guard, as he watched T-Bone walk up to the Range Rover. The window wound down and Harper tensed. His brain went into overdrive as he breathed slowly and evenly, his mind running through all the options. T-Bone had left the keys in the Porsche so if push came to shove he could jump over into the driving seat and drive off. But T-Bone was a friend, and a good one, so if it did all turn to shit Harper would have no choice other than to get out of the car and start shooting. And he was all too aware of how few rounds he had in the revolver. Six shots were more than enough to put down a man, but they wouldn't be much use against a sturdy vehicle like a Range Rover.

The cocaine he'd taken with Smith still had all his senses in overdrive and he took slow, deep breaths to steady himself as he watched T-Bone take out a handful of banknotes and hand them through the front passenger window of the Range Rover. Harper tensed. If it was going to happen it was going to happen now. His right hand tightened on the gun and his left reached over for the door handle. He'd already decided what he was going to do — if they shot T-Bone he'd be out of the car before his friend hit the ground, two quick shots at the driver through the windscreen as he walked towards the car and then he'd have to play it by ear, making each of the remaining four shots count. The gun began to tremble between his legs and he took another deep breath.

T-Bone's hand reappeared, this time holding a small box. Harper caught a flash of white teeth and then T-Bone nodded and turned back to the Porsche. After a few steps the Range Rover's lights came on full beam, blinding Harper. He flinched and turned away, expecting a hail of bullets, but they never came. The headlights dipped and the Range Rover edged towards the exit.

Harper shoved the gun in his pocket as T-Bone pulled open the door and slid into the driving seat. He slammed the door shut and tossed the box of Russian cartridges into Harper's lap. He looked down at the footwell and saw the scraps of plastic from the ammunition box. "You OK, Harpic?"

"All good, T-Bone," said Harper.

"You don't need to be paranoid all the time. There are some good people out there." The Range Rover blipped its horn and turned into the main road.

"Just because I'm paranoid doesn't mean they're not out to get me," said Harper, pulling up the hood and settling back in his seat.

Shepherd's mobile rang and he groped around for it. He was lying on his sofa watching an old Van Damme movie on Sky. Van Damme was undercover but no one seemed to care that he had a Belgian accent or a very dodgy haircut. Shepherd squinted at the phone's display but the number was being withheld. "Yeah?" he said.

"It's me," said a voice. Lex Harper.

"Hello, you."

"I need to see you."

"Bloody hell, it's almost midnight."

"I've got something for you. Can't have them hanging around my place, there's some very shady characters staying there."

"I've got to be up at six."

"You're way past the stage of needing your beauty sleep. It'll only take a few minutes."

"No offence, mate, but I'm not over the moon about you popping around to the flat late at night. Once was OK but it's not cool to make a habit of it. I've got neighbours and there's a little old lady opposite who's big with the Neighbourhood Watch."

"No problem. I can meet you on the Heath."

"At this time of night? They'll think we're cottaging."

"I'll see you at Preacher's Hill," said Harper. "It's well away from Jack Straw's Castle so no cottaging there. I'm here now and there's no sign of George Michael. Put on your running gear and pop over. And don't forget your rucksack full of bricks."

Harper ended the call. Shepherd groaned and rolled off the sofa. He was wearing a polo shirt and jeans so he quickly changed into an old sweatshirt and baggy tracksuit bottoms and pulled on the old pair of trainers.

His rucksack was still in Hereford but he had a small Nike backpack in his bedroom and he put that on before heading out. Preacher's Hill was just a few minutes from his flat, a small triangular section of woodland separated from the main Heath by East Heath Road.

Harper was already sitting on a bench, not far from a children's playground, smoking a cigarette, his face obscured by the hood of his parka. Shepherd sat down next to him. "Yeah, this is good, two men sitting by a kiddies' playground, that won't attract attention," he said.

"It's midnight, all the kids are safe home in bed," said Harper. "Anyway, this won't take long. Take your bag off." He flicked ash on to the path.

Shepherd took off the bag and unzipped it. Harper took a furtive look around then slid his hand into his right pocket and took out a plastic bag. He gave it to Shepherd, who shoved it into the backpack. Harper took another package from his left pocket and that too went inside the backpack.

"What are they?" asked Shepherd.

"Smith & Wesson 629s, they're .44 Magnums."

"Six in the chamber," said Shepherd.

"Yeah, but six Magnums. Hit a guy in the arm and the arm comes off. One head shot and there's nothing else."

"Bloody loud, too."

"Spider, mate, will you stop looking a gift horse in the mouth. There's three grand's worth of chrome in there." He looked around again before reaching into his inside pocket and pulling out two boxes of ammunition. "Four-fours for the Magnums, and rounds for the Makarovs."

Shepherd slid the boxes into the backpack and zipped it up.

"When are we going to do it?" asked Harper.

"We need to have a sit-down with Jimbo and Jock."

"Sure, but you and me are pulling the trigger, right? We've got more invested in this."

Shepherd nodded. "I guess so."

"There's no 'guess so' about it," hissed Harper. "Three of my muckers died out there, shot in the back. And he killed Captain Todd right in front of you."

"I know, but Jimbo and Jock are involved."

"Yeah, well, it's the difference between the pig and the chicken."

"What the hell are you talking about?"

"Breakfast, mate. Eggs and bacon. The chicken's involved but the pig's committed. I'm committed to this. And I think you are too, right?"

"Sure."

"You don't sound convinced." Harper leant forward and rested his elbows on his knees, his left hand cupping his right. His cigarette smouldered and the smoke made Shepherd's eyes water. "We have to do this, you know that?"

"I'm not disputing that. He shot me, remember? Damn near killed me. But we have to do this right."

Harper took a long pull on his cigarette and blew a tight plume of smoke across the grass. "Have you done anything like this before?"

Shepherd took a deep breath and exhaled slowly. "Yeah."

"In cold blood?"

"It's never in cold blood. But shot someone when they weren't a direct threat? Yes. I've done that."

"And we're not talking about sniping?"

Shepherd shook his head. "No. More recent." He sat back and folded his arms, a physical manifestation of how uncomfortable the conversation was making him feel. "But in a way, this is like sniping. If I'd had Khan in my sights back in Afghanistan, I'd have pulled the trigger and thought nothing of it. Half the kills I had in Afghanistan weren't a direct threat to me. Most of them wouldn't even have known what hit them. What we're going to do is payback. It's as if I pulled the trigger back in 2002, it's just that the bullet has taken more than a decade to arrive."

"Sniping's too good for him," said Harper. "I want him to see who puts the bullet in his head. I want him to know who's taking his life and I want him to know why. I want to put the first bullet in him, Spider. You can do what you want, but the first shot is mine."

"It means that much to you?"

"He killed my mates. Shot them in the back. Yes, it means that much to me."

Shepherd stared at Harper. He could see the hatred burning in the man's eyes and for the first time he understood just how Harper felt. Harper wanted revenge, and revenge wasn't always a dish best served cold.

★ ★ ★

Shepherd knew that he had to speak to Charlotte Button, but it wasn't the sort of conversation that he could have on the phone. By the time he got back to his flat it was almost one o'clock so he decided to leave it until the next day. He wasn't happy about hiding the guns and ammunition in the flat but he knew that it would be safer there than in Harper's hotel. There was a bucket of cleaning supplies in the cupboard under the sink and he hid them there, covering them with sponges, cleaning cloths and a bottle of Domestos.

He showered and went to bed, though he slept fitfully. He'd set his alarm for six but he was already awake when it started to ring. He wasn't sure what time Button got up but he left it until he was driving up to The Bishops Avenue before calling her on hands-free. "The early bird?" she said.

"There's a morning briefing at seven each morning and I like to be there for that," he said. "But we need to talk."

"Can you come to the office?"

"Let me see what Grechko's schedule is like," said Shepherd.

"I've got meetings back to back," she said. "It'll be really hard to get away today."

"It's important, but I'll call you back in about an hour," said Shepherd. He arrived at the gates to Grechko's house, wound down his window and waved at the CCTV camera. The gate rattled open and he drove through, waving at Yakov Gunter in the guardhouse. Gunter waved back and went back to reading his newspaper. Gunter was one of the recent

351

additions to the security team, one of the body-builder types who spent most of their time in the gym. His thick neck and overdeveloped biceps suggested that he was also abusing steroids, but Shepherd figured that was none of his business. He drove through the garage doors and down to the parking area in the basement. He left his X5 next to Podolski's motorcycle. She had left her black crash helmet sitting on one of the mirrors.

He used his thumb and four-digit code to get into the security centre, where Thomas Lisko was sipping coffee and watching the CCTV screens. Popov was already in the briefing room with Podolski, Dudko and Volkov. Podolski offered Shepherd coffee and he thanked her and took his place at the table. One of the chefs had already dropped off a plate of croissants and rolls and a platter of assorted meats and cheeses. Shepherd took an almond croissant and had just taken a bite when Tarasov walked in and sat down.

Popov handed around printed sheets and began the briefing. Grechko wasn't planning to leave the house but there were three visitors expected, one of his accountants, a Savile Row tailor and a watch dealer. Popov grinned at Shepherd. "Before all this he'd have been going to see them but he's summoned them here. I think he's quite warming to the idea."

"It certainly makes security a lot easier," said Shepherd. Podolski put a mug of coffee down in front of him and he smiled his thanks. "The visitors, they're all long-standing contacts?"

Popov nodded. "Mr Munroe has been Mr Grechko's tailor since before I joined his security team. Mr Adams is a senior partner of the accountancy firm that handles Mr Grechko's UK companies. And Mr Edwards has been to the house several times before. He is a well known watch dealer."

"Sounds good," said Shepherd. He looked at his watch. "I've got some things to do so I'll leave you to it. I'll be on my mobile if you need me." He went back out to the car, called Button to let her know that he was on his way, then slipped his Bluetooth earpiece into his pocket and switched off his transceiver. He waved at Gunter as he drove out through the gates, then called up Shortt on his hands-free. "Jimbo, can we have a meet at your place this afternoon?" he asked as he drove towards central London.

"No problem, she's at golf until five," said Shortt. "Shall I get snacks?"

Shepherd laughed. "Don't go to any trouble," he said.

He called McIntyre and told him that Charlotte Button had given him the green light.

"That's great news, I'll tell them where to stick their job," said McIntyre.

"I'll fix you up with a room at the house. Have you got a suit?"

"Are you being sarcastic?"

"I was just asking, Jock. We have to wear a suit and tie. Black if you've got it."

"I'll dig out my funeral suit. What other gear do I need?"

"A few changes of clothes. We can buy whatever else you need. Just pack a bag and I'll pick you up at Paddington station in a couple of hours."

"I'm on my way," said McIntyre.

Shepherd's final call was to Harper and he arranged to collect him from Bayswater later that morning.

The traffic was heavy and it took him almost an hour to get to Thames House. It was only after Shepherd had signed in that he remembered that he was still carrying his Glock. He smiled apologetically at the woman who had checked his credentials. "I'm sorry, I have a weapon," he said.

"That's all right," she said briskly. "You can leave it in our secure room. I'll get Brian to take you through."

A young man in a grey suit took Shepherd into a room with metal lockers covered by two CCTV cameras. Shepherd took off his jacket, then slipped off his shoulder holster and put it in a locker with the two extra ammunition clips. He was surprised to see a key in the lock; he'd been expecting something more high-tech. He took the key, slipped it into his trouser pocket and put his jacket on, all the time under the watchful eye of Brian and whoever was monitoring the CCTV.

He took the lift up to Button's office. Her secretary explained that she was busy and kept him waiting for a full thirty minutes before the door opened and two earnest young men in shirtsleeves walked out carrying armfuls of files. She smiled when she saw him and apologised for keeping him waiting. Her secretary put down a cup of tea for her and asked Shepherd if he

354

wanted anything. He declined and sat down while Button went back behind her desk.

"I had something of an epiphany last night," he said.

"That's good to hear."

"This Sasha Czernik. You think he was murdered after the bungled car bombing?"

"I'm trying to get the body exhumed but it's an uphill struggle. The Russian authorities aren't being cooperative."

"But you think he was murdered, right?"

"It's possible."

"So we have a killer who killed two oligarchs and is after a third."

"Assuming that Czernik was murdered, yes."

Shepherd rubbed the back of his neck. "Look, it doesn't seem likely that the Kremlin is going to use a sniper that can't hit his target. Suppose it's personal. Maybe the killer wants to get close when he kills. He wants the victim to know who his killer is."

"But that doesn't gel with a sniper, does it?"

"Here's the thing," said Shepherd. "Maybe the sniper isn't missing. Maybe he's aiming at the bodyguards."

"A killer with a grudge against bodyguards of the world's richest men?"

He grinned at her sarcasm. "Suppose that, as you say, the killer has a personal reason for killing these oligarchs. For some reason he wants them dead. But he wants them to know who has killed them and why. He wants them to see his face. He never intends to kill them with the rifle, or a bomb, because then they wouldn't know why they were dying. The first attempt is set up to deliberately fail so that he can get his man on the team and use him to get the intel he needs to get in close."

Button tilted her head to one side and nodded thoughtfully.

"Hurting a bodyguard, or almost blowing up a car, shows up shortcomings in security. So what does your regular neighbourhood oligarch do when he thinks his security has failed? He brings in more bodyguards."

"So our assassin shoots a bodyguard and then joins the security team? Becomes the inside man?"

"Easy enough to check," said Shepherd. "Get a list of the bodyguards who were on the team at the time of the sniping, and then compare it with the bodyguards in place at the time of the assassination."

"And if you're right, we'll find a common denominator who joined Zakharov's and Czernik's security," said Button. She nodded again. "It's worth a try. I'll get right on it. And you need to take a closer look at the new arrivals on Grechko's team. Find out what changes he made to his security team between the sniper attack and you going on board."

"You think the killer might already be there, in the house?"

"That's exactly what I think, Spider. So you be careful."

Shepherd collected his Glock from the secure room then drove to Queensway. Harper was waiting outside a Chinese restaurant with a line of smoked ducks in the window, his hands deep in the pockets of his parka and his head down. He jogged over to the SUV and climbed in. "So we're doing it?" asked Harper, as they drove towards Paddington station.

"Yeah," said Shepherd. "But we have to talk it through first."

McIntyre was waiting outside the station and he was carrying a black holdall. He tossed his bag on to the back seat and got in after it. He was wearing a black suit and a blue and black striped tie.

Shepherd didn't need the satnav, the route to Shortt's house was imprinted on his memory. The Jaguar was still in the driveway so he parked in the street and the three men walked to the house. Shortt had the front door open for them before they were halfway down the driveway and he hugged Harper and McIntyre and slapped Shepherd on the back before taking them inside.

Shortt made mugs of coffee and put them on the kitchen table, where there was already a bottle of Jamesons. Despite Shepherd's protests that he was driving, Shortt poured a slug of whiskey into each of the mugs. "To the good old days," he said, and they all raised their mugs and drank.

"Come on, sit down," said Shortt. He opened the fridge and took out a plate of sandwiches. He put them down next to the whiskey. "The little woman made us some scoff," he said, taking his seat.

"Remember the coffee in Afghanistan?" said Harper, spooning two sugars into his mug. "Tasted like mud."

"That was because of all the sand in it," said Shortt. "But it was crap coffee, that's true."

"The major always used to have his own private stash," said Shepherd. "Bought it at Fortnum and Mason." He saw the look of disbelief on Harper's face and grinned. "I'm serious. He brought it over in cans. Special biscuits, too. Dark chocolate Hobnobs."

"Now I know you're taking the piss," said Shortt. "The chocolate would melt."

"Swear to God," said Shepherd, sitting down on the sofa next to Harper. Shortt had commandeered the armchair and Jock McIntyre had turned around one of the wooden dining chairs and was resting his arms on its back. He poured another slug of whiskey into his mug. "So, let's get right down to it. It's definitely Ahmad Khan and he's alive and well and living in Hammersmith."

"Not for much longer," said Harper.

"The question is, what do we do now?" said Shepherd.

"We kill the fucker," said Harper. He mimed a gun with his right hand and faked two shots at the window. "Bang, bang. Double tap."

"That's the first thing we need to agree on," said Shepherd.

"Fuck me, if we're not of one mind on that then we might as well all go home," said Harper, throwing up his hands in exasperation.

"Lex, relax," said Shepherd. "This is a big thing and we all have to be absolutely sure of where we stand and where we're heading. If anyone is having second thoughts then now's the time to say so and to walk away with no hard feelings. Because from this point on it's going to be that much harder to walk away."

Harper look at Shortt and then at McIntyre. "Anyone want out?"

The two men shook their heads.

"Fuck, no," said McIntyre.

"Just so we're clear," said Shepherd speaking slowly and precisely. "Everything we've done up to this point is borderline legal. Certainly we wouldn't get sent down for anything that's happened this far."

"Except for the guns, and the ammo," said Harper.

"And breaking into Khan's house," said Shortt.

"And various abuses of the Data Protection Act," said McIntyre. He put up his hands. "Just saying."

"You didn't actually break into the house, Jimbo," said Shepherd. "You stood on the doorstep and asked a few questions." He grinned. "But I take your point, maybe borderline legal is stretching it. But the point I'm making is that anyone who wants to can still walk away. But from now on it's conspiracy to commit murder."

"It'd better be more than a conspiracy," said Harper. "Come on, Spider, get on with it. Let's hear the plan."

"Guys, let's just take a minute here. We've all taken lives before, but this is different. This isn't combat, this isn't kill or be killed. We need to be quite clear about what we're talking about. Murder. Cold-blooded murder."

"Yeah, well, revenge is a dish best served cold," said Harper. "Isn't that what they say?"

"That's what they say all right," said Shepherd. "But that doesn't make it right. Killing someone in the heat of battle, in a firefight or hand to hand, that's all well and good. Hell, that's what we were trained to do. But waiting more than ten years to kill a man when he's not expecting it, that's something else. It's a big thing and it's going to stay with us for ever."

He looked expectantly at Shortt. Shortt shrugged. "Bastard deserves to die," he said. "He killed the captain. He could just as easily have killed me." Shortt nodded at Harper. "He killed three of Lex's mates. Shot them in the back. For that alone he deserves to die."

McIntyre nodded in agreement. "He should have died back in Afghanistan for what he did. He damn well sure shouldn't be living in our country as if it never happened." He put his hand up. "If we're voting, my vote's for doing what we have to do."

Shepherd smiled thinly and nodded. "That's fine," he said. "I didn't want to sound like a wimp but I had to know that we're all of the same mind." He took a sip of coffee and put the mug down. "So the question now is who does what."

"I'm pulling the trigger," said Harper. "I've got dibs on that."

Shepherd ignored him. "We've got four shorts," he said. "Jimbo has two Makarovs and we've got two modern Smith & Wessons as back-up. The Makarovs are from Iraq so if they do get traced it'll muddy the waters. What we need to do now is to decide when and where." He could see that Harper was about to speak

360

so he silenced him with a cold look. "I know, the sooner the better. No question of that. But we can't just walk up to him in the street and put a bullet in his head. This isn't Afghanistan, this is London, and within minutes of a gunshot we'll have ARVs all over us."

"ARVs?" said McIntyre.

"Armed Response Vehicles," said Shepherd. "The capital's full of them. And even if we do slot him in the street, afterwards there'll be a full investigation, which means analysis of all CCTV in the area, speaking to witnesses, the works. Killing someone is easy, it's getting away with it that's difficult."

He picked up his coffee again and sipped it, making sure that he had their undivided attention.

"I'm going to suggest that we don't shoot him in the street, or in his house, or anywhere where there are potential witnesses. We pick him up at his place of work." He looked at Harper. "Where he leaves his car while he's working, right?"

Harper nodded. "It's not overlooked. Providing he's the only one in the car park, no one will see anything. Guaranteed."

"OK," continued Shepherd. "So we take him out to the New Forest, we do it there and we bury him where he'll never be found. That's the key to getting away with this. With no witnesses and no body, there'll be no investigation. Thousands of adults go missing every year and unless there are suspicious circumstances no one cares."

"What about his daughter?" asked Shortt. "She'll report him missing."

"Adults go missing all the time," said Shepherd. "Unless there are signs of violence, he'll just go on the list. If the body never turns up, there's no crime to investigate."

"The New Forest is miles away," said Harper. "There's plenty of places closer."

"We want to be out of the Met's jurisdiction," said Shepherd. "And if it is ever found, the farther away the better. It's driveable in ninety minutes or so and the roads are good."

"Makes sense," said McIntyre.

"So, logistics," said Shepherd. "We need a vehicle, ideally something untraceable, to transport Khan from the pick-up point to the New Forest."

"I'll get the car sorted," said Harper.

"A van would be better," said Shepherd. "No one pays attention to vans. But it can't be traced back to you, Lex. We'll clean it afterwards but that's no guarantee there won't be DNA or something left behind."

"Give me some credit, Spider," said Harper. "I wasn't planning on going to Hertz. I'll pick up a second-hand one for cash and won't bother registering it."

"Then clone a set of plates because these days London is awash with mobile CCTV, not to mention the static cameras. And you'll need somewhere safe to keep it."

"I'll sort out a lock-up," said Harper.

"We'll need something to bind him. We can knock him out but there's no guarantee of how long he'll stay out so we need duct tape and something to gag him with, and something to wrap him in. A carpet. Tarpaulin. Something like that."

Shortt raised a hand. "I've got stuff like that in the garage."

Shepherd shook his head. "No, it all has to be new. And bought from different shops in different areas. And paid for in cash."

"No problem, I'll do it," said Shortt.

"So far as the guns are concerned, we do it with the automatics so that if the body is ever found then the rounds will suggest a Russian or Afghan connection. But they're automatics so we need to pick up the shell casings afterwards. And I can't tell you how important it is that we clean every part of the guns, inside and out. Rounds and clips, too. Clean as a whistle." He looked over at Harper and grinned. "Whatever that means." He sipped his coffee again. "I plan to do it after dark in the New Forest, so hopefully there'll be no one around to hear the shots. But even so I want suppressors on the Makarovs."

McIntyre held up his hand. "I can do that," he said.

"Doesn't have to be too fancy," said Shepherd. "They're not overloud in the first place."

"Pop bottle, cardboard baffles and Brillo pads," said McIntyre. "And Robert's your father's brother. But I'll need somewhere to do it."

"You can use my garage," said Shortt. "Providing the wife's out. I've plenty of tools there, too."

"Perfect," said Shepherd. "And we'll have Jimbo's duct tape to attach them. Now, assuming we get Khan out to the New Forest and slot him there, we've got to dispose of the body. We'll need a hole digging and we'll need that done in advance. It'll need doing at night, the day before the shooting."

"The missus isn't happy if I'm out at night," said Shortt.

"If I'm doing it then I'll need Jock on my job," said Shepherd. He looked at Harper. "You and me, Lex?"

"Sure," said Harper.

"I'll get the spades. Can you get a throwaway mobile with GPS so that we can find our way back to it?"

"Consider it done," said Harper, with a grin.

"So we take Khan out to the New Forest, we do what has to be done, we drop him in the hole and we fill it up. Then we need to dispose of the guns and anything else left over. The duct tape, the suppressors, whatever we use to wrap the body in. Plus the spades, the phone we used to GPS the grave. Everything."

"We could just leave it all in the van and torch it," said Harper.

Shepherd shook his head. "That would draw attention and they'd have SOCO all over it," he said. "Anything not completely burned could be traced back to us. So you should sell on the van. Or leave it somewhere it'll get stolen. I'll take care of the guns and the ammo."

"I'll take the burnable stuff to the quarry I used to use for shooting," said Shortt. "Get a little bonfire. It's well away from London."

"Excellent," said Shepherd. "Now this is important. Everything you're wearing on the day has to be run through a washing machine or destroyed. No arguments. If for any reason our names are in the frame SOCO will look for traces on all our clothes and footwear and if there is anything they'll find it. So immediately afterwards you put all your clothes through a washing machine, twice. Wear trainers and dump them or burn them. And we all shower. Twice."

"Not together, though," said McIntyre. "I've had bad experiences with Jimbo in the shower."

Harper laughed. "Where's the soap?"

All four men joined in, laughing louder than the poor joke merited. It was a way of releasing tension, Shepherd knew. On the surface they all seemed calm and collected with no reservations about what they were planning. But taking the life of a human being was never done lightly and Shepherd knew that they would all be worried about it at some level or another. He waited for the laughter to die down. "Footwear is the most likely to carry traces, so no short cuts there. Don't just throw them in the rubbish. Burning is best, or soak them in bleach and toss them, but again not in your household rubbish, somewhere miles from home. Same with any clothing you decide to throw away." He looked at Harper. "The van will need cleaning, too, inside and out. Best to use bleach on the inside, then take it to a car wash. Make sure the wheels are well clean because if they do get the van they'll be taking a close look at the tyres. They can pretty much match mud in the way that they can fingerprints and DNA. So twice through a car wash, then up to you. If you want to sell it on, do it outside London. If you want to torch it, same applies."

Harper nodded. "Sounds as if you've got all the bases covered."

"It has to be this way, Lex. The smallest thing can follow you around the world. A speck of DNA is all they need. And the phone we use to track the hole, I'll dispose of that and the SIM card. And remember that your own mobile phones always give your position away. I know Lex is covered, but the rest of you, you need to get pay-as-you-go throwaway mobiles. We use them for this operation and then we ditch them. And whenever you're out, you leave your identifiable mobiles at home and switched on. Got it?"

The three men nodded back at him. Harper slapped his hand down on the table, hard enough to rattle the mugs and whiskey bottle. "The bastard has had it coming," he said. "He's finally going to get what he deserves."

AFGHANISTAN, 2002

Ahmad Khan and the three paratroopers drove most of the way to the site of the rendezvous in silence, punctuated only by the terse directions that Ahmad gave them and the Paras' radio transmissions back to base; if they failed to send the correct signal every thirty minutes, the alarm would at once be raised.

The road climbed steadily towards the mountains, its surface increasingly rough and pitted with crudely repaired craters where shells, mortar rounds or IEDs had blasted holes. Their progress was slow, but after driving for an hour and a half they reached a dead-end valley flanked by steep-sided hills. There the road dwindled to not much more than a narrow dirt track, running alongside the bed of a river that a few weeks before had been a roaring torrent of meltwater but was now just a dried-up jumble of rocks.

Ahmad told the driver to slow down still more as they approached the site of the RV with his men, and his keen gaze raked the road ahead and the hills on either side, alert for any danger, anything out of place. As they crested a low rise, he saw ahead of them a group of men wearing Afghan robes, standing at the side of the road in the shade of a clump of pine trees. He frowned. He was an hour early for the rendezvous, but his men were already there.

His frown deepened as they got closer to the group and he realised that most of the dozen or so men were strangers. The only face he recognised was Ghulam, his second-in-command.

One of the men held up a hand in greeting, but Ahmad felt the rising tension from the three Paras and heard the metallic click as the man alongside him slid the safety catch off his M16. "It's all right, drive forward slowly," Khan said, but just as the words left his mouth he caught a brief flash of reflected light from the hillside out of the corner of his eye. His heart began to race. Something was wrong. Something was very wrong. He reached inside his shirt, undid his money belt, and shoved it down the back of the seat behind him until it was out of sight. Ignoring the questioning look from the soldier alongside him, he told the driver to stop.

They were still some fifty yards short of the group of men, who emerged from the shade and began to walk towards them as they saw the Land Rover pull to a halt. "Wait here," Khan said. "Let me do the talking."

He got out and walked up the road, calling out the traditional greeting, "*Salaam alaikum*".

Ghulam returned the greeting. He was smiling but his eyes were hard and Khan began to fear the worst. He stared at Ghulam's face, trying to get a read on the man. Ghulam was tense; that much was obvious.

He slowed as he saw that there were two men among the group who weren't his followers. One he recognised as the commander of another Taliban company. His name, Wais, meant "Night Wanderer". The name suited him well, for he was a dark and elusive character, at home in the shadows and on the margins, seeing everything, saying nothing. The other man was a stranger, but the AK-74 he carried, including a laser sight, and the way the others deferred to him as he stepped forward, suggested he was a powerful figure. "*Alaikum salaam*, Ahmad Khan," he said. "I am Piruz."

"And what wind has blown you here?" Khan said.

"We heard that you were bringing friends with you," said Piruz, waving an arm towards the assembled men. "We wanted to meet them. Will you not introduce us?" He began walking slowly along the track towards the Land Rover.

Khan's brain was racing. He glanced towards the Paras, who were showing increasing signs of agitation.

"The *faranji* are no friend to any true Afghan," he said. "But just the same, they may have their uses sometimes."

Piruz showed his teeth in a smile. "Then let us see what use we can make of them." As he neared the Land Rover, he raised his hand in greeting. "Welcome, English," he said. "Please lower your weapons, you are our guests and we mean you no harm."

The gazes of the three soldiers flickered between Piruz and Khan, clearly uncertain what they should do. Still smiling and affable, Piruz leaned into the back of the Land Rover, resting his arm on the back of the seat that Khan had vacated. "You use the M16, I see," he said. "Do you find that . . ." His voice was drowned by the roar of his weapon. Blood and brains sprayed into the air as the soldier in the back slumped over the side of the vehicle. Without a pause, Piruz swung his AK-74 through a short arc and shot the front-seat passenger through the back of his head. The windscreen shattered as the rounds smashed through it and Khan saw the blood-red smear from what was left of the soldier's head as it slid down the windscreen.

The engine roared as the driver stamped on the accelerator in a frantic attempt to escape, but Piruz's rifle barrel was already swinging towards him and the next shot hit the driver, punching a hole through the back of his seat. The Land Rover swerved and crashed nose down into the ditch at the side of the road, and though the driver, badly wounded, managed to stumble out of his seat, another burst from Piruz killed him stone dead before he had taken three steps.

As Khan brought up his own weapon, he felt a gun barrel in the small of his back and heard a voice hiss, "One more move and you will be as dead as those *faranji* scum." His weapon was taken from him and the next moment blows, kicks and rifle butts began to rain on him. As he sank to the ground, he was dimly aware of Piruz standing over him and he heard him say, "Hold his arms."

There was a momentary pause and then an agonising sensation in his cheek and he smelt singeing flesh as Piruz forced the end of his gun barrel — burning hot from the rounds he had just fired — into Khan's face. "That's enough for now," Piruz said. "There will be time later to deal with the traitor as he deserves, but we need to get away from here before the *faranji* troops come looking for vengeance, and we need him to be able to walk."

Khan was pulled to his feet and his wrists were bound tightly behind him with electric cable which bit into his flesh. Most of the Taliban group moved away from the road, heading up into the mountains and dragging Khan with them, but he saw that a few men were remaining behind, some digging an IED into the ground alongside the Land Rover, others running out a command wire towards a copse of wind-stunted acacia trees a hundred yards away, while still others tracked them, brushing dirt, leaves and gravel over the wire to hide it from view. Khan saw no more as two Taliban fighters took his arms, forcing him along the path that climbed the ridge towards the next valley.

He stumbled on, filled with despair. Even if British or American troops turned up and even if he wasn't killed in the ensuing firefight, the Westerners would assume that he had deliberately led the soldiers into the ambush that killed them all.

He was dragged through the mountains, half conscious and disoriented. They climbed one ridge and descended into a rocky valley only long enough to begin scaling the next ridge beyond. Night had now fallen but still the forced march continued and at every pause along the way Khan was subjected to a fresh beating.

They eventually stopped, an hour before dawn, and laid up to rest for the day in a pine wood near the head of another desolate valley. Through the tree canopy high above him, Khan caught occasional glimpses of the vapour trails of military jets etched across the skies, and once there was the distant clatter of a helicopter's rotors, but the noise grew no louder. He looked around for Ghulam but his friend was keeping his distance. If he was his friend, of course. Khan had no way of knowing for sure.

While most of the Taliban slept, Piruz made sure that Khan had no rest at all. Two Taliban fighters forced him to stand upright and stood guard over him, and whenever he tried to lean back against the rock face or his head sank on to his chest, they kicked him or whipped him with the electric cables they wore as belts around their waists.

The torture began in earnest after Piruz woke up, apparently refreshed after just a few hours' sleep. Sharp

371

splinters of wood were jammed under his fingernails, caustic liquid was forced into his eyes and he was then dragged to the mountain stream running down the hillside, thrown down and held under the water while his feet beat a tattoo on the rocky ground, the blood roared in his ears and his lungs filled with water. Just when he was about to pass out, he was dragged from the water and revived, coughing, spluttering and gasping for breath, only to be interrogated and then forced back under the water again. They wanted to know who he was working for and what information he had given to the British.

He came to rely on the torture to keep himself focused, using the pain to blot out Piruz's questions and his own urge to tell him something, anything that would end his ordeal. The more they hurt him, the more determined he became. He would die without telling them anything.

When the near-drowning failed to loosen his tongue, Piruz had him flogged with the cable-whips until strips of his flesh hung from his back. Eventually he was thrown in the dirt at Piruz's feet. "You are a traitor," Piruz said, for what seemed like the thousandth time. "Confess and by the Prophet's holy name I will be merciful."

Khan knew that he could not win. If he talked he would be killed and if he did not he would also be dead. The truth would not save him, and nor would silence. His only hope lay in a lie.

"I am no traitor," he said through gritted teeth. "You saw for yourself that I led the *faranji* into a trap where

I knew my men were waiting. If I was going to betray my men there would have been many, many *faranji* soldiers with me, not just three, and those little more than boys. But I know who the real traitor is. Free me and I will tell you."

Piruz silenced him with a blow to the mouth that loosened several more teeth and his men then brought their gun butts down on Khan's feet and hands. Piruz had him tied to a tree, the rough bark agonising against the open wounds on his back. Piruz then produced a knife with a wicked, curved blade and held it in front of Khan's eyes. "I shall castrate you, traitor," he said. "You will talk now or you will be no man at all, you will be less than a woman." He cut through Khan's belt and a moment later Khan felt the bite of the knife-edge and hot blood trickled down his thigh. He knew real terror then and for the first time his resolve weakened. That cut might not have been a deep one, but Piruz was ready to cut him again and again, a cruel smile playing around his lips.

Wais the Night Wanderer had remained on the sidelines while Khan was tortured, but as Piruz raised his knife hand again Wais stepped forward. "Don't kill him, Piruz," he said. "Not yet. He will talk, I am sure of it. And when we do kill him, Fahad will want to make an example of him. It will be a lesson that none can ignore. Whether they are warriors or cowards who hide behind the skirts of women, those who turn aside from the path of jihad, no matter what feats of arms they may have done in the past, will feel the holy wrath of Allah — may his name be praised — upon them."

Khan saw Piruz hesitate and he waited, his heart pounding. Fahad — the Lynx — was the Taliban commander for the whole region, and one of Mullah Omar's closest advisers. Piruz would surely not dare risk his wrath. There was a long silence, but then Piruz lowered his hand and strode away, his jaw clenched tight.

As he also turned away, Wais caught Khan's eye for a fraction of a second. His expression was unreadable and yet Khan felt a sudden surge of hope. Perhaps there was still a way that he could survive.

The Taliban group moved on that night, crossing a final mountain ridge, even steeper than those before, and fording a river that was deep enough to reach to their chests and so cold that Khan let out a gasp as he was herded into it by his captors. The rushing water reignited the pain from his shredded back, but he bit his lip and made no other sound. To complain would only reawaken Piruz's cruel desire to inflict more pain, he was sure. As he climbed out of the water he saw Ghulam farther down the riverbank. They made brief eye contact and Ghulam gave him a slight nod, a small gesture but one that filled Khan with hope.

In the middle of the night, Khan woke from an uneasy sleep to find Ghulam standing over him with a bottle of water. Khan's wrists were bound behind his back so Ghulam had to hold the bottle to his mouth. "Piruz found out that you had gone to see the Brits. I managed to warn your men but it was too late for me to run. I don't know what I can do to help you now." After the few snatched words, Ghulam hurried away.

The next morning, the Taliban arrived in a village that they still controlled despite a year-long concentrated effort by the American and British forces to dislodge them. The village dogs set up a chorus of barking as the Taliban fighters approached. Khan was paraded through the streets at the head of the column, covered in dried blood and dust, his clothing torn and his wrists bound behind him.

The frightened villagers peered from behind their doors and shuttered windows as the column of men moved past, too frightened to show themselves in the open.

They came to a halt in the dusty square in the centre of the village, where two Toyota Landcruisers were already drawn up. Standing in front of them, flanked by his personal bodyguard, was Fahad the Lynx, with his ten-year-old son at his side.

Piruz paid his respects to Fahad and he presented the AK-74 he had taken from Khan to Fahad's son. The boy darted a nervous glance at his father and then, at his nod, gave a grave bow of thanks. He began turning the weapon over in his hands, squinting along the sight towards Khan and pretending to pull the trigger. His father gave an indulgent smile and Piruz roared with laughter.

The Taliban fighters then went from house to house, rousting out the villagers and forcing them to assemble in the square. As they watched silently, Khan was methodically kicked and beaten before he was dragged in front of Fahad.

Piruz puffed out his chest, revelling in the moment, his voice carrying to the farthest reaches of the village. "I accuse Ahmad Khan," he said, stabbing the air with his finger as if plunging a dagger into Khan's heart, "of the grossest treachery, the betrayal of the faith, his country, and the nation's protectors, the Taliban, charged by Mullah Omar himself with the sacred duty of guarding the Islamic Emirate from its enemies. I demand death for the traitor, who is not even man enough to confess his crimes." He spat in the dirt at Khan's feet.

A few of the villagers applauded or shouted "*Allahu akbar*" but most remained silent.

"Ahmad Khan, you have one final chance to confess your crimes, before Allah, whose name be praised, sits in judgement upon you," Fahad shouted. He signalled to the guards flanking Khan to untie his hands.

As he rubbed some life back into his wrists and hands, Khan let his gaze travel over the faces of his persecutors. They all stared back at him with undisguised hostility, except for Ghulam, who was looking at the ground. At last he began to speak and, despite his exhaustion and the pain from his wounds, his voice was steady and clear. "Who among you has done more for our country than I? I have fought the Russians, the Americans, the British, the Afghan army and the Pakistani army. I have risked my life scores of times and I bear the scars on my body to prove it. Yet this is how you treat me in return?" He pointed an accusing finger at Fahad's son. "You take the weapons from heroes and you give them to children. And now you even accuse me of treachery? Give me a weapon and I'll show you the real traitor."

"Liar!" Piruz shouted, and raised his weapon ready to shoot him, but Fahad placed a restraining hand on his arm. He stared at Khan in silence, his eyes hooded, then reached into his robe and pulled out an old Makarov pistol that had been taken from a dead Soviet soldier many years before. It was so old that parts of the gunmetal had been worn to a shiny, silver patina. Fahad emptied the magazine into his hand, then put a single round back in the chamber, pocketing the rest of the ammunition.

He threw the pistol to Khan, while several Taliban covered him with their weapons. "Because you fought well for us in the past," Fahad said, "I am giving you this last chance to preserve your honour. Kill yourself now like a man, or we will kill you like the dog you are."

Khan stared down at the weapon in his hand, then suddenly whipped it up to the firing position and shot Wais with a bullet between the eyes. As Wais slumped to the ground, already dead, Khan screamed, "He's the traitor. Search him, if you don't believe me."

The Taliban fighters were screaming at Khan, their fingers tightening on their triggers, but Fahad held up a hand to silence them. "Hold your fire and search the body," he shouted.

Ghulam stooped over Wais's lifeless body, running his hands through his robes. "There is something!" he shouted. He straightened up, holding a bulging money belt he had taken from the dead man's waist. He opened it, stared inside then took out a thick bundle of notes and threw them on the ground. There was a gasp from the watching crowd as the breeze stirred the thousands of US dollars that lay there.

"Wais has been in the pay of the British for many months," shouted Khan. "He has been giving them information about our bases and our leaders. They know him as Abu Qartoob."

Ghulam passed the money belt to Fahad, who flicked through the notes, his face impassive.

"I heard that Wais had been seen talking to a British officer, but I needed you to see that for yourself," said Khan, pointing at the money belt. "I was never a traitor. It is Wais who has been betraying you!"

"We have misjudged you, brother," Fahad said, walking over to him and embracing him. He motioned for his son to give the AK-74 to Khan and the boy sullenly obeyed, clearly unhappy at having to return the weapon.

Khan slung it on his shoulder and then walked over to where Wais still lay and spat on him. He watched the spittle dribble down the side of the dead man's face and drip from the stump of his earlobe — the rest shot away in some long-forgotten gun battle that had earned Wais the Arabic nickname he had chosen as his code name. Khan offered up a silent prayer of thanks for Joshua's mention of Abu Qartoob. He knew that Wais had tried to protect him and had even intervened to save his life up on the mountainside when Piruz was a heartbeat from killing him, but when it came down to a choice of his own life or Wais's, there was only ever going to be one outcome. His fellow agent's reward for saving Khan's life had been to die in his place.

"What now, Ahmad Khan?" Ghulam asked him later.

"Now?" Khan said, loud enough for the other Taliban to hear. "I shall go home to my daughter, sleep — for it has been two days and nights since I last closed my eyes — and give my wounds time to heal, and then I shall return to again put myself at the service of Mullah Omar and his lieutenant, Fahad the Lynx." He made a small bow as he said it, which Fahad acknowledged, but his expression showed that while Khan might have been partly rehabilitated, he was still far from trusted.

As he made his slow way back to his home he reflected on how lucky he had been and knew that time was running out for him. Piruz and Fahad had not been convinced. They would watch and wait, and another slip, however small, would be his downfall. He had to get out. Any lingering doubts that might have remained were removed as soon as he saw his daughter. The dark shadows under her eyes and the way she started as a log shifted in the hearth showed that she still lived in fear.

"We may go on a journey soon, Lailuna," he said. "Somewhere far from the men who frightened you. Would you like that?"

She flinched as if she had been struck, but she nodded and then hugged him with such force that he winced at the pain from his wounds. "Yes, Father, I would like that," she whispered into his chest. "I would like that a lot."

"Bloody hell," said McIntyre as the gate pulled back to reveal the massive mansion. "How the other half lives, huh?"

Shepherd waved at Gunter and drove towards the garage. "That's less than half of it," he said. "It's like an iceberg, most of it is underground."

"How much do you think a place like this would go for?"

"A hundred million, give or take," said Shepherd.

McIntyre whistled softly.

"So, I'll introduce you to Dmitry and get you sorted with a transceiver and fitted up for the thumb sensor. How's your Russian, by the way?" The garage doors rolled up and Shepherd drove slowly down to the first basement level.

"All those hours in the Regiment's language lab paid off," said McIntyre. "But my Serbian's better. Why?"

"Don't let on that you can speak the language. See if you can pick up anything useful."

They drove down into the car park and Shepherd took McIntyre over to the security centre.

Dudko was sitting in front of the CCTV monitors and Popov was in the briefing room with Ulyashin. Ulyashin's crutches were leaning against one wall.

Shepherd introduced McIntyre as Alastair McEwan, a former soldier who had been bodyguarding for more than ten years. The three Russians shook hands with McIntyre and Shepherd could see them all weighing him up. McIntyre grinned amiably as he shook hands.

380

"Can someone fix Alastair up with one of the rooms?" said Shepherd. "And get him fixed up with a security code and a transceiver?"

"He's staying here?" asked Popov.

"Most of the time," said Shepherd. "You can use him in the house but he's up to speed on mobile security."

"But not armed?"

"Not sure we'd trust him with live rounds," said Shepherd. He grinned when he saw the look of confusion on their faces. "Just a joke," he said. "Alastair isn't a police officer so he's not licensed to carry a weapon." Shepherd's phone rang. It was Button. He went outside to the car parking area to take the call.

"I'm having problems getting information on the bodyguarding teams who were looking after Zakharov and Czernik," she said. "We've spoken to the men's companies but they're point blank refusing to help. Their head offices are overseas so there's not much pressure I can bring to bear."

"You want me to run it by Grechko?"

"You read my mind," said Button. "But be tactful, obviously."

"Tactful is my middle name, you know that."

"I thought Spider was your middle name." She laughed, and ended the call. Shepherd put the phone away and went back into the control centre.

"Where is Mr Grechko?" he asked Dudko.

"Pool," said the bodyguard, flicking through a magazine filled with photographs of classic cars. "What do you think about the E-Type Jaguar? A good car, right?"

"A penis on wheels," said Shepherd.

Dudko frowned. "What?"

"It's a substitute for a small penis," said Shepherd. "I wouldn't get one, if I were you."

"But it's a classic, no?"

"It's a classic, but trust me, anyone seeing you in one will think you've got something to hide."

Dudko frowned. "You think I have a small penis?"

Considering that Dudko's physique clearly owed more to steroids than it did to exercise, Shepherd figured that the man probably did have problems in that area but he just smiled and shook his head. "Girls might, though."

"You drive a BMW, right?"

"An X5. SUV. Can't fault it."

Dudko grinned mischievously. "What does that say about your penis?"

"That I look after it," said Shepherd, patting him on the shoulder. He took the stairs down to the third underground level.

Grigory Sokolov was standing by the doors. Despite the fact they were indoors and underground he was still wearing his Oakley sunglasses. "Grigory, I need a private word with Mr Grechko," said Shepherd.

"He doesn't like being disturbed while he's swimming."

"I know that, but this is important." Shepherd pressed his thumb against the scanner and tapped in his code before pushing the doors open. Sokolov started to follow Shepherd but Shepherd put a hand on his chest. "A private word," he said.

"Dmitry says I'm not to allow strangers alone with Mr Grechko."

"I'm not a stranger," said Shepherd.

"You are to me," said Sokolov, folding his arms.

"Call Dmitry, he'll tell you it's OK," said Shepherd.

Sokolov put his hand up to his Bluetooth earpiece as Shepherd went into the pool room. It had been built in the style of a Roman bath with stone columns and carved figures of naked Roman gods. At one end was a huge stone lion with a plume of water cascading from between its open jaws. Grechko was in the water, swimming lengths with a lot of splashing and grunting. Shepherd realised that the Russian wasn't wearing trunks; there was a white stripe of untanned skin across his backside.

Grechko was an uncoordinated swimmer, his legs and arms thrashing in the water with an irregular beat, but he was a powerful man and moved at quite a speed. His turns at either end were ungainly and involved him slapping the poolside with his hand before twisting around with a loud grunt and powering himself forward by pushing with his feet. He would keep his face down in the water until he lost momentum and then he would began thrashing and splashing again.

The Russian swam a further ten lengths before climbing out of the pool at the far end. He picked up a towel, slung it over his shoulder, and walked towards Shepherd with a wide grin on his face. "You swim naked, Tony?" he asked.

"I'm not much of a swimmer," said Shepherd. "I'm more of a runner."

"Then you should run naked. All exercise should be done without clothes, the way God intended." He began towelling himself dry.

"There's something I need to ask you," said Shepherd. "Miss Button is trying to identify the bodyguards who were working for Zakharov and Czernik before they were killed."

Grechko stopped towelling himself. "She suspects their bodyguards?"

"It's too early to say," said Shepherd. "She's been in touch with the people at both men's companies but they're not being helpful."

"And you want me to ask them?"

"I think you'll probably have more luck than she's having. Could you approach them and ask them to cooperate with her?"

Grechko nodded. "No problem. But why?"

"We're starting to think that the assassinations might have been an inside job," said Shepherd.

"One of their bodyguards killed them?" Grechko wrapped the towel around his waist and stood with his hands on his hips.

"It's possible."

Grechko jutted his chin up and looked down his nose at Shepherd. "This is not good," he said.

"It's just a theory."

"And we could have an inside man on our team? He could be in the house right now?"

"It's unlikely," said Shepherd. "I've been through the CV of every man on your team, especially the new arrivals. And everyone checks out."

"People lie on their CVs."

"That's true. I'm in the process of checking all references, and calling them myself. If I spot any discrepancies, I'll act immediately."

The Russian rubbed his chin thoughtfully. "You know what a Judas goat is?"

"I know," said Shepherd. "The bait in a trap. But that's not what's going on here, Mr Grechko."

Grechko stared at Shepherd for several seconds, then he nodded slowly. "I trust you, Tony. I'm not sure why I do, but I trust you."

"I won't let you down, Mr Grechko."

Shepherd spent most of the day in the control centre, reading through the files on the various members of the bodyguarding team. He made more than two dozen calls around the world, checking on references, and found nothing untoward. He decided to go for a run on the Heath and spent an hour and a half running and doing press-ups and sit-ups before running back to the house to shower and change. He was heading to the kitchen to pick up some sandwiches when his mobile rang. It was Button. "Bad news, I'm afraid," she said. "I've checked all the bodyguards for both men and there's no common dominator," she said.

"No offence but you did check photographs and not just names?" said Shepherd.

"No offence taken, Spider, and yes, I had the HR departments send over photographs. There are no matches. I'll email you all the pictures now so you can check them against your team there. But if there's no match between Zakharov and Czernik it's doubtful that there'll be a match with the men there."

"Yeah," said Shepherd, running a hand through his hair as he paced up and down the corridor. "So we're no farther forward?"

"I'm afraid not."

"But that doesn't make any sense. If the sniper wasn't shooting bodyguards to insert himself into the close protection teams, what was he doing it for?"

"That's a good question," she said. "I wish I had an answer."

"It can't be a coincidence," said Shepherd. He stopped pacing. "What if it's not about inserting himself into the team, but getting an intel source in place?"

"Someone to feed him information?"

Shepherd's heart was starting to pound. "That's it. He's got someone on the inside feeding him information on the target. He puts a bodyguard out of commission and when the target boosts his security the killer gets his own man on board. But it's a different man each time."

"That makes sense," said Button. "So we're looking for a connection between the new arrivals, some common denominator."

"The common denominator is the killer, because he's paying them, presumably," said Shepherd. "But he can't be pulling their names out of a hat. They must be people that he trusts, which means he's known them for a long time, worked with them perhaps."

386

"And the killer is a sniper, which suggests military training. The bodyguards are pretty much all Russian, or at least former Soviet Union, so that suggests that the killer is too."

"So what you need to do is to compare the work histories of the new arrivals on all three teams and find a common point."

"I'm on it," she said, and ended the call.

Sheena the chef had prepared a selection of sandwiches and cakes and Shepherd took them back to the control centre.

McIntyre was there on his own when Shepherd opened the door and his eyes sparkled when he saw the food. "I could get used to this," he said. He took a bite out of one of the sandwiches, then wiped his mouth with his sleeve. "I might have something useful for you," he said.

"I'm all ears."

"Last night the guys were talking about another Russian oligarch who was killed a while back. Name of Buryakov. Know him?"

Shepherd shook his head.

"According to the guys, he had a heart attack or something. But two months before he died, someone tried to shoot him. A sniper."

"Where was this?"

"Somewhere in Germany, I forget where." He grinned. "I don't have your photographic memory, remember?"

"So a sniper took a shot and missed?"

"Yeah, just like with Grechko. And just as in Grechko's case, a bodyguard took a bullet. In the arm."

Shepherd nodded thoughtfully. "That's interesting."

"It is, isn't it? Bit unusual for a sniper to hit the wrong target, right?"

"Very unusual," said Shepherd. Long-range sniping was challenging at the best of times, Shepherd knew from experience. It was easy enough to screw up a kill shot and a sudden change in wind could result in the target being missed completely. But hitting a completely different target, even if they were in close proximity, was rare in the extreme. "Who was talking about this?"

"That skinny guy, the one with the shaved head. What's his name? Volikov? Volvakov?"

"Volkov," said Shepherd.

"Yeah, that's the one. He was talking to that big guy, the one who's forever watching porn on his iPad. Molotov."

"Molchanov," corrected Shepherd.

"Yeah, well, Volkov apparently knows one of the guys who was on this Buryakov's team. Apparently the round missed Volkov's mate by inches and hit this other guy. The head of security was fired and the whole thing was hushed up."

"Why?" asked Shepherd.

"Volkov said it was because this Buryakov reckoned no one would do business with him if they thought he was being targeted like that. Fair point, right? You'd hardly want to sit down with him if at any point a sniper was going to take a pot shot. Collateral damage, and all."

"This was all said in Russian, right?"

"Yeah, they had no idea I was listening. I tell you, some of the things they say about me, I have trouble pretending not to understand. When this is over, I'm going to have a few scores to settle, I can tell you."

"Sticks and stones, Jock, remember that."

McIntyre grinned wolfishly. "I won't be needing sticks or stones," he said. "My fists'll do the job just fine." He leaned closer to Shepherd and lowered his voice. "What about the other thing?"

"Soon," said Shepherd. "Lex and I will dig the hole tomorrow night, and Jimbo and Lex are keeping tabs on Khan, making sure we've got his movements off pat."

"Who's Pat?" He laughed when he saw Shepherd's look of contempt. "Just trying to lighten the moment, Spider."

"And don't use my bloody name," whispered Shepherd.

"OK, got you," said McIntyre. "So we're ready to go the day after next?"

Shepherd nodded. "Two days, three at the most. Lex is keen to get back to Thailand. And the longer we leave it, the more chance there is that something will go wrong."

"Nothing'll go wrong," said McIntyre. "That bastard deserves what's coming to him."

The door opened and Popov walked in. "You two are a devious pair," he said.

Shepherd felt his cheeks flush. "What do you mean?"

Popov grinned and pointed at the plates on the table. "You kept quiet about the sandwiches." He grabbed a couple of sandwiches and headed for the briefing room. "As leader of the pack I'm entitled to first bite of every kill," he said.

Charlotte Button arrived at the house at just after midday. Shepherd had called her the previous evening to tell her about the attack on Yuri Buryakov and she had woken him with a 6 a.m. phone call to tell him that she needed a meeting with Grechko.

Grechko was sitting in his study, signing letters with one of his secretaries, a striking Russian blonde called Emma. He didn't get up when Button and Shepherd entered, in fact he studiously ignored them and continued to sign letters with a Mont Blanc fountain pen. Only when he had finished and Emma was gathering the letters together did he look up. "Miss Button, you are becoming a regular visitor."

"Something has come up, Mr Grechko," she said. "Do you mind if we sit?"

Grechko waved at a chair on the other side of the desk. Button sat down but Shepherd went to stand by the window.

Button smiled pleasantly at Grechko. She was wearing a dark blue suit that was almost black and a pale blue silk shirt. "Things have moved on since I last came to see you," she said. "We've taken a look at the case of Yuri Buryakov. You were also a friend of Mr Buryakov's, weren't you?"

"It is a small world, Miss Button. There are not many Russians like us and we tend to stick together."

"But you were aware that he had died, surely?"

Grechko nodded. "Of course. I was at his funeral. But he had a heart attack. He was at a conference and he had the heart attack there and then he died in hospital."

"Why didn't you mention to me that Mr Buryakov had also been the victim of a sniper attack?"

Grechko's jaw dropped. "A sniper?"

"About two months before he was murdered, a sniper shot at Mr Buryakov. One of his bodyguards was shot in the arm."

Grechko shook his head. "He never mentioned it to me."

"Did you see Mr Buryakov before he died?"

"About three weeks before. We were at a racetrack. Ascot, I think. He owns many racehorses." He put up a hand. "I'm sorry. Wrong tense. He owned many racehorses," he said, correcting himself.

"And he didn't say anything about a sniper?"

"I would have remembered," said Grechko. "Are you sure about this? I read nothing in the papers."

"We have since spoken to members of Mr Buryakov's former security team and we have confirmation that there was an attempt to shoot him at long range in Berlin. According to the people we spoke to, Mr Buryakov didn't want anyone to know. He saw the attack as a sign of weakness on his part. One of his bodyguards was hit in the arm and was paid a substantial sum for his silence."

Grechko frowned. "So he was attacked by a sniper, and then he died. Exactly the same as happened to Oleg."

"You see the pattern, then? Yes, Oleg Zakharov narrowly escaped being shot by a sniper. Then he died. And the same happened to Mr Buryakov."

Grechko sat back and folded his arms. His face had gone as hard as stone. "Yuri had a heart attack."

"And you yourself were recently shot at by a sniper. Possibly the same sniper who shot at Mr Zakharov and Buryakov."

Grechko's eyes fixed on Button. "What are you saying?" he said, his voice a low growl.

"I think you know what I'm saying, Mr Grechko," she said. "There is every likelihood that you will be attacked again. Not by a sniper, but by an assassin who is much closer."

"I keep telling you, Yuri wasn't assassinated. He had a heart attack."

"Heart attacks can be induced."

"This makes no sense to me," he said. "If they are using an assassin, why use a sniper first? And how is it that the sniper misses?"

"Well, did he miss, that's the question," said Button. "Did he miss, or was he shooting at the bodyguards?"

"Why would he deliberately shoot a bodyguard?" growled Grechko. "Bodyguards are ten a penny."

"Thank you," said Shepherd quietly.

Grechko turned to scowl at him but Shepherd was already looking out of the window.

"That's a very good question," said Button. "But until we have the answer, I'm going to suggest that you minimise your travel arrangements, and increase your security. After what happened to Mr Zakharov, Mr Czernik and Mr Buryakov, I think you have to be very, very careful until we identify this man and apprehend him."

"Apprehend him?" said Grechko? "When you find out who he is you tell me and I'll have him taken care of."

"That's not how we do things in this country," said Button.

"Which is one of the many things wrong with it," said Grechko. "When you catch him you need to get him to give up the person who is paying him. It won't be enough to just talk to him severely with that stiff upper lip of yours. Some Russian persuasion will loosen his tongue, though."

"We are perfectly capable of handling this, Mr Grechko," said Button, icily.

"You need to get him to tell you the truth, that he is working for those bastards in the Kremlin," said Grechko. "You need him to tell you and then you need to go public."

"If that's the case, then of course that information will be released. But one step at time, Mr Grechko. First we need to catch him." Button took a deep breath, knowing that the Russian would not react well to what she was about to say. "Mr Grechko, we are coming to the opinion that the attempt on your life is personal, not political."

"Of course it's personal," said Grechko. "The dogs in the Kremlin hate my guts. They hate anyone who is richer than they are."

"We don't think it has anything to do with the Russian government," said Button patiently. "What the killer is doing indicates that he is on a personal mission rather than being paid to kill."

Grechko threw up his hands. "You're talking in riddles, woman," he said contemptuously. "A sniper almost took off my head. How can that not be a professional hit?"

"Have you ever paid for someone to be killed, Mr Grechko?" asked Button quietly.

Grechko's eyes hardened and his jaw clenched as he stared at her. "I would be very careful about making allegations like that, Miss Button," he said eventually. "Your prime minister is a good friend. He would not be pleased to hear that you have made an accusation like that."

"I was speaking hypothetically, Mr Grechko. Because if, hypothetically, you were hiring an assassin, would you hire one who could not do the job properly? Of course you wouldn't. And I am equally sure that if the Russian government was using an assassin, they would use the best. There have been a number of very successful assassinations of Russians in the UK over the last few years, as I'm sure you know."

Grechko nodded slowly. "You are saying that the man who tried to kill me is not a professional?"

Button shook her head. "No, that's not what I'm saying. But I am saying that if a professional sniper wanted to put a bullet in your head, it's quite a stretch to shoot a bodyguard in the leg instead." She leaned forward. "We are starting to think that the sniper intended to shoot the bodyguard. He did that for two reasons. To scare you. And to force you to increase your security arrangements."

"Scare me? You think I am scared?"

Button shrugged. "If you know that someone is trying to kill you, you would obviously be apprehensive, wouldn't you? And what did you do immediately after the attempt on your life?"

"I beefed up security."

"You hired more people?"

"Of course. But not out of fear, Miss Button. Do I look like I'm shaking in my shoes?" He held out his hands, palms down. "See, no trembling. I am not a man who scares easily." He sat back and folded his arms, then he slowly frowned. Button said nothing, knowing that it would be better if he worked it out for himself. His eyes widened and he put his hand up to his jaw. "He wanted me to increase my security?"

"We think so, yes," said Button quietly. "We think it is possible that he has put his own person on your team. Somebody who is feeding him intel so that the next attempt doesn't fail."

Grechko pointed at Shepherd. "I already told him I won't be a Judas goat," he said. "I will not be bait in a trap."

"There is no trap, Mr Grechko," said Button. "This is an on-going investigation. So far I have cross-referenced the security teams of all four of you and there are no common denominators."

Grechko scowled. "OK, let's assume that what you're saying is true. That the sniper didn't want to kill me, he only wanted to scare me so that I would hire more bodyguards. Why go to all that trouble? Why not just shoot me at Stamford Bridge? He knew where I'd be, he had a clear shot, why not do it then?"

Button looked across at Shepherd. He was watching her carefully and she flashed him a quick smile before looking back at Grechko. "Because for the killer it's personal. He wants you to know who he is. You've done something to this man, something that he wants to punish you for."

Grechko ran a hand through his hair. "Where have you got this idea from, Miss Button?" he said. "It seems to me that you've been watching too many James Bond movies."

Button picked up her briefcase and swung it on to her lap. She clicked the locks open and took out an A4 manila envelope. She put the briefcase back on the floor and slid three photographs out of the envelope and lined them up on the coffee table. Grechko walked back to the sofa and sat down. He put his head in his hands as he stared at the photographs.

"Oleg Zakharov, Yuri Buryakov, Sasha Czernik. All three men were friends, and business contacts."

It wasn't a question but Grechko nodded and said, "Yes."

"All three are now dead."

Grechko put up his hand to stop her. "Sasha had a heart attack."

"He was, as you say, forty-five and had no history of heart problems."

"He was overweight," said Grechko. "Fat."

"But according to his physician, his heart was healthy, his cholesterol levels were well within the normal range and his blood pressure was fine."

"You checked?"

Button smiled and nodded. "Yes," she said. "I checked. There was no reason for Mr Czernik to have had a heart attack. But there are a number of chemicals which if injected are perfectly capable of mimicking the effects of a heart attack."

"There was an autopsy. They would have found a poison."

"Not necessarily," said Button. "There have been a number of Russian deaths in the UK over the past year or so which have been suspicious but which have shown nothing untoward during the post-mortems."

"The same killer, you think?"

"No, not at all. I'm just pointing out that it's possible to kill someone by inducing a heart attack and leaving no trace." She gave him a second or two to absorb what she had said before continuing. "We have made further enquiries into the deaths of Mr Czernik, Mr Zakharov and Mr Buryakov," she said. "In each case, within the week following their deaths, a bodyguard died. One from what appeared to be a heart attack, one crashed his car into a tree, and one died in what appeared to be a street mugging. All three of those bodyguards had taken their posts when security was increased."

Button sat back and waited for the information to sink in. Shepherd could see that the Russian was having difficulty processing what he'd been told. He kept looking at Button, then at the floor, then back to Button, as the creases in his forehead deepened. "He has inside information," said Grechko eventually. "That's how he kills them. And then he kills the people on the inside. He knows their security details, he knows everything?"

"It looks that way, yes."

Grechko sat back and ran his hands through his hair. "So what do we do? If you're right, the killer already has his man on my team."

"Or woman," said Shepherd.

Grechko looked over at Shepherd. "Woman?"

"Alina Podolski joined your team after the sniping incident," said Shepherd.

"She came highly recommended," said Grechko.

"By whom?"

"Dmitry," said Grechko. "He said he'd worked with her." He turned back to Button. "You haven't answered my question. What do we do? Do I dismiss my whole team and bring in a new one?"

"There's no guarantee that the killer wouldn't have his own man — or woman — on the new team," said Button. "At least now we know we have a relatively small pool of suspects to work on. We're assuming that everyone on your security team prior to the sniping is clean. So we only have to look at the new arrivals, of which there are . . ." She looked over at Shepherd.

"Six," he said.

"So we have six possible suspects."

"I want them out of the house now," said Grechko. He made a fist of his right hand and pounded it into his left. "Actually, I've a better idea, let Dmitry work on them, he'll find out who the traitor is."

Button held up her hands, a look of dismay on her face. "That would be absolutely the wrong thing to do," she said. "It would immediately tip off the killer and he would vanish."

"At least then I would be safe."

"But for how long? You would never know if or when he intended to come back to finish the job." She shook her head emphatically. "No, we need to identify the intel source and follow that back to the killer."

"And how do you intend to do that, exactly?"

"We'll need the mobile phone numbers of all your staff. Plus home addresses, addresses here in the UK if they have one, and any other information you have."

"Dmitry can supply you with everything you need," said Grechko. "I'll talk to him. What about lie detectors?"

"Lie detectors?" repeated Button.

"You have them, surely? To tell if people are lying. We can question everyone and see who is lying."

"Again, that might tip the killer off," said Button, standing up. "I think for the moment at least we should confine ourselves to thorough background checks and phone monitoring." She leaned forward and looked down at the three photographs. "There is something I found a little . . . unusual," she said.

Grechko jutted his chin but didn't say anything.

"Mr Zakharov made his money in finance and property. He started with a small office block in Moscow and grew it into one of the biggest property developers in the country." She tapped the photograph of Yuri Buryakov. "Mr Buryakov made his money in oil. He started with a small refinery and built it into one of the world's biggest independent oil companies." She nudged the third photograph. "And Sasha Czernik. Steel and aluminium. When the Soviet Union collapsed in 1992, he was an assistant manager at a steel smelting plant in Kazan. Within five years he owned a dozen factories, blast and steel-making furnaces, steel smelting and rolling units, pipe-manufacturing lines and continuous casting machines. Now his company is one of the biggest steel and aluminium conglomerates in the world with factories in Italy, Germany and Brazil, and he had just started moving into Africa."

Grechko nodded slowly. "Sasha did well, yes."

"You all did well, Mr Grechko," said Button. She gathered up the pictures, put them back in the envelope and put the envelope into her briefcase. "Amazingly well. In 1992 you yourself were a middle manager in a trucking company that moved building materials for the government."

"Before 1992, everybody worked for the government," said Grechko. "There was no private sector." He grinned. "Not officially, anyway."

"That's right," said Button. "I read somewhere that you made your money selling second-hand jeans."

Grechko laughed. "Not just second-hand," he said. He banged his hands down on to his knees. "You couldn't buy Western jeans for love nor money. So when I wasn't working I used to hang around the tourist hotels and look for Western teenagers. I'd offer them whatever I could for jeans, worn or otherwise. Sometimes I'd do a swap for vodka or some crap souvenirs, but if they wanted money I'd give them money because I could sell them for three times as much on the black market. The Russian kids, they couldn't get enough Levi's and Wrangler's." He laughed and slapped his knees again. "Those were the days."

"The interesting thing about the four of you is that you have all been friends for a very long time," said Button. "And you have all become very, very rich. To be honest, you four are among the richest men on the planet."

"So? We all worked very hard to get where we are."

"I'm sure you did, Mr Grechko. But I do find it interesting that your businesses are all so different. Oil and gas, banking and property, steel and aluminium, trucking and shipping. You were never in competition."

Grechko laughed. "Perhaps that's why we remained friends for so long."

Button smiled thinly and nodded. "Perhaps that's it," she said. "But it is interesting that you all started from nothing, all moved into different businesses, and all became very wealthy, and now three of the four are dead. And it's starting to look as if the same man killed the three of them and is trying to kill you."

Grechko's eyes had hardened as she spoke. "The dogs in the Kremlin hate us all," he said quietly. "And they kill what they hate."

"That may be," said Button. "But the more we look at this, Mr Grechko, the more it seems to us that these killings are not political. They are personal."

Grechko said nothing, but both his hands clenched into tight fists and his knuckles whitened.

"So I have to ask you, can you think of anyone who might want to murder you, Mr Zakharov, Mr Buryakov and Mr Czernik? Someone you crossed over the years, someone out for revenge?"

"That's ridiculous," said Grechko.

"What exactly do you think is ridiculous?"

Grechko leaned towards her. "You know what Putin has been doing? You have seen what happens to people who cross him. Why do you want me to jump at shadows when I know who is trying to kill me?"

"Because if this is personal then understanding the killer's motive means we will stand a better chance of identifying him."

Grechko stared at her for several seconds, then he shrugged. "I can't think of anyone."

"But you have enemies?"

Grechko snorted contemptuously. "The world does not give you money, Miss Button. You have to take it. The strong get rich and the weak stay poor. That's how natural selection works. If it did not work that way, the entire world would be communist."

"So I'll take that as a yes."

Grechko waved away her comment with a flick of his hand. "You wouldn't understand, you have spent your whole life under a capitalist system," he said. "You have a nice car, I have seen it. A BMW. You wear that nice Cartier watch and I am sure that you are treated by the very best private doctors. You have children?"

"A daughter," said Button.

"And I am sure that she is privately educated. You reap all the benefits of living in a capitalist country." He bared his teeth and tapped the front two with his finger. "Do you see my teeth, Miss Button? My wonderfully even, white teeth? They cost me fifty thousand dollars. Why? Because when I was a child I had state-supplied dental care and the drunken dentist they let loose on me was more concerned about his vodka than his patients. By the time I was twelve, half my teeth were rotten. I had a basic education, I had crap food, I wore cheap clothing and I lived with my parents in a flat close to a munitions factory that was exactly the same as the flat of every other family. We had the same furniture, the same cutlery, the same oven, the same refrigerator, everything was the same as our neighbours. The only difference was the colour of the sofa, which changed each year. My parents had the 1983 sofa. It was green."

Button opened her mouth to speak but Grechko held up his hand to silence her. "Every child got the same bicycle. Your parents put your name down for it when you were born and it was delivered on your fifth birthday. Every bike was the same. There was a black economy, of course there was, how else could I buy and sell my jeans. But it was small and it was illegal and, my God, did they punish you if they caught you. So eventually I got a job working in a shitty office for a man who thought his mission in life was to treat me like a serf. Then I got married and was given my own flat and my own sofa, which was blue, and yes, I bought and sold jeans on the black market because it was the only way I could lift myself out of the shit that is the communist system. I did what I had to do, Miss Button, and you would have done the same. Then in 1992, everything changed. The reins were loosened. Finally people were allowed to think for themselves, to act for themselves. But we still had nothing. So if you wanted something, you had to take it. You had to grab it with both hands before someone else took it and once you had it you had to make sure that no one took it from you. No one owned anything before 1992, can you understand that? Everything belonged to the state. And no one gave you anything, you had to take it. Those that took, got rich. Those that sat on their backsides stayed poor. So if you're asking me if I trod on a few feet to get where I am today, then yes, of course I did. And I broke a few heads. So did Oleg, so did Yuri and so did Sasha. And so did all of the oligarchs that you are so quick to welcome to your shores. None of us are angels, Miss Button, but you overlook that fact in your rush to take our money." He could see that she was about to object but he silenced her with another curt wave of his hand. "Not you personally, I'm not saying that, but your political masters. Do you have any idea how much I have paid them over the years? Millions. Literally millions. And like pigs they stick their snouts in the trough and demand more. And not just to their parties. They come in person with their grasping hands out. Members of your House of Lords, the highest office in the land, sticking their tongues up my arse to get what they want. Former prime ministers asking me to hire them as consultants for a million dollars a year." He sneered dismissively. "Money is all that matters to them, so you insult me by suggesting that I have done anything wrong in trying to better myself. Would you rather that I was still working ten hours a day collating timesheets and checking milometers and going home to a flat with a blue plastic sofa and sandpaper sheets and looking forward, if I was lucky, to a week by the Black Sea once a year?"

"Of course not," said Button. "And please don't take offence from what I've said. But with the greatest of respect, can I ask you to just consider that there might be someone from your past who is behind this, someone who might have a grudge against you." She didn't wait for him to reply, she picked up her briefcase, stood up and extended her right hand. "Anyway, be assured we will do our absolute best to protect you," she said.

Grechko stood up and shook her hand. He smiled, but it lacked any human warmth, it was more an animal-like baring of his fifty-thousand-dollar dental work. "I am grateful for all your help with this," he said. "I am sure you are a very busy woman."

"Trust me, Mr Grechko, you are right at the top of my list of priorities."

Grechko released his grip on her hand and walked with her to the door. "I'll show Miss Button out," said Shepherd. "Then I'll go and have a chat with Dmitry."

Grechko nodded and went over to a phone as Shepherd walked with Button along the hallway and out through the front door. Her black BMW was parked in the turning circle. "I thought you were going to ask him if he'd killed anyone on his route to the top," said Shepherd.

"The thought had crossed my mind," said Button. "He won't listen, will he?"

"He's sure that it's the Kremlin behind the killings. But if he has got some skeletons in his past, he's hardly likely to tell you, is he?"

"Well, it's making our job a lot harder," said Button. She took her key fob out of her pocket. "We're going to take a closer look at Zakharov, Buryakov and Czernik."

"He might have a point," said Shepherd. "About the lie detector."

Button wrinkled her nose. "I meant what I said. Anything out of the ordinary might spook the killer."

"I get that, but what if we made it look like the lie detector was for some other reason?"

"I'm listening."

Shepherd chuckled. "That's all I have, unfortunately. But we could handle it so that all the staff have to take a lie detector test. Obviously we're just interested in the six new arrivals to the bodyguard team."

"And we ask them right out if they're helping a potential assassin?"

"We'd need a good operator, that's for sure. But he could be looking for general signs of nervousness. I'm just saying, the background checks haven't turned anything up yet, which means that we're pinning a lot on phone records. But if this assassin is as good as we think he is, I don't see him giving much away on the phone."

"That's a fair point," said Button.

"I don't mean to sound negative. I just think we might need to be a bit more proactive."

Button unlocked the BMW. "On that front, you need to get closer to the six newcomers. See if your Spidery sense tingles."

Shepherd chuckled. "I've met all six of them. And they all seem kosher."

"But then they would, wouldn't they? You need to have a closer look, and I'll talk to our technical people, see if they have any suggestions. And be careful, Spider. If the killer does have his own person on board, he'll probably move quickly." She got into her car, started the engine and waved before driving off. The electric gate was already rattling open. As Shepherd turned back to the house he saw Grechko at the window. Shepherd nodded but Grechko didn't see him, he was staring at Button's BMW as it drove through the gate and turned into The Bishops Avenue.

The New Forest consists of more than two hundred square miles of pasture, heath and woodland and is the perfect place for dog-walking, horse-riding, exploring ancient monuments, and disposing of a body. Shepherd knew that the best way of getting away with murder was to make sure that the body was never found, which was why he and Harper were driving through the New Forest looking for a suitable place for a grave. They had driven there in a white Transit van that Harper had bought from a dealer in Croydon. It still had the details of a plumbing firm painted on the sides and a cartoon of a dog in a flat cap cleaning a drain across the rear doors. Harper had paid in cash and had swapped the plates for a set showing the number of a similar van he'd seen in central London.

Harper had driven the van, leaving London on the M3 as it began to get dark, turning on to the M27 and then following the A31 for ten miles before, on Shepherd's instructions, turning off on an unnamed road that twisted and turned through thick woodland. There were no street lights and no other vehicles around so Harper had the lights on full beam, carving tunnels of light out of the darkness. Shepherd pointed ahead. "OK, let's see if we can turn off somewhere here, some place where the trees are far enough apart for us to drive in a ways." He'd spent an hour or so perusing a map of the New Forest so he knew exactly where they were.

Harper slowed down and indicated he was going to turn, then laughed at his stupidity and switched off the indicator. "Force of habit," he said. He slowed the van to a crawl, then spotted a gap in the trees and turned off the road. The van bucked and rocked and the steering wheel twisted and turned as if it had a life of its own. He managed to get a hundred feet or so before the trees were so close together that he had to stop. He braked and switched off the engine. "What do you think?" he asked.

"Should be OK," said Shepherd. He opened the passenger door and stepped out. The only sound was the clicking of the engine as it cooled. He blinked slowly as his night vision slowly kicked in. There was no way of telling which way the road was, other than by the tracks in the mud.

Harper climbed out of his side of the van. "What about poachers?"

"Poachers?"

"Yeah, poachers."

"You might as well worry about a UFO landing where we are," said Shepherd. "We're in the middle of nowhere. And tonight we're just digging a hole."

He walked around to the rear of the van and opened the doors. There were two brand-new spades there that Harper had bought from a garden centre before picking up Shepherd. Shepherd took them out, handed one to Harper, and shut the doors. "We need to walk a bit farther," he said, nodding at the vegetation. "Fifty feet or so should do it."

He walked through the trees, the spade on his shoulder. He was wearing a leather bomber jacket and had tied a scarf around his neck. Harper, as always, had on his parka, the hood up. Shepherd trod carefully — the ground was uneven and protruding tree roots threatened to trip him at every step. They reached a small clearing and Shepherd motioned for Harper to stop. The two men stood in silence, their breath feathering in the night air. A fox barked off in the distance and then went quiet. Shepherd tested the ground with his spade. "This'll do it," he said.

The two men began to dig and soon worked up a sweat. After ten minutes of hard digging Shepherd took off his jacket and scarf and put them at the base of a spreading beech tree. "The way you've organised this, it's like you've done it before," said Harper, resting on his spade. He looked around. "You got any more bodies buried out here, Spider?"

"I haven't, but it's the disposal area of choice for London's underworld."

"Are you serious?"

"Sure," said Shepherd. "Despite what you see on the TV, we're not awash with serial killers and professional assassins. But they are out there, and the good ones never get caught. And the reason they never get caught is that the bodies are never found." He took a deep breath and flexed his shoulders. He was physically fit but the earth was hard and his arms and back were already aching. "There are anywhere between six hundred and seven hundred murders a year in the United Kingdom, an average of about two a day. The vast majority are committed by a friend or family member, or a neighbour, and are wrapped up by the cops in a couple of hours, a day at the most. More often than not, the murderer's at the scene when the cops turn up, grief stricken and ready to confess."

"Yeah, well, we won't be doing that, that's for sure," said Harper. He took out his cigarettes, lit one and blew smoke up at the night sky. It was a cloudless night and away from the city all the stars were visible overhead, stretching off into infinity.

"See, the key to solving any murder, assuming the killer doesn't immediately confess, is to find the motive. If you know why someone has been killed you almost certainly know who by. And that's why it's almost impossible to catch a serial killer who kills at random, or a professional who does it for money."

"That's why the cops profile, right?"

"Yeah, all serial killers are white middle-aged men who wet their beds and set fire to their pets when they were kids," said Shepherd, his voice loaded with sarcasm. "It's not as simple as that. You watch TV and you think that catching serial killers is easy, but in fact profiling is next to useless. Look at the Yorkshire Ripper. White middle-aged male killing hookers in Leeds. That's as specific a profile as you could wish for. They spent millions trying to get him and they caught him by accident. Fred West? They only got him because he was so stupid he let one of his victims escape. And he buried his victims under his house." He pointed at the hole they were digging. "The real professionals — the ones that think about what they're doing — they make sure their victims are never found. Because without a body it's almost impossible to get a conviction."

"It happens, though."

"Only where there's a clear motive. Which is why no one must ever know why Khan has been killed. With no motive and no body, the cops won't get anywhere, even if they suspect foul play. But if we do this right, it won't even get to that. People go missing every year. Any idea how many?"

Harper shook his head.

"Over two hundred thousand," said Shepherd. "That's how many are reported missing. Now, all but two thousand or so turn up over the following year, but two thousand is still a hell of a lot, and unless there's some sign of a crime the cops just don't have the resources to follow them up. Unless they're kids. Everything changes if kids are involved, obviously."

Harper took a long pull on his cigarette, blew smoke, then extinguished it on the sole of his trainers and slipped the butt into the pocket of his parka. He nodded at the hole. "Isn't that deep enough?" They had dug down just over two feet and shovelled the earth into a neat pile.

"There's a reason that gravediggers go down six feet," said Shepherd. "Any less than that and there isn't enough weight to keep the coffin down. The earth really does give up the dead unless you plant them well deep." He dropped down into the hole and started to dig again.

Harper watched him, grinning. "Sadly there's only room for one of us in there."

"We'll take it in turns," said Shepherd. He worked hard for another ten minutes and stepped out to let Harper took his place. The more they dug the harder it became. The earth was stonier and more tightly packed and once they got below four feet it was hard to move in the hole. It took them an hour to go down the last two feet but finally Shepherd was satisfied. He was in the hole and Harper had to offer him an arm to pull him out. It was six feet deep, just over six feet long and varied in width from three feet to four feet.

"Can you do the GPS thing with the mobile?" asked Shepherd.

Harper nodded and pulled out a cheap Samsung phone. He switched it on and scrolled through the menu. "What the hell did we do before mobiles?" he asked.

"We'd have drawn a map with a cross on it," said Shepherd. "Seriously."

Harper laughed, tapped on the screen and showed it to Shepherd. "All done," he said.

"Bring your spade," said Shepherd, and he headed back to the van. Harper followed him. They tossed the spades into the back of the van and closed the doors. Harper took a deep breath. "I'll be glad when this is over," he said.

"Me too," agreed Shepherd.

"But it needs to be done, right?"

Shepherd nodded. "No question about that," he said.

Shepherd had just got back to his Hampstead flat when his phone rang. It was Button. "Sorry to bother you so late, but our interrogation boys have come back to me about the lie detector idea," said Button. "They seem to think that it's workable. The latest equipment is a lot more reliable than it used to be, and they've had some quite noticeable successes over the last few months."

"OK . . ." said Shepherd, hesitantly.

"They came up with quite a clever idea, I think. If Grechko says that he's had an expensive watch gone missing, he could request that all his staff be put through a lie detector. Everyone, his cooks, maids, serving staff, cleaners — and the security staff, of course. Now, because nobody has actually stolen the watch, everyone should pass with flying colours. But our guys can put in a few general questions, such as 'Have you ever given details about the security arrangements at the house to anyone else', and that should show up anyone who is helping our elusive killer. But in a way that doesn't raise any suspicions. What do you think?"

"I guess so," said Shepherd.

"You don't sound convinced."

"No, it's not a bad idea. You're right, if the maids and cleaners are done first, the bodyguards won't realise it's about them. What about the timing?"

"That's the problem, of course," said Button. "It's best if the same operator performs all the tests. It maintains consistency. And each test will take at least half an hour."

"Grechko has a big staff."

"Exactly. Including gardeners and maintenance workers, we're looking at about fifty people. Assuming two an hour, ten hours a day, it'll take three days to clear them all. And that's pretty hard going for the operator. It can be as stressful for them as for the people taking the test, it requires a lot of concentration."

"And we can't put all the new bodyguards in the first day because that would look suspicious."

"Perhaps not. We could say that we're doing the new arrivals first."

"Except that if anyone was stealing it'd be more likely to be the cleaning staff or the serving staff."

"I agree, it's a difficult line to tread. But we're not having much luck on the phone front and I do worry that if we don't do something, the killer might try again. I'm going to run this by Mr Grechko first thing in the morning and if he's agreeable I'll get our lie detector guy out there in the afternoon. Strike while the iron's hot. If there's anyone you think should be looked at urgently, feel free to put the names forward."

"Will do," said Shepherd.

"OK, we'll talk tomorrow. Sleep tight."

The line went dead and Shepherd put down the phone. He couldn't go to sleep yet. He had to shower to get rid of the New Forest dirt and then he had to put his clothes through the washing machine, twice. And his boots had to be thoroughly cleaned to remove all traces of what he had been doing that night.

Shepherd arrived at the house at seven and got to the briefing room to find that the chef had delivered a plate of egg and bacon rolls, a large bowl of creamy kedgeree and a plate of croissants. McIntyre was already tucking into a roll and he grinned at Shepherd. "You didn't tell me how good the scoff was," he said.

"Scoff?" repeated Popov, who was sitting at the head of the table with a notepad in front of him.

"Food," translated Shepherd.

Grigory Sokolov was making coffee and he looked over at Shepherd. Shepherd flashed a thumbs-up in answer to the unspoken question and Sokolov handed him a mug of coffee.

"What's today looking like?" Shepherd asked Popov.

"Quiet," said Popov. "We have three visitors during the day, and four guests for dinner. I'll run all the details by you but they have all been here before." He looked at his watch. "Where the hell is Leo? He'll be late for his own funeral." At the exact moment he finished speaking the door opened and Tarasov appeared. He apologised for his lateness and sat down, pushing his Oakleys up on top of his head.

After the briefing, Shepherd went out into the garden and called Shortt. "Tomorrow, is tomorrow good for you?" he asked Shortt.

"I don't see why not," said Shortt. "How did you get on last night?"

"Lex had me doing most of the manual work but we've got it done. We've got the van sorted and the guns. So we need to do it as soon as possible."

"Why not today?"

"I've got a lot on and I'm not sure when I'll be able to get away. But tomorrow should be good and I'll send Jock over to yours during the day."

"I'll make sure the little woman's playing golf," said Shortt.

"See you tomorrow, then." Shepherd ended the call. He looked at his watch. It was just after half past eight. He figured that it would be late morning at least before he heard from Button so he changed into his running gear and went for a run on Hampstead Heath for the best part of an hour.

When he returned to the house he showered and changed and went back to the security centre, where McIntyre was monitoring the CCTV monitors. "This is one hell of a system," he said to Shepherd, nodding at the screens.

"The best that money can buy," said Shepherd. "It switches to IR at night, and all the cameras are motion and heat sensitive. Where's Popov?"

"Grechko wanted to see him."

"Did he say why?"

McIntyre shook his head. Shepherd went into the briefing room to make himself a coffee. He was just adding milk when Popov stormed in. "You won't believe this," he said.

"What?" said Shepherd, even though he had a pretty good idea what was upsetting the man.

"The boss has lost a watch. And he thinks it's been stolen."

"I would think he could live without a watch," said Shepherd.

Popov busied himself at the coffee machine. "Not this one," he said. "It's a Patek Philippe worth four million dollars."

Shepherd whistled. "Four million dollars?"

"It's one of his favourites. He's had it for years. He said it was in his study yesterday and went missing some time in the afternoon."

"Is he calling in the cops?" asked Shepherd.

"He's got a better idea. He's bringing in a lie detector expert and he wants everyone in the house to be tested. And he wants you in there supervising."

"Me? Why?"

"Because you're a cop and for some reason he trusts you more than me. I have to say, Tony, this really pisses me off." He turned to face Shepherd. "It's as if he doesn't trust me. Does he think I stole his bloody watch?"

"It's more that he wants an outsider supervising," said Shepherd. "Someone impartial."

"Yeah, well, I'll be the first one to be tested, that's for sure." He grimaced and sat down. "I'll tell you this much, when I find out who stole the watch, I'll personally castrate them."

The lie detector expert arrived at just after three. His name was Jules Lee and he was Chinese but spoke English with a strong Newcastle accent. He was driving a Volvo estate and, to show his displeasure, Popov insisted that Sokolov and Tarasov searched Lee and his car thoroughly and checked his ID before allowing him to drive into the underground parking area. Shepherd went with him. "They're letting us use the library for the tests," said Shepherd. "Is there anything you need?"

"I've got everything with me," said Lee. He was a small man, barely over five feet, and was sitting on a cushion to see over the steering wheel. It was difficult to judge his age as his face was almost unnaturally smooth and devoid of wrinkles or blemishes, but there were dark liver spots on his hands that suggested he was in his fifties. He was wearing round wire-framed glasses and a grey suit and had a thin gold wedding band.

"What about a translator?" asked Shepherd. "Is it better to do it in English or Russian?" He pointed to a parking space.

"Either will be fine," said Lee, reversing into the space. "I'm fluent in both."

"Seriously?"

Lee grinned. "I speak six languages," he said. "What can I say? I had a tiger mother. She wasn't above paddling my backside if I didn't remember a hundred new words by bedtime."

"And Charlie's explained everything?"

Lee nodded and switched off the engine. "It's an interesting one," he said. "Challenging."

Shepherd took a folded sheet of paper from his pocket and gave it to Lee. "These are the six who joined Grechko's security team after the sniping attempt," he said. "Max Barsky, Thomas Lisko, Alina Podolski, Viktor Alexsandrov, Timofei Domashevich and Yakov Gunter. Of the six I think that Domashevich is the . . ."

Lee held up his hand. "Best not to influence me," he said.

"Understood," said Shepherd. "Did Charlie explain that we need to question those six at random so that no one realises they are being singled out?"

"She did," said Lee. He put the paper in his pocket, popped the rear door and climbed out of the car. Popov came walking down the ramp towards them.

"He doesn't seem happy," said Lee, opening the rear door.

"His nose is a bit out of joint, but he's OK," said Shepherd.

Lee's equipment was in two metal cases and he insisted that he carry them both. Popov led the way to the lift. He pressed his thumb against the scanner, entered his four-digit code and walked into the lift first.

When they arrived at the ground floor, Popov led them along to the library. Two tables had been set up in the middle of the room with two high-backed chrome and leather chairs. "Do you need anything else?" he asked.

"This will be fine," said Lee, placing the two cases on one of the tables. "I would like a glass of water if you have it, and perhaps green tea?"

"I'm not a fucking butler," said Popov, but he put up a hand in apology when Shepherd glared at him. "My apologies," he said. "I'll get you tea and water."

He left the room and Shepherd watched as Lee assembled his equipment. Shepherd wasn't sure what to expect — he'd seen polygraphs in movies and they always had lots of needles moving across graph paper, but Lee's kit seemed to be a regular laptop, albeit in a brushed stainless steel case. Lee connected two rubber straps to the computer, and several other attachments, which he laid out on the second table.

Popov returned with a tray on which there was a bottle of water and a glass of ice, and a handleless cup with steaming green tea. He put the tray on the table and sat down. "You can do me first," he said.

"I have a list to work through," said Lee as he tapped on his keyboard.

"If you are to question any members of my team, you will do me first," said Popov.

Lee looked over at Shepherd, and Shepherd nodded. Lee fastened the rubber straps around Popov's barrel-like chest, attached a white clip to his left index finger and asked him to remove his tie and open his shirt. Popov did as asked and Lee dabbed two electrodes with gel and placed them on his shoulder blades.

"OK?" said Popov, as Lee went to sit in the chair and looked at his computer. "Right? I did not steal Mr Grechko's fucking watch. I have never stolen a fucking watch. I will never steal a fucking watch." He scowled at Lee. "Are we done?"

Lee looked at him over the top of his glasses. "I'm afraid it isn't quite as simple as that," he said.

Monotok woke with a start, his heart racing. He stared up at the ceiling and took slow deep breaths. He'd always had bad dreams but the nightmares were visiting him more often now and he didn't understand why that would be. Three of the men were dead and the fourth would be dead soon and he had always believed that killing them would end the nightmares.

The dreams were never the same, not exactly. But they always involved the death of his parents, or the man who had taken care of him after they had died — Boronin, the farmer.

Monotok was six years old when the Berlin Wall had fallen. He'd watched it happen on television with his mother and father, and his father had told him then that the world — their world — was about to change for ever. Monotok wasn't called the Hammer back then, of course, he was little Kirill, a sickly child who caught every bug going, with pale skin and spindly arms and legs that never seemed to get any stronger no matter how much food his mother forced down him. "Kirill, soon the world will open up to us Russians, and we must be ready to take advantage of it." Monotok's father was the manager of a steel factory some two hundred miles east of Moscow, a huge hellish place of flames and smoke that always filled Monotok with a mixture of dread and awe whenever his father took him to visit.

It seemed to the young boy that the factory was staffed by giants, big men stained with soot and sweat with bulging muscles and rippling chests who communicated with nods and grunts but who smiled whenever they saw how scared he was, hiding from them behind his father's legs.

Monotok was eight when the Soviet Union fell apart, and again his father had tried to explain the significance of the monumental event. He had chosen

422

his words carefully, because even as the Soviet Union collapsed, the KGB were still everywhere and the state came down heavily on dissenters. Monotok remembered little about what his father had said, other than that he was excited about the prospect of being given more responsibility at work and that the government would let him run the factory the way he wanted to. His father had big plans, he wanted to expand the factory, seek out export markets, and increase the wages of his staff. All of it would happen in time, he promised his son, all they had to do was to wait and see.

What Mark Luchenko didn't know was that the fall of the Berlin Wall and the subsequent demise of the Soviet Union would result not in a capitalist boost for his factory but in his own death and the death of his wife, Monotok's mother.

Monotok was orphaned shortly after his ninth birthday. His uncle took him away from the house and they never returned. By the age of ten, Monotok had been "adopted" by a farmer, Sergei Boronin, a widower who bought Monotok from his uncle for fifty roubles, as if he was mere livestock.

Boronin's farm, little more than a smallholding, was in a remote area, beyond the Ural Mountains, a thousand miles east of Moscow. He proved to be a vodka-sodden, petty tyrant who beat Monotok, kept him out of school and used him as virtual slave labour on his farm. If Monotok complained or didn't work fast enough, or if Boronin was angry or hung over from one of the vodka-fuelled binges that followed his weekly visits to the small town where he sold his animals and bought his supplies, Monotok would get another brutal beating.

There was worse to come. One night Boronin returned drunk as usual from a trip to town. Monotok was already in bed, and when he heard his bedroom door open, he pretended to be asleep, fearing another beating. There was the shuffling sound of Boronin's footsteps and then a creak as he sat down on the edge of the bed. He spent some time looking down at the boy and then the blanket was pulled aside and Monotok felt the farmer's calloused hand on his thigh. He lay motionless, still trying to feign sleep, though his heart was pounding. He heard the rustle of fabric as Boronin fumbled with his trousers and then the farmer's weight was on him, crushing him and pinning him down, and a moment later the boy felt a burning, agonising pain.

That brutal ritual became such a regular part of his life that he grew to dread the sky darkening into evening because he knew what the night would bring. At first it was just Boronin himself, but after a few weeks, other men began to appear at the isolated cabin in the forest, bringing a bottle of vodka and perhaps a couple of roubles for the farmer. Monotok would hear voices and the clink of glasses, and then his door would open and a figure would be outlined against the glow of light from the kitchen where Boronin still sat, pouring himself another drink.

Monotok ran away twice but both times was found by the police, who ignored his tearful pleas and protests and returned him to his guardian. Each time, after the police had drunk Boronin's vodka and gone, Boronin would wrap the end of his belt around his fist and beat the boy almost senseless.

In the end Monotok became numbed to everything that happened to him. The beatings and the nightly abuse became just another part of his life, as hard, unvarying and predictable as the work of feeding and mucking out the animals that he had to carry out. But, although now outwardly calm and resigned to his fate, inside he burned with dreams of revenge.

He was patient — he had to be — but every day he schemed, planned and prepared for his opportunity. Although Boronin worked him like a dog, Monotok used what little spare time he had to further build his strength and stamina, taking long runs through the taiga — the forest that spread unbroken across northern Russia, spanning nine time zones — and using logs, buckets of water and large stones as primitive weights.

On the rare occasions when Boronin took Monotok with him to town, he grabbed the chance to toughen himself and hone his fighting skills by picking fights with much bigger boys. Inevitably he took a few beatings at first but kicks and blows were too familiar to him to be a concern, and before long, he was flattening any boy who got in his way, landing his blows with a cold, cruel calculation, his pulse rate barely rising above normal as he beat them into submission and then laid them out with a final brutal punch or kick.

When he was fourteen years old, he felt he was ready. He chose his moment well: a midwinter night so bitterly cold that his footsteps rang like struck metal on the ice-bound ground as he crossed the yard from the barn where the animals were housed. He waited for Boronin to return home from the town that night, stumbling drunk through the snow, clutching yet another bottle of vodka. Monotok watched him struggle out of his coat and make his unsteady way to his seat by the fire, but as Boronin turned his baleful, bloodshot gaze towards him Monotok spat in his face and then rained blows and kicks on him, beating him relentlessly to a bloody pulp.

He left him lying unconscious on the floor in a pool of blood while he went through his pockets. He took all the money and valuables he could find, and when he could not pull the farmer's gold wedding ring from his swollen finger, he severed it with a knife, giving a cold smile as Boronin jerked back into consciousness with an ear-splitting scream of agony.

Monotok pocketed the ring, straightened up and booted him in the ribs one last time, savouring the crack of splintering bone. Monotok — measured, unhurried — picked up the bottle of vodka that had fallen from Boronin's fingers as the assault began and poured the alcohol all over Boronin's clothes. Then he pulled a blazing chunk of wood from the fireplace and set fire to him.

He retreated to the doorway as blue flames snaked over Boronin's body, then caught the fabric of his frayed clothes. Monotok watched impassively as the blinded farmer stumbled to his feet and blundered around the room, trying in vain to beat out the flames with his hands. The tattered curtains caught fire, adding to the inferno. Boronin fell to the floor and began rolling on the ground in a frantic attempt to extinguish the flames, and howled in torment as his flesh blackened and burned. Eventually he collapsed in a smouldering heap while the flames began to devour his log-built home. It burned down around him, becoming his funeral pyre.

Monotok left the farm for ever that night. He made one other call, on the uncle who had sold him into his slavery. He flattened his uncle as soon as he answered the knock at his door, cut out his tongue so that he could not cry for help, then hamstrung him by severing the tendons behind his ankles so he couldn't walk. Monotok then slashed him with a knife across his face, torso and arms — enough to weaken him from blood loss but not enough to kill him — and then threw him into the pigsty behind his house. He watched the pigs begin their feast, then moved away through the forest into the night.

Monotok walked through the night, following forest tracks and single-track roads without seeing a single vehicle. He reached a remote station just after dawn, warming himself by the stove in the wooden hut that served as a waiting room and drinking black tea from a samovar watched over by a toothless old babushka, as he waited for the westbound train. He travelled a thousand miles west to Moscow and moved into an abandoned apartment in a dismal Stalinist-era block,

427

where the lifts had not worked in twenty years and the stairs stank of urine and worse. It was one of Moscow's poorest and most violent districts, but his neighbours, mostly drug addicts, alcoholics and petty criminals, who preyed on each other and on the handful of other inhabitants of the block, too old, too poor or too ill to escape, soon learned to stay out of his way.

For almost two years he lived a semi-feral existence, using his wits and his fists to survive, always in and out of trouble with the law for thefts and assaults. Then he made what could have been a fatal mistake, giving a savage beating to a man who richly deserved it, but who was also the son of a Russian mafia boss. With a price on his head and no other way out, though still aged just sixteen, Monotok lied about his age and enlisted in the army. The minimum age was eighteen but he was tough and powerfully built, and his battered face, marked and scarred in scores of fights, made him look much older than his years.

He joined the Spetsnaz — the Soviet Special Forces, or "Special Purposes" troops, as the Russians themselves described them. Unlike the British SAS, the Spetsnaz were not soldiers first who then became special forces by passing a bruising selection process; raw recruits were inducted straight into the Spetsnaz and did their entire military training with them.

Spetsnaz training was designed to break down recruits and then rebuild them, but they never broke Monotok. He never once failed to do what was asked of him, no matter how gruelling the task. When his instructors ordered him to do a hundred press-ups with a full bergen on his back, he did it. When ordered to run a mile through a forest with a colleague over his shoulders, he gritted his teeth and did it. They made him lie fully clothed in an icy mountain stream for two hours, and he emerged close to death but still smiling. He knew that there was nothing they could do to him that was worse than what he had suffered at the hands of his tormentor.

When fully trained, Monotok and his unit were deployed to a barracks north of Prenzlau, close to the Polish border and a few miles from the Baltic coast. They left there only for training exercises and to go on operations, where Monotok proved himself the fittest, strongest and most ruthlessly effective soldier of his entire unit. He was too much of a loner to be a good team player — none of his comrades liked him or trusted him — but he was a cool and cold-blooded killer, who never showed the slightest trace of emotion, fear or panic, no matter what was thrown at him, and he never failed in the task he was set. His talents were noted by his superiors and he began to be selected for special assignments, assignments that more often than not involved assassinations.

Monotok was a skilled assassin, and he killed without remorse or conscience. He had been trained as a sniper but was as comfortable killing with knives, garrottes and handguns as he was with a rifle. After a dozen kills he was sent with his unit to Chechnya. Russia was tightening its grip on the republic following a terrorist attack on a Moscow cinema by armed Chechen rebels that ended with the death of one hundred and thirty civilians. Monotok was part of an assassination unit tasked with killing a dozen of the rebels who had planned the raid. Within six months of arriving in the republic all were dead. In 2006, Monotok was part of a unit responsible for the targeted bombing of Shamil Basayev, the prime mover in the Chechen Islamic rebel movement, but Basayev was only one of twenty Chechens that he helped kill that year. He had become a relentless killing machine, devoid of all emotion or empathy as he carried out his orders.

It was in 2009 that Monotok saw the picture that took his life down a different path. He was still in Chechnya, but Russia was winding down its anti-terrorist operations there and Monotok was preparing to return to Prenzlau. The picture was in a week-old copy of *Komsomolksaya Pravda*, the biggest-selling newspaper in Russia. It had started life as the official organ of the Communist Union of Youth but following the break-up of the Soviet Union had become a tabloid with more than three million readers. One of Monotok's colleagues had returned from leave with the paper in his pocket, and during a break between missions Monotok had flicked through it. He had never been a big reader and rarely watched television. He didn't care about anything that happened in the outside world, his life revolved around the Spetsnaz and his assignments, he cared for little else. Monotok had recognised the man in the photograph immediately, though the name meant nothing to him. Pyotr Grechko.

The story was about Grechko trying, and failing, to buy Liverpool Football Club. Monotok wasn't interested in football, or any sport, but he read and reread the story more than a dozen times. Peter Grechko was one of the richest men in the world, the story said, a man who had fought his way up from humble beginnings to head a transport empire that literally spanned the world. But Monotok knew the truth about how Grechko had started on the road to unimaginable wealth, and as he stared at the newspaper he decided that the time had come to get his revenge. He left the Spetsnaz in the winter of 2010. His superiors offered him all sorts of incentives to stay — promotion, money, more leave, foreign travel — but Monotok refused them all. The only thing he cared about was the revenge that was rightfully his.

Monotok went freelance, working for a former Spetsnaz colonel who had joined up with a former KGB assassin to set up a murder-for-hire company. Assassinations were a common way of solving political and business disagreements in post-Soviet Russia and Monotok had an average of one job a week. Clients included the Kremlin, the Mafia and even legitimate businesses, eager to use a professional service that guaranteed to keep the killings at arm's length. Monotok earned good money, ten times what he earned as a soldier, and he learned quickly. For the Spetsnaz he had been a simple killer, following orders, but as a freelance he learned about electronic surveillance, accessing databases, and gained access to fake documentation that allowed him to move freely around the world under a number of aliases. He hired a tutor to teach him English, and as his fluency increased the company sent him farther afield and Monotok killed in Europe and the United States. When he wasn't working, Monotok dug up as much information as he could on Pyotr Grechko. And it didn't take him long to track down three more faces from his past. Oleg Zakharov, Yuri Buryakov and Sasha Czernik. All four had become rich and powerful oligarchs, men who had the sort of wealth that others could only dream of, men for whom the world was a giant playground. But Monotok knew the truth about the four men, he knew that it wasn't hard work or luck that had brought them their wealth. It had been cold-blooded murder, and for that they had to pay. Now Zakharov, Buryakov and Czernik were dead, and soon Grechko would join them. Then maybe the nightmares would finally stay away and he could sleep soundly for the first time since he was nine years old.

He tensed as he heard a key slot into the front door lock, but then almost immediately relaxed. It was seven o'clock in the morning. It was the girl, returning home. He heard the front door open and close, and then a shuffling sound as she removed her shoes. He smiled as he heard her tiptoe down the hallway and gently open the bedroom door. She paused, then tiptoed towards the bathroom. He let her get all the way to the bathroom door before speaking. "I'm not asleep."

She jumped, and then laughed. "I was trying not to wake you." She jumped on the bed, rolled on top of him and kissed him.

"Alina, you will never be able to sneak up on me, no matter how hard you try. If I had been a heavy sleeper when I was a teenager, I would have died, beaten to death as I slept."

"My wild man," said Podolski. She laughed as he ran his hands over her body. "Are you going to hammer me?" she asked.

He rolled her on to her back and she opened her legs as he moved on top of her. "There's no one I'd rather hammer than you."

She put her hands either side of his face. "Bullshit, Kirill. You're using me. Don't pretend otherwise. You're using me to get the inside track on that pig Grechko."

"You're helping me," said Monotok. "And I'll show you my gratitude." He started to pull off her shirt and slid his hand up to her breasts.

"I'll do it," she said, pushing him off her. "You fumble."

He laughed as he rolled on to his back and she straddled him. "I do not fumble."

She undid her shirt, slid it off and tossed it on to the floor. "You fumble," she said. "But I forgive you." She undid her bra and let her breasts swing free. "Now shut up and hammer me."

Afterwards, he lay on his back staring up at the ceiling, his arm around her as she toyed with the hairs on his chest. She felt tiny lying next to him, soft and warm like a small bird. "Something strange happened today," she said quietly.

"Really? What?"

"We've all got to take a lie detector test. Grechko's orders."

"Why didn't you tell me before?" he asked.

She laughed softly. "Because I wanted you to hammer me," she said. "And if I told you, you'd want to talk and not fuck."

He gave her a small squeeze. His heart had started to race but he forced himself to stay calm and to keep his voice level and soothing. "You're a bad girl," he said, then kissed her softly on the top of her head.

"And you're a bad man. That's why we're so good together."

"You're not a bad girl, Alina. You have no idea what it is to be bad. So who has been questioned so far?"

"The butler. Two of the maids. They did Dmitry first, he insisted."

"And who is carrying out the tests?"

"Some sort of expert."

"Russian? Or English?"

"Chinese. British Chinese. Or Chinese British. But he speaks Russian."

"And he will be questioning everyone at the house?"

"That's what Dmitry says. But it's nothing, it's about a stolen watch. Grechko has lost one of his watches. It's worth four million dollars, they say. It's a Patek Philippe, made of platinum. Old and very valuable."

"And they say someone stole it?"

"From his bedroom. There is no CCTV there. It's not a problem, he's just asking if you stole the watch, I didn't so it'll be OK."

"How long does each test take?"

He felt her shrug. "Half an hour. Maybe more."

"Then he's not just asking about the watch," said Monotok. "This expert, does he seem to know the two British guys who joined the security team?"

"I'm not sure. But Tony is sitting in on the tests. He's in the library all the time."

"And who did he arrive with, this expert?"

"He came alone. Just after three o'clock yesterday afternoon."

"And when did the watch go missing?"

"Yesterday, I think. Grechko called Dmitry in yesterday morning."

"Who hired this expert? Who called him in?"

She shook her head. "I don't know. Dmitry didn't say."

"But it wasn't Dmitry's idea?"

"I don't think so."

"And he's British, you said?"

"That's right. Well, like I said, he's Chinese. But he has an accent like he comes from the North. Not Scottish. It's strange."

"If it was Grechko's idea he would probably have used a Russian. Don't you think?"

"He prefers Russians, yes."

Monotok nodded. "What about the woman who comes to see Grechko? The one who knows Ryan. Has she been again?"

"No. What's wrong? You think this is about you?"

"I think it is unlikely that any member of Grechko's staff would be stupid enough to steal from him. Especially a four-million-dollar watch." He took a deep breath and exhaled slowly. "They know," he said quietly.

He felt her tense. "They know what?"

"They know that someone is passing information on Grechko. At least they suspect. When are you due to be tested?"

"Tonight. After I report for work." She frowned. "It's a problem?"

"They'll be looking for signs of anxiety. Nervousness."

"I'm not nervous," she said, stroking his chest.

"You don't feel nervous but the signs will be there. Respiration rate, sweat, skin conductivity, pulse rate. Things that you have no control over."

"I'll take deep breaths and think sweet thoughts." She laughed. "I'll think about you hammering me."

"That won't work," he said. "There are ways of beating the machines but it takes practice and the right drugs." He kissed her on the cheek. "Did they say when they want to test you? Is there a schedule?"

"They just come and get you. It could be any time."

He nodded as he stared up at the ceiling. "We do it tonight," he said quietly.

"Tonight? Are you sure?"

"It has to be," said Monotok. "If they suspect you in any way they'll move you from the team and then you'll be no use to me."

She grabbed a handful of chest hair and pulled, hard enough to make him yelp. "See! You are using me!"

He rolled on top of her and kissed her. "You're helping me, and I'm grateful. Really grateful. And when this is over, I'll show you how grateful."

"You won't leave me?"

"Alina, I swear I won't leave you. Once I've taken care of Grechko it's over. The four of them will be dead and I can move on."

"With me?"

"With you."

"You promise?"

"I promise."

She smiled and kissed him again.

Monotok returned the kiss and then broke away. "Who is on the shift with you tonight?"

She frowned as she tried to remember. "Vlad, and his bloody porn. He'll be in the security centre for the whole shift. Leo will be there, he's not on shift but he lives in the house. Same with Konstantin. The British guy. Ryan will be there. He's been working with the lie detector guy. And Boris. And Max. And Dmitry. He's always there. Thomas will be on the gate. That's all. Grechko is in all night and there are no visitors expected."

"Max still fancies you, right?"

"He's just a boy," she said. She laughed and ran her hand down his chest towards his groin. "Are you jealous?"

"Of course I'm jealous," he said, and kissed her on the forehead. "OK, we'll use Max. You can call him and tell him you'll give him a lift. Tell him there's something you need to talk to him about."

"OK, but you need to do one thing for me," she said, slipping her hand between his thighs.

"Anything," he said.

"Hammer me again," she said, rolling on to her back and opening her legs.

Shepherd and McIntyre walked across the lawn at the rear of the house. It was lunchtime and Jules Lee was taking a break from his second day of conducting the lie detector tests. They had already done four of the new intake of bodyguards — Thomas Lisko, Viktor Alexsandrov, Timofei Domashevich and Yakov Gunter. Lisko had been one of the first to be done the previous day, and Alexsandrov had been tested just before Lee had left at seven o'clock. Both had passed with flying colours. They had done Domashevich and Gunter that morning and they had also passed. Max Barsky and Alina Podolski were pencilled in for later that evening. Lee had agreed to work until late, though he had dropped heavy hints about expecting to be paid overtime once he went beyond six o'clock. That meant that either Barsky or Podolski was the mole or the test just wasn't working. Or his whole theory was wrong and none of the six was helping the killer.

In a perfect world they would have just questioned the six suspects but that would have tipped off the mole that it wasn't about a missing watch so Lee had to interrogate the bewildered kitchen and housekeeping staff with the same intensity that he questioned the suspects.

438

"This is money for old rope, isn't it?" said McIntyre, taking a pack of Wrigley's chewing gum from his pocket and slotting a piece into his mouth.

"Bodyguarding?" Shepherd shrugged. "It's all good up until the moment you have to throw yourself in front of a bullet."

"Yeah, but the pay's good and that cook is brilliant. Her club sandwiches are out of this world. Chicken, egg, ham, cheese and I don't know what else. And those chips. How does she make them taste that good?"

"She fries them twice," said Shepherd. "She explained how it works, something about cooks them inside and keeps them crispy. Jock, you know this isn't a real job, right?"

"Speak for yourself," said McIntyre.

"You know what I mean. I'm here to catch the guy that's trying to kill Grechko. Once that's done, I'm off."

"And what about me?"

"Jock, you're here to help me. When I go, you go. You're not even here under your own name, remember? You're Alastair McEwan."

"I get that, but a job's a job, right? I can do this standing on my head, and it pays a hell of a lot better than babysitting an empty office building." He grabbed Shepherd's elbow. "I'm serious, Spider. I want to give this a shot."

Shepherd shrugged. "Go for it, then. Your CV's good enough."

"Dmitry was saying that he's got mates out in Cyprus who work with former SAS guys."

"Yeah, I heard that. I didn't get any names, but there are some principals who prefer SAS protection."

"And I can do the old Sean Connery impersonation a treat, that'll go down well." He grinned. "The name's McIntyre," he said in a passable impersonation of the Scottish actor. "Jock McIntyre. Licensed to kill."

"Licensed to bullshit, more like," said Shepherd. "But yeah, seriously, go for it. Now to get to the point, we're doing it tonight."

McIntyre nodded, suddenly serious. "OK."

"You need to meet up with Jimbo this afternoon and get the suppressors sorted. Lex will pick you and Jimbo up in the van and I'll meet up with you in Bayswater."

"How do I get to Wembley?"

"I'll call you a minicab. Get it to drop you at Paddington and then catch a black cab from there to Wembley but get out a few hundred yards from Jimbo's house and walk the rest of the way. I'll tell Popov you have to collect some things from Reading. Remember to leave your mobile here."

"What about you?"

"I'm tied up here with the lie detector test but I'm only interested in one and when that's done I'll drive over in my X5. We'll use the van out to the New Forest then when it's done we'll shower and do laundry at my place and then drive back here."

"Sounds like you've got it all worked out."

"Has to be that way, Jock. We'll only get one go at this and it has to be done right."

Podolski pressed the doorbell and tidied her hair, her crash helmet tucked under her arm. The door opened and Max Barsky grinned at her like a lovesick schoolboy. It was clear from the moment he'd first seen her that he fancied her, especially as they were both from the Ukraine. He was a nice enough boy, but at twenty-three, that was what he was, a boy. And Podolski preferred men. "Alina, come in," he said, stepping to the side. "The place is a bit of a mess, I had hardly any time to tidy up."

"You need a woman to take care of you," she said, patting him on the arm as she walked by him.

"So what was so urgent that you needed to see me before the shift?" he asked.

She put her crash helmet on a table in the hallway and turned to face him. "What do you think?" she said, and smiled.

Barsky frowned, not understanding, but as Podolski unzipped her leather motorcycle jacket, a smile slowly spread across his face. "Are you serious?" he asked, unable to believe his luck.

He took a step towards her, forgetting that the door behind him was still open. Monotok stepped into the hallway and brought the butt of his gun down on the back of Barsky's head. He fell to the ground without a sound. Monotok put the gun away and closed the door, before dragging Barsky into a cramped sitting room that stank of stale pizza and sweat.

He took a handful of long plastic ties from a backpack and gave them to Podolski. "Do his ankles," he said. "One's enough but use three or four. Then find something to gag him with."

As Podolski began to bind Barsky's ankles with the plastic ties, Monotok reached into the backpack again and pulled out a pair of rubber-handled secateurs. Podolski grimaced. "Is there no other way?" she asked.

Monotok grinned cruelly. "It's a bit late to worry about that now, my love," he said. He knelt down next to the unconscious man and lifted up his right hand. Podolski turned her head and closed her eyes as Monotok slotted the blades of the pruning shears either side of the thumb. He pressed hard and there was a crunch like a stick of celery being broken and blood spurted across the carpet. "See," said Monotok as the severed thumb fell away. "It didn't hurt a bit."

"There you go," said McIntyre, placing the two home-made suppressors on the kitchen table. He'd made the two suppressors from plastic Evian bottles packed with Brillo pads. A clear tube made from the tops of bottles formed a passage for the bullets through the bottle, and the wire wool would absorb most of the sound of the round firing.

Shortt picked one of them up and nodded appreciatively. "Nice," he said. "I hope you cleaned up after yourself?"

"All the waste is in a carrier bag in your garage," he said. "We can burn it with the rest of the stuff."

Shortt gestured at the two Makarov pistols on the table. "And we use duct tape to fasten them to the guns?"

"Duct tape works just fine. It'll be good for two or three shots and that's all we'll need."

The doorbell rang and both men jumped. Shortt grinned shamefacedly. "If it was the wife, she wouldn't ring the bell," he said. He went to open the front door. It was Harper. The white van was parked in the street outside.

"Hey, hey, the gang's all here," said Harper.

"Come on in, mate," said Shortt. "We've got time for a coffee before we head off to meet Spider."

The gate opened and Podolski waved at Thomas Lisko in the guardhouse. He waved back. She looked to her left, where Monotok was at the wheel of Barsky's car. Because she had stopped the bike close to the driver's door Lisko wasn't able to see who was driving. As the car moved forward, Podolski matched its speed, keeping herself between the car and the guardhouse.

As they approached the garage the doors rattled up and Podolski accelerated and led the car down into the parking area. The gate closed behind them.

Podolski drove over to the far end of the parking area and climbed off the bike. Monotok reversed into a parking space and switched off the engine. Podolski removed her crash helmet and put it on one of the bike's mirrors. She smiled at Monotok. She wanted to go over and kiss him but she knew that he wouldn't open the window in case anyone was watching on the CCTV. He winked and reclined his seat so that he was almost horizontal.

She flashed him a smile and started walking to the security centre, her heart racing. She took deep breaths to calm herself down, one hand holding the shoulder strap of her backpack.

She took off the glove on her right hand and pressed her thumb against the sensor, then tapped in her security code. Vlad Molchanov was sitting in front of the CCTV monitors. As the door opened he hurriedly switched off his iPad but not before Podolski caught a glimpse of naked flesh. She couldn't tell whether it was male or female. "So what's happening, Vlad?" she asked.

"Mr Grechko's in the pool. He just went in. Dmitry's in the gym with Leo. Konstantin's in the library doing the lie detector thing."

"Where's Boris?"

"In here!" called Volkov from the briefing room. "Glad you made it, I'm gasping for a cup of coffee."

"I was just about to offer," said Podolski. She put her backpack on the floor, then slipped off her motorcycle jacket and hung it on the coat rack by the door. "Where's Tony?"

"The library. He's in on all the lie detector tests. You know they want you in there this evening?"

"Yeah, Dmitry told me yesterday."

"They're doing Konstantin then one of the kitchen workers and then you." He frowned. "What happened to Max?"

Podolski froze. "What do you mean?"

"He came in with you, right? Where is he?"

Podolski forced a smile. "He went to see the chef. Said he hadn't eaten all day."

Molchanov chuckled. "He's always eating, that lad. He'll be as big as a house soon."

Podolski went over to the coffee machine and made three coffees. Volkov was engrossed in a bodybuilding magazine so didn't notice as she took the small plastic vial from her pocket and poured the contents equally into two of the mugs. Both Volkov and Molchanov took two sugars in their coffee so she spooned it in and stirred vigorously. Monotok had told her that the drug was tasteless, fast acting, and would render them unconscious for at least eight hours.

She put one of the mugs down in front of Volkov and he thanked her with a grunt. She took the other two mugs through into the outer room and gave one to Molchanov. She sat down and sipped her coffee as she looked at the CCTV screens. On one she could see Barsky's car. The lights reflecting off the windscreen meant she couldn't see Monotok, but she knew that he was there. Waiting.

Lex Harper looked at his watch for the hundredth time. It was coming up for six. "He'll be here," said Shortt. They were sitting in the white Transit van in the car park on top of the Whiteley's shopping centre in Bayswater. They had arranged to meet Shepherd there at just after six.

"He's always on time," said McIntyre. He was sitting in the back of the van on the floor. Next to him was a holdall containing the two revolvers and the two

Russian pistols with the home-made suppressors now attached with duct tape.

"He'll be here," said Shortt. "Stop worrying."

Monotok took slow, deep breaths, preparing himself mentally for what was to come. In his right hand he was holding a SIG Sauer P227. It was one of his favourite handguns, a high-powered, high-capacity pistol that took .45 ACP rounds and held ten in the clip. In his left hand he held a pair of ATN PVS7 night vision goggles, standard issue to US Army ground troops. They weighed just one and a half pounds and were powered by two AA batteries that would sustain the unit for at least ten hours. The gun was to take care of any of Grechko's security team who tried to get in his way. When he finally came face to face with Grechko, he wouldn't be using the gun. He'd be using the hunting knife in a nylon scabbard on his belt.

There was a dull thud from the briefing room, followed by the sound of a mug hitting the floor and shattering. Podolski looked over and through the open door she saw Volkov slumped over the table. "What was that?" said Molchanov, slurring his words. He put a hand up to his face. "I feel funny."

Podolski stood up. "Are you OK?"

Molchanov frowned as if he was having trouble hearing her. He pushed himself up out of the chair but then all the strength went from his legs and he slumped down. Within seconds he was snoring heavily. Podolski hurried over to her backpack. She put it on the desk under the CCTV monitors and unzipped it. She took out a matt black box the size of a laptop computer and screwed in four rubber-covered aerials of differing sizes, the smallest the size of a cigarette, the largest the size of a fountain pen.

She took it through to the briefing room, where Volkov was sprawled over the table. There were pieces of broken mug and a small pool of coffee on the floor. Podolski placed the jammer on a chair and switched it on. Four green lights winked on. She took out her mobile phone and looked at the screen. For several moments nothing happened, then one by one the signal bars disappeared. The jammer was powerful enough to kill all mobile phone signals within a hundred yards or more, enough to cover the whole house. And its battery was powerful enough to keep it going for at least three hours, which would be more than enough time for Monotok to do what he had to do.

She went back to her backpack and took out a pair of secateurs. They were the ones that Monotok had used to cut off Barsky's thumb and there was still blood on the blades. She headed for the door. First she had to cut the phone lines, then she had to come back to deal with the power, exactly as Monotok had told her.

Shortt looked over at Harper, who was tapping his gloved hands on the steering wheel again. "Lex, mate, will you relax," he said.

"He's late," said Harper.

"He's not late," said Shortt. "And even if he was, we've plenty of time. We don't want to get there early and be sitting in the car park too long. We want to get there just before Khan leaves."

"What if something's happened?"

Shortt sighed. "If something's happened, he'll call."

"I'm going to check, just to make sure," said Harper. He reached into his pocket and took out a Nokia mobile.

"What the hell are you doing?" said Shortt when he saw the phone. "No mobiles, remember?"

"Relax, Jimbo. My phone's in my hotel. This one's a throwaway that we've used to mark the place where we're going to dump the body." He switched on the phone. Shortt put up his hand to acknowledge his mistake. "I know what I'm doing, Jimbo. Don't panic." Harper grinned. He tapped out Shepherd's number but frowned as it went straight through to voicemail. "His phone's off."

"He's probably on his way," said Shortt. "We've got time."

Harper switched off the phone and sat tapping it against his knee. He looked at his watch again. "I just want to get it done," he said.

"We all do," said McIntyre.

Podolski sat back on her heels and looked at the fuse box in front of her. She had opened the metal panel in the briefing room to reveal the wires and fuses that controlled the power and lighting in the house. She took a folded sheet of A4 paper from her pocket. It was a photograph of the fuse box. She had used her Samsung phone to take several pictures of the box a

448

few days earlier and Monotok had blown them up and spent hours analysing them before marking on one of the pictures which wires she had to cut and which fuses she had to trip.

It was important that some of the circuits remained live — Monotok needed the thumb sensors to be working so that he could move around, and they needed the gate to be working so that they could make their escape. But they had to cut the power to the CCTV cameras, the lights and the lifts.

She looked at the photograph, then began to cut the wires.

The lights went out, plunging the car park into darkness. Monotok smiled to himself. He switched on the night vision goggles and slid the strap around his head and adjusted the fit. He could see everything clearly, albeit with a greenish tinge. He opened the car door and got out and headed for the security centre. The door to the driver's room opened and one of the drivers, Yulian Chayka, stood in the doorway. "What happened to the lights?" he shouted into the darkness in Russian. "Is anybody there? What the hell's going on?" He was waving his hand in front of his face. The darkness was absolute and Monotok knew that Chayka could see nothing.

The keypad to the side of the security centre door was still glowing. The power had to be on for the doors to open so he had been very specific what fuses Podolski had to pull and which she had to leave in place.

As he reached the door, he slid the gun into the pocket of his jacket and took out a small plastic bag containing Barsky's bloody thumb. He pressed the thumb against the sensor and tapped in the four-digit code that Podolski had given him. The door clicked open and he put the thumb back into the bag and into his pocket.

He pushed the door open and stepped into the room. She was sitting in one of the high-backed chairs, facing him. Molchanov was slumped in his chair, unconscious.

She smiled, even though he knew she couldn't see him. "It worked," she said. "It worked perfectly." She stood up and held out her arms. "Say something, it's spooky in the dark."

"I'm here," said Monotok.

She smiled, moving her head from side to side as if that would help her see. Monotok looked to the left. All the monitors were blank.

"What about Volkov?"

"In the other room. Out for the count."

"And Grechko's still in the pool?"

"That's where he was when the lights went out."

"And Popov?"

"In the gym with Leo. The only man down on Basement Three with Grechko is Ivan." She waggled her hands. "Give me a hug, I want to feel you."

Monotok smiled and walked towards her. He avoided her hands and walked slowly around her. She continued to waggle her hands in the direction of where she thought he was.

She took a step forward and he moved behind her.

"Kirill, come on, stop messing me about."

Monotok put his hands on her hips and she stiffened, then relaxed. She ground her hips back, pressing herself against him. He ran his hands up her sides and caressed her breasts. She reached behind her with her right hand and rubbed his groin.

"Why don't you hammer me in the dark?" she said, as she felt him grow hard. "How sexy would that be?" She ground against him again, harder this time.

Monotok chuckled and slid his gloved hands up to her shoulders. "You're crazy," he said.

"Crazy for you," she said. "Come on, baby, hammer me. Hammer me good."

He put his hands either side of her head as she pressed herself against him. He slid his left hand up on to her head, his right hand under her chin, then he pulled hard, twisting her head to the right, hearing a loud crack and feeling the vertebra snap away from her skull. He felt her turn into a dead weight and he stepped back as she slumped to the floor.

He bent down and pulled the Bluetooth earpiece from her ear then lifted up her jacket and pulled the transceiver off her belt. "Consider yourself hammered," he whispered.

Harper tapped his fingers on the steering wheel, then looked at his watch. "This is not good, guys," he said. "We can't sit here all night. We have to make a decision."

"He could be tied up in the house," said McIntyre. He stretched out his legs and they banged against the two shovels in the back of the van. "He's organising lie detector tests for the staff."

"He could have changed his mind," said Harper.

"Bollocks," said Shortt. "He wouldn't and even if he did he'd have let us know. Something's happened, he'll get in touch."

"Yeah, but that leaves us sitting here with four guns and our thumbs up our arses," said Harper. He banged the steering wheel with the flat of his right hand. "Guys, it's time to shit or get off the pot."

"Do it without him, you mean?" asked McIntyre.

"I don't see that we've got any choice, do you? If we get caught with those guns we go down for ten years."

"He'll be coming," said Shortt.

"Then he'll be too late," said Harper. He tapped his watch with his finger. "We've got just enough time to get to Shepherd's Bush and pick him up. If we leave it any later we'll miss him."

"Then we'll do it tomorrow," Shortt said.

"Jimbo, the hole's dug. We're all geared up for doing this now. Every day we leave it is another day we can get caught. Do you want your wife and kids visiting you in prison?"

Shortt sighed and looked at his own watch as if he hoped it would show a different time to Harper's. "Screw it," he said. "Try his phone again."

Harper took his Nokia out of his pocket and switched it on.

"Why do you do that?" asked Shortt as Harper waited for the phone to power up.

"It's counter-surveillance 101," said Harper. "Whenever your phone is on you're vulnerable. They can track you and they can listen in."

"Who can?"

Harper tapped the side of his nose with his finger. "Dark forces, mate," he said. He tapped out Shepherd's number and once again it went straight through to voicemail. "It's still off," he said. "Look, I say we go ahead. The three of us."

"I'm up for it," said McIntyre.

"Jimbo?" said Harper. "This has to be unanimous. The three musketeers and all that. We're primed, we're ready to go. Just say the word."

Shortt sighed and then slowly nodded. "Fuck it," he said. "Yeah, let's do it."

Shepherd stood by the window, looking out over the grounds as Lee continued to ask questions of Serov. Serov was the twelfth member of staff to be questioned, the fifth bodyguard, and Shepherd had sat in on all the sessions. Lee switched easily between English and Russian, and while Shepherd couldn't understand the Russian bits he could tell that Lee spoke the language with a strong Newcastle accent. Shepherd had spotted Lee's technique early on. There were basically three types of questions. There were irrelevant questions which were used solely to establish a baseline and they usually involved the examiner asking something like "the sky is blue, true or false" or "when water freezes it turns into ice, true or false". They were simple questions to which everyone knew the answers so lying was out of the question.

The second type of question wasn't related to the investigation into the missing watch and was designed to get the subject to lie. Lee would ask a baseline question and then follow it with something like "I have fantasised about having sex with Mrs Grechko", knowing that the subject would say no but knowing that it was almost certainly a lie. Mrs Grechko, the new Mrs Grechko, was a very sexy woman and the bodyguards — with the exception of Alina Podolski — were red-blooded males.

Once Lee had established the baseline and knew how the subject would react when lying, it was time to ask the relevant questions. In a normal investigation that would be about the missing watch but in this case Lee had to ask about the watch but also ask less specific questions relating to their relationship with Grechko. "Would you ever do anything to hurt Mr Grechko?" was one. "Have you ever given information about Mr Grechko's movements to a third party?" was another.

The skill of the technician was in analysing the responses of the subject while being asked the relevant questions and assessing whether they were more similar to the baseline or to the established lies. It wasn't something that Shepherd could do just by observing body language or listening to their voices. Lie detection was a complicated business, and even a skilled practitioner like Jules Lee had to proceed slowly and methodically. He was now on his third set of baseline

454

questions to Serov, and if previous experience was anything to go by he'd be doing it at least another two times.

Shepherd's Bluetooth earpiece crackled. "What the hell's happening? Vlad, can you hear me?" It was Popov, clearly anxious.

There was no answer from Molchanov.

"Vlad, what the hell is going on?" said Popov. "Boris, are you in the security centre? Will someone talk to me?"

Shepherd put his hand up to his earpiece. "Dmitry? It's Tony. What's wrong?"

"The power's gone down here," said Popov. "Where are you?"

"The library," said Shepherd. "Everything's OK here." The lights were all on and Lee's equipment was functioning perfectly.

"Thomas, do you have power in the guardhouse?" Popov asked Lisko.

"Yes," said Lisko. "And there are lights on in the house, too."

"It must just be underground that has the problem," said Shepherd. "But the emergency lights are on, right?"

"Nothing's on," said Popov. "We're in complete darkness. Vlad, what the hell's going on? Is anyone in the security centre? Boris, Alina, Max? Where the hell is everybody?"

"Dmitry, who's with you?"

"Just Leo."

"Where's Ivan?"

"Basement Three, outside the pool."

"Ivan, are you there?" asked Shepherd.

"I'm on Basement Two," said Koshechkin.

"What are you doing there?" interrupted Popov. "You're supposed to be outside the pool."

"He's doing lengths," said Koshechkin. "He'll be another half an hour."

"Not in the bloody pitch dark, he won't," said Shepherd.

"Where exactly are you, Ivan?" asked Popov.

"The games room," said Koshechkin. Shepherd could hear the embarrassment in the man's voice.

Popov said something to Koshechkin in Russian, clearly giving him a major bollocking. Deservedly, too. Koshechkin was supposed to be a bodyguard and a bodyguard was never, ever supposed to leave his principal unprotected.

"Ivan, can you get down to the pool?" asked Shepherd.

"I'll try."

"Have you got your phone? You can use the light from the phone, enough to see in front of you, anyway."

"It's in my locker," said Koshechkin.

"Get to Grechko as quickly as you can," said Shepherd. "Dmitry, can you get to the security centre?"

"It's pitch black. We can't move around." Shepherd heard a muffled thud followed by a loud Russian curse. "Stay where you are!" shouted Popov. "Leo's just tripped over something," he explained. "Somebody's going to get hurt."

"Have you got torches?"

"No, no torches," said Popov. "There's a back-up for the main electricity supply and there are two emergency circuits. It's impossible for all three to go down at the same time."

"Impossible maybe, but that's what's happened," said Shepherd. "Where are your mobiles?"

"In the changing rooms," said Popov.

"So make your way there and get your phones out. See if you can get out of the gym and into the security centre. I'm with Konstantin, I'll see if he can get some torches down there."

He looked over at Lee. "We're going to have to stop this for the moment," he said.

"Problem?" said Lee, peering over the top of his glasses.

"Power failure downstairs. I need Konstantin to get down there with some lights."

Lee nodded and began removing the straps from Serov's chest. "See if there are torches or candles in the kitchen, then get them down to Dmitry," Shepherd said to him. "He's in the gym. And make sure the security centre is OK, they've gone quiet."

"Will do," said Serov. He took the sensor from his finger and handed it to Lee, then pulled the electrodes off his shoulder blades.

Shepherd went out into the corridor and took his phone out of his pocket. He had to call Shortt to tell him to postpone the Khan business. He frowned as he saw that he had no signal. He went back into the study, picked up a telephone and put it to his ear. There was no dial tone.

Shepherd put a hand to his earpiece. "Ivan, be careful down there, OK? This might be more than a power cut." He started walking to the door. "Dmitry, we might have a problem. The phones are out. And I've lost my mobile phone signal."

"The landlines too?"

"I've just tried the phone in the library and it's down."

"But all the power's on upstairs?" said Popov.

"No problems here at all."

"It could just be some fuses have blown."

"That wouldn't explain the phones," said Shepherd, pushing open the library door. "Something is jamming our mobiles."

"Can you get to Mr Grechko?" asked Popov.

"I'm going to try," said Shepherd.

Monotok walked down the stairs. As he reached the door to Basement Three he heard a noise from above. He froze and held his breath. Someone had opened the door on Basement Two. He heard the shuffle of feet and then a hand brushing against the wall. It could only be Koshechkin, making his way down to Basement Three. Monotok started breathing again and turned to look up the steps. Koshechkin was moving so slowly that he must have been totally unable to see. Monotok drew his knife and waited.

Shepherd walked down the corridor towards the lift, taking another look at his phone. There was still no signal. The killer must have been using a cellular phone jammer. He put the phone away as he reached the lift. He pressed the button but the light didn't come on. He pressed it again but nothing happened. He put his ear up against the door but couldn't hear anything. The lift had been put out of commission, probably by cutting its power. He touched his earpiece. "Ivan, where are you?"

"In the stairwell heading down to Basement Three. The lifts aren't working."

"Yeah, the power's been cut. Get to Grechko as quick as you can."

"Tony, it's pitch black down here. I can't see a thing."

"Quick as you can," repeated Shepherd.

"Tony, if I slip I'll break my neck."

"Just do it, Ivan. Grechko's in danger. This isn't an accident."

"You think the killer's down here?"

Shepherd could hear the uncertainty in the man's voice. "Don't think about that," he said. "Your job is to protect Grechko. Now go ahead and do that."

He put the phone in his pocket and headed for the emergency stairs.

Monotok smiled when he heard Koshechkin ask whether the killer was in the basement. Part of him wanted to whisper "yes, I'm here", but he knew that if he did he'd be making it difficult for himself. As it was all he had to do was wait in the dark with the knife and Koshechkin would come to him. It was almost funny watching the man make his way down the stairs, one at a time, feeling ahead with the toe of his shoe and keeping one hand flat against the wall. He'd reach out with the toe of his right foot, then tap it against the concrete step and only then would he place the foot down. Then he'd put his left foot next to his right foot and then start the whole process again. It was taking him a full five seconds for each step. Tap, step, step. Tap, step, step. With the hand scraping against the wall each time he moved. Monotok gripped the knife and waited.

Shepherd opened the door to the stairwell and looked inside. The light spilled in and he could see the first half-dozen stairs but everything was dark beyond that. He touched his earpiece. "Dmitry, how's it going?"

"We're trying to get our phones out of the lockers." Shepherd heard Tarasov curse as he bumped into something. Shepherd realised that the gym would be a nightmare to navigate in the pitch dark.

"I'm going down to the security centre," said Shepherd. "Ivan's heading to Grechko. Konstantin, how are you getting on with torches?"

"I can't find any," said Serov. "I've got matches. I'm looking for candles."

"Quick as you can," said Shepherd. He took his phone out and switched it on. There wasn't much light but he figured it was better than nothing. He stepped into the stairwell and let the door close behind him. The light from the phone cast a faint glow, barely enough to illuminate the first three stairs.

He moved as quickly as he could down the steps to Basement One. There was a faint diffuse light coming from the keyboard next to the thumb sensor. Clearly it still had power. That made sense because if the power had been cut to the locks there'd be no way of opening them. He pressed his thumb against the sensor, tapped out his four-digit code and pushed open the door.

"Who is it? Is someone there?" Shepherd heard a voice, coming over from his left.

"Who's that?" he shouted. "This is Tony Ryan."

"It's Yulian, Yulian Chayka."

One of the drivers, Shepherd realised. He must be standing at the door to the driver's room. "Yulian, do you have a flashlight?"

"No," shouted the driver. "What's happening?"

"The power's off. What about the cars? Are their flashlights in the cars?"

"I don't think so. What do we do?"

"Stay where you are," said Shepherd. "You'll hurt yourself if you move around in the dark." Shepherd moved his phone around but the light was so weak that it barely illuminated the floor. He took a deep breath and went into his memory. He'd walked around the parking area and the security centre many times, so he knew the layout. The fact that it was pitch black shouldn't make any difference to his mental picture of his surroundings. He headed towards the gym, walking confidently even though he couldn't see his hand in front of his face.

★ ★ ★

Koshechkin continued to move down the stairs. Tap, step, step. Tap, step, step. He reached the turn and shuffled across to the next flight of steps, keeping his left hand against the wall.

Monotok looked up and smiled. Koshechkin's suit was a greenish black in the night vision goggles, his face a pale, almost fluorescent, green, and there was a flash of bright green at the top of his shoes whenever his white socks were exposed. His tongue was sticking out between his teeth.

There was just eight steps between Koshechkin and the knife in Monotok's hand. It was a big knife, the stainless steel blade a full eight inches long, one edge wickedly sharp, the other serrated, with a thick groove along the blade so that the blood would flow out and negate any suction effect. Tap, step, step. A tap with the right foot, the right foot on the step, then the left. Tap, step, step. Six steps left. Tap, step, step.

Koshechkin stopped and cocked his head on one side. Monotok froze and held his breath. Koshechkin licked his lips and then moved his head from side to side, listening intently. For a moment Monotok thought that Koshechkin was going to turn and run back up the stairs but eventually the bodyguard recommenced his descent. Tap, step, step. Tap, step, step. Tap, step, step.

Monotok pulled back the knife and there was the faintest rustle from his sleeve. Koshechkin stopped and cocked his head again, deep furrows across his brow, his right foot poised in midair.

Monotok moved quickly, stepping up and thrusting the knife into Koshechkin's chest, between the fifth and sixth rib, aiming for the heart. He plunged the knife in as far as it would go, then pulled it out and just as quickly stabbed Koshechkin again, slightly to the right of the first wound. Then again. And again. The massive damage to his heart and lungs meant that he bled out in seconds and Monotok moved back down the stairs to give the man room to fall. Koshechkin died without making a sound, a look of confusion on his face.

Monotok turned and went back down the stairs to the door to Basement Three. He took the severed thumb from his pocket, held it against the scanner and then tapped in the four-digit code. The door clicked open and Monotok grinned. It wouldn't be long now until Grechko was dead.

Shepherd saw the faint outline of the keypad to the gym, almost as if it was floating in midair. It was disorienting but he knew it was just his mind playing tricks as it tried to make sense out of the blackness around him. He focused on walking, a strange experience when he couldn't see where he was placing his feet. As he got closer the pale glow from his phone illuminated part of the door. He pressed his thumb against the scanner and tapped in his code. The lock clicked and he pushed the door open.

"Dmitry, over here," said Shepherd, waving his mobile around. "Can you see the light?"

"I can see it," replied Popov.

"Head towards me. Where's Leo?"

There was a loud bang and Tarasov cursed in Russian. "I don't know where the fuck I am," he said.

"Can you see the light from my phone, Leo?" asked Shepherd, waving his mobile around again.

"No, I can't see anything. Wait. Yes. I see it." A few seconds later there was a crash and another loud curse. "Who the hell leaves weights on the ground?" shouted Tarasov.

Shepherd continued to wave the phone around and after a minute or so he heard a footfall ahead of him and then Popov appeared in the faint glow. Shepherd put a hand on his chest. "Hang on for Leo," he said.

It took Leo another thirty seconds to reach them, and he bumped into Popov.

"OK, this is what we're going to do," said Shepherd. "Dmitry, keep a hand on my shoulder, Leo you hold on to Dmitry. I'll lead us to the security centre."

The two men did as they were told and as a group they began to walk to the security centre. The feeble light from the phone was barely any help in illuminating their way.

"How can you see?" asked Tarasov. "It's pitch black."

"I've got a good memory, I can recall the layout, pretty much," said Shepherd. He was moving at a slow walk in what he knew was the direction of the door to the security centre. It was difficult because he couldn't see where he was placing his feet and his brain kept playing tricks on him, persuading him that at every step he was going to put his foot in a deep hole. It was a relief each time his foot hit the hard surface.

Tarasov kept misjudging the pace and banging into Popov, making both men curse.

Eventually Shepherd saw the outline of the thumb scanner and keypad ahead of them, apparently floating in the air. He became disoriented and almost stumbled but he fought to focus and after three more steps he was at the door. He pressed his thumb against the scanner and put in his code. The door lock clicked and he pushed it open.

"OK, guys, we're entering the security centre. Don't move around until we know what the story is," said Shepherd. The three men slowly filed into the room. Shepherd's right foot touched something and he told them to stop. He bent down and there was enough light from his phone to see Podolski, lying face down on the floor. "It's Alina," he said. He transferred the phone to his left hand and felt for a pulse with his right. He knew as soon as he touched her neck that he was wasting his time. His heart lurched. He checked both Podolski's ears. Her Bluetooth earpiece was missing. He patted her down and confirmed that her transceiver was missing. "She's dead," he said, straightening up.

"Dead?" repeated Tarasov.

"The killer's down here," said Shepherd. "He's taken Alina's radio." He put his hand up to his earpiece. "Ivan, this is Tony. Where are you?"

There was no answer.

"Ivan. Where are you?"

Popov interrupted and spoke rapidly in Russian. The only word that Shepherd could make out was "Ivan".

"Dmitry, I think Ivan's in trouble," said Shepherd, though he knew that he was underplaying the situation. Koshechkin was probably already dead. "From now on we're going to watch what we say on the radios, he's probably listening in."

"So what do we do?"

Shepherd went through Podolski's pockets and found her phone. He switched it on and gave it to Popov. "Where are the fuses?" asked Shepherd. "In this room?"

"In the briefing room."

"Find out if he's just pulled the fuses or cut the wire. Either way do what you can to restore power. I'll go down to Grechko."

"Leo can go with you."

"I'll move faster on my own," said Shepherd, taking off his jacket and tossing it on to a chair. "My memory's pretty good, even in the dark. But it'll slow me down if I have to worry about Leo. But see if you can find another phone for him and send him down after me." He stood up and headed for the door.

Monotok walked quickly down the corridor. Ahead of him was the door to the pool room. He took the severed thumb from his pocket, pressed it against the scanner and tapped in the four-digit code.

He pushed the door open and stepped inside, the tang of chlorine stinging his nose. Grechko was at the far end of the pool, sitting on a lounger with a towel around him. "Is someone there?" Grechko shouted. "Who is it? Dmitry?" His voice echoed off the walls.

466

Monotok walked slowly towards him. "No, it's not Dmitry," he said. "It's just you and me."

Grechko drew his legs up against his chest. "Who is it? Who's there?"

"My name is Kirill Luchenko, does that name mean anything to you?"

Monotok could see Grechko frowning as he peered into the darkness. Monotok stopped next to a lounger. He put down the gun then took off his night vision goggles, blinking in the darkness.

"Who are you? What do you want?"

"I told you. My name is Kirill Luchenko, but my friends call me Monotok. And I'm here to kill you." He took his knife out of his pocket and placed it next to the goggles.

Grechko stood up and the towel fell from his shoulders. Grechko stood there naked, his hands out in front of him as he moved his head from side to side in a futile attempt to improve his vision. "You are an assassin, is that it? Someone paid you to kill me and you skulk in the dark like the coward that you are?" He jutted his chin up, his hands still moving through the air.

Monotok reached into his pocket and took out a small Magnalite torch. "No one paid me, Grechko. This isn't about money." He switched on the torch and shone it at Grechko. The light was blinding and Grechko threw up his hands to shield his face. Monotok bent down and picked up the gun. He wasn't planning to shoot Grechko — he was going to use the knife to end the pig's life — but he wanted him to know that he had a gun and that he would use it if Grechko came at him. He shone the torch at the gun, and then back to Grechko's face. "If you take one step towards me I'll shoot you in your shrivelled-up nuts."

Grechko stayed where he was, squinting into the light. "You don't have to do this," he said. "I'll pay you whatever you want. Anything."

"You're not listening to me, are you?" said Monotok. "This isn't about money. This was never about money." He stopped and stared at Grechko. "Actually, that's wrong, isn't it? This is all about money. It always has been."

Shepherd hurried down the stairs, two at a time, keeping his left hand against the wall for balance. The light from the phone was barely enough to see by but his memory stood him in good stead and he knew exactly where he was. He saw the glow of the thumb scanner and keypad at the door to Basement Two but hurried on by.

He put his hand up to his earpiece. "How's it going, Dmitry?" he asked.

"I can't make sense of the wiring," said Popov. "I'm not an electrician."

"We really need lights down here, Dmitry."

"I'm doing my best, Tony."

Shepherd's foot caught on something and he pitched forward. His left hand slammed against the wall and he twisted as he fell, his right hip slamming against the stairs. The fall knocked the breath out of him and he lay against the wall, gasping for air. He pointed his mobile at whatever had caused him to stumble and winced when he saw Koshechkin's pale face, his eyes wide and staring. Shepherd panned the light down the bodyguard's body and winced again at the glistening blood all over the chest. He pushed himself to his feet, then took the last few steps to the door that led to Basement Three.

"There he is," said Harper. "There's the bastard now." They had parked the Transit van next to Khan's CRV behind the supermarket where he worked. Khan had just turned around the corner. He had a carrier bag in each hand and had his head down, deep in thought, as he walked.

"Get the tape ready, Jock," said Jimbo. He was holding a large spanner in his gloved hands. They didn't want to use the guns in the city, even with suppressors fitted. McIntyre reached for a roll of duct tape and pulled off a piece.

Shortt opened the passenger door and climbed out.

Harper wound down the driver's-side window as Khan got closer. "Hey, mate, you got the time on you?"

Khan looked up as if his mind was elsewhere. "What?"

"The time, mate? What's the time?"

Khan looked at him, frowned, then twisted his left wrist to get a look at his watch. He opened his mouth to speak but Shortt came up behind him and slammed the spanner just behind his right temple and Khan dropped like a stone. His carrier bags fell to the ground and one burst open, scattering oranges across the tarmac.

McIntyre kicked the rear doors open and helped Shortt drag the unconscious man into the back. As McIntyre slapped duct tape across Khan's mouth, Shortt picked up the bags and spilled fruit and threw them into the van before slamming the door shut. McIntyre pulled a sack down over Khan's head.

"Nicely done, lads," said Harper as Shortt climbed back into the van and put the spanner into the glove compartment. He started the engine and drove slowly on to the main road as McIntyre wound duct tape around Khan's arms and legs.

"I was too young to know what was going on when the Soviet Union imploded," said Monotok. "My father tried to explain, but I was a kid. He was excited, though. He thought Russia was going to change for the good. He thought it would make his life easier and the lives of the men who worked for him." He shook his head sadly. "He had no idea."

He jabbed the knife towards Grechko and Grechko flinched.

"During Gorbachev's perestroika it was every man for himself. But when Yeltsin took over, everything changed. The rules changed. You had only two ways of getting rich. Yeltsin handed it to you, or you took it. He gave whole industries to his friends, lock, stock and barrel. But you, you were never a friend of Yeltsin. You had to take what you wanted, didn't you? You had to grab it with both hands and you didn't give a fuck who you hurt in the process."

"You don't know what it was like back then," said Grechko. "If you weren't in with Yeltsin or his cronies you got nothing. It was a closed club."

"So you and Zakharov and Buryakov and Czernik formed your own club, didn't you? You decided to take what you wanted. To kill for it."

"You weren't there. You don't understand."

"I was there!" shouted Monotok. "That's the point! I was there!"

He took a step forward. The hand holding the torch was shaking and the beam swept back and forth over Grechko's pale body.

"I was in bed when you came to our house. It was the day before my birthday and I couldn't sleep. Do you remember the house, Grechko? The house of Mark Luchenko? Do you remember him? And what about my mother? Misha? Do you remember Misha Luchenko? You should do because you raped and killed her."

Shepherd moved as quickly as he could in the darkness. He was coming up to a junction in the hallway, he knew that much. The pool room was to the right. Storage rooms to the left. The light from his phone was next to useless and didn't even reach his feet but it allowed him to see part of the wall, which was enough to keep him moving in a straight line. He wanted to talk to Popov to see what was happening upstairs but he couldn't now that he knew that the killer had a transceiver. He didn't want him to know that he was heading for the pool room.

Monotok took a deep breath. He knew that the longer he spent talking the harder it would be for him to escape, but he didn't care any more. He had devoted the last four years of his life to getting his revenge, and Grechko was the final piece of the puzzle. He wanted Grechko to know why he was dying and who was killing him. "I heard you and Zakharov and Czernik and Buryakov come into the house. I heard you shouting at my father, telling him to sign the papers that would transfer the steel plant over to you. I crept out of my bedroom and looked down from the top of the stairs. Do you remember now, Grechko? Mark and Misha Luchenko?"

Grechko had begun to shiver, either through fear or the cold. Either way, Monotok didn't care.

"At first my father refused. He said it wasn't his to give away, but you knew how it worked, back then. Nobody really knew who owned what. Before 1990, the state owned everything. And the local party officials and the police could be paid off. If you had the right paperwork, it was yours. That's what the four of you were doing, back then. You stole steel plants, trucking companies, ships, buildings, factories. You took by force and you killed if you had to."

Monotok waved the knife in front of him. "Look at me, Grechko. Look at me now or I swear to God I'll slice off your balls and shove them in your mouth."

Grechko raised his eyes and stared at him. There was no fear in his eyes, just hatred.

"I saw you rape my mother, Grechko. And only then did my father sign your papers. Then you killed him. And then you killed her. And I had to crawl away and hide under my bed until you'd gone." He gritted his teeth and shook his head angrily. "You took my father's plant. You killed his deputy, too. You gave it to Czernik and within five years how many plants did he have? Ten? Twelve? All of them stolen. That's how you got your start, all of you. You threatened and you killed and you stole and by the time the millennium rolled around you were all billionaires. Did it make you happy, Grechko? All that money? Knowing how you got it? Knowing that it's going to be the death of you?"

Grechko said nothing. His shivering had intensified.

Monotok stepped towards Grechko, holding the knife low. He didn't want the first blow to be a killing one. Or the second. Or the third. He wanted him to bleed out slowly. And painfully.

Shepherd pressed his thumb against the scanner and tapped out his four-digit security code. The door clicked and he gently pushed it open, just an inch or two. The only sound was the hum of an air-conditioning unit and the gentle lap of the water against the side of the pool. He pushed the door open a little more. The darkness was absolute. He pushed the door further and stepped inside.

As soon as he heard the lock click, Monotok switched off his flashlight and put it and the knife on the lounger. He pushed the night vision goggles on and turned to look at the door, just as the man stepped into the room. He was in his late thirties and wearing a shoulder holster. In his right hand he was holding a mobile phone and the screen glowed weakly.

Monotok picked up his gun and pointed it at the man, his finger tightening on the trigger.

"He's got a gun!" screamed Grechko in the darkness.

The man crouched, dropped the phone and reached for the gun in the holster but Monotok had all the time in the world to aim and pull the trigger twice.

The man staggered to the side and fell into the pool with a loud splash.

Monotok grinned. He took off the night vision goggles and put them and the gun back on the lounger. He picked up the flashlight and switched it on. He panned the beam around and found Grechko, crouched like a frightened animal with his back to the wall, as naked as the day he was born.

He bent down and picked up the knife. "Now where was I?" he said. "Before we were so rudely interrupted." He smiled. "Ah yes, now I remember. I was about to kill you."

Shepherd's eyes were stinging from the chlorine in the pool and he blinked several times. The pool wasn't much more than six feet deep and his feet brushed the bottom. The vest had done its job but he still patted his chest with both hands to make sure that neither of the bullets had penetrated.

The Glock was still in its holster, his fingers hadn't even touched it before the rounds had hit him. They had been two good shots. One just above the heart, one below it. If it hadn't been for Amar Singh's vest, Shepherd would have died instantly.

He wafted his arms up to drive himself down to the floor of the pool, then pulled the Glock out with his right hand. The gun would still fire, he knew that there was no way that water could get into the cartridge. The only danger was if the barrel was full of water when he pulled the trigger. He kept the barrel of the gun pointed down as he braced his feet against the bottom. He would only get one chance at this so he had to get it right. He moved his left hand across to support his right around the butt of the Glock, then pushed down hard with his legs.

His mind was totally focused on what he needed to do. He had to keep the barrel down until it was in the air. He had to aim in the general direction of the killer. If the torch was back on he could make the first shot a killing shot. If the pool room was still in darkness then the first shot would have to go high and in the light from the gun he'd see the target and his memory would have to help him go for the kill with the second.

He powered up through the water and burst through the surface, his eyes wide open. He brought up the gun. The torch was on, illuminating Grechko, who was curled up against the wall, covering his face with his hands. The killer had his back to Shepherd, outlined by the light from the torch.

The killer started to turn at the sound of cascading water but Shepherd had already started to pull the trigger. The first shot hit the man right between the shoulder blades. The second was a few inches lower. Shepherd managed to get off a third shot, catching the man at the base of his spine, before he crashed back into the water.

He kicked with his legs and swam to the ladder to climb out. He crawled over to the torch and picked it up. The man he'd shot was lying face down on the floor, blood pooling around his chest.

The knife was by his side and Shepherd kicked it away and then put his Glock back in its holster.

The emergency light by the door flickered into life. Popov must have fixed the circuit, but the main lights stayed off.

Grechko got to his feet and wrapped his towel around his shoulders. "You killed him," he said quietly.

He was in shock, Shepherd knew. But there was nothing he could do for him, right now. He put his hand to his earpiece but realised it was missing.

Grechko walked over to Monotok's body and sneered at it. "Call yourself a killer?" he said. "Look who's laughing now. I'm here and you're dead so fuck you and fuck your mother." He hawked up saliva and spat on the body.

"We need to get upstairs," said Shepherd. "We'll have to use the stairs, the lifts aren't working."

Grechko pointed at the door to the changing rooms. "I need to get dressed," he said.

Shepherd nodded and they went together to the changing rooms. There was another emergency light there with just enough glow to see by. There was a pile of towels on a shelf and Shepherd grabbed one and patted himself down, but his shirt and trousers were still soaking wet and his shoes squelched as he walked. Grechko pulled on his trousers and shirt but didn't bother with his shoes and socks. They went to the stairwell. Before Shepherd opened the door, he warned Grechko about Koshechkin's body. The emergency lighting illuminated the stairwell and the Russian stared in horror as he stepped over the corpse.

"What happened?" he asked Shepherd.

"Knife," said Shepherd.

Grechko shivered, knowing how close he had come to meeting the same fate. "You saved my life, Tony," he said as they headed up the stairs.

"Don't worry about it," said Shepherd.

"Anything you want," said Grechko.

Shepherd stopped and turned to look at the Russian. "Anything?" he said.

The Russian nodded. "Money. Women. A car. Anything. Just name it."

Shepherd stared at Grechko, his face a blank mask. "You know what I want, Mr Grechko?"

"Just name it," repeated Grechko.

Shepherd nodded slowly. "I want to know why he wanted to kill you so badly."

Grechko said nothing.

"I want to know what you did to him that made him hate you so much. I want to know what drove him to kill Zakharov, Buryakov and Czernik and to go to such lengths to get to you."

Grechko remained silent but stared at Shepherd.

"Must have been something pretty important, yeah?" Shepherd met Grechko's gaze and the two men stared at each other for several seconds. When it became clear that Grechko wasn't going to say anything, Shepherd smiled thinly. "That's what I thought." He turned and carried on up the stairs, with Grechko following.

When they reached the ground floor, Shepherd used his thumb and code to open the door. He held it open for Grechko, who walked out into the hallway and headed for the study. "Where is Dmitry?" Grechko said over his shoulder.

"The security centre," said Shepherd.

"Send him to me."

Shepherd scowled at the retreating figure. "Yes, your majesty," he muttered. He went back down the stairs to Basement One.

He heard footsteps below him. "Who's that?" he shouted.

"Leo," shouted Tarasov.

"Is Dmitry still in the control centre?"

"Yes," replied Tarasov, coming back up the stairs. "He managed to get the emergency lights on. Mr Grechko is OK?"

"He's fine."

"And the killer?"

"Not so OK," said Shepherd. "No longer a threat."

"I'll check downstairs," said Tarasov.

"Be careful, Ivan's down there," said Shepherd. "He didn't make it."

Shepherd pushed open the door to Basement One and made his way over to the security centre. Dmitry was in the briefing room, peering into a large metal panel. He looked over when Shepherd came in. "What the hell happened?" he asked, frowning at Shepherd's wet clothes.

"I went for a swim," said Shepherd. He grabbed his jacket and slipped it on over his wet shirt.

"What about Mr Grechko?"

"He's OK. He's in the study. He wants to see you." He gestured at the fuses and wiring. "What's the story?"

"Some of the fuses have been pulled, that's how I got the emergency lights on. Some of the circuits have been cut so we'll need an electrician." He straightened up. "I can't work out how he knew exactly what circuits to interfere with."

"He must have had help."

Volkov was sprawled across the table, snoring. "Drugged?" asked Dmitry.

"Looks like it," said Shepherd. "Alina usually makes the coffee."

"She was helping him? So why did he kill her?"

"So she couldn't betray him." He nodded at the door. "You should go and take care of Grechko. He was a bit shaken up."

Popov nodded at the far corner of the room, behind where Volkov was lying. "Your mobile phone signal should be back. There's a jammer over there, a big one. I switched it off."

As Popov walked out, Shepherd took out his mobile. He was showing two missed calls from a phone that had withheld its number, and one from Jimmy Sharpe. There was one voicemail message, from Sharpe, and he listened to it. It was short and sweet — "Call me back, you bastard."

Shepherd went back out into the car parking area as he called him back. "I've got something on Farzad Sajadi that you might be interested in," said Sharpe.

"That case is closed, pretty much," said Shepherd. He looked at his watch and realised that he'd missed the RV with Harper, Shortt and McIntyre. They would either have put the operation on hold or gone ahead without him.

"He's in witness protection," said Sharpe.

It was the last thing that Shepherd had expected to hear. "Witness protection?"

"The whole witness protection thing is now under the control of the National Crime Agency, which is why it wasn't showing up on the PNC," said Sharpe.

"A witness to what, Razor? The bastard was in Afghanistan."

"I haven't got any details at all," said Sharpe. "There's a rock-solid firewall around the database. All I know is that Farzad Sajadi is there. There's a number you can call where you can speak to a representative, but the problem with that is that all sorts of alarm bells are going to ring."

"Understood."

"It's not a call I can make, with the best will in the world," said Sharpe.

"I'll do it," said Shepherd. "You've done more than enough."

Sharpe gave Shepherd the number and ended the call. Shepherd walked outside and called the number. A woman answered. "Good evening," she said, then remained silent.

"I was told to call this number for information on an Ahmad Khan," said Shepherd.

"I'll need your name, position and ID number," said the woman. She sounded young and had a Home Counties accent. Shepherd gave her the information. The woman repeated it back to him. "And you are enquiring about who?"

"Ahmad Khan. Now using the name Farzad Sajadi."

"Please stay on this number, someone will call you back shortly," said the woman, and the line went dead. Shepherd paced up and down. After a few minutes his mobile rang. The caller was withholding the number. This time it was a man, middle aged and with a Welsh accent. "Mr Shepherd?"

"Yes."

"Can you confirm your ID number please."

Shepherd repeated the number.

"You were asking about Farzad Sajadi aka Ahmad Khan?"

"I need to know what he's doing with a British passport and why he's here under two names," said Shepherd.

"I'm afraid there's a limit to what I can tell you, Mr Shepherd."

"It's important," said Shepherd. He was about to say that it was a matter of life and death but realised how clichéd that would sound.

"I assume it is or you wouldn't be contacting us," said the man. "The problem is that I have only a minimum amount of information on my terminal. Most of the information is protected and can only be accessed at a higher level. To protect the principal."

"He is under witness protection, then?"

"That much I can certainly tell you," said the man. "He came from Afghanistan in 2003 and we prepared the new identity for him. And for his daughter, too."

"They have full citizenship? Their passports are genuine?"

"Of course," said the man. "All his paperwork, and the paperwork of his daughter, is in order."

"Does it say why?"

"Why?" repeated the man. "I don't think I follow."

"He was a Taliban fighter in Afghanistan. How does a man like that get a British passport?"

"I don't have that information in front of me," said the man. "What I can tell you is that there are two contact numbers on the file. One is for our own Defence Intelligence and Security Centre and the other is for the Defense Intelligence Agency."

"The DIA? The Americans?"

"That's correct. It's a number in Washington, DC."

"Can you think of any reason why the DIA would be involved with the relocation of a Taliban fighter to the UK?"

"A Taliban fighter, no. But the relocation of Afghanis with new identities has been going on for years. Usually with translators or Afghan army officers who have been directly threatened. Some politicians have also been relocated."

"With new identities?"

"If their lives have been threatened, yes. It doesn't happen often but when it does it's because the person concerned has done this country a great service."

"A service?"

"Risked their lives to save British citizens, for instance."

"You think that's what has happened in Khan's case?"

"I've no way of knowing," said the man. "All I have is the information on the screen in front of me. If you want more information you will have to either contact the two agencies I mentioned, or make an official request. But I can tell you from experience that such information is rarely released. Everything is geared towards maintaining the anonymity and safety of the principals."

Shepherd realised he wasn't going to get anything else from the man so he thanked him and ended the call.

He tried Harper's phone and it went through to voicemail. So did Shortt's. Shepherd cursed. They were almost certainly on their way to the New Forest, with Khan bound and gagged in the back of the van. He looked at his watch and cursed again.

He hurried back to the control room, knelt down by the side of Podolski's body, rolled her over and went through her pockets. He pulled out her keys and ran to her bike. The crash helmet was sitting on one of the bike's mirrors. Shepherd pulled it on. It was a tight fit but wearable. He inserted the key, started the engine and twisted the throttle. The engine roared and he headed for the exit.

Harper gave the mobile to Shortt. They were driving through a wooded area and according to the milometer they were close to where they needed to turn off. "Switch it on and check out the map," he said. "It'll show where we need to turn off."

Shortt switched on the phone. "What about calling Spider?" he asked.

"Waste of time," said Harper. "This'll be over within half an hour. Khan will be dead and buried and we'll be on our way back to London."

Shortt scrolled through the phone's menu and opened the map application. The map showed the position of the van as a small arrow, and there was a flashing dot to the left of the road some way ahead. "I've got it," he said.

"Let me know when we need to turn off," said Harper, checking his rear-view mirror.

* ★ *

The speedometer flickered at about ninety and Shepherd bent low over the motorbike's tank to lower his wind resistance. He'd been caught by two speed cameras as he sped west but that didn't worry him, he was more concerned about being pursued by traffic cops, but so far he'd been lucky. He was moving faster than the van, he was sure of that, because Harper had Khan in the back so he wouldn't be doing more than the speed limit. There was a chance, just a chance, that he'd get to them before they had an opportunity to pull the trigger. Shepherd didn't need the GPS to tell him where the grave was, his photographic memory was more than up to the job. The question was whether or not he'd be able to get there in time.

There was a line of cars ahead of him waiting to overtake a sluggish coach. Shepherd gunned the engine and pulled out into the opposite lane, flashing past the cars and coach, the wind ripping at his clothes, now almost dry after his soaking in the pool.

A car coming in his direction flashed its lights at him in disapproval but Shepherd wasn't concerned about what other drivers thought about his speed. All he cared about was getting to the New Forest before Harper put a bullet in Khan's head.

Ahmad Khan could barely breathe. The duct tape across his mouth was enough to suffocate him but the sack they'd pulled over his head meant that every breath was an effort. He tried to stay calm and to breathe slowly and evenly because he knew that panic

485

would only increase his oxygen consumption. He began to lose track of time and started counting slowly, marking the minutes with his fingers, but the lack of oxygen made it difficult to concentrate and he began to drift in and out of consciousness. At some point the van began to shake and vibrate and he realised that they had driven off the road and were crossing rough ground. They slowed and the lurching intensified and then they stopped.

He heard the rear doors being opened and a gruff voice. "Get him out."

Hands seized his legs and dragged him across the floor of the van, then more hands grabbed his shoulders. He heard feet tramping across vegetation as they carried him, face down. Then he felt a lurch and he flipped over and he was falling. For a second he imagined that he had been thrown over the side of a cliff but then he hit the ground, hard enough to force the air from his lungs. He rolled on to his back. The sack was pulled roughly from his head and he blinked his eyes. They were outside and he was surrounded by trees. He lay there, staring up at the branches above his head, the duct tape across his mouth pulsing in and out in time with his breathing.

Something moved in front of his face. A water bottle. Evian water. Khan thought he might be hallucinating then he realised that the bottle had been taped to the barrel of a pistol. Khan recognised the gun. A Makarov. A common weapon used by the Taliban, usually after it had been prised from the dead hand of a Russian soldier. It wasn't a common weapon in England. He stared at the gun, wondering what its significance was. He knew what the significance of the water bottle was. It was a silencer, to deaden the sound of the shot that would take his life.

The man holding the gun sneered down at him. "Do you know who I am, you piece of raghead shit?" the man snarled.

Khan shook his head. Maybe they had the wrong man. Maybe this was all some horrible mistake.

"You killed three of my mates and now I'm going to kill you."

Khan looked to his left. There was another man there. In his forties. White. Staring at Khan with cold eyes. The man's face was familiar, but Khan knew very few Westerners. It had to have been in Afghanistan. Which meant that he was a soldier.

"Look at me, you bastard!" shouted Harper. "I'm the one who's going to put a bullet in your head."

Khan looked up at the man again. Three of his friends, he had said. When had Khan killed three men? He had killed many men over the years, which three was he talking about?

"You shot them in the back, you fucking coward. At least you get to see my face."

"Just do it, Lex," said a third man, standing somewhere beyond Khan's feet. Khan tried to get a look at him but all he could see was a gun. A revolver.

Khan tried to speak but he could barely breathe and the only sound he could make was a grunt from the back of his throat.

The man with the Makarov grinned. He was wearing gloves. Black leather gloves.

"The men you killed were friends of mine," said the man. "I'm going to tell you their names so that they are the last things you think about before you die."

Khan blanked out the man's words. There was only one thing he wanted to think about just then. If he was indeed going to die then he wanted his last thoughts to be of his darling daughter, the light of his life.

Khan heard the roar of an engine off to his left. Then a flash of light through the trees. His heart leapt as he thought that perhaps rescue was at hand, that somehow the police had found out what was happening and were coming to save him. The engine noise got louder and he realised it was a motorbike and not a car, and then he saw it, bumping across the rough ground.

The man with the Makarov saw it too and he brought up the gun with both hands and fired.

The bullet glanced against the side of Shepherd's crash helmet and ricocheted off to the side. He swung the handle-bars to the right but hit the curved root of a beech tree and before he could do anything he was hurtling off the bike, arms flailing. He hit the ground hard but rolled and scrambled behind a tree. He flicked up the visor as a second round thudded into the trunk by his head. "It's me, Spider!" he screamed at the top of his voice.

"It's Spider!" echoed McIntyre, holding up his hand.

Harper lowered his gun as Shepherd stepped out from behind the tree. The engine of the bike was still roaring and the air was growing thick with exhaust fumes. Shepherd pulled off the helmet and dropped it on to the ground, then knelt down and twisted the ignition key and pulled it out.

"Sorry, mate," said Harper. "You gave me a shock there."

"You might think about identifying your target before pulling the trigger," said Shepherd, straightening up.

"Yeah, well, we weren't expecting you on a bike, were we?" said Harper. "Anyway, you're here now, better late than never."

He walked over to Khan and pointed his gun at the man's face.

"Put the gun down, Lex," said Shepherd, walking towards Harper.

"What, having second thoughts, are you?"

"We're not shooting him, Lex."

Harper continued to point his gun at Khan's face. Khan stared at Harper, his eyes cold and emotionless as if he didn't care whether he pulled the trigger or not.

Shepherd reached into his pocket and took out his Swiss Army knife. He folded out the blade and stepped between Harper and Khan. "Spider, mate, I'm slotting him tonight, come what may," said Harper quietly.

"He killed Captain Todd," said McIntyre. "And he shot you, Spider. The bastard deserves to die."

"Then let's at least hear his side of the story," said Shepherd, kneeling down next to Khan. He used the blade to sever the duct tape at the back of Khan's head, then pulled it away from his mouth. "Did you shoot me?" he asked Khan.

Khan shook his head. "No, sir, I did not."

Shepherd put a hand on Khan's shoulder. "And Captain Todd. Did you kill him?"

Khan shook his head again. "No."

"Of course he'd say that!" shouted Harper. "He knows we're going to slot him, Spider. He'd say anything to save his skin." He waved the gun at Khan. "Get out of the way. If you don't want to do it, you can leave it to me."

"He didn't do it, Lex," said Shepherd quietly.

"Bullshit."

Shepherd turned back to Khan. "But you were there, outside the al-Qaeda house in Pakistan? It was you I saw. Outside the house?"

Khan nodded. "Yes, I was there."

"We know he was there, we saw the bugger," said Shortt. "And we saw him kill Captain Todd."

"And the three Paras!" shouted Harper. "Let's not forget the three lads he shot in the back."

"Take a breath, Lex," said Shepherd.

"What the hell is wrong with you?" yelled Harper, waving his gun over his head. "We brought him out here to slot him, let's just get on with it."

Shepherd looked over at Khan again. He forced a smile. "Tell him," he said. "Tell him what happened the night that Captain Todd was killed."

AFGHANISTAN, 2002

For a week Ahmad Khan remained at home, working in the fields and regaining his strength, and then he returned Lailuna to the care of his sister. When she realised that he was going away again, Lailuna wailed as if her heart would break, but he promised her, "This is the last time I shall leave you behind. Next time we go together, I swear to you."

He walked away without looking back, knowing that the desolate look on her face would weaken his resolve. He made contact with Joshua using one of the dead drops he had set up on his instructions, and the following night, waiting as arranged in the shadows at the side of a road outside Jalalabad, he was picked up by an American patrol and taken to a meeting with Joshua at the American FOB. "You're not exactly flavour of the month with the British, just now," Joshua said as Khan was brought into the room where he was waiting. "They think you deliberately led their men into a trap."

By way of answer, Khan simply removed his shirt and turned slowly around, allowing Joshua to see the fresh scars that covered his back and torso. Joshua listened intently as Khan told him the story. "So, do the Taliban still trust you?"

"Two of the leaders don't," Khan said. "My time is definitely running out. It is time for you to do as you promised and give me and my daughter a new life in the West."

"I will," said Joshua. "But before I do, I need you to carry out one more task for me. You know the money house you talked about across the Pakistani border? We have intelligence suggesting that some al-Qaeda operatives are based there and are using it as a source of funds and weapons. We've identified the broad area where it's sited but we have not been able to locate it precisely. I need you to locate it, penetrate it and identify who's using it."

"And then? What will you do?"

"And then we'll deal with it, one way or another."

"You will destroy it?"

"That's a decision that will be taken at a higher pay grade than mine."

Khan stroked his beard thoughtfully. "I need a reason to go there, I can't just turn up and tell them I happened to be passing. They're not stupid."

"I've thought of that." Joshua smiled. "We're going to put a price on your head, a large reward for your capture alive. That'll strengthen your credibility with the Taliban and also give you a powerful reason to cross the border into the tribal areas until the heat has died down."

"Even so, why would the Taliban want me to go to the money house?"

"Because we're going to make a large cash payment to the headman of your village to buy his loyalty. You're going to relieve him of it on behalf of the Taliban and then volunteer to deliver it to the money house."

Khan nodded thoughtfully. "And if someone captures me before I cross the border and hands me over to claim the reward you're offering?"

"Then you'll have got your wish because you'll be in our hands and on your way out of Afghanistan."

"I'll do it," Khan said, "as I'm sure you knew I would, but Lailuna must be in a place of safety before I do."

"Agreed," Joshua said. "Bring her to the site of the dead drop at dawn tomorrow. I'll have soldiers there, including a woman, to pick up your daughter. She'll be waiting for you at Bagram when you return."

"And if I do not return?"

"Then you have my word that she will be taken to my country and we will find a good American family to give her a home." He paused. "The drop of money to your village headman will take place at noon tomorrow and you would be well advised to be out of the area and on your way to the border by nightfall, because word will already be spreading about the price we've put on your head."

Khan nodded. "I shall leave before the sun goes down," he said.

"There's one other thing," said Joshua. He held out what looked like a regular 5.45 round for Khan's AK-74. "This is an HOTB — a Hostiles Ordnance Tracking Beacon," he said. "We use them to track and intercept enemy supplies — we just need to insert one of these into a shipment and then we can ambush it somewhere along the line, at a time and place of our choosing. I need you to have this with you at all times.

We'll have an AWAC in the air over the area where you're heading. The HOTB sends out a constant pulse which the AWAC can track. When it stops pulsing, we'll know that you've reached the money house and the point where the signal stops will give us the precise coordinates. There are two ways to stop it. You can fire it in your rifle; put it in your magazine, pull the trigger and it'll seem like a misfire — there's a .22 cap in the base which will go off and destroy the inner workings. A misfire will be perfectly plausible, most Taliban ammunition is made in Peshawar and it's notoriously unreliable. But you can also silence it by crushing it between a couple of rocks."

"So when it is silenced, you'll launch the attack?"

"I'm not sure about the timing. But by killing the signal we will know the exact location of the house. When you silence the HOTB we'll send in surveillance drones to check out the area and we'll then deal with the target."

"A drone, perhaps?" said Khan.

Joshua shrugged. "Given the sensitivity of relations with Pakistan, the attack is likely to be by special forces on the ground, and probably British ones at that, rather than by bombs or missiles. The attack, if it does come, will probably be at night and you would be wise not to be in the immediate vicinity of the building at the time."

Khan was dropped off close to his village later that night and woke Lailuna well before dawn. They slipped out of the still-sleeping village and made their way to the dead drop. Khan told her only that she was going to

494

meet an American woman who would look after her for him, and when he came back, they would be going on the long journey together that he had promised her. As he heard the noise of the approaching American armoured vehicle, driving without lights, he hugged Lailuna, but he was dry eyed and showing a confidence he did not feel as he entrusted her to a young blond woman in army fatigues. While her comrades formed a defensive perimeter around them, she greeted Khan, ruffled Lailuna's hair and gave her a candy bar.

Khan stood watching as they drove away, Lailuna's pale face and uncertain smile peering out at him until she disappeared from sight. He returned to his village and at once went to the house of the village headman, a grey-bearded elder with a face ravaged by smallpox scars. "I know the Americans are bringing money to the village at noon today," Khan said. "If the Taliban hear of it — and we both know they will — they will take all of it. But here is what I suggest. You will give me half the money the Americans bring, which I will deliver to the Taliban, but I — and you, when you are asked, as you surely will be — will tell them that it is the whole of the money that was given to you. You will hide the rest and when you judge it is safe, you will use it to ease the burdens of our friends and families and bring a little prosperity to our village. After today, you will not see me again for a long time, if ever. The *faranji* — the British — have put a price on my head and I must cross the border to escape them."

The headman took Khan's hands in his, thanked him and said, "May you travel safely."

"And may you not be tired," Khan said, returning the traditional greeting.

Exactly at noon that day, there was the clatter of helicopter rotors overhead as a Blackhawk swooped in, bristling with guns and missiles, and hovered above the heart of the village, churning up a storm of dust and leaves. A few minutes later the American military convoy rumbled into the village.

While troops fanned out around them, M16s at the ready, two soldiers, each carrying a sack, ran into the headman's house. Moments later, they emerged empty handed, they and the troops jumped back into the vehicles and the convoy moved off, with the Blackhawk still flying top cover above it.

Khan had already summoned Ghulam from the neighbouring village and they made their way to the headman's house as soon as the convoy had disappeared. For the benefit of any watching villagers, Khan unslung his AK-74 and covered the headman as he appeared at the door. There were still two sacks in the middle of the room, but Khan noted with satisfaction that they were now considerably less bulky than when they had been delivered. The headman made token protests, raising his voice in lamentations as Khan and Ghulam strode away, each with a sack over their shoulder. None of the other villagers tried to intercept them; they knew better than to cross the Taliban.

With Ghulam at his side, Khan made his way out of the village and took the narrow, twisting paths through the mountains. After sunset that night, they reached the safe house, one of several that Fahad constantly moved between. It could have been any farmer or goatherd's house, had it not been for the satellite dish hidden among a copse of larch and pine trees a hundred yards away. Greeted with a faint smile by Fahad and a scowl from Piruz, Khan produced the money at once and told his story. "The British have put a price on my head," he said, "for the deaths of their soldiers."

"I had already heard so," Fahad said, nodding towards the satellite phone that lay on the table.

"With your permission," Khan said, "I will cross the border and live among our brothers in the tribal lands until the *faranji* find other things to occupy their minds."

"Granted," Fahad said. "When will you leave?"

"Tonight. The lure of the reward may be too much for some poor farmer to resist. Shall I deliver these dollars to the money house across the border, where it will be safe from the *faranji?* Ghulam will go with me for added protection."

Fahad thought for a long moment before he replied. "Perhaps that would be wise," he said. "You can relieve my men who are guarding it and send them back to rejoin the fight here, but I will send Piruz and another fighter with you, for poor farmers are not the only ones who may find such sums of money hard to resist."

Khan inclined his head. "As you wish."

The four men left within the hour, travelling light with just their weapons and ammunition, a water bottle and a pouch at their waist containing rations of rice, almonds and raisins. Even in the summer season, the wind knifing through them as they climbed higher into the mountains was bitterly cold and there were ice and drifts of winter snow in the north-facing gullies.

They passed a chai house at the side of the trail, and the smell of cedar logs and the glow of light from inside were as enticing as the thought of hot food, but travellers might already have brought news of the price on Khan's head even to this lonely place and the risk of betrayal and capture was too great, so they moved on into the darkness.

Dawn broke well before they reached the summit of the pass, but this little-used route lay well south of the Khyber Pass and they encountered only one group of travellers, merchants or smugglers herding their plodding donkeys, weighed down with bulky sacks.

They crossed the border mid-morning but did not stop to rest until they had descended below the treeline and found shelter in an abandoned shepherd's hut. Its roof had collapsed, leaving it open to the sky, but the stone walls broke the force of the wind. Tired from their long march, they were able to snatch a few hours' sleep. They moved on again that afternoon, heading steadily south-eastwards through the barren landscape, the brief greening of the slopes at the approach of spring having long given way to a brown, parched wilderness.

After dark that night they approached the money house. It was a tall building in a fold in the hills, surrounded by a collection of ruined outbuildings and a pile of rubble where another one had collapsed. There were a few other occupied farms and houses in the area, but all were at least half a mile away. They did not approach the house at once, but lay up among the trees, observing the guards. There were two of them that they could see, huddled near the doorway, blowing on their hands to warm them from time to time. There was a glow of lamplight from the building and Khan could smell woodsmoke from the fire burning inside.

They watched the house for half an hour, then moved quietly towards it. Piruz waited until they were within twenty yards of the guards, then called out, "*Salaam alaikum*. Do not be alarmed, we are friends and followers of Mullah Omar."

The guards jumped up and pointed their AK-47s at Khan and Piruz. "You lazy dogs!" shouted Piruz. "Be grateful we are not enemies, for if we were, you would surely be dead. I am Piruz, do you not recognise me?"

The guards bowed and apologised. One of them knocked on the door. A few moments later Khan heard the bolts being drawn and a face peered out. They identified themselves once more and Khan, Piruz and Ghulam were ushered inside. There were a dozen men in the house. Khan recognised two of them as low-ranking Taliban fighters but the others were different.

They sat together, their lips moving silently as they studied their Qurans. Five were Arabs and the other five did not look like Afghans to Khan either, but more like the Chechens, Uzbeks and other jihadis who had flocked to Afghanistan to fight the Soviets years before. Khan was sure they were al-Qaeda warriors.

Through a doorway, Khan glimpsed a stockpile of weapons and ammunition and sacking-wrapped bales that could only have been opium.

Khan spoke to the Taliban fighters. He had to find a reason to get away from the others to silence the HOTB, but he also needed a convincing excuse for remaining outside the house during the night. The laxity of the guards at the door had provided him with one. "We've brought more American dollars for the cause," he said, gesturing towards the sacks they had carried. "But my daughter could guard this place better than your men. We walked in here tonight virtually undetected. If we can do it, so can *faranji* soldiers. You need a better guard system, especially at night. I'm going to go outside and find a place from where I can watch the building and the approaches to it."

"Good idea, brother," Piruz said. "We will help you."

The last thing that Khan wanted was to have Piruz outside with him, but he had no choice other than to smile and accept his offer. He went outside with Ghulam. Piruz and Piruz's comrade followed them. They moved around the money house in a gradually expanding circle, exploring the outbuildings and seeking out dips and hollows where they could be concealed and yet able to observe the terrain around them. They eventually chose two sites for guard posts, with a view of each other, the money house and the tracks leading to it. "There are four of us," Khan said. "Shall two watch and two rest, turn and turn about?"

Piruz gave him a suspicious look. "No, we will all watch together," he said.

"As you wish, brother," Khan said. "But will you first keep watch for me while I empty my bowels?"

Without waiting for an answer, he moved away towards the trees. He knew that his fellow Muslims were both fastidious and prudish about bodily functions; even if he had been under guard, they would not have felt comfortable about following him. He slid the HOTB from his ammunition belt, dropped his trousers and squatted down, then blew a farting sound on the back of his hand, using it to cover the noise as he crushed the HOTB under a rock. Unseen high in the night skies overhead, the AWACs would already be relaying back to Joshua the exact coordinates of the place where the HOTB had been silenced and within minutes surveillance drones would be converging on it.

He stood up, poured some of his drinking water into his left hand and washed himself with it in case Piruz was watching him, and then walked back to the others. He glanced at the sky. The attack would not come that night, he was sure, for the first faint glow of dawn was already beginning to colour the eastern horizon, but he was fairly certain that it would happen the following night and he had to be ready for it. Joshua had been reluctant to reveal details of what he had planned, but Khan was sure that the attack would come sooner rather than later.

An hour after daybreak, they abandoned their posts and returned to the house. The other Taliban fighters left at once to rejoin Fahad, leaving the al-Qaeda men to mount guard during the daylight hours. Khan curled up on the floor near the embers of the fire, but he slept fitfully, plagued by thoughts when he was awake and troubled by dreams when he at last fell asleep.

He got up just after midday and at once went outside. He stood in the full sunlight, gazing up at the sky. He knew that drones would be overhead by now and if Joshua had needed any confirmation that they were watching the right place, the sight of Khan's upturned face and the unmistakable milk-white pupil of his left eye would provide it. Piruz emerged a few moments later and gave him a suspicious look, but Khan merely smiled and nodded.

At sunset that evening they again left the building and mounted guard. Khan and Ghulam stationed themselves in the dip just beyond the pile of rubble. Khan lay full length on the ground while Ghulam took a place half a pace behind him. Piruz and the other fighter took up their positions in dead ground where they could see the opposite side of the house.

It was a bitter night, with frost sparkling on the ground. Even men as hardened to the mountains as Khan and Ghulam felt the cold seeping into their bones as they lay in wait.

At just before ten that night, Khan thought he heard the drumbeat sound of helicopter rotors in the distance, but it was snatched away again on the breeze and, though he strained his ears, he heard no more. Half an hour later there was movement on the periphery of his vision near a copse of tall trees. It was a ripple in the darkness, sensed as much as seen. Khan eased off the safety catch of his rifle and slid it forward, sighting not on the area where he had seen the movement, but towards Piruz.

Twice Khan tensed as small groups of dark figures moved down the track towards the money house, but on each occasion they were recognised by the guards at the door and admitted to the house. After remaining inside for perhaps an hour, they left again carrying bundles that might have contained dollars, opium or weapons and ammunition.

A lone figure, perhaps one of the al-Qaeda fighters, left the house shortly afterwards and disappeared up the track towards the mountains, but after that there was only silence, and the lamp inside the building was extinguished before midnight.

Nothing and nobody moved for another hour, but then Khan heard a faint noise, like the rustle of fabric. He strained his eyes into the darkness but saw nothing until two dark shapes suddenly materialised out of the night, no more than twenty yards from him. They carried a ladder between them, holding their rifles in the other hand.

Khan saw the outline of night vision goggles on the men's faces and crouched lower, laying a restraining hand on Ghulam's arm, for fear that he might open fire. For the moment, neither Piruz nor the two guards at the door were aware of any danger, because the two men's angle of approach meant that the building was blocking them from Piruz's sight.

Cloud still blanketed the sky, shrouding the moon and reducing its light to no more than a faint glow. Silent as ghosts, the two figures slipped between pools of shadow, blacker even than the surrounding darkness, until they reached the outside wall of the money house.

As they turned to look back the way they had come, Khan caught a glimpse of their faces. He recognised the man called Spider at once and felt a pang of guilt mixed with unease as he saw that it was Captain Todd alongside him. The SAS men had no reason to trust him, he knew, and every reason to hate him. If they saw Khan, it could cost him his life, but if he allowed them to be ambushed and killed, his ticket to freedom and a new life in the West could well disappear.

His mind raced. There was nothing he could do to alert them. He would simply have to watch and wait. He sensed Ghulam's impatience and motioned for him to be still and silent.

Khan watched as the SAS men placed their ladder against the wall. They paused to listen and scan the surroundings for movement, then Spider climbed up the ladder and fixed shaped charges against the wall on each floor.

Again Khan had to restrain Ghulam from firing. He twisted around and leaned close to Ghulam's ear, breathing, "Not yet, wait."

Spider slid back down the ladder and Khan saw him mime protecting his ears to Todd. Spider covered his own ears a fraction of a second before there was a massive blast and a flash of light tearing the darkness apart. By the time Khan raised his head again, the two SAS men had rushed up the ladder and were disappearing through a gaping hole in the upper storey. Smoke was also swirling from similar holes on the lower two floors. Ears ringing from the blast, Khan barely heard Ghulam's whispered query. "Now?"

Khan shook his head and breathed, "Not yet."

On the far side of the building, he saw Piruz start to rise from cover, then think better of it and sink back down, but a moment later Khan saw twin red dots appear on the house as Piruz and his comrade trained their laser sights on the building.

The minutes ticked by in silence as Khan watched the building. Then flames flared inside and he heard the crackle of flames.

Suddenly a figure burst from the blazing building. It was Captain Todd. At once the red dots flickered across the building. A moment later Khan heard a double tap and saw the SAS officer fall backwards.

There was an immediate answering burst of fire from away to his right and, using it as cover, the second SAS man, Spider, burst through the hole in the wall. Firing as he ran, he dived and rolled and came up alongside his wounded comrade.

As firing continued around them, Khan saw Spider crouching over Todd, clamp a dressing on his wound, then cradle the dying officer's head against his chest.

As Khan watched, Spider looked up and their eyes locked. The SAS man swung up his weapon, oblivious to the red dots now tracing a path across the ground towards him. Piruz and his partner were less than a second away from firing.

Khan turned towards Piruz, took aim and squeezed the trigger once, then twice, and felt a surge of satisfaction as Piruz's head exploded like a melon struck with an axe.

In that same moment, Spider's weapon flashed. Khan heard a double tap from it but also a simultaneous whip-crack from Ghulam's AK-47 behind him. Spider's weapon went flying as Ghulam's shot smashed into his shoulder and sent him sprawling to the ground.

Khan had flattened himself and rolled sideways a few feet, just as return fire from the SAS cordon, zeroing on the muzzle flash from his weapon, ripped through the ground where he had been lying. Although Piruz now lay dead, his comrade was still firing, rounds smacking into the ground and striking Todd's already dead body, half shielding the place where Spider was lying.

Khan zeroed in on the muzzle flashes and then saw the Taliban fighter's face bottom-lit for a moment as he fired another burst. Even before his features had faded back into the darkness, Khan had put a single shot into his brain. He saw the Taliban fighter's head disintegrate, the tail of his turban blowing out behind him as if caught in a sudden gale.

Khan was already rolling across the ground again as a fresh torrent of fire from the SAS cordon blitzed the area. He heard a grunt, choked off as soon as it began, and when he looked back he saw Ghulam spreadeagled, a pink froth bubbling from the hole blown in his chest.

Khan felt sick to his core. Ghulam's loyalty to him had now cost him his life, for one glance at the wound showed there was nothing that could be done for him, and his own life was still in danger. He lay motionless

506

as the suppressing fire from the SAS slowed and then ceased, and he watched as one of them ran to Spider, pulling a field dressing from his jacket. "Stay down," the soldier shouted, clamping the dressing over the wound. Khan heard him cry out, "Geordie, get over here! Spider's hit!" and saw Geordie sprinting to him, keeping low to the ground. The medic spared Todd no more than a cursory glance and then stooped over Spider.

Khan began to worm his way back into the shadows and then rose to a crouch, but as he prepared to creep away, some instinct made him look back and, as he did so, he saw Spider looking directly at him. The SAS man tried to speak but coughed, choked and spat blood, and though Khan saw Spider raise his arm to point towards him, Khan was already moving behind the cover of the rubble heap. He heard a burst of fire and rounds whined and ricocheted from the stones but he was already running fast, keeping the rubble heap between him and the SAS, bent double to stop his outline breaking the line of the horizon.

Lights had now flared in several of the outlying houses and he could see torches waving as villagers and Taliban fighters hurried towards the blazing money house. He dropped into cover and let them pass, then moved on as the glow from the burning house grew brighter and fresh bursts of firing erupted behind him. A few moments later he heard the sound of motorbike engines as the SAS tried to make their getaway.

Khan found the track leading up into the mountains and moved along it, sure-footed even in the darkness.

As he crested a rise, he heard the thunder of rotors away to his left and saw the lumbering shape of a Chinook rising into the sky, its mini-gun thundering, while answering fire struck sparks from its fuselage. He watched until it had vanished into the darkness and even the distant echo of its rotors had been silenced, and then, steering by the stars, he strode on into the mountains, making for the rendezvous with his American handler that would lead him to Lailuna and a new life in the West.

The four men stood in amazement as Khan finished his story. Harper's gun was at his side, his finger no longer on the trigger. "No fucking way," he said. McIntyre and Shortt had also lowered their weapons and they looked over at Shepherd.

"Every word is the truth," said Khan. "May Allah strike me dead if I say one word of a lie."

"He saved you, Spider," said Shortt. He slid the gun into his pocket.

"Looks like it," said Shepherd.

"The guy's a bloody hero," muttered McIntyre. He looked at Khan. "You're a hero, mate. They should have given you a medal."

Khan shook his head. "I am no hero, and I have done many bad things. But I did not shoot those three paratroopers in the back, I did not kill Captain Todd and I did not shoot you."

Shepherd nodded. "I believe you," he said.

Harper turned around in a slow circle, staring up at the night sky. "I came that close to killing you," he said.

He looked at Shepherd. "If you hadn't turned up when you did . . ." He shivered.

"We all came that close," said Shepherd. He knelt down by the side of Khan and used his Swiss Army knife to cut the duct tape from his hands and feet. "Joshua kept his word and got you and your daughter out of Afghanistan?"

Khan forced a smile. "He said we could go to the US, or the UK, or Australia. He could get me citizenship of all three. I chose London because I have friends here. Good friends. They helped me find a place to live, and a job. And my daughter has a place at a good college."

"And Joshua paid you?"

Khan sat up and massaged his wrists. "He gave me money. Not a fortune, but enough."

Shepherd stood up and offered Khan his hand. Khan grabbed it and Shepherd hauled him to his feet. He looked at Khan, overwhelmed by feelings of guilt over the way that he had treated him. Khan had saved his life, and Shepherd and his friends had almost killed him, shot him in the head and buried him in the woods. "I'm sorry," he said, knowing as the words left his mouth that they weren't enough and never would be. "I'll do whatever I can to make this right, I swear."

Khan smiled tightly, and massaged his wrists again. "I understand," he said. "You thought I had killed your friends. If I was in your position, I would probably have done the same."

"Maybe," said Shepherd. "And maybe not. But that doesn't make what we did any less wrong."

Harper, McIntyre and Shortt nodded in agreement. One by one they stepped forward, apologised and shook Khan's hand. Shepherd stood and watched, knowing that it was going to take more than words and a handshake to put right the wrong that they had done. And it was clear from the looks on the faces of the three men that they knew it, too.

PATTAYA. THREE MONTHS LATER

Lex Harper pushed open the door to the bar and looked around. His usual table over by the kitchen was free, and there were only three other tables occupied. Two regulars were drinking Chang beer and watching football on one of the big-screen TVs, there was a large, balding man in a vest, shorts and flip-flops sitting next to a bargirl half his age and a third of his body mass, and a European woman with short chestnut hair and a string of pearls around her neck who was toying with a cup of tea and an iPad.

Harper liked the circular table because it gave him a clear view of the front door, he could sit with his back to the wall, and it was only a few steps to the kitchen, from where he could get to the alley behind the building. He picked up a copy of the *Daily Mail* and took it over to his table. The paper was sent via satellite each morning and printed in Thailand, making it as up to date as the latest edition back in the UK. As he sat down, one of his favourite waitresses walked over. Her name was Nok, which meant Bird, and there was something very bird-like about the way she stood by his side, pencil poised over her notepad, even though he ordered the same thing every day. "Full English breakfast," he said. "Coffee. And French fries on the side."

Nok bobbed her head and scurried away. Harper opened his paper and then realised that the European woman was looking at him. She was pretty and well groomed and he found it difficult to place her age; she could have been anywhere between thirty and forty-five. She wasn't dressed like the normal Pattaya tourist, she was wearing a suit that looked as if it might be Chanel, and on her left wrist was a slim Cartier gold watch, clearly the real thing and not a Chinese knock-off. She smiled as he looked up. "Hot outside, isn't it?" she said.

The question would have identified her as English even if her accent hadn't given her away. "There's only two seasons here," said Harper. "Hot and very hot. Are you here on holiday?"

The woman shook her head. "No," she said.

"Business?"

The woman smiled. "Actually, I'm here to see you, Lex."

She smiled but her cold brown eyes looked right through him. Harper swallowed and realised that his mouth had gone suddenly dry. "Do you know me?" he asked.

"I know of you," she said. "But of course that's not the same thing. We have a mutual friend. Dan Shepherd."

"You know Spider?"

"Oh yes, I know Spider."

Harper stared at her for several seconds. Then he nodded. "You're with Five." It was a statement, not a question.

"There are no flies on you, are there, Lex?"

Harper looked over at the door, wondering whether the Thai police were about to rush in. The woman smiled. "I'm not here to arrest you, Lex. I have absolutely zero jurisdiction here. And if I did want you arrested, I'm sure your police friends would tip you off long before we got to the stage of taking you into custody. I'm sure you already have a fall-back position. Cambodia perhaps? Or Brazil."

"Who the hell are you?"

"My name is Charlotte Button. My friends call me Charlie. I don't think we're ever going to be friends, Lex, but you can call me Charlie."

"He did mention your name, now I come to think about it."

"Really?"

"He mentioned your name, that's all. He takes his job seriously."

Button smiled. "That's good to hear. Does Spider know what you get up to?"

"Some of it."

"The armed robbery, obviously?"

Harper nodded.

"The drugs?"

"Import-export, I prefer to call it. Yes."

"And the killings?"

Harper stiffened. The door to the bar crashed open but it was only the ice-man, carrying a sack of melting ice on his shoulder. He grunted as he walked through to the kitchen, water plopping on to the floor behind him.

"I'm guessing not," said Button. "There are three we know about, Lex. Two in Spain. One in Liverpool. Competitors. Import-export can be a cut-throat business, apparently." She smiled. "Don't look so worried. Knowing about and proving in a court of law are two different things."

"What the hell do you want?" asked Harper.

"You asked if I was with Five. But the lines are all getting very blurred these days. Five. Six. The Home Office. Border Force. National Crime Agency. There's a lot of toing and froing. And a lot of cracks to fall through. I think you might be interested in one of the cracks."

Harper frowned. "Do you always talk in riddles?"

Button smiled. "You would have killed Ahmad Khan, wouldn't you?"

Harper's coffee arrived and he waited until Nok had walked back to the bar before speaking. "You knew about that?"

Button shrugged. "What I know or don't know isn't the issue. But you would have happily shot him and buried him in the New Forest, correct?"

"I thought he deserved it," said Harper. "Turned out I was wrong. Does Spider know that you know?"

Button ignored the question. "And your competitors, they deserved it?"

"What do you want from me?" asked Harper. "Why are you here?"

Button sipped her tea, then carefully put her cup back on its saucer. "Sometimes, Lex, when I'm working in the cracks, I need something taken care of. Or someone. And I rather think you might be able to help me with that."

Harper leaned towards her and lowered his voice. "You want someone killed, is that it?"

Button chuckled softly. "Not right now, no. But in the future . . ." She shrugged. "Who knows?"

"You're offering me a job?"

"With a salary and benefits?" She shook her head. "No. But the occasional contract." She smiled. "Such a strange word, that. Contract. So businesslike and yet at the same time, so *Sopranos*."

"This is what Spider does for you, is it?"

She shook her head firmly. "Spider sees himself very much as the wearer of a white hat, and unless his opponent has a black hat he's very uneasy about crossing that line. But you, Lex, you're very much in the grey area, aren't you? One of your competitors who is no longer with us, he was a friend for a long time. A childhood friend, in fact. But that didn't stop you, did it? You've got a talent, Lex, and it's a talent I would like to make use of."

"And what do I get out of this? If I agree?"

"Money, of course. Though looking at your financial situation, that's not much of a carrot, is it? You're a very rich man, Lex. Well done, you."

Harper nodded and couldn't help grinning. The conversation was making him very uneasy but there was no getting away from the fact that Charlie Button was charming and attractive. "I get by," he said.

"What I can offer you is an assurance," she said. "A sort of 'Get out of Jail Free' card, if you like. If you do accept my offer, you will never be bothered by any of the agencies that I've mentioned. You'll never be stopped at an airport or pulled over by the police or have the taxman trawling through your records. You enjoy being the grey man, Lex, and you're very good at it, but I could help you become the invisible man, pretty much."

"And all I would have to do is the occasional job for you?"

Button smiled but didn't say anything. She sipped her tea again.

"I'll need some time to think it over," said Harper.

"That's OK, I still have to finish my tea," said Button. "But when I get up from this table I need to know whether you are accepting my offer or not."

Harper looked at her for several seconds. "Where's the stick?"

"The stick?"

"I see the carrot. What's the stick? What will you do if I don't agree?"

Button smiled sweetly. "I hadn't even considered a stick, Lex."

"You just assumed that I'd do what you want?"

"Most people do, Lex. Sooner or later." She sipped her tea and smacked her lips. "You know, I'm genuinely surprised at how good the tea is here. It really is quite delicious."